THE
FALL OF HERMITAGE HOUSE

A TWIST OF POE MYSTERY

THE
FALL OF HERMITAGE
HOUSE

A TWIST OF POE MYSTERY

VELDA
BROTHERTON

LAGAN

OGHMA CREATIVE MEDIA

www.oghmacreative.com

Library of Congress Control Number: 2018944178

ISBN: 978-1-63373-385-5

Interior Design by Casey W. Cowan
Editing by Gil Miller

Lagan Press
Oghma Creative Media
Bentonville, Arkansas
www.oghmacreative.com

Thanks especially go to my publisher, Casey Cowan,
my terrific editor, Gil Miller,
and the rest of the crew at Oghma Creative Media,
who strive to make good books possible.

I also tip my hat to Venessa Cerasale, who puts up with
innumerable questions and is always ready to lend a helping hand.

ACKNOWLEDGEMENTS

It's about time I thanked the people who made the Twist of Poe Series possible. Those who contributed to the stories from the first of this series.

For almost 20 years I roamed the rural areas of Northwest Arkansas talking to men and women, boys and girls whose tales contributed to the stories I wrote for newspapers. I'd like to thank the families and the individuals who sat with me and related times in their lives that made my articles and features and columns.

The day I walked into the office of the *Washington County Observer* and sat in Parker Rushing's office, a new and exciting phase of my life began. I already had clips of my work published in several weekly and daily newspapers, but this was the first time I applied for a real job in journalism. He smiled and closed my clip file without going past the first page. Oh well, what did I expect. I had no journalism degree.

"I know your work," he said. "And you want this job?"

Not sure I could speak, for did he like it or was he getting ready to send me packing? He hired me that moment and for nine years I remained with the newspaper. He taught me so much. Those were the days when everything was typed, cut, and pasted. A darkroom in the back of the offices was where photos were developed and he let me watch and showed me so much about photography he was soon using all my photos.

Long story, but I would also like to thank all the people who welcomed me into their homes and shared their lives with me. A list would fill chapters of this books, but being with them gave me stories that I now share in this mystery series. The names are changed, the stories sometimes twisted, murder and mayhem added. But without people like all of you who spent time with me I would not have these stories to share.

So if I ever came into your living room, stood in your compound, flew in one of your airplanes, pet your snakes or tigers, walked through your orchards and blueberry fields, sat at your bedside and held your hand, then I thank you with all my heart for being willing to share your lives with me.

You gave me a look at people, places, and things I never would have found without you.

1
CHAPTER

Dal leaned down to peer into the newspaper lobby where Wendy sat at her desk slicing open one envelope after another. His head thunked on the frame around the opening. Off came his new Stetson.

"Ouch, dammit. Have you seen Jessie?" He retrieved the hat, held it at his side.

"She's not answering her phone?" The envelopes kept right on flying.

He backed off from the new barrier and glared at it.

He'd never yell at her about anything, but sometimes she asked dumb questions. As if he hadn't already thought of calling Jess. Wendy was a cute, plumpish blonde who never lost her temper even when someone else did. A perfect fit for her job dealing with upset or angry readers. Wonder if she was married. She didn't wear a ring.

Parker peered around his office door and interrupted Dal's musings. "Maybe one of the ostriches kicked her. I hear they carry a hefty blow."

"Ostriches?" What in thunder was she up to now?

He rubbed his forehead. The new entryway was a blamed nuisance built after the new fire chief, a fella from Los Angeles with the unfortunate name of Morton Goodscrew, disagreed with one of Parker's editorials, stormed into the place, and punched a hole in his office wall. Though Parker held his tongue until Goodscrew left, he was so angry smoke came out his ears. Later he told one and all that the next pissed off reader could bloody well break his fist on the three-quarter-inch-thick plywood wall he had Wally Claymore construct around the small entry. Anyone wanting into the layout room of the newspaper or the editor's office could wait to be let in, or go screw themselves, as the case might be. A remark that brought down the house, considering Goodscrew's ridiculous name. Jessie had to go to the ladies room to keep from wetting herself.

If he had a name like that, he'd sure as hell change it, but other people's problems weren't his. Dal had enough of his own.

When Wendy was busy, like now, she propped the door open with a chair. An action Parker pretended not to notice. She glanced over her shoulder from the pile of mail. "She hasn't come in yet."

"Did he say ostriches? I didn't know they grew in Arkansas. Besides, what could an ostrich have to say about himself that would be worth quoting? 'I'm a big ugly bird too fat to fly.'?"

At his remark Wendy shrugged and grinned. Dal smiled back and Parker returned to his own desk with only a chuckle in reply to the query. Two phones rang, returning the weekly newspaper office to its typical Monday morning.

When she got off the phone he continued. "Well, if I know Jessie, she'll come up with something. One of those ostriches kicks her, she's liable to wring its neck and have it for supper after she interviews the blasted thing. That is, if she has secretly learned to cook. She comes in, would you ask her to meet me up at Alicia and Jeff's place later today? She can call me for the time."

She waved without looking up from a letter. "Will do."

"Hope one of those giant birds doesn't make the mistake of kicking her." Laughter followed him out.

This spring Sheriff Mac had replaced the deputies' well-worn hats with the snazzier gray Stetsons and Dal wasn't sure how he felt about that. A bit too fancy-pants for his taste. It was said the new Hickok's Western Store in town gave him a hefty discount if the deputies would mention his store at least once every time someone complimented the new Stetsons. So far remarks hadn't been complimentary.

Dal continued to forget that agreement. This morning he tossed the new headgear on the seat and folded himself into the SUV. It was barely ten o'clock, but even with the car windows down the interior was hot as an oven. As was typical for Arkansas, spring blazed toward summer, not losing any time catching fire.

Across the street, Mike Henley and a couple of other volunteer responders washed the town's red fire engine. No doubt Goodscrew watched from the small corner office. Soapy water gathered in the grassy ditch alongside the street. Conversation and laughter joined a blue jay's squawk and the chatter of a squirrel that scolded from a tree behind the newspaper office.

In a town the size of Cedarton that was about the only noise.

Usually.

He stretched while the a/c warmed the interior. Damn, good thing he'd decided to remain here. Since his return, winter had passed with little to break the peace and quiet, with the exception of the hiring of good old Morton, who everyone had grown to dislike pretty quick. It would be much better if folks from California, with their ideas for making Arkansas a better place to live, would just stay where they belonged.

With Jessie around, Dal was far from bored. He liked Cedarton the way it was. Dropping the stick into reverse, he backed out onto the street. Before he could shift into drive a blast shuddered the ground, leaped across the surrounding peaks like a giant fleeing on huge feet. Over at the fire station, alarms cut loose and excited calls broke the silence on his radio. Something had exploded at the abandoned gas station out on Highway 22. Pulling on his blue jacket, Morton—the only fireman on a paid salary—dashed from his office and climbed into the shotgun seat of the yellow first responder truck, almost losing his footing when the driver peeled out before he cleared the pavement.

One of these days someone was going to go too far with poor old Morton. It would've helped had he changed his last name before arriving in town. Or hadn't tried to tell Parker how to write his editorials. All this excitement would teach Dal not to be thankful for a peaceful day. But hey, a harmless explosion could be exciting.

It made good sense to chase after the fire truck. He pulled over and didn't have long to wait before the engine took off, siren screaming. Pickups and SUVs carrying first responders continued to arrive from all directions. Men crawled onto the water truck, some followed in their own vehicles. Parker came out of *The Observer*, leaped in his Range Rover, and tore off down the street toward the station. It was a fine procession to show off the department. Dal followed along, only to hear his radio tell him there was a 10-27 at Hermitage House, Alicia and Jeff Woodson's place. Definitely not the old gas station out on 22 but a call about an armed intruder. Things were getting serious now.

Since he'd been headed that way earlier he'd better get on up there.

Let the firemen take care of their business. When Alicia called she had only sounded a bit stressed, but the 10-27 definitely ramped up the possible danger.

Time to say goodbye to a blissful day. He drove away from the square, fishtailing the unit onto the gravel road that led up the mountain, a spiral of thick dust in his wake. Truth be told, he'd rather clean up after an explosion than answer a call about an armed intruder. Take an ordinary citizen, put a gun in his hand, you got a whole lot worse than something blowing up. And nearly every citizen in Grace County, ordinary or not, was armed. Which was not always a bad thing.

He hooked the mic, replied to the call, then dropped it to concentrate on three miles of winding, steep, narrow road. Another deputy might respond, but he heard nothing on the radio, so he was on his own. Before he reached the stately Southern-style mansion, the only house on this road, another call came through—a 10-46 at the animal farm on Dyer Creek Road.

For God's sake. The animal farm had not opened yet. It was out past Ina Mae's trailer park, where he once lived. The twenty acres would house a collection of exotic animals, each species having its own enclosure inside a larger fenced compound. People would be able to drive through and… oh, hell. That's where Jessie must be. No other place would have ostriches. He shook his head and muttered some choice words.

One thing for sure, he couldn't be in two places at once, and an armed person was more dangerous than a bunch of funny-looking birds, or whatever had got turned loose. And if it was Jeff Woodson fighting one of his battles, he could settle him down. For some reason the blind veteran had taken a liking to him. Could be cause down inside where the demons dwelled they were somewhat alike.

Damn, who offended the gods today? At the moment he skidded around a curve and came in sight of Hermitage House, Colby's voice came over the radio taking the call to follow up on the animals. That would be right up his alley. A veteran of Afghanistan and a farm boy from down in southern Arkansas, Colby would have no trouble rescuing Jessie and corralling a bunch of wild animals. They must've left a gate open or something. Surely not as bad as last fall when Jessie ended up the prisoner of a bunch of nutty cult members trafficking kids. Had to admit though, she had a hand in solving that one. Well, almost. A few members wanted by the FBI continued to wander the woods.

He cared for Jessie a hell of a lot, but in her desire to pursue the very best story she could get herself in some of the worst messes. He'd almost get used to her shenanigans before she pulled another unbelievable stunt.

The tires crackled over gravel and he braked to a stop in front of the mansion. Nothing appeared awry, but because of the armed intruder call, he unlatched the door and crept out, keeping the car between him and the house.

Still quiet.

Boots crunching across the driveway, he hunkered low and scurried to a huge oak in the center of the well-kept yard. From there, hedges were between him and the house till he made it onto the porch and the double front doors. Back hugging the wall, he listened.

Too still, way too still. Every moment he expected to hear gunfire.

Nothing but silence. Not even a curtain lifted at any of the windows in sight. After a moment, he rapped on the wood panel.

"Grace County Deputy. Open up."

Nothing.

He repeated the action, then grabbed the knob, turned it, and shoved the unlocked door open. Once more announcing himself, he pulled out his weapon and slipped around the frame. Held his breath.

Still nothing.

Sometimes you can just tell a house is empty. It gives off an abandoned feeling. Dangerous to pay attention to that, though. It could get him killed. He moved from room to room, heartbeat increasing with each open doorway. A hell of a lot of rooms in this rambling house. Who needed this big a place anyway? Unless they were going to open a hotel.

Once he verified no one was there he reported in. Had to click the damn thing plus smack it one before he finally got through. When Tinkerbelle answered, he gave her the status.

"Who reported someone up here was armed, do you know?"

"Not sure, Dal. I didn't recognize the voice. A female, and she hung up. A cell phone number. You know what? I think Alicia and Jeff are having company, her cousins or something like that. Might have been one of them."

"Well, no one is here. I'm going to check the outer buildings, see if their car may be in the garage."

"You're cutting out. But if you find out anything let me know. Some start for the day, hmm?" Her laughter sounded before she clicked off.

Weird all the way round. An explosion, escaped ostriches, and a phantom call from an empty house. The car in the garage was a bad sign. Maybe he'd stepped into an alternate universe.

Jessie raised the camera with hands so shaky she had trouble focusing. That was one big mother of a cat. Right there, so close she could feel his breath. But she'd asked for the opportunity to get a close-up and July Jones, the keeper of the animal farm, stood guard nearby.

"Steady big fella, just stay where you are a minute longer." The huge tiger stared at her with wide, golden eyes. The camera clicked over and over before the beautiful animal tilted his head back and let out a burbling sound.

"What does he mean by that?" She glanced toward July.

"She's telling you she likes you. Big cats in the wild and house cats exhibit much the same behavior. But she can't meow or purr. It's best if you let me stay handy though, just in case."

Not sure she liked the inference, Jessie took a big breath. "Don't you worry a bit. I'll not get closer. She may like me but with that mouth she could swallow my head. How do you tell she's a she?"

July laughed. "You look, honey. You just look. But I wouldn't advise it."

"Uh, I won't."

"Well, I assure you, she is a she. A few house cats' habits are a bit different because of their exposure to humans. They have learned to communicate with us by meowing and purring. Nature is so very odd, isn't it?" The gun under July's arm related more information than her words.

"That gives them a lot more sense than I ever thought they had. You won't shoot her, will you?"

She moved slowly to one side to let the thirteen-hundred-pound tiger—that was in her notes—stroll by, all the while taking pictures.

July, a woman in her forties, wore an outfit much like the BDUs and boots worn by the military. "This gun fires a dart. Maizie is quite tame, but she's big and could hurt one of us without meaning to."

"If she's so gentle, why knock her out?"

"Cause if she is frightened she just might hurt someone. I called the sheriff and they said a deputy would be here to help corral them and get them back inside the fence. I'm so sorry, one of my new helpers thought she'd fastened the high-pasture gate and it took very little for that mischievous Mexican burro to discover it and turn some of them free. Guess he announced it cause most of them followed. I need to get Maizie back inside. If I can't and she escapes into the woods, they'll have to hunt her down. Can't get her with a dart, they'd have to literally shoot her. That would break my heart."

July scurried off in the wake of the strolling tiger, who seemed to be in no hurry to either escape or hurt anyone. What July did when and if she caught the cat could be more thrilling than the rest of the story. If anything happened good or bad, Jessie would get a picture of it.

The interview she came up here to conduct about this unusual woman and her turning her dream of opening an exotic zoo in the Ozark wilderness into reality was fast growing into more excitement than she'd expected. And she wasn't about to let the keeper and the big cat out of her sight for one minute. She trailed along, working the camera feverishly while several helpers herded the mixed species of animals back into the enclosure and locked them in. A couple of ostriches and what looked like overgrown, over-antlered deer still grazed nearby like they felt perfectly at home.

July kept her eye on Maizie. Her body language alone told Jessie how dangerous the tiger could be. What fun Parker would have with this when he saw the pictures.

A deputy drove up alongside the enclosure herding four strolling camels through the open gate of a pasture that surrounded the inner pens. Colby climbed out, grinning from ear to ear. This was right down his alley. She raised an arm and waved at him, still keeping the tiger in sight.

July spotted him. "If you could just man that gate, I think we can round up most of those who've escaped. We need to funnel them inside. My helpers can then get them inside their own pens. We've got to get Maizie in. She's fairly tame, likes to play, so be careful. If you could just sort of—"

Colby's grin spread, if that were possible. "Gotcha. Act like she's a bony old cow and convince her she wants to go in, even if she acts like she's a man-eating tiger who might take my head off. I can do that. Man, look at the size of those paws."

He took up a position near the gate, removed his Stetson and held it out to his side, moving it up and down as the tiger strolled toward him. Jessie snapped pictures madly. At this rate, she might make the cover of the *National Geographic*. She ignored her phone ringing. Didn't dare take her eyes off Maizie, who stopped dead still right in front of Colby, challenged him for a moment with a low snarl, and tossed her head around, mouth wide open. He stood his ground and Jessie's heart did a fast kick. The roar made the ground tremble. He must be shaking like a leaf, but he just kept waving that hat at the tiger and talking to her, urging her to get her beautiful big butt back where it belonged. Lord she hoped she wasn't going to photograph a tiger chowing down on a deputy. You'd think he'd at least have one hand on his gun.

July approached the cat from behind, closer than appeared safe. One glance over her shoulder and Maizie padded through the open gate and tossed them a look as if it were her idea all along.

"You may shut it now, deputy. There may be a few odd animals running about, but they're not dangerous. We'll get them all back where they belong, don't worry."

The main enclosure was enclosed by what Jessie guessed was a twenty-foot-high fence with barbed wire at a slant around the top. A road circled around the entire acreage so visitors could drive by viewing nearly all the population of the animal farm at any one time. July had made the remark that the gates were getting new latches to hold the clever burro.

"Be glad to give you a hand, ma'am." Colby set his new Stetson back on his head. "Come on, Jessie, let's help the lady get her herd back where it belongs."

With the assistance of several of the young helpers Maizie, as well as two ostriches, three llamas, a mother and baby that resembled large deer with curly antlers, and the burro that had caused all the trouble, were rounded up and guided into their individual enclosures within the main fence. It was quite an elaborate set-up, but one that July promised would receive a few updates before opening day to prevent such an escape again.

"I wouldn't want folks in the area to think this will be a regular event." The pleasant, freckled woman aimed her remarks in Jessie's hearing. "It won't happen again."

Colby headed back to his unit. "Better call in that we've tamed the wilderness. Hey, Jessie, bet this is a story you didn't expect in your wildest dreams. Most fun I've had in a while."

July mopped her sweating forehead with a red bandana. "I do hope you'll be kind to us in your article. I'd hate to get off on the wrong foot and scare these folks. This is really a safe place to visit and we are very careful. I'd like you to come back opening day for a tour and give me a chance to prove that."

Opening date wasn't for another month and Jessie would take her up on the invitation, for she badly wanted to be able to reassure the locals of their safety and she told July so. "I'm surprised Dal didn't show up. He's on duty today."

Colby rubbed the hindquarters of the burro. "He's busy. Well everyone is. That old service station that's been empty for a lot of years blew up and a call came in there was a problem up at Hermitage House. Dal took that one, I believe. Well, gal, you have fun with this. I have to get back before something else happens."

A problem at Alicia's? That didn't sound good. Before the Woodsons moved in there'd been some reports of vandals and break-ins up there, an unusual happening around the small remote town. She'd just detour that way and see what was up before heading back to the paper. It was a beautiful day to be out and about and she'd still have plenty of time to get this story finished. It would practically write itself. Parker would take care of the explosion story. Wonder what caused the old place to blow up like that? Surely all the gas fumes were long gone from the buried tanks.

Singing along with Vince Gill on her CD player, she headed the Jeep toward the Hermitage. Maybe she and Alicia could have tea and visit a while. Hopefully Jeff wasn't in some sort of trouble. He'd come back from Afghanistan blind and a bit troubled, which was the main reason Alicia had brought him off out into the wilderness where he could fight his demons without bothering neighbors. He was an artist, could feel the sweep of charcoal on paper and create visions from his mind. She'd interviewed him for Veteran's Day last fall, and found him quite amazing in his attitude and the ability to handle himself and create lovely drawings. Alicia was an attorney, the only one in town.

When Jessie arrived at the Hermitage, Dal's patrol unit sat empty in front of the big house and it was quiet enough to make her nervous. She parked back a ways, took her camera from the backpack, and hung it around her neck. Considering the call, she'd better be careful. Could be some stranger up here, though there'd been no more trouble since the couple moved in. Burglaries in the area were as unusual as was an entire herd of exotic animals going walk-about. Dal would be pissed at her for showing up at the scene of a call, but she was accustomed to that.

She detoured around the house, paying more attention to the barn and garage. Dal came from the latter and signaled her to stay back. She scuttled to the edge of the porch where she waited. It was a few minutes before he showed up.

"What are you doing up here?" He took her arm and moved her toward the cars. "I thought you were chasing ostriches or something."

"Got done. Colby helped. Said you were up here so I came on up. What's going on?"

"Nothing, it looks like. The car's not here, so I figure they've gone to town or somewhere else. Don't know what the call was about, but I can't find anything out of sorts. Some kid without enough to do, I guess. Alicia called earlier, asked to have you come up, she wanted to talk to you, but it didn't sound like an emergency. Sort of strange, though, when I get this call that someone up here reported an armed intruder." He shook his head. "Weird. Sort of adds to a very odd day."

She leaned back against the porch railing. "What're you going to do?"

"Still want to check the barn, then I'm going on back to town. You're working late tonight, I reckon."

"You know it. Monday and Tuesday are killers. I'll give Alicia a call when I get a break." She moved closer to him. "I'll be home about midnight tomorrow though, if you've got nothing else to do."

He tilted her chin up and gave her a quick kiss. "And just what would we do at midnight? McDonald's is closed."

"I'll bet we can come up with something. I give good leg rubs."

"Yeah? Well, I could use one. And maybe a few other things rubbed, if you're so inclined. I'll let you know. You going on back now?"

"Guess I'd better. I'll text you about my inclinations later. Parker will be looking for me, so I'll see you." She touched his arm and walked back to the Jeep, humming "Go Rest High on that Mountain." Sort of an odd choice for such a beautiful summer day, but Vince had just finished singing it for her so she probably wouldn't get it off her mind the rest of the day. Nor would she get images of that Cherokee hunk out of there, either.

Dal moved carefully in the gloom of the barn. Might as well be night with no windows or open doors to let in the sunlight. Something had gone on here. Surrounding thoughts, feelings of anger and violence tore at his senses. Danger, but something else as well. He couldn't put his finger on it, but it told him something wasn't right. That he needed to beware.

The dirt floor was all scuffed up like there'd been a fight. In the powerful beam of his flashlight, he searched inch by inch. Sifted his fingers through the hay-strewn soil and dried dung. It'd been years since anyone ran this place as a ranch with animals housed in the barn. Years in fact since anyone lived here. Everyone had been surprised but pleased when the attorney and her veteran husband moved in. It was told around town that a Saint Louis company owned the property and had for a few years now.

Back and forth on his hands and knees looking for something, anything that might show him who had been here and what had happened. Voices caught up in disagreement. Some angry. A few cigarette butts. What kind of fool smoked in a barn with leftover hay? Someone who wasn't familiar with the explosive danger. The butts were new. The Woodsons didn't smoke, or never had in his presence. He placed several in an evidence bag and laid it on the shelf where tools were scattered. Wished he could bag his perceptions as well.

A couple of candy wrappers turned up, also recently discarded. Signs of oil drippings indicated an ATV of some sort might have been kept in the small stall not long ago. Wadded up pieces of paper with pencil sketches that made no sense. Looked like maps not easily made out. Everything went on the shelf. And then, buried under a boot print, one of those purple flags, symbols of the Rising Moon cult the Grace County deputies had broken up last fall along with help from the feds. What was this doing in a barn at the Hermitage?

The flashlight beam skittered across the wide plank walls. Always look head high was a rule and so he did. Near the small back door close to the tack room something white fluttered under the moving light. He took it down with a gloved hand.

We have the Woodsons. Will be in touch.

That was all. No explanation or demand. Odd. Even a bit stupid.

At least something halfway explained the purple symbol. For some reason Robert Kimble, the ex-sheriff from Nolton County, and Taylor Bainbridge, leaders of that cult being used as a cover-up for trafficking children, might have been here and recently.

But why? And what were they looking for? Once fleeing arrest, why hadn't they lit out? What in the world did this cryptic message mean?

It had to be connected to the child trafficking. Obviously something had been left undone. Worst of all, had the Woodsons somehow found out about what was going on and been grabbed up?

He had some choices here, but didn't like most of them. The tracks of an ATV led off out the back way and into the woods. Taking the patrol car to run them down wasn't an option. The trail was narrow and overgrown. If these assholes had Alicia and Jeff, he needed to get to them fast. The only way to do that was on foot. He could travel as fast that way as they could in the ATV. Except for one thing. The damned leg might give out on him halfway through.

The walkie on his shoulder or the radio in his car? Call someone, get help doing the tracking. First choice. He keyed the walkie. Nothing but static, no answer. A few minutes later, he sat in the unit working the radio. Nothing there at all, not even static. What the hell? The radio was dead. Had been giving him trouble for the last few days. He should've had it fixed. Dammit. He tossed the mic into the floorboards.

Down to one choice. His cell phone. They had the Internet here from a satellite connection because there was no cable or phone connection. Popping the glove compartment, he palmed another magazine for his gun and stuck it in his pocket. Locking the evidence bags in the glove compartment, he headed out. He had to get on their trail and fast, before whoever had them decided to get rid of the Woodsons.

Off to the northwest a bank of black clouds grew, smothering the afternoon sun.

"It figures." He spat the words at the rain-scented air and headed along the double tracks cut through the weeds and into the thick-wooded Ozark National Forest. A rising breeze dried the sweat on his face.

Jessie didn't hear from Dal the remainder of the day and no one answered up at the Hermitage. Odd, but still she thought nothing of it. He got busy, knew she was too. A storm moved through later that afternoon, but by nightfall it had settled into a gentle rain. Along about midnight she hurried to the Jeep, the air cool and wet on her face. A nice relief from the earlier heat. She was on her way home to her cabin outside of town when Tinker called.

"Say, is Dal with you or meeting you?"

For a moment her heart sped up, but she calmed herself. "No, haven't seen him since this morning up at the Hermitage. I tried calling Alicia several times but there was no answer. Even the voicemail isn't working."

Tinker didn't say anything for a minute. "Well, it's probably nothing, but we haven't heard from him since he went up there either."

Why had they waited this long before getting curious? "Tink, what the hell? He never came back?"

"I know, but there was so much going on, and he's a grown man. So many places with no signal. The HazMat guys came in to clean up the mess out at the service station, and they've been in and out all day, tracking stinking mud through the station. Well, anyway, Mac asked me to call you cause we both figured he'd met you at the paper or something."

"Have you tried calling Alicia?"

"Yep, got the same as you." Tink sounded far away.

"I'm going up there. You'd better tell Mac to send someone up too."

She tossed the telephone into the seat to the sound of Tinker hollering at her, slammed on the brakes, and did a U-ey in the middle of the road. Dal did not do stuff like this. Not anymore. He'd learned his lesson when he laid on that mountain so long. Now he always let someone know where he was going. Last she knew he was looking for an armed intruder. Holy crap. What could've happened?

The Jeep rocked and rolled all the way up to the Hermitage and skidded ten or fifteen feet to a stop in front of the house. His car sat where it'd been when she left him this morning. Rain drops glimmered in the yellow glow of the yard light.

Now what? Since last fall when she'd been grabbed by members of the Rising Moon cult she'd taken advantage of her carry permit. The .38 revolver went with her everywhere. Two men had escaped arrest by the FBI when the cult members were taken in for child trafficking. No one had ever found them or any recorded evidence of the cult members or the traffickers. The case was bogged down under the weight of red tape.

One of the men missing was Robert Kimble, the ex-sheriff of Nolton County, the other Taylor Bainbridge, thought to be the leader. Some folks believed they were hiding out over there in the wilderness while organizing another cult to continue their business of stealing and selling children. Funny thing, though. The FBI had Bainbridge's wife.

This situation made her glad she carried the .38 and she dug it out of the backpack. Other than the yard light out front, the place was dark and quiet as a tomb. Where the heck were the Woodsons? They usually stuck close to home at night. Alicia had an office on the square in town, but her main office was here at the Hermitage where she handled most of her clients.

Jessie slipped the gun in her pocket, took a powerful flashlight from her backpack, and hung the camera around her neck. In the soft yellow glow from the yard light, she headed toward the barn. The last place Dal was going when she left him here this morning. She hadn't gone more than ten feet when the power flickered and went out. There was no moon so it was dark as the bottom of a well. After she swallowed her thudding heartbeat, she clicked on the flashlight with a shaky hand and followed its path toward the barn.

It really wasn't unusual for the power to go out in the country. Especially with storms frolicking from peak to peak like gigantic fireflies. The darkened valley cradled Cedarton, revealing unlit homes only when the lightning flashed. She'd never been much afraid of anything, especially the dark, but since her few close calls chasing stories through the wilderness she'd learned a bit of caution. According to Dal she was foolishly fearless, but that's just cause he suffered from a man's need to protect women, her in particular.

High weeds swished around her ankles, wetting her skin. The Woodsons had no cattle so all kinds of grass and brush grew up around the outbuildings. The barn door was wide enough to drive heavy equipment through and hard to move, but there was a smaller one to the side and she opted to drag it open. A musty smell washed over her when she stepped through the threshold into the cavernous structure.

A huge bird flew down from the hay loft, stirring up a noisy wind. Only an owl. She ducked and let out a breath. What next? The empty stalls had dark corners and she crept past them. In the trail of light, spider webs hung from large beams like gossamer drapes. Tiny critters scurried underfoot. Barn rats and mice, shrews no doubt. No telling what sorts of bugs lived in here. None as frightening as the two-legged variety of creatures who walked this earth.

Where in the world had Dal gotten to? At the far end of the barn, the ground was clear of strewn hay and tire tracks led into one of the stalls. Inside, the smell of gasoline, oil, old machinery. On the ground, a soaked-in puddle. Liquid of some kind. She knelt, rubbed her fingers in it, and sniffed them. Greasy. Someone kept a vehicle of some sort parked here. And recently. The space wasn't big enough for a pickup or even a full-sized car. But a four-by-four ATV, like was used by just about every farmer in the state, would fit here just fine. Trouble was, it was not here. On a shelf along one side lay a few wrenches along with a gallon jug of oil and some coolant.

The wooden handle on the back door allowed her to slide it open easily. Outside, her light picked out tire tracks leading out across the overgrown pasture. Not once, but many times, a vehicle had been in and out here.

What was it Alicia had told her once? Jeff spent a lot of time in the barn when he was having a difficult time with his demons. What if someone was using this barn for something illegal? And he'd heard something he shouldn't have? It was far enough from the house to keep its secrets from the couple. The Hermitage had been empty for a long time before the Woodsons bought it. This place ought to be searched. Dal could be in trouble, or he could have gone off on foot to follow those tracks. Either way he needed backup.

She hurried down to the house where there was a WiFi signal, took her phone from her pocket, and called Mac. No telling what was going on here, but someone needed to check it out.

2
CHAPTER

The trail of emotions was clear.

Confusion, thoughts strange under the circumstances. But Dal followed the scent emanating from Jeff and Alicia like a trained dog. It led him finally over a fairly well-beaten path to a shack deep in the woods. Odd. Someone had traveled this way numerous times. Though not a road or constructed trail, it was beaten down by many feet and some smaller vehicles. Perhaps ATVs.

Within the dilapidated walls of the shack two people waited. Perhaps a bit too calm, but anticipating something he couldn't quite read. Under duress, some people reacted that way in a tight spot—wondering what to do yet, not terrified. Whoever had brought them here had left.

Not trusting his senses, he checked the perimeter thoroughly. Sensed no one lurking about. At last back at the door, he jerked on the padlock.

"Alicia. Jeff. You in there?"

Odd sounds. They were gagged somehow.

The shiny new lock looped through a rusted metal hinge was hardly sufficient to hold against a sturdy kick, which he delivered. Some of the wood panels shattered as it slammed open and bounced off the inner wall.

Inside, he nearly fell over the couple huddled together on the floor. The man kicked out and shouted, then rolled away, holding the woman close.

"Jeff, it's me. Dal Starr. Don't kick me, buddy."

Alicia joined him in calming the explosive blind Marine. It took a while. Finally, he slumped forward, convinced.

"Okay, you're safe. Where did they go? When?" Neither could reply since their mouths were taped. He shrugged at his own stupidity. "I've got to get you out of here before they come back."

He took Jeff's arm first cause he had such a protective hold on his wife it was near impossible to get to her. "Jeff, she's fine. Just fine."

With some struggling, he managed to remove the tape holding their wrists and covering their mouths. "Come on, let's go. Now."

Stumbling toward the door, a sliver of light in the darkness, he dragged them out into the night. "Sorry if I'm hurting you, but we gotta split. I don't know where they're at. Figure they're armed. We're going in the woods. Jeff, if you'd let her go, we can get you between us and then you won't stumble or run into anything."

"Yeah, okay. Just don't let anything happen to her." Jeff got it together, hauled up and turned loose of his wife. Pawed the air and cursed under his breath.

Dal grabbed him as soon as he could. A marvel that someone totally blind could trust him and let go of the only thing keeping him stabilized in an unfamiliar environment.

"Gotcha. Got her. Now let's boogie. It's getting light enough I can keep us from ramming into a tree, but these woods are still dark most places. I'm gonna hush now. We're headed downhill with some rocks along the way, so lift your feet. And let's move." The moonless night was on their side. But nothing else was.

Damn, they sounded like a stampede, rocks tumbling and brush snapping. The deep woods still so dark they might as well all have been blind. The path narrowed and he urged Alicia out front so he could make sure Jeff had enough guidance. If he was to be yanked loose the guy wouldn't have a prayer. Maybe none of them would.

It took forever to reach the ridge he intended to follow to the backside of the Hermitage property. The rising sun hid behind the mountains, but light crawled over the land. Everyone gasped for breath so he brought them to a standstill. His face and arms stung from being slapped with branches pushed aside then released by the two in front of him.

"Come on, let's rest just a minute. No sign of either of them. They may have figured to just leave you there and get on out of here. There's still a steep drop from the woods to the back pasture so catch your breath. Sit here." He moved Jeff to a huge boulder. "Sit by him, Alicia."

From the way he shook, Jeff was about to lose it. She wrapped her arms around him, murmured against his ear. He lowered his head to her shoulder.

Keeping an eye on them, Dal sat on the far side of the boulder and rubbed at the burning in his leg. By the time they reached that incline he might be the one who needed carried out of these woods. When he could get his breath he broke the silence. "Dark here under all these trees, though the sky is lightening. Back there I couldn't see a darned thing."

"Now you know how I feel." Jeff chuckled under his breath.

At least the guy had a sense of humor about their dilemma. It would help get them out of here. Someone in panic mode almost always did something stupid.

Despite the darkness, his eyes grew accustomed to the dim light so he didn't drag them into any trees or off a bluff. Just kept going even when Jeff stumbled. Had to hurry, no telling if or when they'd come looking for them. What had they wanted anyway? Time to question the couple after he got them safely back home.

Approaching headlights twinkled like a brilliant diamond necklace along the curving road to the Hermitage where Jessie paced in anticipation. Mac arrived first and she ran to meet him.

"Looks like you brought everyone."

He took her hand. "All but one. Your friend Tinker, and she's romping and stomping down at the station. Someone had to take care of the phone. She'll probably quit again. Heard or seen anything?"

The note she'd found on the shelf in the barn burned a hole in her pocket. "I found this on a shelf near the back door where there's signs of a struggle and small tire tracks headed off up the mountain."

Mac shined his light on the crinkled piece of paper. "Read it aloud."

Around them cars skidded to a stop, doors opened and slammed shut, men conversed low.

Mac shouted above the din and everyone settled down. "Note from Dal reads '*Follow the tracks out back on foot. Don't shoot me.*'"

A ripple of nervous laughter.

Colby stepped into the glowing ring formed by the headlights. "Sure hope someone told him not to shoot us."

More chuckles. Men preparing to go into danger often made jokes. She'd learned that well in the past few years.

"I want Duggan and Les to stay here in case they double back. Colby, Burt, and I will go out back and follow the tracks. One of you tie Jessie to a tree. I don't want her wandering around out there." Mac pointed at his adopted granddaughter.

Seeing the orders coming, she hightailed it through knee-deep, rain-soaked weeds toward the barn, even as the two deputies who were to stay looked around for her. Heading out the back door, she followed tracks visible in the shimmering dawn. No way was she staying back like a good little girl. Dal was out there, and besides that, so was her story. Mac could get ripped and he probably would.

Once under the shelter of the thick canopy of oak, hickory, and black walnut branches, she clicked on her flashlight. Kept the beam low to the ground and scrambled up the rocky path, cut by exposed roots that threatened to trip her. Behind her, three deputies followed. They didn't catch up to her till she was well along the old logging road on top of the ridge. And then only because she kept having to stop and check the trail to make sure she hadn't lost the tire tracks.

Mac took her arm. "Dang nab it, girl, I told you to wait below."

She pulled away from his grip. "Hush, they'll hear you."

The look he gave her could've set fire to her hair. She ignored him and flounced on down the trail. Colby and Burt went along, one at either edge of the tracks crushed by the tires.

Early rays of sunlight brightened the sky, sending tiny rainbows sparkling over the rain soaked forest. Alicia, Dal, and Jeff stumbled out of the upper woods onto the lower pasture and almost ran over Colby, who managed to catch Dal by the arm and slow them before all went sprawling. Jessie snapped images with the camera when all she wanted was to throw her arms around Dal. All three looked a bit the worse for wear.

Mac remained speechless for a few seconds, then addressed Dal. "Are they on your trail, boy?"

Dal righted himself, hanging on to Jeff, who in turn refused to let go of his wife. "Don't think so. We never saw them after we escaped our bonds and took off. "

More pictures, then she released the camera—letting it hang around her neck—and took Alicia's place on Dal's arm. Alicia grabbed hold of Jeff, who looked a bit lost.

"All the same, it'd do to keep our eyes open." Colby turned a slow circle, checking out the woods. "Let's get these folks down off this mountain. I'll bet we can brew up some coffee at the Hermitage. Keep an eye open, though, in case we're being watched."

Mac agreed. "Going after them will have to wait for another day. They ain't enough of us. "

Returning on the trail they had climbed earlier proved even more difficult. Boots stumbled on rocks and caught under roots so they were forced to slow down to keep from tumbling one after the other into the flat pasture below. By the time they all made it back to the Hermitage, everyone was complaining about running all over hell and creation, and who the hell had they'd been after, and what in thunder did Kimble and Bainbridge mean coming back here with warrants out for their arrest by the feds anyway?

And most important, why hadn't the feds picked them up?

Sprawled over the comfortable furniture in the main room, everyone looked dog tired. Jessie slumped against Dal on one end of the large sectional. He had a good hold of her arm, his eyes closed.

She patted his thigh. "Gonna help Alicia get the coffee and some food. It'll be microwaved, not cooked, but then you're used to that."

He grinned without opening his eyes and let her go. The deputies were spread out in recliners and overstuffed chairs. Colby sat near the front door next to Jeff as if guarding him. She wouldn't be surprised if that's precisely what he was doing. There'd been talk when they first came inside about those two fugitives hiding out in the woods not being done with them yet. Jeff recalled the names Taylor and ex-sheriff and Dal verified the ID with his own investigation.

It was definitely Taylor Bainbridge and Robert Kimble.

Alicia attempted to explain. "I saw someone cross the porch and thought it was Jessie or Dal. But when I peeked through the door window it was these two men I didn't know and they were trying to get in. I dialed nine-one-one but didn't get much said before they busted in. Grabbed me and before I could warn Jeff, they had him, too."

She ran out of steam and Jessie put an arm round her shoulders. "That's enough for now, guys. Let her rest."

Pacing, Mac finally settled in a comfortable chair among his deputies. "What I can't figure out is what they are doing back here anyway. Reckon there's something they left undone. Gotta admit I'm a bit worried what they may be up to. We'll just keep an eye out."

Alicia wiped her eyes and rose. "I need to help Jeff." She left and returned with gauze and antiseptic, got busy dabbing cuts and scratches on his arms.

"I hate to ask, but can you spare a deputy to keep watch up here till we find out what's going on? Or until those two are in custody?"

Mac assured her he would do just that. She didn't head for the kitchen till Jeff settled down and insisted he was fine and everyone was hungry.

Jessie followed, took coffee mugs from the cupboard, and found sugar and cream. "I'll assist but I'm still learning to cook."

"Let's just stick a couple of frozen pizzas in the oven. I know they're not real good, but they'll do, don't you think?"

Jessie smiled at Alicia's embarrassment over not cooking something. "Sounds fine to me. Shall I get something to drink and some ice? The coffee is ready, and that'll hold them till the pizzas are done."

Alicia closed the oven door, turned toward Jessie, and buried her face in both hands, shoulders shaking. "I just knew they were going to hurt him. I couldn't stand that. He's been through so much."

Jessie put her arms around Alicia. "Hey, everything's okay. Look at him, he's telling jokes and laughing. He's fine."

"That's how he reacts when he's gone through something that frightens him, or when he gets past one of his 'bad spells,' as he calls them. He doesn't like anyone to think he's scared of anything."

Jessie patted her back. "Well, they say laughter is good for the soul."

"I don't know. I hope he gets through the night okay."

"Do you want me to stay here with you? I know a deputy will be here, but sometimes a woman wants another woman around."

Alicia sniffed and shook her head. "No, he'd be so embarrassed. Could you ask Mac if Colby could stay? The two of them have formed a bond of sorts. You know, that Semper Fi thing."

"I'm sure he can. You sit. I'll get the coffee passed around."

"Thanks, Jess."

Maybe thirty minutes later, everyone gathered around the table, grabbing hot slices of pizza.

Jess glanced at her watch, took a bite, and fanned her mouth. "First time I ever had pizza for breakfast."

Nervous laughter broke the tension. "Then you never been in the service or on an all-night stakeout."

Several stories followed while they wiped out two huge pizzas and a couple beers each.

Colby agreed to take the rest of the day shift there with Jeff and Alicia.

Mac said he'd spell him for the night. "And you be watchful, boy. Those men are bad news, and we know at least one of them has some training. We don't know exactly what they wanted with Alicia and Jeff. Maybe just to scare them, but for what reason doesn't seem clear. Does anyone know much about that prissy Taylor Bainbridge?"

"We ought to let the FBI know those fellas are traipsing around in our neck of the woods. I'll call Trey, he'd surely know something about him, being a US Marshal."

"Why don't you do that, Dal? Meanwhile, I'm getting on down to the station. I've still got a department to run. If y'all'd come on in we can get shifts re-set for today and tonight. Meanwhile, I'm headed out of here fore Tinker gets so pissed she won't talk to me for a week. Not that that's a bad thing, exactly." Mac donned his brand new Stetson and lifted a hand in farewell before leaving to the sound of laughter.

Jessie wanted only to go to bed and sleep, but best if she went on in to the office and did some writing while everything was clear in her mind. Experiencing things without taking notes, there was a danger of leaving out some important facts. Especially if other stuff came up to distract her.

Was it still Tuesday? If so, she had one heck of a long day ahead of her. She told everyone so long. The house emptied out quickly, leaving Colby, Alicia, and Jeff to the silence.

Outside she leaned into a long embrace with Dal. "Come on over tonight at midnight if you want to. You never did get that leg rub. "

"I could sure use one, too. Reckon I'll be there if I don't curl up somewhere and fall asleep."

She offered her lips for a kiss, then trailed a hand down his arm, turned, and strolled to the Jeep. Before going to work she stopped by the cabin and put down food and water for Brad. The little pit bull was happy to see her, happier to see the food.

Around midnight she drove home, dead beat from a long day at the paper, parked close to the porch, and dragged her weary body inside and as far as the couch.

Lips touched her cheek and she startled awake, swinging a fist that contacted flesh with a solid thud.

"Shit."

A fierce barking and she struggled to her feet, ready to do battle. "What? Who?"

"Dang, woman. I can go away and come back some other time."

Dal stood back from her a ways, a hand over his nose. Blood seeped between his fingers.

"Oh, honey, I'm sorry. I was dreaming." She stood on tiptoe and eased his hand away from his bleeding nose. Touched it gently. "I don't think it's broken. Too bad, though. They say a crooked nose adds to character." She giggled, then covered her mouth. "Sorry. So damned tired. You hadn't ought to sneak up on me, you know."

She took his hand, led him into the bathroom, and sat him on the stool. Wetting a cloth in cold water she gently wiped the blood off his face. Kissed his chin. "I'm so sorry."

"It's okay. I shouldn't have scared you like that. It's my fault."

Grabbing a fistful of tissues, she took his hand, urged him to his feet, and led him into the bedroom. He dropped to the edge of the mattress and she sat beside him. For a long few moments they sat like that, him dabbing a tissue to his nose.

"It's stopped. I think I'll live. I'll just remember never to kiss you awake again."

"I'm really sorry. Tell you what. I'll get you undressed if you can do the same for me." She didn't wait for his reply, but rolled the hem of his t-shirt up and off over his head.

He grinned. "My turn?"

"Uh-huh, most definitely. But don't count on this leading to anything."

Without replying he ran both hands up under her shirt, tweaked her nipples with his thumbs, then peeled the fabric over her head.

"Oh, my. Hmm."

"Britches?" He shoved her to her back, slipped off her shoes and ragged jeans.

His boots hit the floor, the mattress jiggled with his movement. She didn't open her eyes.

Lips on her bare stomach, tongue warm, tasting, nibbling. A big sigh joined her moan. "If you could just scootch around till your feet are... yeah, like that."

Lying lengthwise, eyes still closed, she waited. He crawled over her, stretched out, and took her in his arms.

"I'm dirty." With no idea when, she awoke held securely against his chest, sunlight warming her skin. She took a deep breath, snuggled into the curve of his shoulder and went back to sleep.

The phone rang and rang. The noise invaded Dal's dream, but search as he might he could not locate the damned thing. And it wouldn't stop that blasted noise. He slapped a hand against the table, but it was soft. Not a table at all. Something lay across his chest. Something warm and cuddly.

Whatever it was moved, groaned, wiggled closer. "Answer the phone." The words muffled against his bare skin.

He hugged her closer. "Let it ring. I can't find it."

Whatever he had snugged up close to him was causing all sorts of reactions from his body. An ache in his groin that grew intense. He slapped at that. "Goddamn."

"What?" She jumped up and away from him.

Coming awake, he rolled toward her. "I about broke my prick off. C'mere fore something busts."

She crawled to him, slipped one leg over his, and rubbed her breasts on his chest, barely touching him.

"Not helping." He laughed, spread his hands at her waist and zigged and zagged her till everything fitted together. "Oh, yes. That's good. But could you... well jump up and down or something?"

It was her turn to laugh. "Jump up and down or something? Well, I can try." She made a weak effort, just enough to stir him up even worse.

"Ah, well, now you got me in a predicament."

She rose on her knees and made a valiant go at fixing his problem.

"Shit, you're just making it worse."

"I'm making it worse? It's him down there that's making it worse. I was going to get up and make us some—"

He grunted in a final effort, rolled her over so he was on top, and went to work. It didn't take but two or three or maybe it was four ups or downs or both, he lost count, and a glorious release. Damned glorious. Evidently okay for her too, cause she did that little humming thing she always did when she came and her insides gripped him so tight he couldn't even move. Waited for it to happen again, cause it was so sweet when she did that. He'd had some women, but none of them ever did that thing while he was up inside them that felt like she had a hold with her hand and was squeezing with all her might. Holding him in that sweet, warm, wonderful place.

"Ah, love, you are something. Okay if I just stay here awhile?"

"You're mashing me. Couldn't we just sort of roll to one side without disconnecting? Would that work for you?"

"I reckon we can try. Roll this way or we're going off the bed. You push me off of you and I'll do my best."

Again she got tickled and tried to shove him off while he made only a little effort to accomplish the feat. Then Brad got in on it, obviously tired of waiting to be fed. He jumped on the bed and licked Dal's bare butt, then barked.

"I think you'd better get off me before he decides to take a bite." He pushed with one arm, rolled off her and off the bed, landing with a thunk. "I thought you said roll that way."

Between hysterical bouts she tried to talk, but he couldn't understand her. Brad jumped onto his chest, did his little foot stomp bark, then licked his face while Jessie lay on the bed, helpless to do anything but laugh.

"Wish you'd cut that out, woman. It's plumb embarrassing. He's staring at my… at me. Hell, I can't even get up from here, and I'm telling you I badly need a shower."

"Yep you do." She barely got the words out. "Tell you what, I'll get up, help you up, and we'll maybe make it to the shower. Damn it, Brad, stop licking my feet. Dog must like dirty skin."

"Hmm, don't blame him. I think I'm broke for life."

"Just wait a minute, hon. Get on your knees and use the bed to lean on. I can't pick you up."

After groaning for a while, he hoisted himself to his feet and went ahead of her into the bathroom where he turned on the shower and stepped in. "Oh, that feels good, come on."

"It can't be hot yet."

He reached out, grabbed her hand, and pulled her under the icy spray. She objected by hugging herself. "Crap, that's freezing."

"Just right for a summer shower. Feels good."

He took pity on her and wrapped her in his arms, rubbing her prickly skin until the water warmed some.

"Oh, that feels good."

"Trade you a back rub for a leg massage. Damn thing's killing me."

"Deal." She grabbed a washcloth, soaped it good. "I'll wash you first."

That worked out well, but took more time than she'd imagined. Finishing with his toes, she handed it to him. "Boy, I never realized how much, uh, skin, you've got. Sort of like it, though." She rubbed her naked butt against his thigh. "Back rub, if you please."

Her back rub turned into an all-over body rub that had her aching for more. He smacked her bottom. "Fetch a couple towels and back to the bed. Where I intend to keep you the rest of the week."

"Oh, yeah? Do I have any say about it?"

"Okay, say."

"Hmm, sounds pretty good to me, if we're allowed to break for food."

In the bedroom, he fell onto his face across the mattress. She grabbed a bottle of body lotion, crawled in beside him, and gently massaged the damaged leg. Only since he'd come home from Frog Pond had he consented to letting her touch the scars that laddered up the back of his thigh and across to his spine. Bullet wounds that had almost put him in a wheelchair for life. She'd finally convinced him how good it would feel after a sexy romp that involved lotion, her hand, and his erection.

Later that day, while they took a break from bed for sandwiches and beer, the phone rang and Jessie answered it.

"Where you been?" Tinker, sounding either excited or scared, it was difficult to tell which.

"With Dal, where do you think I've been?"

"Oh. Ah. Can't blame you."

The silence puzzled Jessie. "Well, you called me and it sounded really important."

"Oh, yes, it was. Is. I got distracted thinking of the gorgeous hunk. Hope I didn't interrupt anything."

"Nope, we have to come up for air once in a while. You're married to quite the hunk yourself. So rein in that imagination and tell me what's up."

"We have a mystery."

"Good. I mean, as long as no one is dead."

"Nope. A couple of the guys went out trying to track those two idiots who taped Jeff and Alicia up. Mac thought maybe they could track them. Instead they came across a cabin way off the beaten track."

"Well, not too unusual. Someone wanting to be left alone. Deputies are lucky they didn't get shot at."

"There's a man living there and they thought he was alone but guess what they found?"

"A bear. Bigfoot. Amelia Earhart. Elvis Presley. How do I know till I get more clues?"

"Get this. They found two girls. His daughters, he claims, and they call him Daddy. So am I just being overly suspicious? What with all that's going on."

Her ears perked. A possible connection with the child trafficking? Maybe they hadn't rounded them all up. "How old are the girls?"

"They didn't know, but young. Maybe three and six, but that's just a guess and you know how men are."

"Old enough to know who their Daddy is. A bit young for the traffickers. Did they try to take them aside and question them?"

"They radioed it in to Mac and he said they couldn't do anything unless there was a reason to bring them in."

"Sounds true, but how I'd love to interview them. I smell a story. Which deputies went out there?"

"It was Les and the new guy, Duggan. Why?"

"Cause I'll want to talk to them. Would you tell them? Say I'll be by the station Monday. I'd like one of them to take me out there. If it looks hinky we can notify the FBI."

"Sounds good. Meanwhile, we thought you and Dal might like to come out tomorrow afternoon for a BBQ. Some of the guys are coming with their girls. We all think it's time we had a party."

"I'll talk to Dal. What can I bring?"

"Oh, you talked to him already and he said okay?"

Jessie laughed. "You know Dal. He's agreeable."

Dal had watched her during the conversation, and his eyebrows climbed his forehead.

"Okay, you guys can bring the beer."

"Will a truckload be enough?"

"Maybe. See you then. Sometime around four. It'll be cooling off by then. But you can come early if you want, and help me get stuff ready."

"Sounds good to me. See you then."

She hung up, grinned at Dal. "We've been invited to a barbecue."

"I got that much. Sounds good." He took a bite and studied her while he chewed. "When you gonna tell me the rest?"

"What?"

"The mystery. The one you're going to go chasing after Monday."

"Oh, that."

"Oh, that."

"Not today. We have other things to do, and I'm not letting you out of the house till we go to Tinker's tomorrow afternoon."

He finished the sandwich and grinned. "Sounds like a deal to me. But you will tell me about the mystery."

"Maybe."

"You will, I have my ways."

She laughed. "You certainly do."

And in the end, she did tell him.

His reaction? "We can't go busting in on everyone who likes to live off the grid unless there's a good reason. I'd say leave em be."

She had no intention of doing that.

3
CHAPTER

The first to arrive at the barbecue in Tinker and Burt's yard, Dal and Jessie went to work. He headed toward the garage where Burt was stacking chairs on a dolly. Carrying two pies from Grandma's on the square, Jessie climbed the steps to the back door and rapped before entering through the screened-in porch. Tink started talking to her even as she stepped into the kitchen.

Wow, what a difference since she'd been here last.

Jessie halted. The old-fashioned kitchen had been replaced by new appliances of black and stainless steel. On the outside wall, bay windows looked over the valley and distant mountains. A round dining table of polished cherry wood held preparations for the barbecue. "This is beautiful. I kind of hate to walk across that shiny floor."

"Isn't it pretty? But you can't hurt it. It's some kind of black bamboo. Treated so it doesn't scuff."

"Impressive." She put the pies on the table and went to the sink where Tink washed dirt away from the roots of green onions from the garden.

"Mmm, those smell good." From a nearby bowl, she plucked up a pod of snow peas and bit it in two. The sweet, crunchy taste was one of her favorite fresh vegetables.

"Last of the spring crop. So glad you guys could manage to crawl out of bed to honor us with your presence." Tink turned and gave Jessie a hug, the smell of onions fresh on her hands.

"Oh, cute. Wouldn't have missed it. It'll be good to see Dave and Kathy too. They've been gone way too long. So, what can I do?"

"See those cans of baked beans? Open them, dump them into that casserole, and sprinkle bacon bits over the top. Everyone will think they're homemade if you throw the cans down in the bottom of the trash. Don't you dare tell anyone my secret. Stick em in the oven at three-hundred-fifty degrees."

"Oh, I like your methods. Maybe you can teach me how to cook."

"Smart aleck. The wise woman learns what's good and already cooked, then she disguises it as her own. For instance, take those pies out of their wrappings and heat them up. Give 'em that just-out-of-the-oven taste."

"And all this time I thought you were a damn fine cook. Now I find out you're one heck of a good actress."

"Liar, you mean. You want to wash those peas and let them drain in the colander? They're best eaten raw. Les's wife is bringing her famous three-tier Mexican dip, and Kathy promised her potato salad, the best in three counties. The rest, I don't know, but there'll be plenty of food. Burt has deer and beef steaks all ready to throw on the grill."

"All sounds good enough to eat. Is Parker coming?"

"Uh-huh, and he's bringing a lady friend."

"About time he crawled down off that celibacy perch. Who is she, do you know?"

"Nope, he just told me he was bringing someone."

"I can't wait to meet her." Jessie picked up a tray stacked with plates, napkins, paper cups, and silverware. "I'll take this out to the table. Be right back."

Tink nodded and stood the onions in a glass.

Jessie found Dal scattering chairs around the lawn in the shade under the huge oak trees. "Guess what? Parker is bringing a female friend."

"No shit? I thought he was a monk or something. Women always making eyes at him and he never turns a hair. Acts like he doesn't even know they're alive. Who is she?"

"Tink doesn't know."

"Poor Tinkerbelle. And here I thought she knew everything that happens in Cedarton."

Kathy and Dave arrived, giving hugs all around and chattering about their trip to Egypt. A couple more cars and the gang was all there. Including Parker and his lady friend, who showed up last and made quite an entrance.

Parker's companion waited in the Rover while he hurried around to open the door and take her hand to help her down. Her long gray hair blew in the breeze, revealed a wide purple streak the length of one side. The waiting crowd hushed all conversation and stared like a bunch of country bumpkins.

Relieved the woman wasn't a youngster, she couldn't help being one of the gapers. Seemed he'd kept the woman a secret from one and all. Jessie was just a tad hurt that he hadn't told her. Still she was happy for him. Just like him to keep secrets close to his chest. No one spoke while he led her by the arm to their hosts.

"Beth, this is Tinker and Burt Sample." He raised his voice so all could hear. "Everyone, this is my friend Beth Lavender. You can introduce yourselves."

A shouted *hi* resounded. No one dared laugh at the name, considering the streak in her hair, but there was an undertone of humor in the conversation that followed.

Even though Deputy Duggan hadn't shown up, the feast got underway precisely at four o'clock, because that was the way Tink was about things.

The crowd seated at two redwood tables centered the conversation on the Spaceys' adventures at several digs, then moved to Beth, who answered questions about where she'd come from. No wonder no one knew her, she was from Little Rock, visiting a great aunt in Clifty, and had dropped by the paper the previous Saturday when Parker was there alone. Evidently the two hit it off immediately.

"I was smitten." Parker took her arm and beamed like a kid.

Sam Watson, who must have been eighty years old, couldn't take his eyes off her. Looked like he wanted nothing but to haul her off to bed somewhere. And not to sleep, either.

No matter what the topic, Sam continued to gaze off and on at the woman. Conversation moved on to the strange appearance and inexplicable actions of Robert Kimble and Taylor Bainbridge, the two fugitives still on the loose. Alicia related the frightening kidnapping her and Jeff experienced.

"Neither of us can figure out why they took us. They never threatened or harmed us in any way. Just kept talking about us keeping secrets or we'd be sorry."

"Weren't you scared?"

"Keeping what secrets?"

"Sorry how?"

Questions came from around the table, then paused so the couple could reply.

"Sure, I just knew they were going to kill us. I have no idea what secrets. Funny, their threats were implied and not spoken. Believe me, I'll keep their silly secrets, whatever they might be." Alicia took Jeff's hand and he smiled but didn't say anything.

Mac shook his head and frowned. "Looks like the FBI could've caught them by now. I just figgered they were long gone. Spect we'll have to go out there and arrest them ourselves before they get busy and start up their cult again."

Dal told them he had spoken to Marshal Trey Ledger about the continued freedom of the two fugitives, but had received no satisfactory reason they weren't in custody.

"What if they start stealing kids again?" Mac scratched at his already messy hair. "Something needs to be done."

It was indeed a mystery that kept the conversation going until dessert. The two pies Jessie had brought, one blueberry and one peach, were served with ice cream and the subject drifted on to the latest mystery.

"I swear if this place hasn't become a haven for all the weirdos, present company excepted." Les was retired from the police department down in Fort Smith and worked as a deputy in Grace County. "We heard tell about this man down in the holler keeping two young'uns captive. We going down there to check him out?"

"Hold up." Mac raised a hand. "Nothing says he's keeping them captive. And we sure can't accuse him of it, less we get more to go on. Colby, why don't you get on that machine of yours and do your magic? If you find something solid we can go on, why then we'll do something."

As the party progressed Sam continued his fascination with Beth.

Parker better keep an eye on those two, for she had noticed and shifted her dark eyes in Sam's direction, preening under his attention. This was a triangle in the making.

Dal was obviously concerned about the man living in the woods with two girls. Could they be a part of the ring that stole children to sell? Even if not, what could the guy be up to? It wasn't a good situation and Jessie would check it out too.

"I'm thinking we ought to look into it, Mac. There's just something suspicious about a grown man keeping two little girls in a cabin off in the woods, even if they do seem okay with it."

Good thing Dal felt uneasy, at least that meant they'd follow up on it.

"You thinking he kidnapped em, uhm, and they might be under that syndrome?" Mac appeared reluctant.

Dal nodded. "The Stockholm Syndrome. Maybe I ought to pay them a visit, see what kind of vibes they put off. It's mighty suspicious."

Mac eyed Dal for a minute or two. "What reason you going to give them for showing up at their door uninvited? Duggan and Les didn't have a search warrant."

"And they weren't invited in. Only heard about this, didn't actually see it for themselves. How about if I tell them we're looking for a kidnapped woman? That won't be far from the truth and it'd give me a chance to feel out their thoughts, so to speak. "

"Seems to me like that's close to being illegal. Sort of like taping them in secret." The words escaped before Jessie could stop them. Dal might not be too happy about what she'd said about his peculiar way of eavesdropping.

The discussion grew louder and several of the deputies put in their two cents' worth, siding with Dal. It wasn't unusual among the group to disagree and once in a while someone got angry. Fistfights had never happened. Yet.

Tinker and Jessie could get into it over some topics but always stopped short of raising their voices. This one, though, they agreed on in theory. Dal listening in on people's thoughts might be considered by the law as illegal as taping them without consent. However neither cared if he did it if it was to catch lowdown dirty scum. As for Dal, he really preferred not to.

Jessie returned Dal's frown. "It's just illegal, is all I'm saying. Not wrong. There is a big difference."

"Not if you wear a badge there's not." This from Mac. "If it's against the law then it's wrong. Sounds like you ain't gonna leave me be about it."

None of the deputies would argue with their boss in public, though it was clear by their expressions some of them would have liked to on this subject. Mac was always ready to use Dal's abilities when it came to crimes. Catching scum was what it was all about.

The disagreement went on for a while, with no solution, then died out when someone brought up planning a Fourth of July celebration in the city park. Les's wife was in charge while several of the deputies' wives were on the planning board for that event and welcomed suggestions from everyone. The celebration was pretty well planned by the time the party broke up around nine o'clock.

The crowd pitched in to help carry and stow everything away, then headed out hollering and waving goodbye as if they lived hundreds of miles apart and wouldn't see each other for a year.

Jessie and Dal went to his car holding hands. She was curious about the missing deputy. "Did anyone ever find out why Duggan didn't come today? It was mentioned a couple of times. Did you call him?"

"Nope. He's sort of an odd guy. Being the youngest in the department, I think he feels out of place sometimes. Maybe thinks we're a bunch of old fogies."

"Hmm, well, he's not too far from wrong." She dug an elbow in his ribs. "Old man."

"Hey, that'll do, woman."

She didn't think of the young deputy's absence again.

Horny as hell, Dal went home with Jessie. He'd left his patrol car at her place and rode over to the Samples' in the Jeep with her. Though he had rented Tinkerbelle's old apartment above the garage of the Five Bs when he returned from Frog Pond last fall, he often stayed at Jessie's place when he had the urge to make love off and on all night. Or, for that matter, when she was horny. This was one of those nights for him. Sometimes he couldn't keep his mind or hands off her for more than ten minutes at a time. Other times, he'd be so pissed off at something she'd done he didn't want anywhere near her. They would never be able to live together, of that he was sure. Both of them were too volatile. Set in their ways, Mac often said.

Along about midnight he rolled off her, contented and ready to sleep. Moonlight through tree branches laced in the window and across the bed, outlining her relaxed features. When his phone rang, he was unable to take his eyes off her, reached for the blasted thing, and knocked it off in the floor.

"Well, shit." He hissed the words to keep from bothering her, scrabbled around under the table and bed till he came up with the noisy nuisance. Was a time no one could find him if he didn't want them to. Cell phones had changed that for good. He peered at the display to see who was calling at this hour. One thing he could do was ignore the damned thing, not answer if it wasn't important.

Duggan? What the hell?

He clicked it. "Starr, what's up?"

Static, a voice cutting in and out. Hard to make out the words. Dal rose his voice. "Can't hear you. See if you can get a better signal."

Nothing but white noise. Then a sound he had no trouble discerning. What sounded like a gunshot, then another, then nothing.

He sat up, called the deputy's name a couple of times. Still nothing. He disconnected and called the station. Sam Watson answered.

"Hey, Sam. Where's Duggan supposed to be now?"

"Hold on." Silence, then he came back. *"Schedule shows he's doing Sector Five, but he hasn't checked in."*

A year or so ago Mac had dragged out a county map, divided it up, and numbered the sections so he could keep better track of where the deputies were and how to assign them. Better than trying to remember what highway or road they were on. Dal had to think about it for a minute or so.

"Five? That's—"

"Southwest. Down around Lizard Lick. No cell signal down there. On and off on the mountain. You get down in the valley there ain't none. Why? What's going on this time of night?"

"Not sure it's anything. Got a call from him, couldn't understand what he was saying. Don't know why he would call me."

"Might be cause he tried to call here and I couldn't make out anything either. He may have thought he might have better luck getting you."

"Well, I'm pretty sure I heard a gunshot before we got cut off completely. Think I'll call Mac."

"Good idea. That don't sound good."

"Isn't that where the guys were talking about finding that man living with those two little girls? Wasn't that down below Lizard Lick?"

"I believe you're right. Er—Section Five that is. You gonna call Mac? You don't, I will."

A sleepy Jessie roused beside him, looking so sexy in the moonlight he almost forgot all about Duggan's call. "Dal, what's going on?"

Reluctant to do so, he dragged his attention away from her and assured Sam he would call Mac. He hung up, leaned over and kissed her, even managed to keep from touching her otherwise.

"Something going on with Duggan. I heard gunshots. Think I'm gonna check with Mac. We ought to send someone down there. Too much of a coincidence that he's patrolling the area where that man has those kids in his cabin. I don't like the sound of it."

Mac's phone rang several times, but he didn't answer. He sometimes left it up to the deputies on night duty to take care of things and didn't take calls after ten o'clock. Dal left him a message, then pulled on his jeans and t-shirt and slipped on a pair of moccasins.

"Can't get through. I'm going on down there."

Jessie wiggled into her shorts and t-shirt and bent to pick up her sneakers. "Guess you don't mind if I keep you company."

"You're just afraid you'll miss something." Like it'd do any good to tell her she couldn't go along.

"True. Hate to miss a good story cause I was too lazy to get out of bed. You don't care, do you?"

He raised his shoulders and grinned. "Guess not. I welcome the company. That's one of the more deserted parts of the county. Nothing down there but trees and rocks and bluffs."

"And lizards." She trailed along behind him, hooking up the backpack she kept sitting by the door. "What do you think's happened?"

He crawled in behind the wheel and keyed the ignition. "Not sure. Whether it was Duggan's weapon or someone shooting at him, I couldn't pick up on much from this far off."

She remained quiet till he headed south on state road 19. He sensed her staring at him.

"What?" He didn't take his eyes off the twisting pavement.

"Just wondering if it's bothering you, all that mind reading and poking around in other people's murderous thoughts. I didn't mean to put you on the spot earlier. You know it's not so much that I think it's wrong. I just wish you didn't have to do that stuff cause of what it does to you."

That was something he had to think about. Since returning from Frog Pond everything had been pretty quiet around Cedarton so he'd been spared touching the ghosts, or *asgi'na* spirits of his people. He could shut off the mind reading and usually did. Walking onto a crime scene, the violence and red hot fury transmitted by the evil spirits, the *anisgi'na*, often drove him to his knees. He struggled dealing with the lingering thoughts of anything from despair to rage.

"It's been okay. I think I can keep it in check till it actually hits me, then I'm not sure. But it's better here than while I was in Dallas. At least murder and mayhem are few and far between here. I don't think I can escape it unless I become a hermit. Best I learn to live with Grandfather's occasional influence much as I can."

He slowed, turned onto a narrow road marked by a county sign containing four numbers which meant the road was unpaved and accessed only a few residences.

"I'm sorry you can't just shut it off. You're a good cop without it."

He chuckled. "How do you know that?"

"I just do, that's all. You're tough, and I watched you with those kids when you brought them down off that bluff last year. You not only know how to handle people, you notice things most people don't."

"You're giving me a lot more credit than I deserve." He slowed, leaned forward to make out the sign in the headlight beams. It read Lizard Lick and pointed to the left along an even narrower road that coiled its way down the mountain. Folks who lived down there existed off the grid by choice. No electrical power, no services of any kind. That way they left no footprints. It was like driving into a black hole. To make matters worse, clouds drifted over the moon, leaving only the cones from the headlights to show the way. Trees grew closer and closer to the road, gathering over it like a canopy. Branches scraped the sides of the car.

The night was filled with the chitter, click, and saw of hundreds of bugs and frogs and night birds. Lightning bugs signaled each other, thick in the darkness. Without warning, a bird, a mere shadow with widespread wings, swooped over the top of the car and flew ahead of them, as if a portent of what was to come.

"Damn, what the hell *is* that?" Dal braked so the bird disappeared into the distance.

"A whippoorwill. Your first one?"

"I reckon. I think I'd remember something like that."

"They're reclusive. You may never see another one."

He chuckled, nerves showing. "Glad you were with me, or I might've took it for a warning from the other side."

"Well, sweetheart. It might well be." She pursed her lips and made a *woo-woo* sound.

"Cut that out." He finally let up on the brake and the car moved forward again.

"Sort of like going into another world, isn't it?" Her voice was a bit jittery, whether from the roughness of the road or her sensibilities, he wasn't sure.

"I was thinking more like driving into a good horror movie." He had to laugh when she shuddered and hugged herself.

A pair of eyes stared at them from the center of the road and he braked again. "Good heavens. Dare I ask what the hell that is?"

"I don't know everything."

"Huh. First I heard of that."

Whatever it was lumbered away slowly as if to say I'm in charge down here, not you. And it well could be. Black bears, cougars, coyotes, and an occasional wolf pack lived in these woods. And no telling what else. No telling at all.

"Still glad you came?" His low chuckle sounded funny to his own ears. It was the atmosphere, the strange noises, the imagination that, turned loose, could come up with all sorts of monsters.

"When I was a kid I loved to be scared in the night. Used to beg my dad to take me with him when he went coon hunting. Probably seems pretty wild to a Texas boy, huh?"

"Just a different sort of wild is all. Why do people want to live out this far like this?"

"Oh, I'm sure they have their reasons."

"No doubt. It'll serve you well to lock yourself in. Only thing, if I come running out of the woods hollering, you make sure you let me in."

Both of them managed to laugh, but it was a nervous jittery sound.

No. she didn't want to wait in the car like a good little girl, but something told her to do just that. Something deep in her mind echoed over and over. Stay here. One of them had to stay safe in the car just in case. Maybe she'd end up being the hero.

She laid a hand on his arm as he opened the door to get out. "Be careful. Don't take any chances. You'd never live it down if I had to rescue you from the clutches of a wild hillbilly."

His smile flashed an instant before he shut the door and was gone. The dome light faded slowly and she leaned her head back. Time to take some deep breaths and relax. Not easy. In her imagination, the lumbering monster that had appeared in their headlights snuck up from behind the car. Not a bear nor deer, but a slobbering, moaning monster. Her childhood delight in being frightened had been dissolved by having faced some cruel realities.

She shivered and turned on her iPhone, more to light up the interior than to check her email. Good thing because there was no service. All she had was a flashlight that would take pictures. Ah, well. No problem. She'd never been afraid of the dark. That was Tinker. She on the other hand loved the dark. Embraced it. Nothing bad lurked there. No indeed. If she closed her eyes she could pretend it was daylight.

Get off this nonsense. Try to figure out just what's going on with this business. It made absolutely no sense. Going to all the trouble of sneaking back into a county where everyone knew them, taking Jeff and Alicia, then without harm leaving them tied up in a shack in the woods. Why hadn't those two left the county, hell left the state and country? The FBI and US Marshals were looking for them. How crazy did they have to be?

Okay. Reasons. Coming back for someone or something left behind. Or someone knew something about them. Enough with the someones and somethings. Uh, more to the point, Alicia and Jeff knew something about them. If so, why didn't they know what they knew? And why were they left behind without being asked? Or threatened? Didn't even torture them, for goodness' sake. What if they were coming back to do that? She shivered, changed the subject.

More reasons. The men had left something here they wanted. Left it in the barn. Before the Woodsons moved here last year. The place had been empty for quite a long time, leaving it a super location for dark goings-on. Though mostly kids making out, or as they put it today, hooking up. That made more sense, in a skewed way, only if one considered that people who committed crimes were not the brightest bulb in the lamp.

Her phone played a few bars of *Polonaise* and she jumped, hitting her head on the side window. Took a few deep breaths and glanced at the display, expecting something ghostly to appear there. Instead it was Tinker's picture. A signal after all.

"Hey, what's up?"

"You okay?" Tinker sounded down in a well.

"Yeah, just sitting in a car. In the dark. Waiting. You okay?"

"Fine. I couldn't sleep so thought we might talk. What are you doing sitting in a car? I thought you'd be in bed all cozy and satisfied watching that gorgeous hunk sleep."

"Oh, that's right. Sam is on duty and you're home. Duggan called and talked to Dal, all jumbled up. Then there were gunshots, so he called Mac, who didn't answer, so then he talked to Sam and told him we were coming down here cause Sam said this is where Duggan was scheduled to be."

"Uh, okay. You're babbling. Could you tell me where down here is? And do you need backup?"

Something banged on the rear end of the SUV, the phone went dead, and Jessie couldn't help it, she yelped. While she was proud she didn't scream like some stupid Hollywood actress, she did yelp and she did wish she were somewhere else. Anywhere else. No matter how hard she tried, she couldn't get a signal on the phone.

The footpath to Lizard Lick petered out in less than a mile. Just sort of narrowed to nothing but an animal trail. Left him wishing he'd worn his walking shoes. Dal glanced behind him. He'd never been down here. What the hell happened to Lizard Lick? Had he blinked and missed it? Maybe there were some buildings back in the woods. Hard to see more than a foot or two in the darkness. The moon hung behind clouds that glowed but didn't help much showing him the way. If it weren't for the shots he'd heard, he'd be using his flashlight, but it would be damned foolish to make a target of himself till he figured out the lay of the land.

If anyone had told him when he searched the alleys of Dallas that he'd one day be tromping through the wilderness where no lights, not one goddamned one, shined, he'd have told them they were certifiably nuts. Instead here he was, and more than likely he was the one who ought to be certified. Nothing out here. No one. He'd know it if they were. Wouldn't he? What in the hell was he doing here? For the only time in his life, he wished he could hear someone else's thoughts.

He stood still, closed his eyes. Concentrated. Not even Grandfather. A critter skittered across his path, scolding him in a language he didn't understand. He chuckled just to add to the sounds. How crazy did he have to be?

Gritting his teeth, he pulled the flashlight off his belt, turned it on, and lit up his surroundings, searching in a full circle, finding nothing but trees and rocks and a trail. So, okay, he'd follow it for a little ways. It was probably useless, but he keyed his walkie and hailed Duggan with a 10-20.

Nothing but static.

Someone keyed a walkie. *"Dal, is that you?"*

"Jessie?"

"Oh, hi. I thought that was you. Could you come back?"

"Jessie, honey. This isn't a telephone."

"What? Oh, I know. Do I need a number to talk?"

He laughed. "No, I don't suppose you do. Why should I come back?"

"Well, something banged on the trunk and then I heard you say ten-twenty."

"What was it?"

"I don't know. Scared me to death, but it went away."

"I'll be back shortly. Stay in the car. Don't get out. If Duggan came this way, his car has disappeared in thin air. I'll need daylight to find him."

"Okay. Don't be too long."

"Remember, you insisted on coming."

"Yes, I know. I'll wait." She sounded petrified.

Served her right. He couldn't help grinning. Leaving the flashlight on, he headed down the trail, occasionally scanning the surrounding woods. Where the hell had Duggan got to? There must be lots of old roads in this area, and the deputy could be anywhere.

Something glittered through the trees. He held the light on it. Couldn't make out much. Shined the beam down, headed toward the object. Looked like glass reflecting light. The last hundred feet or so he fought his way through brush and armpit-high shrubbery and finally came up on a patrol unit with Duggan's number on it. It was roof-deep in thick growth, but he finally made his way close enough to light up the inside. No one in the front. High stepping, he checked the back. Empty.

Puzzled, he stood there for a while staring at the vehicle. A walk behind it revealed it had indeed not appeared out of thin air. It had plowed its way through the brush, leaving a broken trail behind. With some difficulty, he followed the tracks left by the car where it had gone between trees, dodging here and there. Driven in, not just pushed off out of the way.

Exhausted from high-stepping through the heavy brush, he leaned against a tree for a moment. Then made up his mind. He went back to the car, climbed in fighting the thick growth, and reached for the key to start it. Not there. A quick search and he came up with nothing.

Well, shit, the least they could've done was leave the key. Who would steal it way out here? Now what? He could hot wire it, but didn't like the idea. Some of these cars could really be fucked up.

Here he was, in the middle of the night—hell almost morning now—had walked as far as he could manage for a while, sitting in an abandoned patrol car with no keys, no radio. Maybe his cell had a signal. He dug in his pocket, took it out.

And what was he going to say? Help me, I can't walk out. Never would live that down. Actually, couldn't even tell them where he was. Except if he had a signal they could find him. Damn, he hated to call for that kind of help. Would rather someone was pointing a gun at him than that.

Get out of the car, get back to the trail, and back to your car. What are you, some kind of sissy? If the damned leg gives out, then sit and rest for a while. Thing was, he didn't want to admit defeat. He studied the phone, tried to call Jessie to tell her he was coming back but he'd be a while. Sure hated to leave her there alone this long, but it was her insisted on coming along.

No signal.

Nothing for it but to go back the way he'd come in. Dawn silvered the sky, even though the woods were still dark.

He climbed out, stretched for a moment, stared aimlessly into the distance. And there, nestled in the woods sat a cabin and it looked like someone lived there. Maybe their unknown friend and his children? The windows reflected the dawn light so he might have to wake someone up, but he was going there.

Just as he stepped onto the stoop, the door swung open, revealed a man holding a rifle. Pointed at him.

4

CHAPTER

Jessie jerked awake, opened her eyes to sunlight filtering through leaves onto the windshield. She'd fallen asleep, of all things. Out here in the woods in the car. Alone. What time was it and where was Dal? He'd been gone for ages. Waiting for him through the dark of night in the woods was becoming habit forming.

Static sounded from the other seat. She dug around and found the walkie. Keyed it. "Hello? Is anyone there?"

More static, then a male voice. Vague and unrecognizable. *"Who is this?"*

"Well, who is *this?*" Chattering from outside. A gray squirrel sat on a limb, telling her off. She had to smile.

"What are you doing on this channel? This is Sheriff Mac Richards." A pause. *"Is that you, Jessie? What are you up to, girl? Everyone is looking for you and Dal. Rumor has it you eloped."*

The squirrel stared at her, darted away as if shocked.

"You and me both, fella."

"What? Jesse?"

Concentrating on the walkie, she spoke to Mac. "I was talking to a squirrel. The day we elope will be the day. He went into the woods looking for Lizard Lick. I thought that name was a joke but it appears to exist, even if in name only. And it's where Duggan disappeared last night. I hope this isn't one of those woo-woo stories. Anyway, Dal left me in the car if you can believe that. And he hasn't come back."

"We know Duggan's gone, too. Figgered he went with you two to be your witness. Why is Dal looking for Lizard Lick?"

"Long story. I'll shorten it. He was talking to Duggan on his cell, heard gunshots, then nothing. Called Sam who said Duggan was out here somewhere on patrol. We couldn't find him, now I don't know where Dal is. Maybe they both dropped into a black hole."

"Okay, I'll send Colby out. Do you at least know where you are? A road number or something?"

"I saw a number where we turned off the main road, but after a while there was this sign said Lizard Lick and we turned there. Now the road's petered out and Dal's traipsing around on foot somewhere. And I'm talking to the wildlife. You know how easily he gets lost. City boy in the woods. Be funny if you send Colby and he disappears too."

The sound of Mac laughing. *"Here's Colby, girl. Talk to him. He knows that area pretty well. Maybe he can place you."*

She did and almost an hour later, when she'd about given up hope, the patrol car pulled up. Colby crawled out and stomped his way to her. He always looked as if he were marching.

Before he reached her she opened the door. "You have any water? I drank all mine, and I'm dying of thirst."

He retraced his steps and fetched a bottle, waited while she drank most of it. "Which way did Dal go?"

"Off down that path that disappears into the woods." She pointed. "I'm going with you. I've been in this frigging car most all night."

"Well, come on, then." He frowned. "Seems odd Dal just walked off and left you here. Odder still he hasn't returned."

"You just don't know him. He's been trying to leave me somewhere ever since we met." Colby laughed along with her. She wasn't sure it was that funny. "He wants to handle everything on his own."

Colby's long legs thrashed through the brush like it wasn't even there. Insects fogged up around him. She had to run to keep up. After a brief walk he stopped abruptly in front of her. "There's Duggan's unit. What the hell's it doing off out here?"

He waded waist deep through poke bushes, the purple berries staining his gray pants. One look at her ragged jeans and she shrugged and followed. Time to throw them away anyhow.

"Looks like someone drove it in here. No way it rolled in between all those trees. Dal found it." Colby gazed in all directions, turned back to her.

She shivered. "He's not inside dead is he?"

"Nope. Guess he could be in the trunk."

"Well, can you get it open?"

He opened the door and popped the trunk. She refused to go look, left him to do it "Nope. No blood or nothing." He gave her that familiar teasing grin that made her grit her teeth.

"How do you know Dal saw it?"

"Cause, he'd have to be blind to miss it."

She stopped dead in her tracks. "That's it."

He looked at her like she'd farted in church. "What?"

"If you're blind you might miss what's staring you in the face unless you can hear or smell or feel or taste it."

"Well, sure. Everyone sort of knows that."

"I just didn't apply it. We need to find Dal and get back up to the Hermitage. Now."

"Okay, but why?"

"I'll explain it, or at least talk it out once we find Dal and get back up to Jeff and Alicia's place."

Colby searched the perimeter around the patrol unit while they talked. "Come this way, Jessie. I think Dal took off here."

"How do you know that isn't the tracks of whoever left the car?"

"It is but Dal would've followed. And besides, it's the only tracks through these weeds other than those we made. Two possibilities. The guy who brought the car walked away in the car tracks, or he went this away and Dal followed him. Or he teleported outta here. I guess Dal could've gone off this way by hisself. Anyhow, someone went this away. Come on." He grabbed her hand and she practically ran to keep from being dragged.

Weeds waist high on either side of the trail let loose fogs of big grasshoppers that perched on her arms, then flew off, a few as big as hummingbirds. The trail headed down into a small stream. They would've lost their way then except off to the right as they waded out of the water sat a cabin and a small ATV parked nearby. Dal wouldn't have missed this place. Would definitely have stopped to check it out.

Colby slowed, paced the ground under several large pine trees. Nothing grew there. The ground was covered with pinecones and needles. Couldn't really tell if someone had walked there recently.

He palmed his gun and took a few cautious steps toward the silent cabin. She followed, breathed deeply of the pine-scented air.

"Here, looks like he went this way." He leaned close to whisper his findings. "Keep quiet. These folks live out here for a reason. They don't appreciate being bothered."

"So maybe we ought not to bother them." Her skin prickling with the possibility of being shot at, she followed along behind him. Trees and brush grew up around the place, not leaving a yard of any sort. Colby approached the side away from the porch. Held an arm up to stop her.

"Wait here."

"Huh-uh."

He took a deep breath. "Okay. Come on, then. Anybody home?" His shouted words echoed back from the surrounding peaks.

No one replied. For a moment the woods turned quiet as if the critters waited for an answer. In the silence, her empty stomach rumbled.

Colby raised an eyebrow in her direction. "They're hid out. Probably watching us. I'm gonna knock. They gotta wonder what the hell we're doing out here. This doesn't help." He patted his side arm. "Best if I'd a come in plainclothes too. I'll try once more." He yelled again, this time identifying himself, then trotted up the steps to rap on the sagging wood.

Someone approached, the door scraped open. A figure stood beyond the screen under the shadow of the porch roof so it was hard to make him out. Till he spoke. "Hey, Colby, come on in. I told em you didn't come to arrest anyone. Want you to meet this fella. Jessie, what are you doing here?"

"Dal, I could ask you the same thing." It would've suited her to throw something at him.

He sure had a lot of nerve. Spending hours out here visiting in comfort while she waited, half-starved and dying of thirst. Well, maybe that was an exaggeration. She favored him with a glower and stepped inside along with Colby.

The man who closed the door behind them looked as if Dal might have invited a bear into his house. Easy to see he wanted them gone. His long pale hair lay against the shoulders of a white robe-like garment so he looked like pictures of Christ she'd seen in churches. But that wasn't all. The vibes he gave off tiptoed through her depths where she tucked away secrets. And as sappy as that sounded, she accepted it when she glanced at Dal and saw his expression. This man who spoke to spirits looked as if he was in the company of one.

"Colby, Jessie, this is Marcus, and he says he has no other name. I'm sorry I let the time get away from me. We've been talking."

Jessie nodded toward Marcus and Colby followed suit. He didn't offer his hand so neither of them did either.

"Did you find Duggan?"

"Your friend isn't here." Marcus spoke and everyone listened.

She couldn't explain it, except that he had a charismatic approach that demanded attention.

"I suspect he will return shortly though." His eyes, so light a blue they appeared silver, locked on her and, despite sweat running down her spine, she shivered.

It was as if someone or something had her trapped in a spell and she didn't much like it. "Do you have some water? I'm dry as a bone after sitting in the car half the night then walking all the way up here." She shot a harsh look in Dal's direction.

Colby stared at her, no doubt remembering she had drunk almost an entire bottle of his water.

Marcus smiled, moved to a dry sink where a bucket sat and, using a metal dipper, filled a glass with water that glittered with clarity. When he handed it to her, their fingers touched and a spark snapped between them. She jerked away. If he hadn't kept hold the glass would've fallen. With no reaction whatsoever, he set it on the table as if he knew all along what would happen when they came in contact.

Whatever game he was playing, she was uncomfortable that he could have such control over her thoughts. But he did, and she couldn't take her gaze off him while she drank.

Colby watched the interplay in silence, then turned to Marcus. "So did you talk to the deputy? Did he tell you how his car got off out in the woods? And where did he go?"

"I understood he was searching for someone who might have kidnapped two children? Is this true?" When the man turned, dust motes danced in the sunlight around him. He failed to admit that he'd talked to Duggan.

"You wouldn't happen to know someone like that? What did you tell him?" Dal acted plumb silly, as if he'd been off somewhere and was just returning.

"I did tell him of a man who lives off down in the holler. I've seen two little girls with him on occasion when I'm walking in the woods, but they do not act as if they are afraid. However, your deputy decided to check it out. He couldn't get his radio to work, so he went down there alone."

Dal looked surprised. "Did you hear gunshots?"

"No, I did not."

Something really odd about this guy and also about Dal's reaction. She had to talk to him alone. "I need some air. Dal, would you mind going with me? I don't feel well."

Dragging his gaze from Marcus, where it'd been locked for some time, he moved to her side, took her arm, and guided her out the door.

Outside, she turned to him. "What's wrong with you?"

He shook his head as if coming up out of deep water. "Jesus Christ."

"Come on." Despite her doubts, she cast a furtive look into the cabin.

"No. Didn't mean it that way. You don't want to know where I've been with this guy. He's... uh." He put his arms around her tight. "Jessie, he took me places I'd rather not have gone. And no way could I pull loose. Until just now. He knows about me and about Grandfather."

"That's ridiculous. You're hurting me."

"Sorry." He loosened his grip.

"What has he done to you?"

"I'm not sure. I don't remember except fire and howling wind and blood flowing in a place I don't ever want to be again. You know I would never have left you in the car all night. Until you walked in with Colby I didn't know the night had passed or that you were waiting for me."

She stared up into his eyes, swore flames of a fire flashed in them before they went back to their forest green. Dal possessed some frightening abilities and he had learned to deal with them, but this man must have cracked the protective shell he kept around those mysterious powers. As long as she'd known him, he'd pretty much kept that part of his life in protective custody. Oddly enough, she liked it that way, wasn't anxious to deal with what he kept hidden away in that secret part of his psyche.

What if this enigmatic man living in a hidden cabin in the woods had opened that box? What might come out of it could be destructive to Dal and her.

A breeze rose, lifting her hair against his bare skin. With a shiver, Dal held on to her, fearful of what had happened in those hours he'd spent with

Marcus, because he didn't remember anything but the visions, the taste of the howling wind, the sound and smell of blood, the godawful heat of the fire. Good God, where had this guy come from, and what did he want? Grandfather would know, but he was absent and silent. So like him.

Colby came out the door looking a bit confused. He shot a gaze over one shoulder as if something wicked might be coming. "I've heard about these woods being filled with oddities, but this one caps them all. Does this guy really think he's the Second Coming?"

All Dal wanted was to clear his head of the man's ability to enthrall. He led Jessie down off the porch and away from the cabin. The man was dangerous, the type who could convince a person of just about anything. Perhaps like lead the innocent into a cult existence.

Impossible to read him, though. He possessed a barrier Dal couldn't break through. It'd been a while since he'd gone spirit hunting, seeing as how violence was pretty much a rarity around Cedarton. But this one was scary as hell. The shoe on the other foot, more or less. He prodded around inside Marcus's brain till all he wanted was to get far away from him and this place.

"Let's head on down into the holler." Dal turned to Colby, not anxious to hike into this wilderness, yet desperate to leave Marcus behind. "Do you have any idea where this place might be?"

"Nope. You know what I'd suggest? That we go back to town, rent some horses from Parker, and then search. Hearing shots doesn't bode well, though there isn't any blood. We have no idea what could've happened to Duggan."

"Sounds like a good idea to me."

Relieved Colby had been the one to suggest that, Dal headed back toward the cars, still grasping Jessie's hand. She was looking at him sort of funny. In an effort to ease her mind, he grinned and she appeared to relax. Still, he didn't turn loose till he opened the car door and guided her inside.

Colby backed his car around and Dal followed suit, letting the deputy lead them out to civilization. Jessie was unusually quiet all the way to Cedarton. He expected her to ask if she could go along on their manhunt, but oddly enough she didn't bring it up. Not like her to pass up the opportunity to live out her next story. Maybe she thought he wouldn't let her go.

At the station, he parked next to Colby.

Jessie gripped the door handle. "Are you going to ride out there today? You must be tired after being up all night."

"Funny, I'm not tired. But we'll have to talk to Mac. Once he knows about the gunshots I'm sure he'll want to follow up. But no body. Hell, someone could've just taken pot shots at a deputy's car for the fun of it. Mac may not like the idea of us renting horses to go on some wild goose chase. These people might or might not exist. We've only heard some vague talk about the situation. Duggan may walk out on his own. He's not exactly a greenhorn. Besides, we still need a deputy to protect Jeff and Alicia Woodson until that threat's sorted out. Let's see what Mac says."

He ought to offer to let her go, but he didn't. Danger existed in those woods, and he'd rather she didn't get exposed. And he was going back, in spite of what Mac might think.

She slid out of the SUV. "I had a thought about that business with the Woodsons. Someone needs to talk to Jeff. I have a feeling he's heard or knows something he just hasn't thought about yet. Those guys were obviously using that old barn before the Woodsons bought the place. It was empty a long time. Maybe they came back for something left behind. And Alicia told me that Jeff goes out to the barn often when he's caught up in a flashback or just feeling bad. Sometimes those experiences mess with his memory. He might not remember what he knows."

Dal swung the glass door open and stood back to let her go first. "You may be right about that. You know, you'd make a good detective. Still it's odd. Leaving them in that shack like that."

She paused outside. "I can't believe you said that, the way you run me off from crime scenes. I'll remind you of it next time you do. I think I'll go on over to *The Observer* and get a story started for this week. Then I'm going home and take a nap. Unlike some people, I can't exist on a few hours' sleep." She stood on tiptoe and kissed him on the cheek. "See you later?"

He nodded and watched her walk away till she went around the corner behind a row of Rose of Sharon bushes.

Masses of gold, purple, red, and white flowers of all descriptions lined the sidewalk around the square. Overhead the pink and white blossoms of dogwood trees nodded in a morning breeze.

As beautiful as it was, he couldn't pull his mind away from what they'd found out in those woods. Something terrible was going to happen as a result of their meeting with Marcus. He'd give anything to be blissfully ignorant of what was coming, but he sensed it with every fiber of his being. And he was going to have to stop it. If only Grandfather would show up.

Somehow Jeff and Alicia and what was going on up at the Hermitage were all tied into it. Be damned if he knew how or why yet, but he did know and it scared him.

Tinkerbelle sat behind the desk in the station, a place she hated to be. Mac kept her there most of the time, finding it hard to let her go into the field. She looked up, eyes sparkling.

"Hey, Dal. So glad you're back. Everyone was worried. Where's Jessie?"

"She went to work, thought she ought to. Oh, and stories that we eloped are exaggerated, in case you wonder."

"Did you find Duggan?"

"Just his car. Is Mac here?"

"He's getting coffee. Colby is back there with him."

"Sounds good." Dal headed for the break room. Even that cop coffee would taste good after a night awake doing whatever it was he'd been doing. It would be good if he could remember what happened all night, cause Mac might just be a bit curious. And Dal was more than a little concerned about drawing a blank.

"Well, son, I understand there wasn't a wedding after all." Mac chuckled, clapped him on the back, and waited till he'd fixed his coffee.

Everyone was sure having a lot of fun out of this.

Mac led him from the break room. "Let's get ourselves into the office where we can talk more privately. You come too, Colby. We need to figure out our next move. With a deputy missing and those two yahoos running around loose—thanks to our brilliant FBI—I'm thinking trouble is brewing."

He headed down the hallway, Colby and Dal at his heels. In the chair behind his desk, he punched the intercom. "Tinker, would you please bring me the duty roster for the next twenty-four hours?"

After a few minutes, she came through the door holding out a sheet of paper. Dal shook his head. The roster was kept in the computers, which were linked, and it would've been easier and faster for her just to punch a button. Mac held tight to some old-fashioned functions. As he put it, he wanted "to hold that blamed piece of paper in his hands." It had only been a year or so ago that they'd talked him into an iPhone.

Tinkerbelle glanced from under her brow at Dal, acknowledged him with the barest twitch of a grin, and scurried out.

The sheriff spread the paper on his desk, sipped at his coffee, and studied it through reading glasses perched on his nose.

"Mac, we could—"

The old sheriff waved his fingers toward Dal. "Hold it, son."

Dal held it. Colby cleared his throat. The office was so quiet their coffee sipping sounded loud.

"Okay." Mac looked up from his perusal between the roster and the county map he kept taped to the corner of the desk. "We can have a couple of men back here shortly to put together a search team. How quick can we round up some horses? That place is not fit for vehicles or traipsing in on foot."

"I'll call Parker." He could've done that half an hour ago, but Mac would do things his way, so Dal didn't mention the fact, just took out his phone and called the editor and owner of *The Observer,* who also owned and rented out several riding horses.

"Four enough?" Dal glanced at Mac.

"Make it five, I'm going along. It's been a long time since I've been in on an honest-to-goodness manhunt. It could prove exciting." He squinted at Dal. "Seeing as how I missed the last one." He glanced from under furrowed brows. "See that Jessie remains here, would you?"

Under his stare, Dal squirmed. Suddenly, he was supposed to have control over her? Worse, it appeared he wouldn't live it down that he'd kept Mac out of the loop last fall when they went out to round up members of the cult of the Rising Moon.

Parker answered and Dal made the arrangements. They could meet him at his ranch in thirty minutes and saddle up. Mac had Tinker contact the deputies who were on their way back and have them go straight to Parker's.

"Mac, do you think we need extra eyes for this? No telling what kind of trouble Duggan is in."

"I think we can handle it. We'll give it a quick go and if we don't come up with something real soon, we'll call for help from the community. Lots of folks have riding animals and could pitch in."

Colby looked thoughtful. "Sheriff, I'm wondering, considering we know those two men are on the loose and dangerous, I was thinking maybe we ought to alert a couple of marshals besides everyone who could help us be on the lookout. Someone might just spot them."

Mac appeared to mull over the suggestion. "Good idea. We do that, though, the blamed FBI will get in on it, but guess it can't be helped. Let's have Tinker call ARKC radio to make an announcement. If they ain't caught by evening, it won't hurt to have the television station put it on the six o'clock news too."

Easy to see Mac was really jazzed about taking part in this manhunt. Dal wasn't so happy about the old man going along, but he was in good enough health they didn't have a reason to exclude him. It certainly wouldn't be as dangerous as last year's event.

"Okay, let's get. Beat the danged feds." Mac grabbed his Stetson off the rack near the door and headed out, followed by Colby and Dal. "Might as well all go up to Parker's in one vehicle."

Dal fetched his hat from a nearby desk. "Mac, the feds are liable to be pissed off we didn't let them know. Couldn't we just…?"

Mac's pale eyes twinkled. "After we leave Tinker will do just that."

The ornery old man. He actually wanted to be a step ahead of the feds. Dal really couldn't blame him. Sometimes those guys were so big-headed they couldn't screw their hats on straight. Marshal Trey Ledger was more on the ball, though.

Before Mac could get to his vehicle, Dal made it to his and so they all loaded up in it.

Fifteen minutes later, he pulled up near the stables where several horses were already saddled. Someone was mounted on one of them, but with their back to him Dal had to make a quick guess who it was. He was right the first time. Jessie reined the gelding around when they piled out, lifted a gloved hand, and waved at him.

Dammit, girl. He wanted to shout at her, but didn't dare. Besides, Mac did it for him, giving her a thorough cussing out in front of everyone. She paid him little attention. Far as Dal was concerned she'd more than proven herself with that deal last fall. Besides, she would go where the story was, no matter what he or anyone else said. Mac might be able to stop her, but he seldom acted out his decision. Funny too, since he wouldn't let Tinker in the field. No sense in arguing with Jessie, though, and they both knew it.

While they were stuffing bottles of water, nature bars, and rain gear in their saddlebags, two more deputies drove up. Les and Tink's husband Burt climbed out of their cars and went to work adjusting stirrups and packing up.

Dal glanced at his watch. It was eight thirty-five, light from the sun peeking over the mountains to the east and last night's cool air rising from ponds and creeks in pillars of mist. They needed to get on the move. It would take at least an hour to get to the freakoid's cabin, another to organize and head into the treacherous wilderness.

"Y'all be careful now and come back safe. I'd hate to have to write about anyone getting hurt." Parker stood in the corral and watched them ride off.

When the riders moved along Hunter Road adjacent to the square, Tinker flagged them down and passed around steel thermos jugs filled with steaming hot coffee courtesy of LaNita's. She passed out six. Dal stared from her to Jessie then back again. Tinkerbelle smiled and wiggled her fingers.

Little minx. She had to've made sure Jessie got in on this. Parker would never have let her know about the manhunt.

When Tinkerbelle passed beside Dal she spoke in a low tone. "Be wary of that FBI fella. He's out for blood over this. Says those two are his lookout, not yours."

"Oh, he does? Well, if he shows up here and gives you a hard time, you just tell him we're on a manhunt for one of our own who may be in jeopardy. This is still our jurisdiction. We'll let him know if we happen to spot his escaped most-wanted. Might even take them into custody to do him a favor."

Dal hung back and tucked in behind Mac and Jessie where he could keep an eye on them. Colby could lead them back to the cabin with no problems. He had an innate sense of moving around in the wilderness, and Dal wanted to keep an eye open for Grandfather. The old man was just nosy enough to want to be in on this hunt. And for once Dal wanted him there. Marcus was a viable opponent, but despite that, he looked forward to facing him.

5
CHAPTER

Having been involved in chasing around Lizard Lick on several occasions, Colby led the way. Dal rode behind Jessie, Mac followed, and deputies Les and Burt brought up the rear.

Dal shifted in the saddle. "Hey, you guys realize I'm the Indian here. Just cause I wear a classy cowboy hat and Justin boots doesn't mean I'm a cowboy. I really only like to show off."

Jessie dropped back to admire his butt before replying. "All the same, you look pretty good on a horse."

"I think I got a bony one."

She laughed. "Your butt or your horse?"

Muffled hilarity passed through the group. It was more like a weekend outing than a manhunt. If Dal resented her remark, he didn't show it. Since his return from Frog Pond he'd been a lot more easygoing. Yet in some ways, she liked the old unique Dal better when she never quite knew what he'd say or do. It seemed nowadays he tried to please everyone, never did something unexpected, like he was unhappy.

All in all she hoped the old Dal would come back soon. Should she tell him that?

Amazing how Colby led the way without hesitation. His innate sense of direction was present even in the dark. She was pretty good in the woods, but nothing like Colby.

The sun climbed and the temperature followed. Mac mopped at his neck with a bandana. "Gawdamn if it ain't gonna be a hot one."

Colby contemplated the sky for a minute. "Hell, you call this hot? This isn't hot. After three tours in the sandbox I'll take this anytime." He looped the reins over the saddle horn and rode hands off. "Jessie, when we were down at Lizard Lick you mentioned how you had an idea about what might be going on at the Hermitage."

"Yeah. I thought about how, Jeff being blind, he's really an expert with his other senses. However, that might make him ignore thinking about what he couldn't see in favor of touching or hearing, for instance."

"Uh, not sure I'm getting your drift."

"Suppose what Bainbridge and Kimble were doing out there in the barn, probably in the dark of night, could only be seen, not heard or felt, smelled or tasted? Jeff might miss that altogether."

Dal got in on the conversation. "So you're thinking that those two were so silent with whatever they were up to Jeff didn't know they were doing it?"

She nodded. "Might not even have known they were there."

Dal spoke loud enough to be heard this time. "What about the ATV? They had to come in on it. There's signs of it being parked in there. Jeff would've heard that."

"Yes, but we can't presume they brought it in once the Woodsons moved into the Hermitage. Surely they wouldn't be that stupid. The place was empty for quite some time while those perverts were stealing kids. We don't know how long or even when they began doing that. What if the barn was a meeting place back when the Hermitage was empty? They could've put those kids up in the big house while waiting to meet with the others. It was an ideal situation."

"Even if that's true, how does it help us figure out why the Woodsons were kidnapped and then let go?"

"Hey, I don't know. Still mulling that one. You guys have to figure out some of this stuff. I'm just a reporter. You're supposed to be crime busters."

"Wait a minute. She's right. What we need to do is search that barn better. We might find out what motivated them. Did anyone go up in the loft or check out the storage rooms?"

Dal swung around and stared at Les. He seldom said anything, but when he did, he caught everyone's attention. "I never once thought of checking out the loft. Us city fellows don't know anything about barns and lofts."

Les shook his head. "Boy, oh boy."

"What? Put you in a dark alley in south Dallas, see how much you know."

"Now, now boys. Let's not get in a measuring contest." Jessie laughed and the sound rippled from one to another.

"First thing when we get back then." Les grew quiet again.

Probably all he'd say the rest of the day.

Colby made a sound in his throat. "I'll swear if I don't think maybe I'll get to know Les on this ride. I didn't know he talked till just now."

Mac threw in his two cents' worth. "I had a brother who never spoke a word till he was fifteen. Ma and Pa didn't think much of it, just figured he didn't have anything to say. Maybe Les is that way. Come to think of it, I heard him remark on the sad condition of the coffee at the station once."

Les appeared to ignore them.

An approaching vehicle came up from behind. They moved the animals to one side to make room. Brush scraped the sides of a rust-ridden pickup. Slouched in the center of the seat, the driver pulled alongside, kept pace with the riders.

Burt leaned down and peered in the window. "Hey, Dooley."

Dooley lifted a hand out the passenger side of his pickup.

It was a puzzle how rural mail carriers could drive all day sitting in the middle of the seat. Must use their left foot on both the brake and the accelerator. An idle thought, but she'd always wondered. On a good day she could write an entire four-inch, two-column article on the subject. Anything she wondered about became fodder for a story.

Dooley moved on before she could ask. There went her story cause she'd need a good quote from the man.

"We're coming up on the road to Lizard Lick." Colby interrupted the chatter, touched the reins to guide his horse off the main road and onto double ruts marked as *2552*. Three sagging mailboxes sat at the turnoff. None had a name on them, only a number. A brown sign at the turn read Black Creek Wildlife Management Area.

Jessie was nervous approaching the cabins. They'd better get the joking out of their system. They must've read her thoughts, because after a few minutes the only sound was the rhythmic thud of hooves on the narrow dirt road and an occasional snort from one of the animals.

A sloping ditch on either side of the winding track grew thick with wild daisies, the white petals nodding in a slight breeze. Whoever lived out here must walk or ride horses or ATVs. There wasn't room for a full-sized vehicle on the path. It was so quiet the singing of tree leaves was accompanied by the splat of horse dumplings hitting the ground. The sun climbed high into the sky and sweat trickled down her backbone. Though she was hungry and wished they'd take a break, she didn't say anything. Being the only woman along, it wasn't a good idea to complain. In less than a minute, as if reading her mind, Mac called a halt and she let out a groan of relief. They all agreed it was time to eat and drink something before heading deeper into the rugged wilderness.

Happy to be off the horse, she hunkered down on a huge boulder, removed a wet wipe from her pack, and cleaned her face and hands before taking out a health food bar and a bottle of water. She wanted to talk to Dal, but he and Colby were engaged in a low conversation. Too bad she couldn't hear what they were saying. It looked serious.

The day had progressed slowly and it wouldn't get any better. She rubbed her aching butt. Riding for an hour or two for pleasure was a lot more fun than spending half a day in the saddle. And they were only getting started. She sort of regretted her decision to come along. The idea of the air-conditioned office and helping Wendy typeset was real tempting.

The men remained involved in a discussion too soft for her to hear. Probably football or something equally inane. She finished eating and strolled closer to listen to what they were saying. Just as she got near enough to make out their words, something buzzed past her ear like a gigantic bumble bee and cut a chip from a nearby tree. A loud bang echoed off the surrounding hills, fading as it bounced from peak to peak.

"Holy hell. Get *down.*" Colby hit the dirt face-first.

And it didn't look like he was having an episode from his time in battle either. This was real. She didn't know she could move so fast. She landed on her belly and crawled behind a large boulder. Several more shots cut chips from a nearby rock.

My God, were they shooting at her?

A great deal of shouting and scrambling took place while everyone sought cover in the thick trees along the path, the horses scattering into the woods. While the deputies had drawn their guns, none opened fire.

All went deathly still after the first fusillade. In the long few minutes that followed no one said anything, then Colby broke the silence. "Must've got too close to their marijuana patch."

When she could finally find her voice, she showed her fear and anger. "Why didn't someone shoot back? Just let them target practice on us. What the hell?"

Dal moved to put an arm around her. Whispered in her ear. "Not a good idea to shoot at something you can't see. Could be kids. No telling. Wouldn't want to kill someone. Especially when they clearly were shooting just to scare us. No one was hit."

"Well, maybe they're just lousy shots." Her mutterings were mostly ignored, so she said no more.

Colby and Burt snuck around behind trees in the direction of the shooters while Mac and Les stood guard. Dal kept an eye out and continued to hold her till the thumping of her heart slowed somewhat. Colby and Burt returned in a few minutes.

"Nah. Whoever it was clearly wanted to scare us off. We heard them scurrying through the brush away from us." Colby shrugged. "Think we ought to keep going if we're going to talk to that fella who saw Duggan. His cabin is just yonder the other side of that bluff."

They rounded up the horses while she watched. Men. Someone shoots at you, you ought to hightail it out of there. Not these guys. They'd just wade right on as if gunfire wasn't warning enough to leave the country. For two cents she'd mount up and ride out. Leave them to it.

Sure. In a pig's eye. She could no more retreat than they could.

When they rode around the promontory, Dal spotted Marcus first. He appeared as if out of thin air, spatters of sunlight reflecting off the white robe he wore giving him an ethereal appearance. A surge from the man's intellect washed over Dal like a wall of heat from a forest fire. After spending the previous night in the man's company, he wasn't a bit surprised. Still he sucked in a breath.

Hell, what was this man about anyway? He shook his head, concentrated on avoiding the shimmering eyes that pinned him as if they were all alone. What did he want from him and why was he hiding out like some hermit when he obviously thrived on manipulation? Didn't one need a constant audience for that type of control? The entire thing made Dal nervous as hell. More and more he wanted to connect the man to the vanquished cult.

"Won't you come in? Join me where it's cooler." He still appeared to be addressing Dal with that said-the-spider-to-the-fly implication.

He pulled away from the stare, studied the faces of his companions who seemed unaffected by the white-robed man's eerie presence. Indeed, Mac's expression was one of sneering disbelief, like he was on the verge of laughing at the stranger's appearance.

Was it all in his head, this perception that sent his thoughts back to the influence his grandfather's beliefs held over him? Something he ought to escape to live a normal life.

Whatever *that* was.

The sheriff stepped forward but made no move to go inside. He introduced himself. "We're looking for one of my deputies. Name of Duggan. I understand you might have seen him earlier yesterday."

Mac took off his Stetson, wiped his brow with a red bandana, and stuffed it back in his pocket. He glared at Marcus, waiting for him to reply.

"I'm afraid you've been misled, Sheriff."

"You didn't see him?" Mac shot Colby a quick glance, to which the deputy shook his head.

Marcus reached out a hand. "Come, let's get up on the porch at least. Out of the burning rays."

"We're fine right here. We didn't come to visit, sir. Did you or did you not tell my deputy there that you saw Duggan?"

"No, I did not. I told him the man was not here."

Colby stepped forward. "And you said he would return shortly."

"Not precisely." Marcus smiled, an expression so peaceful it was hard not to relax.

The man was a goddamned mesmerist.

Shaking off the grip Marcus had on his mind, Dal pushed past Mac, determined to put an end to this.

"Unless you want to be charged with obstructing an investigation, you'll answer our questions. Our deputy is missing. You so much as admitted having seen him. Now, where did he go? And what was he doing here? I don't think you'd fare very well in jail, and if you don't answer my questions, that's where you'll be. There was gunfire, and if Deputy Duggan is somewhere injured you're in deep shit."

A vicious evil thought tore into the darkest recesses of Dal's mind. Promised brimstone and hellfire. It was all he could do to keep from smashing his fist into this idiot's peaceful countenance.

His voice level and without emotion, Marcus spoke as if to the beyond. "I have no knowledge of your missing man. You will leave this place and not return or I shall see you pay in a way you will regret."

Dal took a step closer even though he preferred to keep his distance. "Oh, what will you do? Smite me?"

Behind the shimmering vision of this man, Grandfather appeared, holding up a hand and shaking his head solemnly. Exactly what he feared. Dal backed away. This was a warning he'd best obey. Too often he had walked into the world peopled by the *asgi`na* and *anasgi`na*. Faced their wrath in order to deal with the evil of some men. He wanted none of that unless given no choice. Had hoped to be a good detective on his own, not have to call on the supernatural to keep his job.

Jessie stared at him like he had frogs coming out of his ears. At this very moment he wouldn't have doubted it if he had. Jesus, he had to get hold of himself. He almost laughed at the turn of words, considering the way this man looked. He was nothing more than another screwed up character hiding out in the woods. Belonged in jail, no doubt. He sure didn't fold under Mac's bluff to put him there, though.

Jessie moved closer to Dal, touched his arm. He jerked as if bitten. She entwined her fingers through his, tugged him away from the altercation. Must've thought he was about to light into the man. She wasn't far from the truth.

"Let's go check around. Maybe you can come up with something proving Duggan was here."

He ought to be angry with her, but she was right and he was better off out of the influence of this pseudo Jesus figure. He was getting to him big time. Maybe he needed a shrink. They probably both did.

If he could've shaken himself mentally, he would have. Instead, he stepped away with her and walked slowly around the perimeter of the cabin, hoping to find something, anything, that would lead him to Duggan. Colby swore the deputy had been here, and if he had there might be some sort of sign. Be damned if he'd step into that other world in search of a leading spirit. He wanted no more to do with that.

Mac's angry voice carried and he would let the old man handle this. Toward the back corner of the cabin, weeds grew with more abundance than out front where pine trees kept the ground clear of growth. Here there was a definite path. On his knees, he fingered the crushed stems. Not yet dried from being broken by someone rushing down the path, it headed downhill toward the valley. Worth following just in case. Only a few feet farther on he spotted boot prints. Doubted Marcus wore boots. He was more the sandal type.

"What?" Jessie had been so quiet, he'd nearly forgotten she was there.

"Want to go fetch Mac and the guys? We need to follow up on this."

She turned to leave, stopped when he said her name. "Don't tell them anything in front of that spooky character. Just say I want to talk to them and make sure they all come. I don't think it's a good idea to leave any of them here with him. Okay?"

"Of course. I'll be right back."

He nodded, let her start toward the cabin before kneeling to examine the prints. Sure enough someone had been afoot here and recently. Could have been Duggan, or maybe the man who lived down here with those two girls. He would check for more sign of Duggan's presence. Something had happened to the deputy. There was no reason for him to just walk away and not come back. And there was the gunshot.

Dal looked pale and shaken. Jessie'd never seen him like that. She hurried around the cabin to give Mac the message and no one was there.

What the hell?

Where'd they go? She hadn't been gone more than five or ten minutes and Mac had not seemed inclined to go inside with that Marcus dude. She'd never wanted to laugh hysterically at anyone like she had him. What a pretender he was. Didn't he know how foolish he looked?

She ran up the porch steps and peered through the screen. Rapped on the frame. "Hello? Anyone in there?"

The man who called himself Marcus appeared without making a sound. He didn't say anything, just stared at her through the rusty woven wires.

"Well, where are they?" She had little patience with his silly actions.

"Who?"

"Jesus Christ."

"Is that a joke of some kind?"

"No, fool. Is that better? Where'd the sheriff and his men go?"

"I have no idea. They got a call on that radio thing they carry and took off. Said tell you to get back to the road. They'd leave your horses."

"Shit. They say why?"

"No. Wouldn't have done them any good. I'm not a message carrier."

If she'd had a gun handy she'd have fired a warning shot over his head. Instead, she took hold of the door handle and yanked. It must've been locked, for it didn't budge. Marcus slammed the heavy door, yelling something she couldn't understand.

She turned and ran back to where she'd left Dal, found he'd moved slowly on, still following what he must think was Duggan's trail leaving the cabin. He was almost into the thick woods that circled like a fence built by nature.

"Dal, wait."

"What, Jessie? What's wrong?"

"Do you have your walkie?"

He fingered it off his shoulder. "Yeah, why?"

"Spooky told me Mac got a call and they rushed off, asking him to send us back to the road."

He compressed the button and called in. Waited longer than normal, tried again. "I'm not getting anything at all. Not even static. These damned analog units. Not worth pitching in the creek out here in the wilderness."

"Well then, how did Mac get a call?"

He looked at her for a minute, his expression one of dismay. Then he shrugged. "I really don't know. Sometimes they work in one place and not ten feet in either direction." He stood there a few more minutes, tried one more time, then hooked the thing back on his shirt. "Useless piece of junk."

"What do you want to do?" She waited, ready to do whatever he thought best.

"I want to follow this trail. It's fresh and could belong to our missing deputy unless Jesus in there traipses around through the brush in his nightgown wearing boots. I have no idea what Mac's call could've been about, but he has some men with him. You might ought to run back and catch up with them. I may be down there a while."

That's what she ought to do, for sure. But it wasn't what she was going to do. Leave Dal out here on his own? Never happen. Sure, she wasn't his keeper and he was a grown man, but lately he'd been acting really strange. It might be best to stay with him. Besides, as it looked now, that's where her story was. And that's why she came. To get a story.

Wasn't it?

Sure. Tell yourself that. Go ahead.

But you know you want to be with him out in the wilderness all alone. They hadn't had much togetherness this year, and he'd sort of shied away from her till this past weekend when he finally began to act like himself again. In bed anyway. She wanted more of that. Definitely.

After one more glance over her shoulder toward the cabin, she took a step in his direction. "You want me to go get the horses?"

"I don't think so. The going will get really rough and I'm better off on foot."

"We're better off on foot."

He watched her, forest-green eyes shimmering in the sunlight that filtered through the oak leaves. "You're coming with me?"

Lips compressed, ready for battle, she nodded. "Yep."

He didn't even hesitate. "Well, okay then. Let's get a move on."

For quite some time she moved along behind him, keeping an eye open for anything he might miss. He didn't talk, and though she wanted to discuss her feelings, she kept her mouth shut.

He was right. The ground became rough and steep where it dropped off into the valley. A horse might've broken its leg there. She cringed at the thought that she could do the same. At times, they had to back down an incline hanging on to small trees. Finally, he stopped at a flat place, maybe three feet wide, that overlooked the tops of trees and announced a water break.

He scooted onto a boulder, eyed her till she joined him. "You okay?"

"Long as I can stay upright."

"You've been really quiet."

"Figured that's what you wanted."

He chuckled. "Since when do you pay any attention to what I want?"

"That's not very nice. I always care what you want. Why are you being so weird?"

Water bottle up toward his mouth, he paused. "Am I?"

"Ever since we talked to old Spooky up there you've acted… well, yes, weird." He drank and swallowed and she laid a hand on his arm, stared up into his face. "What's wrong, Dal?"

His attempt to look innocent didn't work. His gaze was distant, his eyes shiny. "Nothing."

Something was bothering him, but he wasn't about to say what. Just kept his mouth shut and studied her in that way he had that was so disturbing. It said *don't be nosy*, and at the same time urged her to care. Hard sometimes to read him. So she did the only thing she could think of.

Lifting her butt off the rock, she touched her lips to his. Fingers tangled in her hair, he deepened the kiss. Something wet fell on her cheek. His tears. He was crying, his tongue tracing her mouth. She let him in, dropped into his lap where his erection nudged her thighs.

Humming against his warm skin, she locked both arms around his neck. Without warning, he enclosed her waist, lifted her onto her feet, and pulled away.

"What is it? What's wrong?"

The ground evidently held more fascination for him than she did. When his hands dropped she backed up a step, bumped into a tree. "You going to tell me what's going on?"

"Not now. We need to find Duggan. There'll be time later."

"I just don't want you to—whatever it is, we need to talk about it."

"Why?"

"Sometimes you—never mind. Have it your way."

He gave a curt nod, picked up his water bottle from the ground where he'd set it when she climbed into his lap, capped it, and stuck it into his backpack. "You ready to go?"

"Whenever you are." Even in the heat she felt cold and devoid of feelings. Sometimes he could vacuum her empty, leave her wondering what the hell had happened. Just all of a sudden. Later he would take her in his arms and hold her close to his heart. She might never find out what had happened. Or *why.*

Following him down off the mountain, keeping her eyes glued to his broad back, she ran possibilities through her brain till it was numb. Was there any sign to follow or were they just going blind? He hadn't pointed out any clues in a long while.

Entranced by the search, she ran into him when he came to a fast halt.

A man stood astride the trail, a rifle cradled across his middle. Ordered them to stop in a commanding tone.

"Put that gun down." To hear Dal's demand one would've thought he had a gun pointed at the man, but he didn't. His was still in the holster on his thigh.

"I'm not making a threat. I'm here to ask you to turn around. Do so, forget you ever saw me, and I'll send your man out to you. I don't want any trouble. I just want to be left alone."

She moved to one side to get a look at him, but Dal reached out and stopped her. For a split second she saw him, memorized his description as quickly as possible.

"Stay back, Jessie." He never took his eyes off the man blocking the trail. "Once you threaten or detain a lawman, you've already got yourself trouble. I'd suggest you lay your weapon on the ground. Then maybe we can talk about what's going on here."

"I can't do that." He glanced back over his shoulder. "Deputy, come on out here. Show these folks you haven't been hurt in any way."

Duggan stepped out of the woods. His holster was empty.

"Stop there." The man gestured toward Dal and Jessie. "Turn and walk away. He'll follow. And don't bother to look for me, cause you won't find me."

"Duggan, you okay? Where's your weapon?"

"Yep, I'm fine. Do what he says, Dal. We don't need no dog in this fight. Believe me, it's best left just like it is. This man offers no threat to anyone. Just head on back and I'll catch up shortly."

Duggan stepped up even with the man, shook his hand, and patted him on the shoulder. Acting like old friends. She didn't hear what he said, but the man thanked him.

What in the world was going on here? Duggan must be drugged or hypnotized. He'd proved a fair deputy, so why was he acting this way with an armed man who had probably earlier taken shots at all of them?

"Turn around, Jessie. Move away. I'll be right behind you."

"Dal? What's wrong with you?"

"Just do it." He addressed the man. "We're gone, mister."

This was beyond her understanding. But Dal sounded so serious. Besides, she didn't want to do anything that would make the man unsling that rifle. Chances were he'd already shot at them once. So she turned and hurried away, feet slipping over rolling pebbles on the incline. She grabbed a sapling alongside the narrow trail and pulled herself up, then skittered further on hands and feet, all the while expecting to be fired upon just for good measure.

Close behind her, Dal urged her to keep moving and she did.

"Is Duggan coming?" Breathless, she gasped out the question.

"Yep."

"I'm right here, Jessie."

How long it took to reach the top and head toward Marcus's small cabin, she had no idea. She didn't take to being herded by a man with a gun, but Dal and Duggan were so calm. What was wrong with the two of them? Letting an armed man get away with such actions.

Once on level ground and getting close to the horses Mac had left, she couldn't hold her tongue any longer.

"Who was that guy? And why did the both of you just do what he said without question? I can't believe you didn't arrest him."

"There's only two horses. Duggan, you and Jessie take that big sorrel. He'll carry your combined weight, both of you being lightweights."

Jessie stopped and whirled on Dal. "What is wrong with you?"

"Nothing."

"Then why won't you answer my question?"

"Jessie, I don't know the answer. What I do know is I trust Duggan. If he thought we ought to simply leave, then that's what we needed to do. I'm sure he can explain himself once we're well away from any danger that man might offer. He had a rifle, Jessie. There'll be time later to investigate."

Duggan eyed Dal for a long moment as if puzzled. "Glad you trusted me, Dal. I assure you, we did the right thing. I can't tell you anything yet, but I'll explain it all when we get back to the station. I can't chance Jessie here putting it in the paper."

"Wait a minute. You know I can be trusted."

"Hush, Jessie." Dal touched her arm, but she yanked away.

"Wonder where Marcus is hiding out." Ignoring her, Duggan peered around as if he expected at any moment for Spooky to burst out the door. "You want a story, there's one for you." He pointed at the cabin.

"There's the horses. Let's get out of here. Good idea to get home before dark if at all possible." Dal mounted a sturdy Appaloosa and started up the road while Duggan climbed on the sorrel, kicked loose a stirrup, and pulled Jessie up behind him.

"Don't let her talk your ear off, man." Dal kicked the apple into a trot.

Jessie locked her arms around Duggan's waist. "Just wait till we get back. There'd better be a good explanation for this, and none of that not talking in front of the press. I'd like to remind you of the First Amendment, to mention only a few freedoms we have in this country."

"I have the right not to talk till I see my lawyer. Besides I'm tired. So if you could just hush up and hang on." Duggan kicked the sorrel in the ribs and the long-legged horse stretched into a trot.

Hush up, indeed. Lawyer. What in the world was he going on about? Whatever it was, she would find out.

6
CHAPTER

"I'm telling you, Parker. There's something really strange going on out there. First Mac gets a call and leaves us to find Duggan, that's strange in itself. When we do find him, he's chummy with a guy who's all but pointing a rifle at him. Then Dal goes all woo-woo on me like he's living in another world. I began to think I'm the only one who's sane."

Her boss stopped midway, blue pencil poised to edit her article. "In a place called Lizard Lick? Something strange? Sounds like an ordinary day to me."

She slanted a glare at him, ought to bop him one. "I wanted to interview Deputy Duggan but he wouldn't talk to me."

"So you really don't know anything strange happened. Maybe the man is a friend, they spent some time together and it's none of your business."

"Huh. So why did he literally threaten us with a rifle? And why was Duggan walking around without his sidearm?"

Parker read down through the piece. Shook his head. "It doesn't say anything about him threatening you. Just that he had it slung over his shoulder. As for the shot that Dal heard fired over the radio, maybe they had squirrel for supper. I had the scanner on and Mac and the deputies had to come back to handle a drunk running around in Walmart threatening to beat up on his wife who was in there shopping. It was quite an uproar.

"Honey, this is Grace County. What would've been strange would be if that fella didn't have a rifle over his shoulder. You were trespassing on his land. Deputies or not, he has that right. Now, you want to edit this yourself, or let me finish it the way it is?"

She sighed and backed out of his office. "I'm going to go home now, unless you need me for anything else."

He glanced up. "What? Nope. Not unless you have something to add to this. It's late, you've had a long couple of days. Go home, get some rest. I'll cover the Walmart fiasco. Oh, and by the way, I really liked your story about the new animal farm, and the pictures were superb."

"Yeah, thanks." Even though she had great plans for some of the images, it was hard to get too enthused about the praise. All she could think of was that spooky Marcus and the mysterious man with Duggan. And most of all, Dal's odd behavior. That's where the real story was, and she wasn't about to give up on it. Dal might have some input, if she could drag him out of his recent funk. Something was bothering him. Maybe a night together would cheer him up.

In the Jeep, she pulled out her phone and punched his number. It was only eleven. He should still be up. Lots of times, they met at midnight after she finished at the paper. It went to voice mail and she invited him to meet her at the cabin and bring a pizza, she was starved. Only one place in Cedarton stayed open this late, and it was the new café out on the recently opened Tulsa to Branson highway. It had a number, but she couldn't remember it.

After feeding Brad and showering, she slipped on a sheer gown and snuggled down on the couch with the happy pit bull. After an hour, she gave up on a return call from Dal, grabbed a quick sandwich from the fridge, washed it down with iced tea, and crawled in bed.

The next morning, she sat on the deck soaking up sun and drinking coffee while waiting for the wash to finish. Brad leaped up from a patch of sunlight, did his happy dance bark, then disappeared around the house. He and Dal soon came out the sliding glass door sharing a Honey Bun.

Funny how glad she was to see him after yesterday. "Hey, hi. You know you're spoiling him rotten, besides making him fat."

"Too late to stop that. How you doing?" He leaned down, kissed her on top of the head, and sprawled into the chaise opposite her. "Sorry I missed your call last night. I was looking into something and didn't... uh, couldn't answer my phone."

"Oh? And what might that be?"

"I got to thinking about what you said. Jeff and that business at the barn up at the Hermitage."

"And you went up there without me?"

He chuckled. "When did you become my partner? Besides, you were working. But no, I didn't go without you. I was checking something else."

"Okay. All right. And it won't do any good for me to ask about that either, huh?"

The last bite of roll went in his mouth. He picked up her coffee mug and took a sip. "You're right, since it's an ongoing investigation."

She grinned, punched him on the shoulder. He seemed back to his old self from the way he'd acted during their ride out to locate Duggan. "You don't know what you missed not showing up here last night. I had exciting plans for you."

He put down the mug and took her hand. "It's not too late. Or too early, or whatever."

She would never tire of the gentle caress of his long fingers. Or the way he could turn on his sexy vibes. Even just taking her hand in his sent shivers through her and switched on all the erotic signals she could never resist. Gaze locked to his, she rose, pulled him to his feet, and led him into the house. A good thing the first door inside was the bedroom, because he had pulled her shirt up over her head and went to work on the zipper of her shorts even as they made it that far.

She turned, fell backward on the mattress, unfastened his belt, and yanked down his jeans, all in one swift move. Looked like she was just in the nick of time too. He was more than ready so that she had a hard time getting his jockey shorts off.

"My, looks like you came prepared."

Eyes glazed with passion, he shoved her knees up and pushed deep inside her.

"Whoa, sweetie. Slow it down. What happened to foreplay?"

He didn't or couldn't either answer or slow down. He finished so quickly she barely had time to enjoy what was happening. Silent, he grabbed her around the shoulders and hugged her up so tight she could barely breathe.

Lips against his neck, his heartbeat throbbed against her skin. He was so still, held her so tight, like he feared she would disappear. After a long while, his breathing slowed, but still he held her, saying nothing.

"Honey, talk to me."

He made a sound down in his throat.

Fear skittered through her. She was losing him. Before he took off last year he'd acted this way, going all quiet in the midst of making love or just discussing their feelings.

She slipped her hand between them rested it over his limp cock. He made a sharp uh sound down in his throat.

"Want me?" She folded her fingers ever so gently around him.

"So damned much it scares me."

"Do I frighten you somehow? I don't understand." Gently she worked her hand over his warm, satiny flesh. Despite his reluctance, he grew to fill her palm. Lips against his ear, she whispered. "Want that, huh? Whatever you want. Just say. I want you to be happy."

"Why, Jess? We can't make other people happy. Don't you know that?"

"Why aren't you happy? Tell me. We can fix it."

"Tell me why you feel this way about me. Hell, tell me how you feel about me. We just go at each other, can't keep our hands off each other, yet we never talk about how we feel." He chuckled bitterly. "Supposed to be the woman who wants to talk, but I have to know. Jessie, I can't let you mean the world to me. I can't. And yet, here we are, in each other's arms."

"I'm not sure I understand."

Instead of turning her loose, pushing her away, he continued to hold her, which sent the opposite message his words did.

"I don't know what you want here, Dal. Don't know what to tell you."

"You, Jessie. Goddammit, I want you. But…. Shit."

He rolled onto his back, locking her on top of him. She opened to his need, though her mind said wait, figure this out.

He turned her loose, the deep green of his eyes flashing in a stare so intense she shivered.

"Make love to me." She rocked slowly, palms flat on his chest, keeping him deep inside. Forward, backward, her insides quivering with passion. Taking her time to build to the first orgasm, on to the second, and into the third. When she came near to passing out from the sheer joy he came, heat shooting into her. He never moved to put his arms around her, just laid there panting, sweating, gazing at her through eyes shining with moisture.

They reclined together in a silence so profound even their heartbeats faded into space. No wind, no light, nothing but the rhythm of their hearts. The whisper of his skin sliding across the sheet, a sigh from his lips, the ripple of his muscle beneath her palm. Sprawling across his chest, his heart thundered in her ear. He massaged up and down her back and planted a long kiss under her jaw. He could keep right on doing that forever, carrying her into another world reserved for lovers.

His words cut through the fantasy world. "Dear God, I'm sorry about all this shit. I have ghosts, and sometimes they mess with me. Worse, I let them. She died despite everything I did to save her. No matter how much I took off the streets, I couldn't keep her safe. And somehow she couldn't leave the dope alone."

A pause, still she kept quiet. He went on in a different tone. "When I think of going almost an entire year without you I feel like a total fucking idiot. I'm afraid to care for you, to want you. Despite all I do you are under my skin. I can't protect you. I tried to get away from it, but it didn't work too well."

His words were like cruel slaps, but at the same time she understood in an odd way. Losing someone you love is hell, it creates a fear you can't get rid of that you are never going to have that wondrous feeling again. Then when you do, it scares the hell out of you cause, hey jerk, you're about to lose this one too.

Yes, she understood, because she had almost killed the man she loved, had killed their love.

But how did she explain this to Dal?

So instead, she rested her head on his chest and remained there, stretched over him, touching from head to toe. Silent, breathing in unison.

Finally he laid a hand across her back and rubbed a thumb slowly up and down her spine. "Sorry. I'm sorry. I'm just being moronic. Things haven't been going well in this crazy brain of mine for the past year or so. I need an attitude adjustment or something. I'll get through it."

Sure was hard loving a man who kept everything locked away in the darkest corner of his brain. But it was harder when he revealed the fears he lived with. Either way, she cared too much for him to let it break them apart. This too would pass.

She rolled to his side and he turned to enclose her in his arms.

Afternoon sunlight poured through the bedroom window, stirred her from her nap, and warmed her naked form curled around his bare butt. They'd slept the morning away. She stretched against him and he turned over, wrapped his arms around her. For a long while, she lay cuddled against his chest, content to remain right there. All too soon he would be off somewhere else in body and mind. Till he got the hots again.

Strange what women put up with. She chuckled against his chest.

"What?" He cupped her breast, tweaked the nipple.

"Just wondering what men put up with to keep a woman warm in their bed."

"Oh, yeah? I'll make a list."

"Me, too, sweetheart. Me, too."

The reflection of Jessie in the rearview mirror waved at him and grew smaller. Dal blipped the horn in farewell. Time to get back to the real world. A man could only take so much poking about in his feelings. It got the better of him sometimes.

Best to get to work. Ever since she'd talked about what Jeff might have missed at the barn, he'd been anxious to get back out there and take a look at the scene from a different perspective. One that did not include the visionary world inherited from Grandfather. The one he no longer wanted to count on. Her mentioning it reminded him that this might be just the time to investigate the place. She had realized something he hadn't thought of because he relied too much on those powers he hated so much. That was pretty funny, made him sound like Superman.

At the Hermitage he drove past the empty house, weeds scraping the undercarriage, and parked near the barn. Ever since the Woodsons had been grabbed and kept prisoner, they'd been staying in Cedarton at The Five Bs. Alicia was concerned about Jeff's safety until the FBI could arrest the two men responsible. Jeff, on the other hand, was unhappy being in a place he was unfamiliar with.

It was an unfortunate situation and the law needed to get on the ball. No one was absolutely sure who the kidnappers were, even though they suspected Kimble and Bainbridge, the leaders of the Rising Moon Cult who continued to escape capture. They were wanted by the FBI for running a human trafficking ring using the cult for cover while they transferred the stolen children to buyers around the world.

So far the kidnapping episode was confusing to say the least. It seemed to have no reason. Despite it being an FBI case, Dal wanted to take a better look around the barn. As far as he knew, no one from the FBI or the US Marshal's office had checked out the place. They were too busy running about trying to find their asses with both hands.

Leaving the bright sunlight to go inside the gloomy barn, Dal was struck temporarily blind. In those few seconds before his eyes adjusted, he experienced what Jeff lived with all the time. A bird song out of the darkness. The smell of old hay and a lingering odor of horses. The heat of trapped air. A foreign taste on his tongue. All in total darkness.

None of it lasted long. Strips of sunlight sent bars through the cracks in the siding. The barn must be nearly a hundred years old. He trod past rows of individual stalls, empty since the former owners had moved out long before he came to Cedarton. At the back of the barn was an empty tack room with a few strips of leather reins and harnesses hanging on the wall. The opposite corner had an open area large enough to hold a small tractor or one of those vehicles called UTVs that had taken the place of horses on many modern farms and ranches.

Jeff had said when he and Alicia were grabbed they were transported from the barn on one of those. He heard the engine running, smelled the fumes, and felt the rough ride that carried them into the woods to the shack where they were kept. Unfortunately he couldn't see his abductors but said he would know their voices if he heard them again.

Switching on his flashlight, Dal checked the dirt- and hay-strewn floor of the tractor space. Drippings from an engine left stains that had leaked there only recently. A shelf along the back of the room held wrenches, pliers, screwdrivers, and the like. An empty, red plastic container smelled of gasoline, and in a metal barrel under the shelf were two discarded quart oil containers. It was plain that whoever had been using this barn had been here recently, long after the Woodsons moved in.

Yet Alicia had said Jeff often escaped to the barn when he needed some peace from his demons. He must have heard something and didn't remember. What other reason could there be for their capture? On the other hand, why were they released without questioning?

Colby had mentioned a loft and he swept the beam of light around, searching for a ladder or some means to access the upper floor. He found it in the darkest corner, one-bys nailed across exposed two-by-four framing supports. To make movement easier he removed his utility belt and hung it over a half-wall leading into an adjoining stall. Thick spider webs swayed from the roof down to the half-wall, but there were none on or across the makeshift ladder. Someone had been up there recently, brushing aside whatever webs would have accumulated over the months since anyone had climbed it.

He shut off the flashlight, stuck it in his waist band and started up, cursing once more the man who had used a MAC-10 to cut him down in that back alley in Dallas. If it weren't for Mac Richards he'd be retired on disability now. Some days felt as if he should be. At the top, a pain shot through his leg and he paused, let out a grunt before moving on. A wide opening just under the peak of the roof let in more than enough light for him to search all but the farthest corners, which he lit up with the flashlight.

The beam showed peculiar scrape marks across the hay-strewn floor, like someone had dragged a four-legged piece of furniture. Nothing like that was in sight. The room was empty except for a few bales of moldy hay, some old wooden chairs piled against the wall, and what looked like a chest, broken into pieces. He bent to examine something sticking from under one of the slabs of wood. A scrap of thick paper was caught between the wall and floor.

What the hell was that? He got hold of it and pulled. It was a manila folder like files are kept in. It appeared empty till he got it worked loose. Inside was a folded up paper, the top portion of a letter head. Over in the light he held it up to examine the words. Bainbridge and Lofton, a phone number and a fax. Carefully, he rolled the file and paper and stuffed it inside his shirt front. After another thirty minutes of finding nothing, he lowered himself down the crude ladder, being extra careful. Be just like him to fall and break something. After being in a wheelchair for the better part of a year, he wanted no part in that sort of helplessness again. He was lucky to be on his feet at all, even luckier to be alive.

Make the best of it and quit being such a cry baby. How often did he tell himself that? Just about every day.

So, did he have himself an honest-to-God clue with that letterhead, or had it been there since a rancher had ordered something and received a bill of lading for it? Naw, no such thing as a coincidence like the name Bainbridge. Wonder why the man didn't use a fake name when he moved his trafficking here? Or maybe he was now using a fake name and they'd never find him.

The sun set while he drove back to town, but he went on over to the station. Time he talked to Mac about this whole mess. They needed to get together with the FBI and try to clear this up so the Woodsons could return to their normal life. Besides, he wanted to find out more about the two guys living down at Lizard Lick. Something weird was going on there too. He'd argued Jessie out of that because he didn't want her poking around and getting in trouble, but she was right. She had a nose for such stuff. He'd never tell her that. He'd pretty much given up keeping her from underfoot while he investigated what few crimes occurred in Cedarton.

When you really thought of it, the small town and its couple of thousand population was only a portion of what the sheriff and his deputies were responsible for. Out in the county itself lived ten thousand or so, as widespread as if someone had thrown them out like a handful of rice. All the towns, and there weren't many, were insignificant when taken individually, but on the whole represented a lot of people who needed protection under the law. And also represented those who stole, mugged, shot, cheated, abused, grew and dealt dope, and worst of all, murdered. He could go on, but one thing for sure. You never knew what sort of crime would occur or when or where.

Lunch was a hardboiled egg, some slices of ham, a celery stick, and a glass of iced tea. All munched on under the shade of a tree near the deck. Given the chance, Jessie would live out there most of the year. Under the blue sky or the night sky, with only a blanket to lie on. But of course that wasn't feasible what with ticks, snakes, mosquitos, an occasional wandering black bear or wild cat. Brad lay in a spot of sun near her feet. He liked the outdoors too, and he liked it more when she was with him. Yet he took his duties of being on watch seriously. She gave him the last bit of egg and a piece of ham, finished off her tea, and leaned back for a moment to study a bank of dark clouds off to the northwest. Where the worst storms came from.

A breeze kicked up, carrying the smell of rain and distant jags of lightning reached for the peaks. "Guess we'd better gather up our things and go inside."

The faithful pit bull followed her inside, nails clicking across the hardwood floor to the front door where he took up his station, nose resting on both paws. The landline she kept because it was the only way to acquire the Internet in the county jangled. She'd left the ring-setting like an old fashioned telephone because it reminded her of her childhood.

A flash of her father, looking up from his newspaper and smiling, came and went. With a sad smile, she picked up the cordless.

"Is this JJ?"

A chill fisted her heart and she couldn't take her next breath.

Finally, when she could make a sound, she cleared her throat. "You've got the wrong number."

"Have I? This isn't JJ Stone? I'm sorry, I'll try again."

"No—wait." Better if she found out what was going on. If this person hung up, she might never know what the deal was. "What do you want?"

"I want to speak to her about Stephen."

A harsh swallow. The gun in her hand. Going off in the confines of the car, the blast so loud her ears rang, the stench gagging. His blood all over her. "Stephen is gone."

"Gone?"

"That's what I said. Who is this and what do you want? Stop fooling around or I'm going to hang up." Though gone, he was not dead. Not to her knowledge anyway. But he sure as hell wouldn't be coming back here anytime soon. What did this person know?

"I need to speak to JJ. God, that's awkward. What does it stand for?"

"It's not a real name. It was a pseudonym. For writing purposes."

"Ah, so I do have who I'm looking for. You wrote for a newspaper out in California. Some tough stuff. I need help and when I found out you were living in Cedarton now, considering your history, I thought you might help me."

This didn't sound threatening at all and she relaxed, dropped to the couch, eyes turned toward the window that framed billowing black clouds. A bit bothersome someone could locate her, but she let it go for now.

"I'm sorry. I really don't handle that kind of journalism anymore."

"My husband has stolen my children and I can't get help anywhere.

Oh, their picture is on milk cartons and flyers that go out once in a while but nothing else. There are so many lost children. It's not a very active investigation and I need someone who knows how to stir up things. You broke up those men out in LA who were dealing in selling prostitutes to some of the richest men in town. Your stories uncovered the whole mess."

She closed her eyes. Shuddered, knuckles white where she clutched the phone. How had this woman found her? And why did she think her kids might be around here somewhere?

Good Lord, she couldn't do this.

"I'm sorry. I can't. Let me give you the number of our sheriff's department. If you think they are in this area they can help you. I don't do that sort of thing any longer." Investigative journalism had broken up her love affair, destroyed her career, almost gotten her killed, and ended in her shooting the man she loved when he came here bent on killing her. She couldn't go through this again. Not again. "I'm sorry, no. Here's a number for you to—"

The caller hung up.

The phone fell from her trembling fingers. Was there no place to hide? Here where she was raised felt so safe. Mac taking the place of her grandfather, who was his best friend. Coming back here gave her a family, a bevy of cousins scattered all over Grace County. Who was this person that she presumed she could come and ruin her life?

After crying for a few minutes, she mopped her face with a tissue, tossed it along with a pile of others into the trash. The storm whipped the tops of trees and rain slashed across the yard and hit the house with a vengeance. A streak of lightning cracked the air sharply and sent Brad scurrying under the table where he lay staring at her as if she were responsible for the mayhem.

Children stolen. My God, was this a hoax or could it be connected to the stealing of foster children that had prospered until the combination of sheriff's deputies, US Marshals, and a few FBI agents shut it down? They hadn't caught the head honchos, Robert Kimble and Taylor Bainbridge. Both still roamed free. How could the two possibly be connected?

The woman had said her husband stole her children. That wasn't quite the same, was it? But maybe she just thought he took them. Was there someone she could talk to about this? Not Dal, for he would see the danger and want to post a guard around her. Parker would do about the same, insisting she move into his ranch until the danger was past. That she wasn't about to do, considering their history. Who could she trust? Did she need help from anyone?

The questions bounced back and forth in her mind while the storm raged on. A limb blew from the tree in the front yard, slammed onto the porch roof, then one end skidded to the ground. At the same moment the power went off. No flicker or warning, it just went off. Brad yelped and leaped into her lap, where he lay trembling. The only danger in Jessie's mind was from her caller or perhaps those two men who were mean enough to make slaves out of children and sell them as such. Nothing like a storm scared her much. Being without power was more inconvenient than anything else. Suddenly, she needed to run water but the pump in the well wouldn't allow that, or there was something really interesting on television she could watch. Even these new phones didn't work, and of course the Internet was useless. Both of which she found a dozen reasons to want to use. Funny how that worked.

It could be minutes, hours, or overnight before it came back on. Could be a tree down or a semi running off the road and knocking down a pole or an untrimmed limb lying across lines or a transformer hit by lightning. In case it might be a while, she scrounged up some candles and matches and put them at hand on the living room table.

Once prepared, she relaxed and went back to earlier thoughts about Spooky and the stranger with Duggan. She had the next two days off before returning to work. Time to do a bit of nosing around, and she'd do it alone because anyone she tried to talk to about it would only want to shut her up somewhere so she'd be safe. She was sure she could find Spooky's place on her own. Maybe she'd ask Parker to loan her a horse. Tell him she wanted to go riding alone. He'd understand that. Maybe.

The fury of the storm passed over by dusk, but a steady rain set in and it grew dark earlier than normal. She sat in the dark, finding the utter silence soothing. No sense in lighting out tonight. She might be fearless like Dal said but she wasn't stupid.

After lighting a couple of candles she made a sandwich and sat down to eat it when headlights swept across the front of the house. The only drop-in visitors she ever had were Tink or Dal and since he'd left with something important on his mind, it must be her good friend. Her husband Les was probably on duty.

Brad greeted the visitor at the door with his happy dance. He never knew a stranger, which made him less than a good watchdog, except that he did bark at every intrusion. Since she'd never wanted a watchdog that would go around biting everyone, that didn't bother her much.

Sure enough, Tink bounced in, scooping the mutt up in her arms so he could give her kisses. "Dark in here. When did the power go out?"

"Been out here for several hours. Not in town?"

"Nope, must be a tree between here and there."

Jessie greeted her friend with a hug. "You need to get yourself a dog, you like him so much."

"I only like other people's pets. Too much trouble. Not even sure I want kids, though Les is talking about it. I told him he wanted one he could raise it. I burned out on that taking care of my five half-brothers after Mom died."

"It crossed my mind you might get pregnant. But knowing how much you love your job, I wasn't sure."

Tinker plopped down on the couch beside Jessie. "Me either. Mac is never going to let me out in the field and I'm fed up with sitting at a desk. I've been thinking of applying to the FBI. I've had the training to get accepted."

"Oh, honey. That would be fabulous. But what does Les think?"

She shrugged. "Haven't asked. It's just a thought so far."

Might be a good idea to change the subject. Get Tink's mind on something else. She sounded depressed.

"I had a strange phone call earlier and I need to talk to someone about it."

Tink perked up. "Well, give. I'm right here ready to talk about something strange."

After her quick rundown on what the woman had told her, Jessie studied her friend's face, hoping for the right reaction. Mostly hoping she cheered up.

"Sounds like a story to me, unless it is a hoax. You're the reporter, can't you find out if she's telling the truth? Maybe get some information from her and check it out?"

"I almost made an appointment to interview her, but then with so much going on right now, and it coming right on top of the arrests, I'm suspicious of her."

"Well, why would that stop you? Where'd the call come from?"

Jessie shook her head and shrugged. "Area Code three-one-six. Isn't that up around Wichita?"

"I think so. Why would she think you'd be able to help? Did she say?"

"Nope, just hung up when I started asking questions."

"Probably a prank."

"Could be. Besides, I can't get my mind off that spooky guy we ran across in the woods the other day."

"Oh, Les told me about him. He did sound very strange. I can see where he'd be more interesting than a woman who's lost her children." The sarcasm sounded like the old Tink.

"Okay, you're right. These woods are full of spooky guys." She put the dead phone back on the table. Glanced at her friend whose features were spooky themselves in the flickering candlelight. "Would you be interested in going down there with me? You're always wanting to do stuff like that."

"Hmm, well, I do have tomorrow off. Sounds like fun."

"At least Dal couldn't accuse me of going off on my own if I had an officer of the law with me."

Tink snorted. "Yeah, right. When would you want to leave?"

"I was going to borrow a horse from Parker, but knowing how you feel about riding, we could take the Jeep, drive to the end of the road at Lizard Lick, and walk the rest of the way. It isn't far. I can't get either one of these guys off my mind."

"These guys?"

"Didn't Les tell you about the guy Duggan was with? And how odd the whole thing was? Must be the water down there or something." So Jessie told her about the man and how strange he and Duggan acted when they appeared in the woods. "I'm telling you, something is going on down there and both those men are involved. Everything so secretive."

"Honey, this is Grace County. Everything is weird here."

"That's what Parker said."

"Did they ever get the patrol car out of there?"

She nodded. "Yeah."

"That's good. And you're sure you remember how to get there."

"Oh sure. One thing I can do is find my way around in the woods. Thanks to my grandpa."

"Okay, sounds like fun. As long as you're sure nothing will happen to us. I'd hate to get kidnapped like the Woodsons."

"Don't be silly. We'll be armed." Maybe she ought to tell Tink about the gunshots. Or maybe not.

"Armed? You?"

"Sure, remember I have a carry permit. We'll leave at eight o'clock in the morning. It'll be fun and nothing will happen." She stared out the window into the darkness, excitement sending shivers through her. Dal would kill her.

7
CHAPTER

Even though it was close to 8:30, Mac's SUV was still parked at the station when Dal drove into the parking lot. He cut across the empty street to Grandma's café, bought two large containers of coffee, and headed back. The dimly lit hallway was as deserted as the streets of the square. Duggan sat behind the intake desk at the end of the hall to his left. He waved and Dal hesitated. Maybe he ought to stop and question him some about the guy he'd been with down at Lizard Lick. But it was more important that he talk to Mac about the Woodsons so he returned the wave by lifting one cup of coffee and moved on.

The only sound was the occasional burst of cursing or laughter from the cells along the far side of the building. There were only a few county prisoners at the moment, some waiting for transfer, others for their hearing to come up. It was a pretty normal situation for Grace County. The jail was never empty but seldom overcrowded.

He leaned in the open door where Mac sat behind a battle-scarred desk. "Brought you some coffee. Need to talk to you."

The sheriff looked up from an open file and smiled. "Be good to have the company and a decent cup of joe. What're you doing out and about this late?"

He set Mac's coffee down, pulled a chair over, and settled in. "Couldn't get my mind off the Woodsons. Been out to the barn looking around. Figured since it was the scene of the crime I had as much right there as one of the feds—which by the way, it looks like that hasn't happened yet."

Mac sipped at the coffee. "Thanks for this. It beats the very devil out of that in the break room. Most men just can't seem to learn to brew this stuff. It's either thick as oil or so weak you could read the newspaper through it." He took another long sip, set down the cup and, hands locked behind his head, studied Dal.

"Something ragging you about that situation?" He tilted his head and squinted at Dal. "You look tired, boy. Been burning the candle at both ends, or is that little gal keeping you way too occupied?"

"Ah, neither. I'm okay. This case is so damned confusing. I keep wanting to tie everything up in a bow, but I can't get it to fit together. Too many pieces missing or out of kilter. I found something odd in the barn."

He stretched his legs and dug the stained file from inside his shirt. "Tell me what you make of this."

Someone shouted down the hall, laughter responded. Mac opened the manila folder and pulled out the half sheet of paper with Bainbridge/ Lofton in the letterhead. "This was where?"

"Up in the loft. It appears at some time in the past someone has had an office of some sort up there. Not exactly a classy location. I'd guess something illegal before the Woodsons moved in. My next guess would be they forgot something and when they came back for it Jeff was out in the barn. They had to have walked in or he'd have heard them."

Mac snorted. "Snuck in, more than likely. They could've used a flashlight and if they were quiet enough Jeff wouldn't have known they were there. Hell, they probably didn't know he was there till he made a noise of some kind. Didn't Alicia say he went out there to vent sometimes?"

Dal nodded. "I suppose him hollering or holding some sort of battle aloud would've warned them he was there. Maybe too late and caught them by surprise. They didn't think but acted and dragged the two of them off. If they didn't know he was blind then they'd think he'd seen them. Alicia said she went out to check on him and they grabbed her too. Hell, if they'd had good sense they could've snuck back out and no one been the wiser. Now we've got a big problem. Did they just leave them there cause they realized the stupidity of grabbing them? It just doesn't fit together."

Mac studied the scrap of paper. "Did you get any uh, you know, your woo-woo messages while you were there?"

"Nope, deader than a tomb." He tapped his temple. Not entirely true, but he couldn't exactly read what he had sensed.

Mac pinched his lip and peered at the torn letterhead a while longer. "This ain't worth kidnapping someone for. Whatever they were there for wasn't this piece of paper, that's for sure. And chances are, whatever it was, they found it, which means we won't."

Dal sipped at his coffee and stared off across the room. "I tend to agree with you. Still, it had to be Bainbridge and/or Kimble, so we need to notify the FBI."

"Yep. They've been in tight scrapes and held off on violence every time. Why resort to it now? I think they grabbed them just to scare them, then maybe didn't know what to do next so they left them there. But you're right. It's still quite a puzzle. Did you check out this firm on this letterhead?"

"Not yet. I thought you might recognize it."

"Naw. I don't think it's local."

Dal finished his coffee, stretched both arms above his head. "It'll do till morning. I've got to get some sleep."

"Then you'd best head to your place at The Five Bs cause you go to that gal's bed you'll not get any."

Dal laughed. "You been spying on me, sheriff?"

"Nope. Ain't necessary. This being the small town that it is. I believe I'll head out too. Gonna watch the ten o'clock news, then get me some sleep."

"Sounds good. I'll work on this in the morning."

Dal rose, waited for the sheriff to get his fancy Stetson off the rack and screw it on his head, then walked out beside him. Duggan waved them a goodbye when they passed the hallway to intake.

Dal stopped. Hell, they'd been so involved in the grabbing of the Woodsons, he and Mac didn't get into the strange disappearance and reappearance of Duggan. Seeing him sitting at intake reminded Dal, but he was too blamed tired to get into it. It would wait. The man was back and unharmed, whatever his reason for being with that man. A lot going on there that needed investigating.

Mac hauled up, turned to see Dal standing there with what was no doubt a goofy look on his face. "You be alert, boy. Don't let one of these bad'uns get the best of you." Mac laughed and so did Duggan and Dal.

Out in the parking lot, Dal stared back at the jail for a moment. He'd get Duggan alone and in the right mood, maybe he'd tell him just who that man was. The both of them had sure acted funny, like they'd been caught with both fists in the cookie jar.

He shrugged and opened the car door. There was no real hurry, he was just curious. It wasn't like they'd been breaking the law. Had they?

The power came back on at Jessie's in the middle of the night. Naturally, the lights were on so it jerked her awake.

"Crap." Rubbing her face, she pulled the covers over her head and closed her eyes. Time ticked by but sleep wouldn't return. Might as well get up as lie there wide awake. She and Tink would need food and water for their trip. Could get everything ready, then go back to bed and catch some winks.

When Dal found out about this he'd be so pissed. He wasn't her boss and she was doing it right. Not going alone. With a shrug, she crawled out of bed, dropped a sleep shirt over her head, and went to the kitchen. Were they being foolish confronting those people down at Lizard Lick? People living off the grid were sometimes a bit touchy about uninvited company.

Energy bars, water, and a few other snacks went into the backpack. It was otherwise always ready, and she set it on the table.

Out on the deck with darkness a soothing cloak, she breathed in the sweet night air. Gazed upward. How beautiful the stars were, thickly scattered across the velvety sky, looking so close she might reach up and pluck a handful down like a brilliant bouquet. From the trees nearby, an owl posed a long series of questions, another added a few from across the way. No one knew the answer, it seemed, but they discussed it for a while.

That poor woman who had called her about her lost children must be going through hell. If indeed the call wasn't a prank. But why would anyone go to the trouble to find out her journalism pseudonym from California as a joke? Too bad she hadn't made more of an effort to talk to her. Maybe she'd call back, or maybe her number wasn't blocked and it was in her phone.

After a while, sleep caught up with her and she went back inside to crawl into bed. The alarm was set for 7:30 and the glowing hands on the clock pointed at 4:10. She curled up and hugged her pillow. Knew no more till the alarm went off and woke her. A quick shower while the coffee perked and she was dressed and ready to go by five till. Tink must've been anxious as well, for she drove up about the same time.

Jessie shrugged into the loaded backpack, poured coffee into two insulated containers, and handed one to Tink at the door. "You nervous?"

A silent nod.

Brad showed his desire to go along, but she instructed him about keeping guard on the house, made sure he had food and water, and left him looking a bit forlorn. Behind the wheel of the Jeep, she hesitated, fingers gripping the key.

"I left a note where we went. Just in case."

In the light from the dome, Tink threw her a glance. "In case what? We've got our phones."

"They're as useless as a can and string where we're going." She didn't mention the Wi-Fi booster cause she hadn't wanted to bother with all that. Besides, what could happen they'd need hooked up to the outside world? For just once forget it. Be out of touch.

Tink pulled out her phone. "Tell you what. I'll leave a message. If anyone calls they'll know where we're at. How would that be?"

Jessie smiled at her friend. "I knew you'd be nervous. But go ahead if it'll make you feel better."

Tink did, then leaned back.

"Ready now?" Jessie didn't wait for a reply but started the Jeep. "This is going to be some adventure."

"I certainly hope so."

The storm from the previous night had left a wash of sticks and dried leaves in a curve alongside the drive. The morning held leftover lavender streaks against a sky of crystalline blue. The air smelled of honeysuckle and wild roses.

Jessie drove without hesitation while an unusually silent Tink gulped coffee down. When it was gone she fit the empty cup into the console. "I told Burt you and I were spending the day together. He's working out in the northwest corner of the county."

"That's good."

"Do you have a plan when we get there?"

"You mean A, B, or C?"

"Well, sort of, like it might be good if we're on the same page. Do we just walk up and knock on the door of this Spooky's house and ask what the heck he's up to?"

"I'd like to know what him and Dal did for those hours they spent together leaving me to cool my heels alone in the car, but I guess you're right. We can't just come out and ask him that."

Tink tapped her front teeth with a fingernail. "Why don't we treat it like an investigation? I have a badge. I can tell him we're looking for some lost hikers and see if we can get him talking about whoever he might have seen around. Or maybe he'll tell us where someone else lives who might know something. Like that man you saw with Duggan. What was that about, anyway?"

"You got me. Okay, that'll work." Jessie slowed at the brown and white sign for the wildlife management area and pulled onto the grassy ruts. Obviously, very few vehicles used this road, though there must be several homes out here.

Heavy brush on either side hemmed them in, branches screeching along the doors. About the time the road narrowed and brought them to a halt, Tink pointed.

"There's the sign for Lizard Lick."

"And this is where we get out and start walking. Let's reload our packs. We can leave some of our food and heavier stuff we won't need till we get back and just carry water and snacks. I want to take my camera and a notepad. Maybe the binoculars. Can you think of anything else?"

"Our phones." She waved her fingers at Jessie. "Oh, I know they're useless but I feel naked without mine, so I'm taking it anyway. I might want to take some pictures. How come you carry that big heavy camera when there's a perfectly good one in your phone?"

"I need to have more control over my picture taking than that little old thing in the phone gives me. In case Parker wants to use them in the paper, or sometimes I write a magazine article and the photos have to have more pixels."

Tink nodded like she knew what Jessie was talking about, but her knowledge of that sort of thing was limited. After they sorted through the backpacks, Jessie locked the Jeep and led the way down the narrow winding trail toward the valley below and the cabin of the spooky man called Marcus.

They had walked for what seemed like forever when Tink called a halt. "You sure you know where we're going? And if people live out here how do they get in and out?"

"It's just around that next bend. The path flattens out and a cutback off to the right is where his cabin is." Jessie shoved back a low-hanging limb and held it for Tink. "I would imagine they ride horses or have one of those all-terrain vehicles."

The cabin was exactly where she remembered it being. Tink walked boldly onto the small porch and rapped on the door with Jessie urging her to be careful. When no one answered, she ignored Jessie's signaling her to stop and knocked again. "Grace County Deputy. Sir, we need to ask you some questions."

Jessie stared open-mouthed at her friend who sounded so official, so commanding. She must've learned that during her brief stint in the field last year. Probably better to lay back and use the law approach. Some people hated reporters worse than they did deputies. Good thing she brought Tink along.

The door finally cracked open enough to reveal one eye and a mouth. The smooth voice Jessie remembered. "What do you want? Could I see some ID?"

Tink held up her badge. "Deputy Mattawan. We're looking for a group of lost hikers. Thought perhaps you might have seen them."

He revealed a slice more of his face but remained silent, then scratched at his head like he was trying to remember something. "If I saw strangers wandering about out here I would've called the authorities immediately." He tilted his head. "Or took a shot at them. There's no legal hiking trails around here. What are they doing trespassing?" The tone a little sharper. "For that matter, what the fuck are you doing out here?"

Not the sort of language Jessie had expected. She poked Tinker. This was public land and, if anything, he was squatting here illegally but she kept her mouth shut and jerked her head, trying to get Tink to come away.

"Sir, if you see them, I would—uh—hope you'd assist them in finding their way out."

"Well, I might do a bit more than that. Could you describe them to me?" The edge hardened some more.

Jessie tightened both fists against her thighs. For God's sake, were there crowds of people wandering by that he had to have a description?

"Perhaps you could tell us if there's anyone else who lives around here we might talk to?"

"People live out here so no one will bother them, and so I don't poke my nose into their business."

He opened the door to reveal the white robe and long hair, but the charismatic personality was gone and he aimed his threatening tone at Jessie. "I believe I've seen you before. You were out here looking for a missing deputy. Has this suddenly become the land of the lost?"

Tink backed off the porch. "We thank you sir. If you do see these people we'd appreciate it if you'd call the sheriff's office."

Spooky laughed and Jessie shuddered. Sounded a bit like a hyena. "No phones out here but I'll point them in the right direction, that's for sure."

"Wonder what would happen if you fell and broke your leg." Tink's tone was less than friendly.

"Don't you go worrying yourself about that, young lady. I'd like it if you'd get off my property and leave me alone."

Jessie moved out toward the trail. "Come on, Tink. I think we'd better be on our way. I thought I heard some people off through the woods there." She pointed vaguely and Spooky craned his neck to peer in that direction before hustling back inside and slamming the door.

"Friendly sort. I thought you said he reminded you of Jesus Christ. He sure didn't seem very forgiving to me." Tink snickered and trotted to catch up with Jessie.

"He must've had a personality transplant since yesterday."

"Where we going now?"

"Down the hill. Where we found Duggan and the other guy."

"The one who was carrying a rifle?"

"That's the one."

"I hope he's a little more friendly than Spooky there."

"You gotta admit, it's a beautiful day for a walk in the woods."

"Yeah, if we don't get shot."

A voice came out of the thick growth of cedar off to their right. "That's about what you're gonna get if you keep goin the way you are. You weren't women I'd already have put a bullet in each of you. And I might do that yet. Just haul up right there, the two of you." The man who'd been with Duggan earlier stepped out into the open, a rifle carelessly pointed in their direction. "And oh, you might just lay that gun down on the ground real easy like, little lady."

Tink curled a palm over her weapon.

"Yeah, that one. Real easy. I'm nervous as all get out today. Go for months without seeing anyone in our neck of the woods, then two days in a row, once in the middle of the night, the law shows up." He studied Jessie with squinted eyes. "You been down here before, with that other deputy. I haven't done anything and I'd appreciate it if you sort of walked on out of here the same way you came. And don't keep coming back." He waved them away and snatched up Tink's gun.

"Hey, you can't keep that."

Jessie tugged at her friend's arm. "Hush."

"Listen to your friend, little lady." Odd, this guy was trying to act like a backwoods hick, but he just couldn't cut it with the language or the accent.

"Daddy, where you at?"

At the sound of the childish voice behind him the man swung around. "Go on back to the house, Ellie. I'll be right there."

Like most kids, the little girl just kept coming and calling for Daddy till she appeared beside the man. Hanging on to his britches leg, she tugged at a lock of long blonde hair and grinned at Tink and Jessie. She wore boys' pants held up by suspenders over a ragged t-shirt and was barefooted.

"Who is them ladies, Daddy? Do they know Mommy?"

He spread a big hand over the top of the little girl's head, aimed a dark gaze at Jessie and Tink. "Well, this does indeed produce a predicament, doesn't it?

Stiff with fright, Jessie snugged an arm around her friend. The man was right, it did indeed.

Dal awoke to a rain-washed morning so peaceful he yearned to light out, find a quiet spot preferably near a waterfall with its soothing song, sit with his back against a tree, and let his thoughts wander. If it weren't for work he'd just walk off into the woods for the day.

Shit, he hadn't contemplated doing that since he'd been in the hospital, what, five or six years ago? His doc called it meditating and it had gotten him through a long painful rehab. One of his buddies in rehab called it brain masturbation. Funny, the stuff that would come back when he just let it all go. Doubts, fears, love, hate.

So why this was going on in his mind now, he wasn't real sure. He might ought to go fetch that crazy Jessie who he couldn't keep his hands off of and take her with him. Being with her could heal a lot of problems and she was always up for something wild. They'd make a day of it where no one would interrupt whatever they wanted to get up to. Only the birds and bees, and heaven knows they knew all about such goings on.

He called Wanda at the Red Bird Café and ordered a big lunch to go, told her he'd be by in an hour or so to pick it up. He wouldn't call Jessie. Better to surprise her and drop in all ready to go on an outing, picnic and all. She was always saying how he used to surprise her but now he didn't seem to have it in him. Well, she was wrong. This kind of day was just the sort that filled him with surprises. Still, she was right too. He needed to get back his blamed mojo, wherever it had gone off to. Definitely her word, not his. He just wasn't much fun anymore.

Basket and blanket in hand, he left his apartment at The Five Bs an hour later, went by the Red Bird, then headed out to Jessie's place, the fragrance of fried chicken filling the car's interior.

At the cabin he found no Jeep and Brad shut up inside the house, Tinkerbelle's car nosed up under the oak tree. Out somewhere on a ladies' day. Turned out his surprise was ruined. Where those gals had got off to he had no idea. Something to do with a story, maybe. Or shopping up in Fayetteville. Hard to tell. They shouldn't be gone too long, so he opened the door and let Brad out, sat down on the porch and shared his drumstick and thigh with the happy little pit bull.

An hour later, he gave up waiting, put Brad inside, and drove over to the newspaper to see if she was there. Turned out no one was, which wasn't all that unusual. It was a day off for everyone. That'd teach him to plan a surprise. So back to the station and see what he could find out about the company on the header of the scrap of paper he'd found out at Hermitage House.

Bainbridge and Lofton was buried on page forty-three of similar listings on Google. One day he'd get someone to teach him how to narrow down his searches. Focus on the subject. He and computers just barely got along and he usually managed to get someone else to do that

Google trick while he took over some of their duties. Today most of the guys were out, probably driving around the county on make-work just to enjoy the beautiful day.

He had promised Mac he'd check this out so he sat there scanning down page after page of the listings for Bainbridge and Lofton in Google till he finally found one that showed the company. It had claimed bankruptcy four years earlier. Located in Saint Louis, the CEO listed was Clarence Bainbridge, not Taylor, but in the other officers, he found Taylor as Financial Officer. The company didn't produce anything, but handled investments of some sort. What wasn't exactly clear.

That figured. A company that had no actual value, just shifted piles of money around from one place to another while borrowing from Peter to pay Paul and cheating shareholders. Why in the world would they be messing about out here in a county filled with folks, most of whom were broke or bent? Maybe Taylor fell into involvement with the child traffickers to pay his bills after the company went broke. Now he was in the wind along with Robert Kimble.

Dal went to the break room for a can of pop and found Duggan lolled kicked back in a chair eating a sandwich. This was his chance to question him about the man in the woods. Sure a lot of mysterious goings on lately, but he couldn't help thinking they were all connected in some way.

After the usual guy greetings he sat, trying to figure out a way to bring up the odd occurrence of Duggan's disappearance. Turned out he didn't have to, for Duggan must've decided to try to explain it before Dal got his own ideas.

"Say, I'm sorry about that mix-up on the radio the other night. Me and my friend were sitting out in his yard when I called you. The reception was lousy and while I was shouting and carrying on trying to get you to hear me, he took a shot at a squirrel. Then we lost contact altogether. I apologize for the scare. Mac already lectured me about getting half the department out hunting for me."

Well, that sounded like a full-blown lie if anything did. "He a pretty good shot at night, is he?"

"Uh—oh, yeah." Duggan chuckled like some kind of idiot. "You know what? He likes to put them in a spotlight. Big braggart, he is."

Dal almost choked. "How in the hell did your patrol unit get crammed halfway down the hill in all those trees? For that matter, how did you even get it back in there in the first place?"

Duggan stared at the table. Clearly he'd forgotten all about that detail. Still, he flushed and stammered into a quick explanation. "I hope you won't tell the sheriff, I'll catch hell. Truth is we were drinking and reminiscing and when I got in my car to come home, I must've been way out of it. Went the wrong way off down that mountain. Goddamned car just kept rolling and dodging trees. I don't even remember much of it, but Randy laughed like a blamed fool when he told me how he dragged me out of the car and took me up to the house after it run off down through the trees. Jest kept slapping his leg and saying how the fucking car must've had eyes or something the way it dodged them trees." Duggan stopped the tale, eyes wide, took a breath, then went on. "That's why I was gone all night. I passed out and didn't wake up till the next morning."

What a bullshit story that was. Dal didn't know Duggan very well, but he was lying through his teeth. Dal didn't have to read his mind to figure that out. Trouble was, he worked so hard making up his lies Dal wasn't sure what the truth might be.

He would find out, but for now he just grinned and nodded his head like he believed every word. Be fun to fish around and see just how much Duggan could invent.

"I guess your friend missed that squirrel and shot a couple of holes in the door of your car."

Duggan stammered around that one then grinned. "Must have."

A bark of a laugh escaped before Dal could stop it. "I hope Mac is gonna bill you for the repair."

Duggan shook his head. "Could be, but I hope not. I'm flat broke."

Good God. The man was unbelievable. He prodded some more. "Don't believe I ever saw your friend around here. Is he just visiting or has he moved in out there? You said his name is Randy?"

"What? Uh, well, he lives off down in the valley. Closer to Harrison than Cedarton, so he don't come to town up here regularly. Think he's been there a few years though. I only got acquainted with him when—" He scratched his ear. "Funny thing, I stopped him out on the highway with a burnt-out taillight. We got to visiting, found we had a lot in common, so I go out and see him once in a while."

This was getting worse by the minute. A lot in common? A hermit and a sheriff's deputy? Some people thought if they told a convoluted enough lie, it wouldn't be questioned, but just the opposite was true. Keep it simple, stupid. He had to work to keep from saying that out loud.

"Well, I guess you were lucky all the way around then, huh? Say, you still didn't say what your friend's name is. Randy what?"

"Uh, Drain. Yep, that's it. Drain."

"Well, I'm going to have to go down there and talk to this Randy fellow. You know those two guys the FBI is after are still wandering around somewhere close. He might have seen something."

"Oh, shit no." He dragged splayed fingers through his hair. "If he had seen them he'd have told me."

"Why is that? Did you tell him about the cult and the child trafficking?"

Gaze turned toward the window. Look long enough, maybe you'll come up with more story, lamebrain.

"Can't remember, I was drunk. But he gets riled if he sees anyone around down there. He'd a been sure to tell me. You saw how he carries that rifle."

"To hunt squirrels. At night."

Duggan held his watch up, leaped to his feet. "Look at that, I'd better get back to work or Mac'll have my ass."

Boogie on outta here, you fool. How in God's name did he pass the tests to get hired? Time to talk to Mac about this guy. Unbelievable. He'd have his ass all right, but not for the reasons this idiot thought.

He finished his drink and headed down the hall toward the sheriff's office to have a little talk with him. Maybe by then Jessie would be back from wherever she went and they could at least have the evening together. She'd get a kick out of Duggan's tale.

After hearing Dal's story, Mac declared he'd have Duggan on the carpet. "You know, when I had his unit pulled out there were dents and scratches on both sides. He said he was run off the road by a pickup truck that didn't stop. Blamedest story I've heard in a coon's age. May just have to fire him."

Dal grinned. "Another lie, huh?" He rose, fetched his Stetson off the battle-scarred desk, and plopped it on. "I'm going on out to Jessie's. She's been gone all day and I need to see her."

Mac laughed. "Can't say I blame you, but in my day it would've been time to make an honest woman outta her stead of bedding her and leaving her."

Sure couldn't say Mac pulled any punches, but he was right. It just wasn't something Dal could consider. "I reckon you might be right. But that's not the way it's done anymore. We live in a whole new world."

"Yep, sad to say we do. Well, tell her hello for me and don't you hurt her or you'll have me to count."

Dal walked out into the warm evening. Mac had a good point. He'd get on out there. She'd surely be home by now and they could soothe each other's itches.

8
CHAPTER

Staring into the barrel of a rifle was not even close to one of Jessie's favorite things. But once there, the choices narrowed down. She picked the safest one. Don't do anything stupid.

"What are you going to do with us?"

Crap. Why couldn't she at least sound brave? Fear made her voice quiver. Hard to act brave with a rifle pointed at your nose. That dark hole looked big enough to fall into and blacker than hell. It didn't help that she'd once been shot and knew what it felt like. Her feet grew roots deep into the ground. Even given the chance, she couldn't run.

A girl of maybe two or three toddled out of the woods. "Daddy, Suzie won't play with me." She grabbed his leg, stared up at him.

Tink appeared to be a little more calm, her words coming clear. "You wouldn't want your little girl to see something bad, would you?"

A sorrowful expression crossed his face. "I'm afraid she already has."

"If you're in trouble maybe we could help." She reached out, palm down. "Just put down the gun. Nobody wants to hurt you."

His head shook back and forth. "Why did you have to come out here and ruin everything? I haven't bothered anyone. All I want is to be left alone." His hand clutched the rifle so hard the knuckles turned white.

Jessie cleared her throat and found her voice. "I was with the deputy who came by yesterday. Don't you remember me?" This man was hiding from something or someone, that was clear. And he might panic and shoot them, but hopefully not in front of the child.

"Sweetheart, why don't you go back to the house and stay with your sister? Daddy will be home in a minute."

The child broke from his leg and ran to Jessie, grabbing her hand. "I want the lady to come with me."

"Ellie, get away from her and do like I asked."

The little girl stomped her foot. "No, I don't want to."

A baffled look crossed the man's face and he glanced around as if not sure what to do.

Jessie knelt and fingered the tangles of hair off the child's face. "Honey, maybe you'd better listen to Daddy."

Tears filled Ellie's eyes. "I want my mommy. She's gone and I can't find her."

"Goddamn it." He dropped the rifle, took two long strides, and yanked the child away. Hugged her up tight and kissed her on top of the head. "It's okay, sweetheart."

Tink moved so quickly it surprised Jessie. She had the rifle and was back out of his reach before he saw what had happened. "Stay right where you are."

He raised to gaze at Tink, cheeks wet with tears. "Please don't do this. You don't understand what's going on."

"I know what it looks like, mister. You pointed a gun at us." Tink sounded so official Jessie was amazed. "You're out here in the back end of nowhere with two children and no wife, you hold a gun on us and this little girl is crying for her mommy. What conclusions would you draw if the situation were reversed?"

"I know how it looks. Please. Talk to Duggan, he'll tell you the truth."

Jessie stared at him. "You steal these kids? Kidnap them? We've just gone through some sad stuff with child traffickers and we're not exactly in the mood to listen to anything you have to say."

"Child traffickers? Good God. These are my girls."

Tink made a rude noise. "Then prove it. Where's Mommy?"

"Duggan is a deputy and he's family. I don't want to get him in trouble, but he can straighten this out fast. Please, don't do anything till you talk to him."

Jessie studied the man's face, the expression so distressed she tended to believe he was telling the truth. Except he hadn't told them enough.

She was good at getting that. "Okay, start at the beginning. Who are you and where are you from?"

"I tell you and you go back and tell someone else and first thing I know their mother will have some ape friend of hers out here dragging my girls back to that hell hole."

"No, look. If that's true, if your kids are in danger, we will make sure they are protected. Just tell me about it. I'm ready to listen." She turned toward Tink, gestured for her to put down the rifle.

"You sure? You believe this guy, just like that?"

"Tink, I've interviewed hundreds of people and I've learned when someone is outright lying. This guy is frightened. Let's at least listen to his story before we make a decision that might hurt those little girls."

"You always are too trusting. You sure about this?"

"Please." His voice was ragged with despair.

"Tell you what. I'll just sit over here against this tree with the rifle right beside me. Then you can talk to him all you want. Just don't get close enough for him to grab you and hold you hostage. Then if we both decide to believe him, we'll figure out how to help him. How's that?"

Jessie looked from Tink to the man, then back to Tink. Nodded. Turned back to him. "That okay with you?"

"Okay with him? I've got his gun. It's either that or I cuff him and we take him in."

"No, good God no. Here, let me show you something." He held Ellie out away from him and lifted her dress to bare her midsection. There were three round inflamed marks there. "That is what my wife did the last time she was high and I couldn't take it anymore. I can't even leave the house but what she isn't at one or both of them with some sort of torture."

Jessie's throat closed till she couldn't swallow.

"How do we know he didn't do that to her?" Tink wasn't quite ready to give up yet.

"Ellie, could you tell the ladies how you got those marks?"

She nodded, those big blue eyes overflowing. "She burned me with her 'grette."

"Who, honey?" Jessie's voice came out a squawk and she went back to kneel near Ellie again.

The child sobbed, then broke down and cried.

"She doesn't want to tell you who did that to her. She loves her mommy and it's confusing to her that someone she loves would hurt her."

"Well, she did say she, so unless she calls her daddy she we've got a part of the truth. Tink, I think if he wants to tell us why he's out here, we should listen. I don't want to do something that will get these kids hurt."

Tink lifted her shoulders in a sigh. "Okay." She relaxed against the tree, but kept a hand on the butt end of the rifle. "Talk away, but like I said Jess, stay out of his reach."

Jessie touched Ellie's cheek. "Honey, do you know your way back to your house?"

She nodded.

"Why don't you go back and make sure your sister is okay? We need to talk to your daddy. Would that be okay?"

After rolling her eyes up to look at her dad and seeing him nod, she turned and ran back the way she had come.

God help them if this man was lying, but Jessie had to hear his story before making a judgment call that had so much riding on it. The woods around them was filled with sounds of life, birds singing, squirrels digging about in the leaves for nuts, the peaceful noises of other creatures going about their business. It was hard to believe danger lurked so near, but something crawled up her spine when she turned to face the terrified expression of this man.

Damn. That woman had gone off on some dangerous tangent again. Dal read the note she'd left. He'd missed it before. The wind when he opened the door earlier must've blown it on the floor. But when he returned to see if she'd come back there it was under the edge of the table. The only hopeful thing was that Tink was with her, if that helped any. The two of them together was almost twice as scary.

He called the station to see if Duggan was still there, but Colby answered, instead.

"Just on the desk till Tink gets here. She's late." The explanation from Colby was less than satisfying.

"Did Duggan say where he was going?" He'd get the truth out of him about the so-called Randy and what he was doing in Lizard Lick if he had to slap him around.

"Home, I think, but he didn't say. Why? What's up?"

"Les or Burt around anywhere?"

"Nope, in fact it's almost quiet as a tomb in here. Mac's been gone a while. Again, what's up?"

"I don't want to bother him."

"Sam Watson's on his way to take over for our absent Tinker. When he gets here I can help out, whatever it is."

"Appreciate it. I'll let you know." If he'd pick anyone to help get this mess cleaned up, it would be Colby. "Hey, listen, when Sam gets there could you meet me out here at Jessie's? If I'm not here, wait for me. I'm going to see if I can round up Duggan. He's got some explaining to do."

"Sure thing. You might try After Hours. I think his girlfriend is a bartender out there."

"Thanks. I'll keep in touch." Dal was halfway to the unit when Brad skittered between his legs and waited at the door. "Okay, buddy, you can go. Maybe you'd be able to follow that mistress of yours."

The pit bull leaped in the car and across the console to claim shotgun like he always did. The drive to After Hours, a recently opened bar out at the edge of town near the new highway, took maybe five minutes with lights flashing. The sun hung low in the west behind a blaze of orange and gold clouds. Off to the north, lightning played through an ashen sky. It would storm before full dark. Jessie had picked a heck of a day to go running around on one of her quests.

Sliding to a stop in the gravel parking, Dal left Brad to guard the car and headed for the bar. The Open sign in the window flashed off and on. Two guys came out talking and laughing, but were silenced when they spotted a deputy headed their way.

"Evening, boys." Dal nodded and the two men nodded in return, each moving on their way.

Thunder rumbled and rolled closer. Damn. Chasing around in the woods in a storm wasn't his idea of the way to spend an evening. He ought to let Jessie make her own way through this. If she had better sense he would. If he had better sense he would. The odor of beer and cigarette smoke greeted him inside.

Duggan leaned on the bar about halfway into the gloomy room. A pretty girl in a low-cut shirt stood on the other side laughing up into his face. The room was crowded with after-five workers and he shoved his way through to get to the deputy.

Their eyes met. "Hey Boss." Duggan's voice held a false gaiety.

He held off clocking him one so he could answer his questions. "Need to talk to you a minute. And don't call me boss."

"Okay, whazupp?"

Damn, he hated that greeting, but bit back his annoyance. Probably anything this man said to him right now would stir his anger. "Could we get out of here so I can hear myself think?"

Duggan glanced at the girl, who frowned and murmured something Dal couldn't hear. He gave her a cold stare. "He'll be right back. Maybe."

Outside, Dal pinned the younger deputy with a glare. "I want to know everything you can tell me about that fella you called Randy. The one that lives off down at Lizard Lick. Now."

"Shit, Boss. I mean Deputy Dal."

"That's not any better."

"Okay, yeah, I know. I'm just nervous. I ain't done nothing wrong and neither has Randy, so why do you wanna know about him?"

"Cause I do. Get started."

"He's a good guy trying to do what's right. I don't wanna get him in any trouble."

"If he's doing what's right he won't be in trouble."

Duggan scuffed at the gravel with a booted toe. "His wife is a drunk and a junkie, and she was hurting his kids and she sued him for custody and he took off with the girls to keep them safe." The explanation tumbled out.

"Holy shit, man. That's kidnapping." The reference to her being a junkie tightened Dal's stomach.

"They're his own girls. How can he kidnap his own girls?"

"Well, he's figured out how."

Duggan stared down at the ground, then glanced up, anger crossing his round features. "She burns em with cigarettes and other worse stuff. What would you do?"

I'd probably kill the bitch. Dal didn't voice the thought, but gritted his teeth. "There are ways to get them lawfully."

"He tried, but she convinced ever'one he was doing the hurting, and no one would believe him cause—cause…." He screwed his mouth and refused to look Dal in the eye.

"He's got a record, hasn't he?" Duggan nodded, didn't say anything. "How do you know this for sure? And who is Randy to you?"

"He's my cousin. We grew up together up in Salem, Missouri. He got in trouble once when he was a kid, not old enough for it to go on his record. Nothing violent. But everyone knew. Small town. Stupid stuff, that's for sure, but he come out of it. When all this went down he come to me for help. I knew he could hide out down in Lizard Lick. Never thought anyone would ever find him. Shit, Boss. Hell, I'm sorry… about calling you boss and ever'thing."

Dal wadded Duggan's shirt in his fist. "You're coming with me." He dragged the younger man across the parking toward his unit. "Just leave yours here. Is it locked up?"

"Huh-uh. Where we goin? What you gonna do to me?"

"Lock your unit up. Now. You're taking me to Lizard Lick and we're going to get this fixed, one way or another. You can't facilitate someone breaking the law. Jessie and Tink are off down there, doing no telling what, and if he hurts either one of em I will put the both of you in jail if I have to make up charges. Now move."

The goof-off locked his patrol car, then hunkered by the passenger door peering in the window.

"Well what are you waiting for? Get in."

He tapped a finger on the glass. "There's a dog in the seat. He looks like a pit bull. I ain't ridin in the seat with no pit bull."

"Oh, for God's sake. Brad, get in the back." Brad cocked his head, rolled his brown eyes, and lay down. "Duggan, you get in the back. That seat is taken."

Once he was settled, Dal sped off, grumbling under his breath. He just might dump this fucking idiot over a cliff before this was over with.

Accompanied by wind and rain, storm clouds darkened the sky. Tink and Jessie and the man who called himself Randy were drenched before

they made it to the cabin. A truce of sorts didn't keep Jessie from being nervous about the situation. If she was wrong and this guy was lying, no telling what could happen. The only comforting thing was Tink had both the rifle and her sidearm and the man showed no inclination to attack or escape.

He burst through the cabin door and held it open for them.

"Wait here while I light some lamps." He felt his way into the darkness, only a shadow in the gloom.

Jessie huddled next to Tink. Even though it had been a pleasant day, the rain was cold and they hugged each other to get warm. A soft glow spread from the lamps, one on a small table where Ellie and an older girl sat, another on the wall above a worn recliner. In one corner were two beds, a chest, and clothes hanging on hooks on the wall. While the place was spare, it was clean. A pot steamed on top of a small potbellied stove that gave off enough heat to warm them. For some reason the smell of soup of some kind made the room more comfortable.

Randy opened a drawer in the chest and took out two towels, gave one to Tink and Jessie, used the other to dry his face, hair, and bare arms. "You'll have to share and please hang it on the line behind the stove to dry."

His tone had lost its earlier surliness and was quite calm. Jessie studied him after she handed the towel to Tink. The way he regarded his daughters, his body language, and the constant glancing at her as if she held his fate in her hands led her to believe him.

But what if she was wrong?

He divided the soup into two bowls for the girls and gave them each a glass of milk from a small ice chest. "I'd offer you something to eat, but there's not enough. The girls have to eat."

"We need to talk, Mister—"

He didn't supply his last name. "Yes, I know. But I'd appreciate it if it could wait till the girls eat and go to bed. You're surely not going anywhere in this storm anyhow."

As if to reiterate his statement, a limb slammed into the side of the cabin and the wind and rain slashed the window panes.

"I have some snacks in my backpack. We can eat those and I have water." Jessie dropped into one of the beanbag chairs and opened the pack, shared out the nature bars and apples with Tink. Held some up toward the man who refused to tell her his last name. He shook his head no, but looked as if he'd like some. "There's more. These are good."

His shoulders slumped as if someone had said they were going to give him twenty lashes, but he took the offered food, dropped into the recliner, and practically inhaled the bar and apple.

Tink watched the entire episode in silence before she took the other chair and unwrapped her food. Her eyes were guarded and it was hard to tell what she was thinking.

Jessie finished her food and leaned back. "How long have you been out here?" She aimed the question at Randy, but he acted as if he didn't hear till he finished off the apple, core and all.

"It's been a while."

"In the winter?"

"Ah, no. Why do you need to know?"

A long rumble of thunder shook the floor under her chair. Ellie cried out and Randy rose and went to her. Hugged her close. "It's just the angels bowling. You finished?" She looked up at him and nodded. "Well, let's get you ready for bed then."

Jessie studied her surroundings once more. When this was over and done with, a solution reached, she wanted to remember everything for the story she would write. The way the wood burning in the stove crackled and smelled blending with the aroma of rain in her hair. The man's big hand gently undressing his young daughter and dropping a gown over her head, lifting her and laying her in the bed. The older girl, whose understanding of what was happening darkened her blue eyes. And Tink's confusion as her gaze darted from Jessie to Randy and back again, trying to gauge just what would happen next. She didn't agree with Jessie's approach and it showed in her disapproving expression.

The noise of the storm died away, but rain continued to hammer the roof and window. Randy finished getting the girls in bed and came back to where they sat, straddled one of the wooden chairs at the table. His work boots were worn and muddy from the trek back to the cabin.

"I want to tell you a story and I hope you'll be kind enough to listen and believe what I say."

Jessie nodded. "I'll promise to listen, but that's all. What I believe depends on the story."

"Fair enough. About nine or ten months ago I happened to get away from my job early, so I stopped and picked up take-out to surprise my wife so she wouldn't have to cook. She worked at home and I knew it was difficult working and taking care of the girls. They are home-schooled. Her idea, not mine. I'd rather they learn to be with other kids."

He took a big long sigh as if he wasn't sure he could go on, and he didn't for a long pause.

"I decided to go in real quiet and holler boo at the girls. It's a game they loved to play. I'd pop out of a room and yell boo and they'd fall down giggling. Anyway, I shoved the door open and just as I did I heard Ellie scream. Suzie was sobbing in the background. Thinking someone had broken in I dropped the bags of Kentucky Fried and raced up the stairs toward the sound. It was coming from behind the girls' bedroom door. Afraid whoever was in there would hurt them if I scared him, I eased the door open gently."

He stopped, covered his mouth to hold back a sob. "She… she had a cigarette and was holding the burning end against Ellie's tummy. Suzie was huddled in the corner of her bed crying. I was so in shock for a minute I could do nothing but stare. Hard to believe my wife, always so soft-spoken and sweet, would do such a thing. Maybe I was imagining it. Of course, I came out of it and leaped across the room, pulled Ellie out of her arms and flat-handed my wife in the chest, knocking her off the bed."

He stopped, tears streaming down his face.

"But how could this go on and you not know it till then?"

One hand came up, signaled her to stop. "Same thing I asked myself. She swore she'd lost her patience when the girls talked back, that it was the first time. She'd already done the same to Suzie." He barely choked out those words, swallowed, and took a deep breath. "Please try to understand, because I need you to believe me and help me if you can. Or in the least not tell anyone I'm here till I can find another place to hide them.

"When I thought back on it, I asked myself what kind of father I'd been that this could go on under my nose. And she begged me, swore on her mother's grave she'd never done anything like that before. Never would again. I had given the girls their baths, changed their clothes. Knew I would've seen burns like that, so I believed her. But I kept an eye on the girls after that. Turned out she was using other forms of punishment that didn't leave scars. When I found that out I took my girls out of the house one night after my wife finally went to sleep, put them in the car, and took off. I finally landed here because my cousin—you've met him—had this cabin and I figured she'd never find me.

"A few days later he told me she'd swore out a warrant against me. Said I'd been molesting the girls and when she accused me I ran off with them."

"But didn't anyone, friends or other family members, miss the girls? Wonder what had happened to them?"

"Duggan told me she said that I threatened to kill them both and myself if she told and so she was afraid and had told everyone that they were visiting my parents for a short while to get acquainted with their grandparents. The woman has a lie for every single thing that happened. For a long time Suzie wouldn't talk about what had happened and when I finally got her to say anything, she said Mommy said she would kill all of us if they ever told it was her that hurt them."

"How could you have been married to someone like that and never suspected anything? My God, you should've reported her right then."

"We don't always do what we should. Not when someone we love is in danger. Don't you think I've asked myself that question hundreds of times? She was pregnant with Suzie when we married. I didn't love her but I was old-fashioned and wanted to do the right thing. We made the best of a bad situation, but I thought we were managing. Then Ellie came along and we had these two precious little girls. I swear I never saw anything that even hinted at what she was doing." He broke down then, covering his face with both hands to muffle the crying.

Headlights reflected the rain and flashed across the brown sign marking the wildlife management area. Dal braked, backed up, and made the turn.

"We're gonna drown walking in this." Duggan wiped the sweat off the inside of the door window. "Can't see nothin out there."

"You should've thought of that before you pulled this stunt. What were you thinking, protecting someone who's breaking the law? A deputy sheriff, for God's sake. You could lose your job. Probably will."

"Shit, man. He's family. You telling me you wouldn't help your own damn family?"

"The kind of help he needed was to see a lawyer and handle this the right way."

"Sometimes the right way don't work out so good. You know that. Look what they did to Mac and he didn't even do nothin."

Dal clamped his lips tight. Duggan might be a fucking idiot, but he was right. Still, this could've been taken care of better. Yet he had no choice but to serve the warrant against Randy. He sure hoped the man didn't lose his kids over this, especially if the woman had been abusing them. For all he knew, it could be the other way around, and it was Randy abusing them. It had to be cleared up before either parent was allowed to have custody.

This coming right on top of Kimble and Bainbridge running amok through the county gathering up kids to sell and the Woodsons being uprooted out of their home was most annoying. Either nothing happened in Grace County for months, or when something did it was one thing piled on another. He hoped Mac had Les, Burt, or Colby checking on the couple over at The Five Bs. Wished he'd of thought to make sure of it before taking off. Mac was getting more absentminded and he'd been trying to take some of the load off the sheriff since he'd returned from Frog Pond last year.

"Stop, man. Stop."

Duggan's shouting cut through his reverie just in time to keep him from running off into a mud hole at the end of the road.

"Dang, thought you was going to sink us up to the axles. Then we woulda been in trouble for sure."

"Yeah, well I didn't." Dal cut the lights and reached for the door handle.

"Why'nt we wait till this slacks up a bit fore takin off? It's near half a mile to Randy's place."

"Aw, hell, you made of sugar? The storm has moved off and it's just harmless rain. I want to get down there and make sure your cousin hasn't taken the law into his own hands and harmed Tink and Jessie. I'd think you'd be concerned yourself. I've got a couple of slickers in the back. Look behind the seat there."

"Randy ain't violent. He won't hurt them women." Duggan came up with the rain gear and handed one to Dal.

Dal shrugged into it. "You sure? He might if it was to save his girls."

Duggan went silent while he put on the coat. "Well, shit, then. Let's get going."

Dal had to chuckle, cause he'd already opened the door and was getting out. Brad barked and he turned. He'd forgotten all about the little fella. Bringing him along had been a mistake and now he had to figure out what to do with him. Duggan hunched nearby, grumbling and griping. Dal leaned in, gathered Brad up and tucked him under his arm, sheltered from the rain. He pulled out his flashlight and clicked it on. The powerful beam sent a circular cone out in front of them that bounced with each step he took.

Drops splattered on the plastic rain gear, their boots squished in the mud, and Duggan continued to curse all the way down the hill and around the bend. Neither spoke until he spotted the lamplight through the trees.

"Well, thank God. I thought we'd never get here." He led the way, stomped up onto the porch.

The man bitched more than anyone he'd ever known, but Dal did his best to ignore it. "Knock, tell him it's you."

"He's gonna be real sore at me for betraying him. I hope he don't shoot us."

"Hey, I thought you said he isn't violent." Just in case. Dal tucked the flashlight into his belt and replaced it with his .44 sidearm, holding on to the wiggling dog. "Go ahead, knock and tell him it's you."

"Aw, hell. All right." He rapped on the door. "Randy, open up, it's me. Duggan."

All was quiet. Shifting from one foot to the other, Dal had enough. Suppose Jessie and Tink were tied up or worse, hurt?

"Open this goddamned door or I'll kick it in." Also having enough of this nonsense, Brad struggled loose and let go with a series of barks.

The door swung open, but it wasn't a man Dal pointed the gun at but Tink, eyes wide in the dim light.

"No need to shoot, deputy. We're fine. Git in here before you drown."

Holstering his gun, Dal shoved Duggan in ahead of himself and Brad skittered between their legs, nails ticking madly on the wood floor. Tink slammed the door behind them. The noise of the storm died away some.

For a long silent moment everyone stared at everyone else. All ready to pounce. Dal wasn't real sure who to watch the closest.

"Daddy, where did the puppy come from?" The childish voice from a darkened corner broke the silence and the mood. Brad stared with innocence from the arms of the little girl who sat on the bed. Laughter trickled through the room, setting a relaxing tone. Leave it to a kid and a dog to set things straight.

9
CHAPTER

"What do we do now?" The words Jessie spoke echoed with those of her friend Tink, who slumped next to her in the larger of the bean bag chairs. Both turned toward Dal with the question.

Long legs sprawled across the cabin floor, he shrugged, glanced toward the bed where the two girls and the little pit bull slept. Randy and Duggan sat at the table sharing what was left of the health bars and apples, not saying much.

"I honestly don't know what's the best or right thing to do here. We all know there are times when the law comes down on the wrong side. But that doesn't make it right to ignore it."

Tink ran a fingertip along Jessie's arm. "Could make it the best thing to do though."

Rain continued to pepper the roof, a soothing sound now that the wind had laid and the storm passed on.

With a subtle glance at Randy, Dal considered the question. "I don't know what to do. His story is plausible, he seems to be telling the truth, but you both know as well as I that some folks are such good liars they can make us believe anything. Mostly cause they've convinced themselves."

Tink nodded. "And if it's his wife who is the liar, then what? We're turning those two sweet babies over to someone who will make their life a living hell."

Jessie brushed her hair back. "I wish we had a lie detector."

"Do you believe him?" Dal pinned her down with the question.

"I, uh, yes. I do."

But did she really, or wasn't she only afraid of coming down on the wrong side of this in a story that could do irreparable harm? Dear God, she needed to be right about this or not write the story at all. She'd learned the hard way that hurting people just to get what seemed the most exciting story to write could ruin lives.

"Tinkerbelle?" He swung to look at her.

"I'm on the fence leaning toward not believing him."

Jessie tapped a fist on her friend's shoulder. "Why do you say that?"

"I'm really not sure. It's something about his story that bugs me. That he could claim to be a good husband and father, yet let that abuse go on under his nose for months and months without knowing it. I have trouble with that."

"I have to go with that for now." Dal held up a finger before Jessie could object too hotly. "To be on the safe side, I'd like to find someone who knew the family all along and get their opinion. Did they go to church? We could talk to their minister. Belong to clubs or scouts or the like? Find out what they think. I just can't say let him have those little girls without checking this out further. It's a dangerous step, breaking the law. And if we're wrong and he's lying, it's so much worse."

Jessie gazed at the girls asleep across the room. Okay, that was a safe way to go. "So in the meantime what do we do? Take them in and let Social Services put them in the system? I don't like that idea."

"Well, I have another idea." Eyes closed Dal leaned his head back. Went all quiet for a while.

Jessie studied his worried expression, waited for him to say something. Lost her patience. "Well, what is it?"

"I'm trying to think it out. I'm not sure it will work, but I think it's worth a try."

Okay, so give him some time to do that. He could be so frustrating sometimes she wanted to shake him. "So?"

"I just don't know if we should do this without first consulting Alicia."

"Maybe when we're old and gray. Spit it out, Dal. We're all dying here."

"What if we take the girls and their dad into town to Hermitage House and see if Alicia and Jeff want to move back home? I'm sure they're ready to do that by now. They can give these girls and their dad a place to stay while we look into this. Try to find evidence that will support one or the other side of this issue. And Randy can look out for everyone in case Bainbridge or Kimble show up. What do you think?"

Not a bad idea. "I think we'd have to ask a lot of people to cooperate, but it sounds like a good idea. Do we try to keep it secret in a town like Cedarton, though? You know it'll get out somehow."

"We can make up a story that will satisfy the gossips. If we're the only ones in town who know the truth, then it can't get out. Right? Randy can just be a man looking for peace and quiet after separating from his wife. A place to lick his wounds. And the girls won't go to school since it's summertime, so we wouldn't have to worry about them telling anyone."

Jessie stared at Dal. "We can say his wife died, then we won't have to explain why he has the kids and not her. Mom almost always gets the kids in a separation or divorce."

Tink and Dal both nodded. "Good thinking."

"There's only one flaw in this." Tink glared toward Randy and Duggan.

"What's that?"

"If he's lying then he's apt to jump and run the first chance he gets. He would be the last one who would want to hang around while we checked out his story."

Randy jumped into the conversation. "I'm not lying, but I don't know any way to prove it to you."

"I believe you, Randy." Jessie appeared not to understand why the others didn't.

Dal continued to cling to his doubts. "There's got to be a way to guarantee he'd hang around. Maybe Alicia can come up with something legal that would convince him to stay put till we get it all figured out."

"What do I have to do to convince you?" Randy kicked back his chair, paced to the window, and stared out into the night.

Ignoring the outburst, Dal patted Jessie on the knee. "Let's try it anyway. Maybe we could start by asking Alicia and Jeff since Hermitage House is their home." He dug around in his pocket, pulled out his phone, pecked on it. Messed with his walkie, still got nothing but silence. "Does anyone's phone have a signal, so we could call them and get this underway? Wish to hell we had those new digital walkies. These analog units are useless out here."

"What about the car radio?"

"No tower. The fire department has tried for years to get another tower to carry the signal off out here. We're in a black hole as far as communications are concerned."

Jessie rose, paced back and forth. Stopped. "I have an idea."

"About time." Tink patted Jessie on the shoulder. "Give."

"I'll walk out to the cars, drive in to The Five Bs and talk to Alicia and Jeff about this, then I can come back and let you know what they say and we can go from there with Randy and the girls."

Expression cloudy, Randy stood. "Wait just a minute. I appreciate your effort on our behalf but you can't keep me and the girls like prisoners no telling how long. She'll hear about it. You start going around talking to people who know us and she'll send someone to take the girls away. I won't let her take them, I'll kill her first."

Duggan, who had been quiet throughout the discussion, grabbed his cousin's arm. "Sit down. You don't go sayin things like that in front of deputies."

Randy jerked out of his grip. "Well, I'm packing my girls up and leaving, and you're gonna have to shoot me to stop me. I won't be a party to something like this cause you choose not to believe me."

Disappointed and impatient, Jessie jumped up and faced Randy. "You got a better idea, tell us. Your running is not going to solve anything. You can't drag those two little girls from pillar to post. Even here they're hungry and scared. They need a place they'll feel secure, and I can't understand why you don't see that. There are ways to talk to these people that no one will be suspicious. I can interview them on the ruse that I'm writing a story about families going through this sort of thing. For all they'll know I'm on your wife's side and don't know anything about you at all. It'll work. I can make it work and you'll all be safe at Hermitage House." She went to Randy's side, patted his shoulder. "We're trying to help you, can't you see that? You run now and get caught, you'll lose those girls."

He dropped into his chair, buried his face in both hands. Everyone waited. At last he looked up. Nodded. "Okay, for now, but I want to know who you talk to and everything they say."

Aware that Dal didn't like this turn of events at all because it put her out in the open, Jessie glanced at him. If the wife was like Randy said, she was dangerous and could hurt Jessie. But it couldn't be helped. She yearned for a chance to face the woman, challenge her, prove herself right about Randy, despite the danger. Working for the small rural newspaper didn't give her many opportunities to be involved in something like this that could grow into a major story. She had to reassure Dal.

"Don't worry about me, I'll be extra careful." She still hadn't told Dal about the phone call that might have been from Randy's wife. Something odd there though, but at the moment she couldn't think what it was.

"I know how you're careful, Tiger Lady." Though he sounded angry, he wrapped her in his arms, gave her a shelter she could not deny. The rain had slackened off, leaving behind a stillness that was suddenly and viciously broken by the roar of what could only be a tiger.

"My God, what was that?" Tink ran to the window and peered out. "Can't see a thing."

Jessie joined her. "You know what? I think one of July Jones's tigers has gotten out. Nothing else could make a noise like that."

"Will it attack?" Duggan's eyes bugged wide and he backed up into a corner.

Tink pointed at the window. "Whoa. What is that?"

On the other side was the face of a white tiger, head larger than the pane of glass. Its great mouth opened wide, the roar rattling the windows. Brad hit the floor barking and jumping up and down. Ellie and Suzie woke up crying. In the small cabin, mayhem reigned. In turn, the tiger reacted to the excitement and tossed her head, letting out a series of growls. Her nose traced circles on the wet window.

"It's just Maizie." Jessie went to the window and ran her finger along the marks.

"Well, I guess that puts the icing on the cake. Try telling this and no one would believe a word." Dal chuckled in a weird sort of way and Jessie, obviously the only one who heard him, laughed under her breath. It certainly had been one crazy day and it wasn't about to get any better. July Jones was apt to be having a fit about now.

There were times in his life when Dal believed the universe was purely random. This was one of them. What could possibly be the reason for a tiger running around in the Ozarks and appearing here, for God's sake? Obviously it just happened, and that, by God, was all there was to it. If Grandfather were hanging around, he'd ask him, but the old man had been mysteriously missing for most of the time. That sort of pleased him till the tiger showed up. Now he had no clue what purpose the old man served. And desperately wanted to talk to him. Perhaps set this straight. For purpose was the one important point in anyone's life. The one thing he had to understand.

"Shoot him." Duggan made as if to draw his gun and danced around like he expected the huge cat to come in through the walls. Best he disarm him and fast. Dal moved so quickly the frightened man had no idea what he was up to till he slapped a palm over his gun and jerked it from the holster.

The man was badly flawed and sometimes acted like a ten-year-old girl. How they missed that when he took his tests to join the department was a mystery. Once all this was settled, he was going to have a talk with Mac about him. Under duress, he would not react properly and someone could get killed.

It finally dawned on the stunned deputy that he'd been disarmed. "Hey, wait a damn minute now. What's that about?" Palm cupped over the empty holster, he jumped up and down. "Give me back my damn gun. That thing gets in here I wanna be armed."

"Sit down and calm down. There'll be no shooting in here."

"Who put you in charge?"

Dal ignored him and shoved Duggan's sidearm in his waistband. Just till he could find a place to put it where the madman couldn't lay hands on it. No one with any sense walked around with a semi-auto tucked into their belt. Could shoot his foot off, or worse. Another good reason to get this guy out of the department. His connection to Randy Drain could be a worse problem however.

The tiger disappeared from view, but the disruptive growl continued to be heard as the cat prowled around outside.

Dal took Jessie's arm and walked her to the far corner away from everyone peering out the window.

"What are we going to do?" Her mouth close to his ear gave him the shivers. Or maybe it was the tiger. Nope, it was her touch. Definitely.

"Not sure yet. Thought you might have an idea. This is about as freaky as it gets. For a while there I thought I was hallucinating till everyone reacted. I guess July didn't get the gate fixed as well as she hoped."

"Maybe the burro opened it again." She giggled, probably a result of the absurdity of the situation. She rarely giggled.

"Hey, you okay?"

"Sure. Why wouldn't I be? I'm shut up in a cabin with a wild man, an escapee from the law, a man I'd like to jump in bed with, and we're being stalked by a tiger. What could be more fun?"

"Oh, I don't know. I sort of like the one about jumping in bed as long as I'm the man referred to." He wrapped an arm around her waist and snugged her up close, her breasts molded against his middle. "Hmm, nothing like a hard-on while being considered as lunch by a man-eater."

"Oh? I thought that might be the gun."

"Well, probably that, too. Almost forgot, I've got to put it where he can't get his hands on it. Damn me, what a day."

Against the wall above her head was a cupboard. The .45 would fit in there and Duggan wouldn't know where to find it since at the present he was facing the corner making odd noises. Quickly Dal tucked the weapon away behind an assortment of dishes and clicked the door shut.

"All we need now is for Mister Spooky to show up accompanied by Kimble and Bainbridge."

"Bite your tongue. Under the circumstances it's entirely possible." Shifting a bit, he gathered her closer. Might as well get some enjoyment out of a ridiculous predicament.

Obviously she liked it, for she settled in with a sigh. "Looks like we're here for the night. I'm in no mood to wander around in the dark with Maizie out there. Won't be very comfortable, but I'm so tired I could bed down on a rock. Maybe something miraculous will happen overnight."

He gestured toward the tiger in the window. "When you think about it, that's pretty hard to beat. Odd name for a tiger. Maizie. Sounds like an old maid. Maybe she'll go elsewhere while we sleep." He slid down to the floor with Jessie, spooned their bodies together in the dark corner. She laid her head on his shoulder and relaxed.

Seemed like they hadn't had much time together and he'd missed that. More his fault than hers. A strange place to make up for it, but he held her close and shut his eyes. It'd been his experience that people in danger had a tendency to want sex but she was already dozing off. Might be something he'd said.

Maizie grew bored staring in at the humans and wandered off. For a while the others chattered and argued a bit about the possibility of being eaten by a tiger, then they must've taken a page from Dal's book and all found a place to relax. Even the argumentative Duggan finally shut up, slid down to sit cross-legged in his corner. It wasn't long before Randy put out the lamps and stretched out on the bed next to that of his daughters.

Something awoke Dal just as it grew light enough to make out shadows in the small room. One of those shadows moved. Jessie slept in his arms and he didn't want to awaken her. But the figure snuck around exploring every nook and cranny. Had to be Duggan looking for the .45 Dal had hidden. He raised his head enough to watch him search a few places, then give up and plop down in the empty bean bag chair. Too bad Mac had to hire someone like him. There'd be a hole in the roster till they could find someone else willing to work on the small force. It wasn't easy finding good help considering the pay and lack of much excitement. Most men training to be lawmen were Type-A personality and needed the surge of adrenaline that came with the chase and capture of bad guys. Maybe like when a tiger had them cornered. They could always use that as an incentive.

The very reason Dal liked this town was the lack of too much excitement. After the shooting in the alley in Dallas, his type-A personality had collapsed into a C or D. They'd only had three murders in the four years he'd been here. So far this year was winding up to be exciting enough without any killings. Hopefully it would stay that way. He'd hate like hell for there to be a death by tiger, so he had to figure out how to get them all out of here safely.

First thing was to find out if Maizie still prowled around out there. Only one way to do that. He eased Jessie's head off his arm and slipped away from her. Be best if at least two of them could clear the perimeter. That way they could have each other's backs. Too bad Colby wasn't here, but maybe he could trust Randy. It was a cinch Duggan was not in the running. He trusted Jessie the most, but wouldn't put her in that kind of danger.

Before he could make a decision, someone tugged on his shirt sleeve. He looked down into Tinkerbelle's face, barely discernible in the early dawn light.

"We need to go out there and see if the tiger's still here." She voiced what he was already thinking, except the we part.

"That's the plan, but I was thinking two of us. Maybe Randy would be up to it?"

"You're as bad as Sheriff Mac. You and I are the armed deputies with any sense about us. So we need to do it. We can't put a civilian in danger."

Funny. It was a stretch to differentiate between deputies and non-deputies in that way. Tinkerbelle was very serious about her approach to this deputy thing, and Mac was a fool not to let her out in the field. As an officer she beat Duggan out so far it was pathetic. But should he let her put herself out there? Dammit, she was right. He'd turned right around and sounded just like Mac.

"What did you have in mind?" She was simply too serious for him not to consider her idea.

"Well, we go out as soon as it's light enough to see well and we check the surroundings, back to back so Maizie can't sneak up on us. We can scare her away by firing into the air if she does come at one of us. We don't have to kill her unless she charges, do we?"

"Maybe if we make enough noise she'll either come out into the open or run off."

A familiar voice entered the conversation and Dal hunched his shoulders. Damn it, he'd wanted to keep her out of this. But it was Jessie and naturally she had some ideas of her own.

"Three's better than two. I can use this." She held up Duggan's.45. "Maizie is fairly tame and certainly not a man-eater, though she could hurt one of us."

"We have to presume she might then. But put that back. I'm not letting a civilian in on this."

She sputtered with laughter. "A civilian? Come on."

Swelling as tall and broad as possible he stared down at her. "Not a weapon like that, you're not. Yours is a pissy thirty-eight revolver. You pull that trigger, you'll take out the top of a tree."

"Hsst, what's going on over here?" Randy joined them.

They were getting louder and louder. Bound to have Duggan in on it soon. Dal was about ready to hogtie him. He sucked in air, let out a big sigh. "Okay, here's the way we're gonna do this. The two of us" —he indicated Tinkerbelle and himself— "go out there, make sure the tiger has gone, then you two" —he pointed at Randy and Jessie— "bring the girls out and we'll stay on either side of you while we walk back to the car. I'm pretty sure Maizie is gone since we haven't heard her in a while."

Randy nodded, then glanced toward his cousin. "What about him?"

"I'm seriously thinking of shooting him, but I'll probably just tie him up and leave him here. We can always send someone in to get him after the tiger is safely back home. July's going to have to do something about that big cat. She can't keep up this escape plan. Someone will shoot her."

Jessie shuffled around a bit, looking unhappy. Dal decided to ignore that and check with Randy. "You okay with this? Taking you up to Hermitage House for a bit till we can get things straightened out?"

With a shrug, Randy agreed.

"Then get your stuff packed. Whatever you brought in with you in case anyone checks here. We don't want them to know where you've been staying. Duggan gonna keep quiet? He's the wild card here, as I see it."

Already busy gathering up their few belongings, Randy cast a quick look at Duggan. "I'll talk to him. He's helped me all along. Brought me and the girls out here. I know he's missing some tools in his box, but he's a good ole boy and I don't think he'd betray me for anyone. We need to take him with us."

"Okay, but he better behave or I will tie him to the nearest tree. Maizie might find that delectable. Everybody get your junk together, soon as it gets a bit lighter we need to get out of here and get you guys hid out better than this. You have no food or anything."

Obviously fearful of being left behind, Duggan piped up. "Hey, I'm goin with you. Someone has to carry that ugly dog. I can do that."

"Get ready then and don't cause any trouble."

In a few minutes everyone was ready to go. Dal led Tinkerbelle to the door and creaked it open slowly. All appeared clear and he motioned her to move out. Glanced at Jessie. "Watch for our signal to follow."

Jessie and Randy each had one of the sleepy girls in their arms and waited in the doorway. A bit nervous about how this was going to work, Dal took one last look at Duggan, who sullenly remained with Jessie and

Randy, an unhappy Brad in his arms. Dal and Tinkerbelle began their sweep of the surrounding area.

Once Tink and Dal did a wide walk around the trail that led back to the car, his hand came up in a gesture to follow and Jessie, Randy, and Duggan hurried to do just that.

Jessie was less worried about Maizie attacking them than she was what that fool Duggan might get up to. There wasn't much telling, but he appeared to be going along at the present.

The climb up the incline out of the valley was a tough one. She had the smallest of the girls, but after a while the backs of her legs burned. She'd crawl before letting the others know, though. At last, up ahead on the left, was old Mr. Spooky's cabin. They had to hurry past or he'd be out there coming down on them about something screwy.

Ellie squirmed and whimpered in her arms. "Shh, baby girl. We'll be in the car soon. You're safe."

"Mommy, Mommy." Her legs stiffened in battle and Jessie struggled to keep her from getting away.

Randy drew even to her. "Hush, baby girl. She has nightmares sometimes. Won't tell me what they're about, but I suspect they come from the abuse. Always sounds like she's hurting."

Jessie nodded, but wasn't sure at all that's what the little girl's cries sounded like. It was more like she wanted her mommy than that she feared her.

Dear God, what if she'd been wrong in believing Randy's story?

What if it *were* him who had abused these girls?

She cast a quick glance in his direction, but could tell nothing by his expression of concern.

Dal and Tink stepped up their pace and she was happy to do so as well. They didn't need for Spooky to spot them.

A few first rays of sunlight leaked through the trees and birds set up their serenading. The morning sounded much more cheerful than she felt.

From behind her, Duggan cursed loudly. Brad barked. She whirled in time to see the deputy rolling around on the ground. Another bark and Brad ran to her whimpering.

"That damned dog bit me." Duggan struggled to his feet. "Where is he? I'll wring his damned neck."

"I suppose he tripped you, too."

The door to Spooky's house slammed open and the white-robed man stood there, arms spread as if extolling the wrath of his god. It was like someone had magically called down an automatic freeze. Even Dal and Tink turned and stopped to stare.

Before any one of them could recover two shots rang out in tight succession. Dal and Tink hit the ground, as did Jessie and Randy. Duggan went down on his face in the dirt.

Where had the shots come from? Not the white-robed man in the doorway, he appeared as shocked as anyone. An answer was imminent when two men strode from the woods, their features not discernible in the early morning light. At least not till one of them spoke.

Former Nolton County Sheriff Robert Kimble's harsh voice identified him immediately. "What in thunderation are y'all doing out here?"

Dal made a move and Kimble swung the barrel of his rifle toward him. "Ah ah, I wouldn't do that were I you."

"I wouldn't do this if I were you." Dal spread his hands away from his body. "You must know the two of you are wanted all over the state and since it's federal, I'd guess all over this great country of ours. The one that makes it illegal for you to take and keep prisoners, let alone sell them. Slavery has been outlawed way over a hundred years."

The other man stepped farther out into the light. "Well, it would seem that whoever is looking for us isn't having much luck. When we first heard you we thought it was them coming in after us. But it don't look like that at all, now that we can see your rag-tag asses."

Dal looked fit to be tied. "Just cause they haven't caught up to you yet doesn't mean they won't. It's just a matter of time. Why haven't you both lit out before they do? Do you not have good sense? Or have you misplaced something?"

Jessie set the wiggling Ellie down and grabbed her hand. She opened her mouth and wailed. The noise woke Suzie who joined her. Randy knelt and gathered both of them close.

"Shut the brats up or I'll do it for you." Bainbridge may have been small, but he sounded vicious.

Jessie could hold her temper no longer, but appealed to the one person she thought might be willing to calm things down. "Sheriff Kimble, you were my grandpa's friend and are close to Mac. Can't you see how foolish this entire thing is? It's getting out of hand and someone is going to get killed. I know you don't want that. Let us take these little girls to safety. We don't pose any threat to you two. You can be long gone before we can tell anyone we saw you."

"Hush up, woman."

Kimble jumped when his friend spoke. "She's right, Taylor. Let's just get the hell out of here. No need to hurt anyone."

"And suppose Slopes finds out? Then what?"

"How will he? He lit out for the hills long ago. Anyway, he does we'll be long gone. Let these folks go about their business. They have nothing to do with our problems. We do what we discussed and poof. We're gone."

The two men let their attention wander from the group while they discussed their problem just long enough for Jessie to step between them and the two little girls, the .45 Dal had neglected to take from her pointed at the deadliest of the two, Taylor Bainbridge.

She said nothing, just aimed at the ground in front of him and squeezed the trigger. The barrel of the large semi-automatic jumped, Bainbridge folded up.

Dal was already next to her and he slammed his hand down over the top of the gun in time to keep her from firing another shot. Terror gushed through her and she turned loose of the weapon.

"I didn't mean to hit him. Oh, God, is he dead?"

"Hardly, not the way he's screaming."

The roaring echoed in her ears.

"Bitch shot me in the foot."

"You're lucky. Kimble, take your friend and get the hell out of here before I arrest the both of you. Too damned much trouble. The FBI will have you soon enough and I don't want the hassle."

Knees ready to dump her, Jessie leaned against Dal. The two high-tailed it into the woods and disappeared from sight but she feared the danger they posed still hovered over all of them.

10
CHAPTER

Dal moved among the group milling about as if they were lost. Someone had to take over. "Okay, everyone, let's settle down and get moving. It's not very far to where we left the cars."

Tinkerbelle followed his example, soothing Randy and the two girls, even giving Duggan an atta boy before swooping Brad up off the ground and nuzzling him against her neck.

If he could, Dal would make sure she received a commendation from Sheriff Mac when they got back. She had stepped right up as a deputy and he was proud of her. Without being told, she brought up the rear, doing a good job of keeping everyone moving.

He took one last look at the man in the white robe, who remained in the doorway of his cabin, arms outstretched like a Christ figure. He was still there when they went out of sight around a curve in the trail. At least there was no sermon. There were other things to worry about, like where that tiger got to. He might ought to have shot her, but he'd give July a chance to catch up to the big cat first. He might live to regret that.

If the animal didn't go back to the compound they would have to hunt her down, anyway.

Jessie trailed along behind him as they single-filed it up the narrow path to the flat spot, the end of the road coming in from civilization, where Dal's SUV and her Jeep waited.

Only they weren't there.

Dal came to an abrupt halt. What the hell? There weren't enough people running about in these woods to steal one car let alone two. And who stole a deputy's car anyway? He turned a couple of circles to make sure this was where he'd left it. Maybe he was confused and it was around the next bend. But no, this was where the road ended.

It didn't take long to find the Jeep, for the tire tracks led off the road and right out to the edge of the bluff where they disappeared. He leaned out and sure enough, there was what was left of Jessie's Jeep looking like a great wad of metal piled among huge boulders.

He stomped back, following the tire markings. The patrol car had been turned around in a wide spot and driven off.

"Son of a bitch." He only muttered the words, but everyone heard him, cause they'd all halted to watch him pace around like a fool. What was it? Ten, twelve miles back to town? On a road hardly ever traveled? Goddamned random universe, anyway. That'd break him of the bad habit of tossing his key ring under the front seat. But who was stupid enough to steal a deputy's car? How was he going to tell Jessie about the Jeep?

"Somebody steal your car, deputy?" Duggan grinned like an idiot.

He grabbed the man by the arm, fingers gripping vice-like. "If you had something to do with this, I'll have more than your job."

Duggan shrugged in innocence. "What could I've done? Been with y'all the whole time."

"Dal, we need to cool it. Only one person could've done this, and that's Mister Spooky." Jessie gazed back down the road toward the cabin where the man in white who called himself Marcus lived. "Where did he hide them both, do you reckon?" She studied Dal's expression. "What?"

He took her arm and led her beyond the flat place to the edge of the bluff and pointed.

"Is that—? No, Dal. Not my Jeep."

"Fraid so." He held her in his arms while she used language he seldom heard from her.

Duggan had trailed along behind them, spouting words he might soon regret. Once Jessie came out of her funk.

"Sort of odd though, isn't it? Member what happened to my car when I come down here the other day to visit with Randy?" Duggan sounded more sensible than he had in a while. "And y'all thought I got drunk and drove it down through them trees. Hell, I began to think the same thing. But just lookee here." He flung out an arm and turned a circle where the tire tracks ended. "I believe we got us a serial car thief."

Jessie exploded from Dal's arms and hit Duggan full tilt in the chest, fists pounding at him. "If you had something to do with this I'll toss you down there with her."

By then everyone had gathered to stare down and mutter as if offering a eulogy to Jessie's Jeep.

Dal scratched his head in thought. "There's someone else who could've done this. Kimble and Bainbridge. Even with Taylor's wounded toe they had time to get here before we did, and more reason to leave us afoot. Plus they needed transportation."

He pulled out his phone. "Anyone have a signal on their cell?"

He waited while everyone fished out their various brands of phones and paraded around with the damn things above their heads. Like a scene out of some silly comedy movie.

Finally Jessie hollered. "I've got two bars. Might be enough to get a message through to Mac. I'm trying it now. Dang, why didn't I bring along the MiFi? Started to, but—Mac, that you? Listen, don't talk. Send someone out to Lizard Lick to pick us up.... Mac?" She dropped her hand to her side. "He's gone. Hope he heard me. Shall we start walking or wait here for him?"

Dal studied the situation. Randy and the girls sat on the ground leaned up against a big rock, Duggan nearby. Tinkerbelle had called for a break and was out of sight behind some nearby bushes. Jessie sprawled against a tree and dug around in her backpack. She was still reasonably upset, but appeared to be moving on.

"Let's take a five-minute rest. Drink some water. Relax. Then we need to start on to town. Only one way in here from the main road. Someone will be along eventually even if Mac didn't get my message." She set her jaw. "Those bastards wrecked my Jeep better find a deep hole to hide in."

He held up a hand and Jessie broke off. He went to her side and lowered himself, favoring the bad leg. "No sense in scaring them." He spoke softly and she massaged his thigh, watching his expression.

"You're right. Wouldn't want to scare anyone. There's a tiger out there somewhere, two fugitives wanted by the FBI, who in turn are oddly absent from the manhunt, and a crazy man with a gun hovering in a cabin waiting to see if his god is going to give him orders to send any one of us off to kingdom come. And, oh, I almost forgot, we've got at least one crazy in our midst, perhaps two." She offered one of her crooked grins to show she was only halfway serious.

If anyone was frightened, it wasn't her. Hell, she was too angry to be scared. "Reckon you're gonna have one heck of a story when we get back from this."

"Sure looks that way. I'd rather not have lost my Jeep, though."

"Suppose you'd like to go off into the woods for a quickie just to top things off."

She grabbed his hand. "I'm willing if you are."

He cupped a palm behind her head and drew it to his shoulder. "You're one wild-ass woman, you know that?"

She laughed and gave him a playful nip on the neck. "Doesn't pay to be too serious."

Tinkerbelle waded out of the woods through hip-high weeds to rejoin them on the road. "Well?" She gazed all around eyes lingering on Dal and Jessie.

"Water break. Sit." He gestured around.

"Don't look like no water break to me." She dug out a water bottle from her backpack and drank deeply, standing spraddle-legged.

At least he had two women with him who would not panic or need pampering. They weren't exactly stranded in a deserted forest filled with wild, hungry animals. Well, maybe one. It was a simple inconvenience being without wheels. He closed his eyes and leaned against Jessie's head, her hair tickling his cheek. Just her touch soothed him. Her fingers interlaced through his and she brought his hand to her lips. What did she really want with him? A bit off center, beat, bent, if not quite broken, yet from the moment they'd laid eyes on each other she'd sent that message he couldn't deny.

You are mine, I am yours. And that's all there is to that.

Beauty went to her core, as did her strength. And she gladly shared that strength with him with nary a whimper. How could he be such a fool as to deny what she offered? But that wasn't it, was it? He took what she offered, just didn't give back. His reluctance to reciprocate hurt her, but she never turned away.

He whispered her name, wishing he could voice his thoughts. She replied with a "Hmmm?" And he chickened out, like he always did. A dead woman with scorn in her eyes stood between them. Guilt built a fence he couldn't tear down. Not all the way, anyhow.

"What, honey?"

"Time to go, don't you think?" He unwrapped from her grip and stood, leaving her to follow along, which she did. Of course she did.

You are a *bastard*, Dallas Starr. A pure and simple bastard.

There was nothing she could do but follow Dal. Well, not really. It was more like there was nothing else she wanted to do. Except maybe get her hands on whoever had trashed her Jeep. Not like she put up with abuse from him. It was just that she understood him. He wanted to get past his hang-ups. When he made love to her it was like going to someplace both serene and primitive. Seemingly for both of them. And if she could admit it, she loved him.

Just best not to tell him.

The older of Randy's daughters ran to her side and wound small fingers around hers. "Okay if I walk with you?" Brad showed his happiness and trotted alongside the child.

"Sure, keep me company."

Her touch gave Jessie a feeling of hope and how strange that was. It had never occurred to her to want a child of her own. She was too self-involved to be a good mother, yet it was something to think about, that warmth that crept from Suzie's hand to hers.

"Where are we going? Daddy wouldn't tell me."

"He doesn't know for sure, but we're going to find you a safe place to live, okay?"

"Does that mean we'll have a TV and frigerator?"

Jessie couldn't help but laugh. "Yes, I guess it does."

"And will Mommy be there?"

"Well, do you want her to?" Hard to tell if that was fear or desire in her tone.

Silence for quite a long ways. Then, "Not really. I don't think she loves me and Ellie." Two or three steps. "I know she doesn't love Daddy. She yells at him all the time. I wish we all loved each other, then we could live together and Mommy wouldn't be so mean."

"Aw, honey, sometimes grownups make mistakes and do things they shouldn't do. I'm sure she loves you and your sister." She stopped short of assuring the child that her mommy loved her daddy.

"Huh-uh, no." Suzie sobbed. "You just don't know."

Unable to come up with the right answer, Jessie plodded on in silence. She'd never been very good with children and didn't want to traumatize the kid by saying the wrong thing. She probably shouldn't even have told her about a safe place. What if that didn't work out? Then Suzie would think she'd lied to her.

After a while, the child broke away and ran to the side of the tracks to pluck a few daisies, which she took to her sister. Brad trailed Suzie everywhere she went. Odd, how dogs and children banded together.

Jessie hurried to catch up with Dal and clasped his hand much like the little girl had taken hers. How very strange it made her feel when she thought about it. Needing some sort of stability, a child sought out an adult and that same adult sought out another adult. And all each one of them needed was a caring touch.

By the time she spotted the sign for Lizard Lick, the sun had climbed high enough to heat up the day. Her clothing was soaked in sweat and clinging to her. The two-lane dirt track led up toward the main road back into Cedarton or on out the mountain to Red Rock, one of the stops along the Ozarks Hiking Trail.

She shuddered with the memory of Steven shoving Dal off the mountain there and how he'd almost died before she found him.

When they reached the main road Dal called a halt, dragging her thoughts back to the present. "If Mac got our message he'll come out this way, so we might as well relax for a while. He doesn't show up pretty soon, I think our best bet is to head on back toward town. It's a long walk, but hopefully someone will come along."

Everyone settled in patches of shade alongside the dirt road, each finding their own way of relaxing and cooling off. The exhausted pit bull sprawled on his belly in a shady patch of dirt. After Jessie gave him a drink by filling her cupped hand with water, Dal pulled her down beside him.

Everyone sucked on their water bottles a while before a few conversations grew between them. Almost like a friendly Sunday outing.

Jessie screwed the lid back on her bottle, stuffed it in her backpack, and gazed up the road. "What I want to know is did anyone happen to see Lizard Lick? I kept hoping to get a glimpse of a place worthy of that name, but nothing. Nothing at all. Did I blink and miss it?"

Randy sat cross-legged against a tree with his daughters nested in the crooks of his legs. Easy to see they weren't afraid of him. But she'd heard that children often desire the approval of the parent who mistreats them.

He twirled one of Ellie's curls around a finger. "I don't think it's here anymore. All that's left are some rock foundations and a couple of fireplaces. Lots of these settlements that were once scattered throughout the Ozarks are long gone, but people still call where they were by their name."

Tinker picked up a perfectly formed dry leaf from last year's fall. "I read that at one time when people were settling down here, there was a town every eight to ten miles. A church/school house, a mercantile, maybe a blacksmith. People had to walk just about everywhere. Some had a horse or mule, but that animal was usually for work, pulling a plow or a farm wagon."

Suzie sat up and stared at Tinker. "Where did they all go?"

"Well, when we got cars and people could drive from one place to another, they built bigger towns farther apart and moved away from the little places."

"When I grow up I want to live out in the woods in a cabin like we did. Only with TV and a frigerator."

Randy ruffled her hair. "Oh, you do? And what about all that talk about wanting to go see a movie or get some ice cream?"

She puffed up and frowned at her daddy. "Well, couldn't there be an ice cream store and a movie place down the road a ways?"

Everyone laughed. Finally, she asked him if where they were going to live had a movie place and an ice cream store like Mountain Home where their old house was.

"I'm pretty sure they have an ice cream store, but we'd have to drive to Harrison or someplace bigger to see a movie. We could do that though."

"Soon as we get a car, huh, Daddy? Cause Mommy run off in ours?"

Wow, that shut everyone up right quick.

Suzie and Ellie jumped up and ran in circles hollering the names of cars. Brad joined in, barking wildly. After a while, they changed to crying out movies.

Dal leaned close to Jessie. "Kids and dogs sure do make lots of noise, don't they?"

"It certainly sounds like it."

He regarded her for a long silent moment. "Ever want any? Kids, I mean."

It was hard to know how to answer that. "Never really thought about it, since there hasn't been a man who—" She broke off and picked up an acorn to examine. Good thing Dal didn't push the issue.

Randy stopped watching his daughters and unfolded his legs. "I know it's hot, but don't you think we ought to start on down the road? I'd hate to be out here after dark with the girls and that tiger on the loose."

Dal agreed and pulled her to her feet. The last thing Jessie was worried about was Maizie, for she'd been in the compound with the enormous cat and knew her to be tame around humans. Probably was more scared of being lost in the woods than they were. She did wish she could let July know about where her tiger was though.

It seemed they'd walked forever, though Dal's watch showed only the passage of a bit more than an hour, when a county patrol unit topped the hill down the road a ways. Sunlight flashed bright off the windshield so it was hard to tell who the driver was until it pulled up and stopped next to Dal and Jessie. Mac lowered the window and grinned out at them.

"A bit hot for an afternoon stroll, ain't it?"

Another SUV rolled up just behind him. Tinker's husband Burt was at the wheel, relief clear on his features when he spotted her bringing up the rear of the weary group.

She ran past everyone to greet him. "I sure hope you've got the a/c cranked up."

"Sure have, Babe. Hop in."

"Let's get you all loaded up and back to town. Where's my other patrol unit?" Clearly Mac made an effort not to sound too perturbed.

After Randy and the girls crawled in the backseat of Burt's vehicle, Duggan reluctantly got in the front seat of Mac's. He looked like he expected trouble from the sheriff. Dal and Jessie—with Brad in her arms—climbed in the backseat and the caravan swung around and headed toward Cedarton. Dal filled Mac in on the occurrences of the previous day and night, with Duggan interrupting once in a while like he had to make sure Mac understood the connection of the disappearance of Dal's unit with his earlier.

"Well, we'll get a party out to look for it after we get everyone home. Sorry about yours, Jess. What about those kids and their dad? You figger out what's going on with that?"

Jessie let Dal do the explaining, she was simply too tired to try to make sense of the situation for Mac. Instead she leaned against Dal's chest and closed her eyes. He wound an arm around her shoulders. His voice rumbled pleasantly so she was almost asleep when they pulled up to let her out at her place.

Dal dropped his arm away, kissed her on the temple, and told her he'd be out the next day. She stood in the shady yard while Mac turned a circle, then took Brad inside and shut the door behind her. All she wanted was a shower and a bed. Tomorrow would take care of itself. Be nice if it took better care than it had so far.

After Mac dropped him off at The Five Bs, Dal called Tinkerbelle to find out what was going on with Randy and the girls. She told him she'd talked to Alicia about making arrangements for them to stay at Hermitage House for a while and she was pleased with the idea that she and Jeff could go back home. In fact, Burt and Tinker were waiting for the Woodsons up there.

"So they must still be here at the bed and breakfast?"

"I expect so. Alicia said she had to pack their things, then they'd drive on up to the house. She told me where the spare key was and we're airing the place out now."

"You're sure they're all right with strangers staying up there?"

"She seemed to be. Why, you worried about it?"

Dal stretched out his throbbing leg and rubbed it. Hurt like the devil.

"Dal?"

"Sorry. I'm a bit concerned. We don't really know these people that well and Jeff and Alicia have already been through a lot."

"Aren't they still there? Why don't you go talk to them about it? See if you can get a grasp on their true feelings. We can always put Randy and the girls up at The Five Bs for a few days."

"I think I will." Dal only wanted to shower and eat something besides health bars, but he told Tinkerbelle goodbye and limped down the stairs and across the drive to the main house where the Woodsons were rooming.

He rapped on their door and while he waited for an answer his phone buzzed. It was Deputy Les Howard. *"Dal, Tink just called me and told me your concerns. If it would make you feel better, I'd be glad to spend some time up at Hermitage House when I'm not on duty. Mac says I can drop by there when I'm working just to make sure things are okay."*

Alicia opened the door before Dal could reply and he held up a finger. "Sounds good, Les. I'll talk to Alicia about it. I'm with her now. Thanks."

"Be glad to help. I hate to see those little girls without a place where they'll be comfortable.

"Me, too."

"Well, okay. Just let me know."

"Will do." Dal smiled at Alicia and disconnected.

She smiled back. "You okay? You look a bit frazzled."

"It's been quite a long couple of days."

"Come on in and sit down. I heard a little about it."

"I'm dusty and sweaty, so I'd better not sit. Wanted to make sure you're okay with this arrangement. I'm not so sure I like putting strangers in your house with you."

"He's not a criminal, is he?"

Dal wasn't sure how he should answer that. "Honestly? We don't know. He's breaking the law, but it may be for a good reason. In my mind that alone doesn't make him a criminal."

Her eyebrows rose. "Tinker told me a bit about it, but I didn't understand how he's breaking the law. She did say she wasn't sure he was telling the truth, but I didn't think lying was against the law."

He outlined the situation, surprised that Tinkerbelle hadn't done so, since she had been the one who wasn't sure she believed Randy was innocent in the situation. "Les says he'll keep an eye on the place and you guys cause he hates to see the little girls without a place to live. To tell you the truth, all I'd worry about is Randy taking off with those girls before we can get this all straightened out. I don't see him hurting either of you, but that's entirely up to you."

"So he's not technically under arrest, is he? I wouldn't want to have to be his keeper."

"Nah, nothing like that."

Jeff came in from the bathroom. "Sweetie, let them come up to our place. It's been way too quiet up there lately. Might be good to have kids running around laughing and playing."

Alicia turned to Dal. "You heard the man. So it's settled. If anything seems amiss we'll let Les know immediately. How would that be?"

Dal raised his shoulders. "Okay, it's entirely up to you. I'm sending Les's number to your phone. I'll call Tinkerbelle and let her know. Now I'm going to shower and eat something before my stomach caves in."

Alicia took his arm. "Thank you for caring, Dal. We really appreciate all you've done for us. Come up for supper sometime. I'm curious to know more about what's going on with the child trafficking situation and our odd kidnapping, but I can see you're too beat to go into it today. You know you're welcome. And don't worry, we'll be fine."

Jeff held out a hand and Dal shook it. "See y'all later, then."

"Can't say the same." Jeff chuckled.

Every time Dal met Jeff, he admired him more. Haunted by a war that had taken his eyesight, he did his best to face up to the reality of his situation without bitterness. He ought to take a page from the veteran's book for himself and get on with his life.

His bed should've felt good, but in the middle of the night he sat straight up like he was sleeping on rocks. Couldn't lay there another minute. A dream? Maybe. But more like a memory, something he should have thought of but hadn't. He rubbed his stomach. Must've been the warmed-over, left-over pizza he'd grabbed when he came out of the shower. Yet he kept thinking of a man in white and something so damned familiar he ought to well know what it was. Something Marcus said or did? What did he really have to do with anything? He couldn't get a handle on it, but it would come to him.

He sat hunched on the mattress for a while, then plumped up his pillows, lay back down, and tried to go to sleep. The clock read 4:30, way too early for him to crawl out of bed. Yet, when it read 5:15 and he still hadn't dozed off he sighed with regret, swung his feet to the floor, and pulled on his jeans.

The early morning was already warm so he didn't put on a shirt or shoes, but padded into the bathroom, then on to the small kitchenette and started a pot of coffee.

His apartment over the garage next to The Five Bs Bed and Breakfast was comfortable, neat, and suitable for a bachelor. If he and Jessie spent the night together they did it at her place because she didn't like flaunting their relationship in front of the owners of the B&B, Bob and Barbara Blake, a retired fussy little couple who wouldn't have approved.

Funny, you wouldn't think a woman like Jess would be concerned over what others thought. She was made up of equal parts prudent and reckless. Often, it was difficult to tell which one was going to come to the surface at any given time.

Lost in reverie, he watched the coffee pot fill. His cell jittered along the countertop and he stretched to reach it. The voice was at once familiar but for a minute he didn't recognize it.

"It's Trey Ledger. Hope I didn't wake you, but we've got a situation concerning Kimble and Bainbridge, so I thought you might want let in on it since you were involved with this case originally."

"Hey, you bet. I was sitting here watching coffee make. What's up?"

"As you know, the US Marshal Service hunts fugitives, and even though this is an FBI case, we're involved in the search for these two slithery snakes. We got a call a while ago that our fugitives were spotted at a gas station on US Sixty-five in western Grace County. Seems they stopped to gas up a Grace County Deputy's vehicle. One of your deputies must be mighty red-faced."

Dal laughed. "Afraid that's me. A good story for later."

"I'll just bet. Well, anyway, if the kid inside hadn't been vigilant they'd have got away without being spotted. I'm headed in that direction now."

Dal came to his feet. "Well, hell. I'll have to call the sheriff."

"We're about ten miles from the station. Catch up if you can."

Ledger clicked off and Dal headed for the bedroom and the rest of his clothes while he punched in Colby's number. He ought to have been on duty all night. He'd rather have him along than wake Mac.

What in the hell were those old boys thinking, driving a deputy's patrol unit into a lit gas station and blatantly filling it up? What had he been thinking leaving it in the woods with the keys tossed under the seat? Guess they could all get a dummies award. Still, they had been smart enough to steal the car in the first place as well as shove Jessie's Jeep off into a ravine, leaving the group without a vehicle.

He filled Colby in while stomping into his boots, shuffled into the kitchen, poured a thermos full of coffee, and went outside to wait by the road so the lights of the arriving car wouldn't wake the Blakes. His heart skittered about in his chest at the thought of catching these guys, but there was still the head honcho who ran the organization as well as the Woodsons' kidnapping. So far as he knew no one had an inkling who the top guy was or where he was. It was supposed he'd moved on somewhere else and continued to run his child trafficking organization.

Every lawman in the state had to want that filth shut down. Slavery had been abolished a hell of a long time ago, but these kids were nothing more than slaves being stolen, bought, sold, and shipped all over to fill the perverted needs of the assholes of the world.

Kimble never knew no one who talked so smart and acted so blamed dumb. Bainbridge would dig a hole in the ground looking for his ass. He was about as useless as a sidesaddle on a hog. But he'd put up with him cause if he turned him loose first thing he'd do was get caught and his mouth would go into high gear. His so-called wife was already caught and God knew what she was blabbing about. Smart as she was about business, she didn't have much good sense. If he himself was a killer he'd'a already buried her and Bainbridge and been done with it.

But what took the cake, and he still couldn't believe it, was him going inside that filling station big as a monkey with brass balls to buy a candy bar. The kid looked up from his funny book, spotted Bainbridge in his dirty britches and tore shirt and bloody foot wrapped in a rag, then glanced out the window, saw the cop car sitting right there at the pumps, big as you please. Right away the kid's brain kicked in and told him this man didn't belong in no deputy's car. Not unless the deputy was dead somewhere. His bright sidekick then grabbed a handful of Snickers, didn't pay for the gas and come running out yelling, "Start the car! Start the car!" Sure as shootin the kid called the police fore they was in the car good.

There surely coulda been a better way to get gas, though now that the deed was done, all Kimble wanted was to clear out of the county, hell outta the state, and never come back. But if he wanted paid, that couldn't happen. Not yet anyway.

There was the money to consider. And consider it he would, even if he did have to go back on his vow to his sweet wife to never take another man's life. She'd a never put up with him being a sheriff and carrying a gun without that promise. The smartest thing she did was clear out when everything got too hot. Leaving with that remark that she knew better places to cool off when the going got tough. He'd never seen her again. She died out there and him not even able to leave for her funeral. Meanwhile, Anna took her place as far as the community was concerned.

Best if he cut off the main highway and lit out into the wilderness before the cops could start blocking roads. There wasn't enough cops in three states to block all the back roads that meandered about through the national forests of the Ozarks. Hell, a fellow could stay lost back in here for a year if he put his mind to it. What folks did live back in the boonies was there to stay off the grid, so they left everyone to their own business.

Two or three times while he drove in and out of creek beds and literally climbed rocky roads one tire at a time, Bainbridge had to say something more about that blamed shot foot of his. He didn't shut up so help him God, Kimble would toss him out in the road.

"I need a doctor. I might have blood poisoning."

"Shut right up. You ain't got no blood poison. I don't want to hear it."

It was middle of the night and him falling asleep at the wheel when he spotted the sagging rooftop of what looked like an abandoned school building or church hiding in bunches of trees growed up all around it. He drove into saplings, weeds, and bushes till the car couldn't be seen from the road.

Had to shake Bainbridge awake. "Git yore ass outta there and inside. I saw an old well out back. I'll see if there's a bucket or something we can draw up some water. We ain't got no food, but I spied some blackberry bushes coming in."

"I have an armload of Snickers."

First thing right off he whopped the idjit with his hat. "You almost got us caught getting them Snickers."

"Then it makes sense that we eat and enjoy them, doesn't it? How you plan on getting in touch with the others so we can collect our share for that last delivery before everyone got caught?"

"I'm gonna have to think on that. Right now we need to get ourselves something to drink and sleep a while. Them gals can well take care of themselves. We got our troubles to take care of." At least he hoped to hell that would be the way it worked, yet knowing full well that good things didn't work out just cause you hoped they would.

It was plumb dark with no moon when he heard a funny, snuffling sound. Almost right on top of him. Before he could scramble backward, a huge tongue lapped across his face rough as sandpaper, a smell fetid like raw meat. What the hell?

He kicked and flailed his arms, then started screaming when the most godawful roar in the world shook the air and the ground and probly was gonna make the old building fall down. By then he was on his feet, running pell-mell for where he thought he remembered the door being. Bainbridge kept shouting incoherently until Kimble slammed face-first into a wall where he was just sure a door should be. Everything turned black.

11
CHAPTER

Jessie sat at her desk staring at the computer screen, Brad curled nearby. Hard to come up with the best way to tell this story. Maybe her Jeep being rolled off the bluff and turned into a bundle of scrap metal wouldn't really be a good place to start, though right now she couldn't think of anything but how she was going to replace it. Her insurance company was not happy when she reported the loss, but then the only time they were was when they collected premiums. You'd think that was the only reason they were in business.

Like always, she gazed at the blinking cursor for a beat or two, hovering over the keys waiting for the story to unfold from her brain to her fingertips. Forget the damned Jeep. Uh-huh, that wouldn't happen soon. Parker said she could borrow his. Seeing herself herding that left-over from some long-closed Army base created a nightmare of sorts. Oh, well. Onward and upward.

So far her hands hung above the keyboard like wounded doves while she squinted off into space. Beats four, five, and six. Visualize the setting, the characters. Forget the first line. Writing that wasn't the issue. That would only come when the piece was finished. First figure out just the right way to approach the story of the continuing search for fugitives. Randy's story had to wait until Dal's investigation revealed the truth about the situation.

An hour later she produced two small news stories Parker assigned plus her weekly column and a draft of their adventures in the deep woods, pursuing the still-missing Kimble and Bainbridge. If she hadn't been involved in the chase she wouldn't believe some of it.

Parker stopped behind her, hovered to read. "Hmm, sounds great so far. Could it be you might need to wait till the story ends before trying to put it together? That may take a while."

"I don't know. It's never-ending. I'm thinking of writing it in parts. The ongoing series of the pursuit of Grace County's fugitives continued from last fall. There's no telling what will happen next."

"You're right there. Doesn't sound like a bad idea. Go ahead and polish this and we'll run it this week with a promise of more to come. What are you planning to write about Randy and the girls?"

"I'm going to wait till Dal gets some more digging done, then I'll interview some of the people he and his wife knew so I can write it without revealing where Randy and the girls are. Can I go to jail for keeping that a secret till all the truth is uncovered?"

He scratched his chin. "Sort of doubt that will happen. Where is he doing his research? Online?"

A blank wall for a moment, then. "Holy crap. Wichita. I knew there was something. I need to get in touch with Randy. Now. The call came from Wichita, but that's not—"

Parker had continued to talk over her whispered musings. "You know, if I were you I'd set that aside altogether till it's settled, and you have your interviews. Once the investigation is finished and you know those girls will be safe from whoever has been abusing them, then's the time to think about the slant." He grinned. "Reporters rarely go to jail."

"Sometimes they should. But forget that for now. I rarely go to Kansas for interviews. I don't think that's where Randy is from." She grabbed the phone. "Sorry, gotta call him. We have to talk about something I completely forgot. It's important."

She dialed Alicia's number but no one answered. They probably weren't up there yet. As soon as she could reach Randy she'd find out where his wife was. At least that would let her know about the anonymous caller. But it wouldn't let her know who it was or why the woman made the call. Just another mystery.

Parker remained quiet for a moment. "Uh. You and Dal on the outs?"

"Why would you think that? And how does that matter to the subject?"

"Doesn't, not at all. Does it? What does he think of this Randy and his story about his wife?"

"He tends to believe him. Otherwise, he would already have gotten in touch with her. He says technically the man has illegally kidnapped his daughters. Yet he's not anxious to notify her till he knows if she was abusing the girls."

"Well, why don't you go on home or go see Dal or something? I'm gonna take off here in a minute. I can drop you by home, or we can go out to the farm and drag Gertie Jo out of storage. Up to you."

She laughed. Brad raised his head, regarded the two of them, then went back to sleep. "You actually named that ugly green thing Gertie Jo?"

"Hey, look out or she'll get back at you. She's very touchy. Besides, that's not green and she's not ugly. She's khaki and beautiful."

"If I looked like she does I'd be touchy too."

He raised his shoulders, a wide grin spreading. "If you don't want her, just say so. I'll loan you a horse."

"My butt is still sore from that experience, thank you. I'll go with you and you can give me a quick lesson in shifting the gears and dragging my feet to stop her."

"Ha ha. Funny. Give me ten minutes to clean up some stuff."

"Okay." She put the finishing touches on her story, then while she waited on her ride she called Dal and told him what was up with her transportation. His laughter could be heard for miles. "Smart ass." She hung up on him, peered into Parker's office.

"Since you think it's okay to be so nosy about my relationships, I've been meaning to ask, how is Beth Lavender? You guys still an item?"

He didn't turn around, just shrugged. "Maybe an obit. You could ask old Sam Watson since you're gonna poke around till you find out, anyway."

Uh-oh.

Not sure what to say, she bit her lip. "Uhm, sorry. I really like her." Surely Beth couldn't prefer Sam over Parker. But there was no accounting for taste.

"Yeah, me, too. We might patch it up. To tell you the truth I don't think old Sam can keep up with her, if you know what I mean."

Having been in Parker's bed on one long, lovely occasion, she knew exactly what he meant. "I hope you're right."

"Yeah, me, too. I'd appreciate it if you didn't—you know—spread it all around."

"Of course."

He and Beth seemed to hit it off so well and that was unusual for him. He'd been a confirmed bachelor for so long, limiting his liaisons to two or three dates before he found a reason to break it off. He and Beth had been an item all winter.

After the one night together when Dal was iffy, she and Parker decided being good friends was best.

With that thought, she tossed her things in the backpack and settled to wait for him to finish. Sensing they were about to leave, Brad ran to the door and took up his post. He'd be the first out and fight her for the shotgun seat.

The sun hung low in the summer sky when they arrived at the ranch. She followed Parker to the barn, Brad trotting along happily. The silly little dog would go anywhere with her if she'd let him and he especially loved outings that involved horses or cars.

"There she is." Beaming, Parker whipped the canvas cover off the Jeep, sending dust and dead insects flying. "Know where the name came from?"

Great, he was about to give her a history lesson. "I don't know much about cars at all."

Brad hopped happily into the shotgun seat and watched the two of them with his tongue lolling out.

Parker practically spit in the dirt at her comment. "This, my dear, is not a car, nor even near one."

She held up a palm. "Just show me how to drive it so I can go home. Tomorrow is time enough to get the research done."

He laid the flat of his hand on the front fender. "This is a Ford GPW four-by-four. This particular one was built in nineteen forty-two."

Parker climbed in the driver's seat and demonstrated the gears. "Please don't grind them, okay?" He showed her the peculiarities and started the engine, wiggled the gear shift into neutral, and hopped out. "Try it."

She tossed her backpack in beside Brad and climbed into the seat.

Clutched and moved the shift into low. "My Grandpa had an old nineteen forty-nine Ford pickup, one of the first to be built after the war." She used the clutch and slipped into second. "I kept begging him to let me drive it when I'd been driving maybe a few months. Thought I was real smart cause I could drive a stick shift. He grinned at me, and sent me down to the store to get some bread. I did just fine till I came out and tried to back it out of its parking space." She grimaced and shifted into third, still not braking. "Couldn't find reverse. No matter how hard I tried. Had to walk home, that was before cell phones, and he got the biggest kick out of it. I was so embarrassed. He'd been waiting on me to show up on foot, cause I'd been so smart alecky I didn't ask where reverse was in the five speed gear box. Bet he told that story a million times over the years." She gently worked into reverse and this time slowly backed the Jeep out of the barn with only a bit of a jerk from the transmission. She grinned at him. "Do I pass?"

"Just don't let someone roll it off a bluff, okay?"

Waving, she drove off, the evening wind blowing her hair.

Dal dragged himself up the steps to his apartment, gestured a thank you at Colby, and made it across the floor to the couch before collapsing. They'd spent a large portion of the day crisscrossing the entire area around the gas station where Kimble and Bainbridge had been seen. Sometimes on foot through the woods, other times following a lead on some godforsaken backcountry road. He had a sneaking suspicion the bastards had slipped away once more. They were as slick as pond slime. They finally agreed to leave it to the Staties and returned to Cedarton.

Before crashing, he called July to see if she'd found Maizie. Her low chuckle was good news.

"Funniest thing. We were all set to go looking for that crazy cat this morning when she showed up and waited at the gate to be let back in. Acted a bit spooked like something might've been chasing her. But what or who would chase a thousand-pound tiger, you tell me?"

A man with a gun, most probably, but Dal didn't say that cause he didn't want this nice, hard-working lady all upset. "Main thing, July, if you don't mind my saying, is either move that lock-picking burro into a different compound or put on a lock it can't figure out. I'd hate it if someone shot Maizie."

"We'll handle it right away, and I appreciate you, Sheriff."

"Deputy."

"Right, Deputy."

It was nearing dark when Dal came awake with a jerk. He'd been back in that damned alley in Dallas again. Was he stuck there forever in his nightmares? He padded into the bathroom to wash his face and when he came out Jessie stood in the hallway, a big smile on her face. The light from the bathroom made it all too clear that was all she wore, that smile.

He jumped a foot. "Christ, woman. You scared ten years' growth out of me."

"Just thought I'd surprise you."

"Well, guess what? You succeeded."

Stepping forward, she bumped up against his bare belly, her nipples firm as beads against his skin.

Sucking in a tortured breath, he spread both hands at her hips and pulled her tight between his legs so that his excited member worked at fitting where it belonged.

She trailed her fingers over his chest. "Good evening, sweet man."

Goosebumps followed the same route and peter made another go at breaking into place. Her wiggle up close turned his world sideways, left him dumbstruck.

"Mmm, oh my. Just what I came for." A nuzzle and her teeth nibbled on his nipple, her tongue tended to the bite.

That right there was enough to get him in the mood fast. Her head resting on his chest, the heat of her breath on his skin, and he was well past go. A deep-throated grumble rolled out of his throat and he swooped her up in his arms, headed for the bedroom, tossed her on the bed, and buried his lips on hers. He wanted in and couldn't decide where to go first.

"Okay, woman, you just started something you'd better be able to help me finish."

"I noticed you're well-armed." She slipped the flat of her hand between herself and him, grasping his swollen cock.

"Less we do something there's bound to be an accident." His words fell out in gasps.

"Well, then I suggest we do something."

Her hand wrapped around him was warm and strong and he grabbed her, yanked her across his lap.

"Easy, boy. We got time."

"You might. I haven't."

"Okay, then. You first, then you know what you're in for." She rotated until he slipped inside her, then came down hard.

The noise he made probably woke the dead off in the graveyard the other side of town. Keeping her deep in place, he flipped over. Her legs locked around his waist and he went at her with a furor.

She was hot and wet and frantic, making little uh uh noises each time he came down hard, then pulled away. He shouted, held her tight, and gnawed at the sweet flesh of her shoulder while he spilled his seed.

She wasn't done yet, and when his grip lessened, she pulled him down to cover her. "Just one more push. One more." He obliged though he wasn't sure he had it in him until she came and gripped him so tightly up inside that old peter took a definite interest with a few weak nods that did it just right for her.

Rolling to his back, he crooked an arm over his forehead and hugged her up close with the other.

"Jess, I'm sorry. I am so sorry I can't be... or do things right with you."

She kissed his temple. "Shh, it's okay. Believe me it's okay."

Fingers intertwined, neither of them moved, as if the world had stopped turning.

After a while Jessie slipped out of bed quiet-like so as not to wake him, went into the bathroom, and turned on the shower. Steam covered the mirror, disappearing her reflection. She wiped it clean, expecting to see a new her there. His words, the closest he'd ever come to admitting a bond of any sort between them, had tangled around her heart. Drawn her even closer to him than she'd ever been. And she had no idea what to do with the feelings that rushed through her. Even so, it was still the her she knew, the one who was not so sure what her life was all about.

She stepped under the hot spray. Love juices needed washed off, but she wasn't done with him by a long shot. They hadn't had sex in at least two weeks. The other night, botched as it was, didn't count. To make up for it she'd keep him in that bed with her all night and to hell with the Bs knowing about it.

Soaping both hands, she rubbed suds all over her body, slowing at each erogenous zone to make herself ready for more loving from him. She'd go back in there on the edge of a passion that would last far into the night. She had reached between her legs when the curtain rustled, then moved aside. He couldn't wait.

"Ah, do you want some more? I'm ready, sweetie." She reached for his hand, took it between hers. Something wrong, or at least not quite right.

The hand.

Crap. Definitely not his.

She choked on her own fear.

Swiping wet hair off her face, she stared into a stone-hard, pale-eyed gaze. Not Dal's. One hand clamped her mouth so she couldn't scream and he shook his head. Didn't make a sound.

Bastard. She lifted a leg to kick him in the nuts but he moved aside, slapped her so hard her teeth rattled. Blood filled her mouth.

He took his hand away. "Swallow it. I'll break your jaw you try anything again. Got it?" When she didn't react but gagged on the taste, he shook her hard. "Got it?" Harsh whispers from lips against her ear. He was shorter than her, but strong, wiry, muscles like steel cords, fingers with the grip of metal claws. Something vaguely familiar.

For now, you son of a bitch. I've got it for now. But she kept the thoughts to herself and nodded hard. Fighting this man wasn't the way to go if she wanted to live. Who the hell was he and what did he want?

Dal would hear. Wake up and come in here. Beat this son of a bitch till he begged for mercy.

"Make a sound, I'll kill you. And I'll do it the hard way. Got it?"

Thoughts rushed wildly through her head. Beg him to just drag her out of here and go. Leave Dal alone, let him sleep. Don't hurt him. Through the steam and water running from her wet hair, she couldn't see a weapon of any kind.

He turned off the tap and jerked her from the shower, handed her the jeans and a shirt she'd taken off earlier and dropped on the floor in the bedroom. How the hell he got those she didn't know. My God, he'd been in here when Dal came home, when she came in. When they undressed and made love. Only way he could've gotten the clothes she'd taken off earlier. The struggle to pull them on over wet skin annoyed him, but he waited. How did this guy get in? Dal wouldn't go off and leave his place unlocked. She'd had to use the key he gave her last time she was here.

Nails biting into her palms, she tried to calm down, shake the pain and fear. He'd hit her so hard it had rattled her brain.

Hand plastered over her mouth, he dragged her into the main room. Only lit by the glow from the yard light beyond the window, his silhouette was all she could make out. A smell in the palm of his hand, familiar but puzzling. Waxy, like a sweet candle. What did he want? At least he wasn't going to rape her or he surely wouldn't have had her dress. Not unless he had some fetish about tearing off a woman's clothes. If only he'd let her talk she could ask him what he wanted. As if he'd read her mind, he breathed into her ear. Words muffled.

"Promise not to scream? You do, I'll kill you, then him."

Her head bobbed up and down like a bobble-head doll and pain shot across her jaw where he'd hit her. Tears spurted but she ignored them.

The hand, damp from her breathing, slipped off her mouth and he lifted his head just enough so his pale eyes gleamed. She believed what he promised. Gritted her teeth to keep from making any sort of noise.

"Okay, this is it. You listen, I speak. Got it? He wakes up and comes in here you're both dead. I'm not messing around with this anymore. The two of you stop coming around, messing with…."

He broke off, clearly about to get wound up in an explanation he didn't want to voice. Left her hanging on the edge of hope. Of getting some sort of explanation. Maybe if she could clear the jumble in her brain, she could figure out what this could be about, but all she could think was she didn't want to die, she didn't want Dal to die, and this guy was serious.

Then a sound from the bedroom, a word or two. Like a question. Dal was waking up. Maybe he'd hear. Know there was trouble. He had his gun in there. Maybe. Yes, sure he did. He never left it lying around, but put it in the drawer by the bed.

But had he done that this time?

Frantic, she gazed everywhere but into this maniac's face to keep from revealing her hope. He didn't seem to have heard the small noises. It was Dal's voice she was so accustomed to, low and soft most of the time.

Don't be foolish. She couldn't handle this. Needed Dal to help. Sent him thoughts to read.

Please, don't go back to sleep. Please come in here. Together we can handle this guy. He's strong, mean, determined.

If Dal is warned, maybe. But what if she got him killed? To cover the muted words coming from the bedroom, she spoke under her breath. "Tell me what you want and I'll get it for you. Money? What?"

He must've heard something, for he glanced up, giving her a quick peek at his shadowed face. Yes. Familiar, but still yet, nothing. Grabbing her arm with that steely grip, he dragged her toward the front door. Toes shuffling, she stumbled after him. Out the door and onto the small porch with its set of steps down to the yard a full story below. He pulled the door shut with a soft click.

He didn't want to have to deal with Dal waking up and challenging him. Okay, so he was smarter than she thought. Must be afraid of him. He shoved her back against the wall. It would pay for him to be wary of her. She wasn't about to let this happen.

"Now, pay attention. I need you to do something for me."

A glance at the door. Had that been another word spoken from the bedroom? Hurry, say something to cover it up.

"Tell me, I'll do it if I can." She stepped away from the wall so he had to turn and face her, which put his back to the waist-high railing of the small porch.

He appeared not to notice the position she'd put him in. "You can get inside Hermitage House without suspicion?"

She nodded but asked nothing. Waited.

"There's something in there I need. And there's no way I can get in there with deputies around all the time."

The girls. *Randy's* girls.

Was *that* what he was talking about?

Oh, God. Did he want her to get them out? Was this man hired by Randy's wife? Well, she'd agree to anything he asked, but did he really think she wouldn't go right to Dal or Randy or both? He must be out of his mind to think she'd have any part in something like this.

"Uh, what do you want?" It was all she could say and sounded so stupid she couldn't believe he took it at face value.

"In the attic in a trunk under the side window is a ledger. It's black with maroon corners. Alls you have to do is get it and bring it to me. No looking inside or anything."

That was really a great relief. Prepared to be asked to steal those two little girls, she let out her breath in a huge sigh.

"Can you do that?"

Odd, his demeanor had abruptly changed from pressure and threats to gentle persuasion.

Maybe she'd test him, so she closed the gap between them. "How much will you pay me to get it for you?"

"You get it I don't come back and shoot you." He paused, glanced around. "Or them pretty little girls."

Her heart slammed against her chest at the audacity of her own actions. What was she trying to do? But something about the way he'd done an about-face, he must be desperate to have that ledger and saw her as an easy way to get it. But he knew about the girls and threatened them. Yet neither hand held a gun. Still, things were escalating. Lord, some people were dense. What if this was what those two were looking for when they grabbed Alicia and Jeff? If so she could go along with him, find the ledger, and turn it over to the FBI. And maybe get herself or someone else killed. Geez.

"Well?" The word poufed out of his mouth while he made an obvious effort to keep quiet.

Okay calm down. Ask questions. "Why don't you simply ask Jeff and Alicia to find this ledger and give it to you? I presume you can prove it belongs to you. They're nice people." As she spoke, the sound of her voice rose.

"Be quiet. You'll wake your boyfriend and I'll have to shoot him."

She dug her elbows into her sides, moved close to him. Nose to nose. "With what, your finger?"

"What are you, some kind of crazy cunt?"

That did it. Bitch or broad she could take, but not the c-word. Without thinking anymore about it, she shoved him with the flat of both hands. He yelled something, fingers barely slipping over her shirt front, and went over the rail backwards.

Just like that.

At that moment the door burst open and Dal stood there, filling the opening, a looming, dark, dangerous shadow. She screamed and leaned out to see if her attacker was lying broken down there. Maybe even dead. And her next story would be how she'd killed a man.

Before she could get a good look Dal crossed the porch, encircled her with one arm. "What's going on? What happened?" He pulled her away from the edge. "What happened? I heard you talking to someone, thought I was dreaming. Who was that? Jessie, say something."

But she couldn't. Not yet.

Her mouth opened, her lips moved, but nothing would come out but a croak.

"Shh, it's okay. You're okay? It's dangerous to be out here in the dark. It's a long way down." He held her close, as if it were her who'd been in danger, when all along she'd killed someone.

Finally, after letting him hold her for a while, she found her voice. "I killed him. He was going to kill us and I pushed him and—uh—he said…." Once more she buried her face against his bare chest. "You're naked." Something she'd only then noticed.

"Well, sure. I heard—like you were calling me." He gazed into her eyes. "Who did you kill?"

She turned, pointed down toward the concrete drive that led into the garage below his apartment. He leaned out, peered down. "I don't see anyone, dead or alive. Jessie, are you sure you're okay?"

"It's dark. He's down there. All smashed up and dead. He... he said he was going to kill us both. And the girls, so I had to do it. We'd better call the police."

"Honey, look. It's not dark. The light in the yard is on. There's no one down there, dead or alive. Not even a grease spot. Who was this guy?"

She leaned over, squinted as if that might make him appear in all his squashed glory. He was right. No one was down there. "He must've crawled away. I wasn't dreaming."

"I know. I heard you talking, like when I sense danger. I've been closed to that, but your fear woke me. Thank God I paid attention to it. He could've killed you."

Flashing blue lights lit the night sky and a deputy's car pulled into the drive, headlights sweeping across the yard. The empty yard. No one crawling. Les Howard jumped out.

Oh, God, no. She'd go to jail. They'd find a body out there somewhere. Her hands slipped down Dal's chest.

He covered them with his. "Nothing is going to happen to you. I'd better get some clothes on. Don't tell him you killed someone cause you didn't. Just report what this guy did and that he ran off. You hear me? We'll straighten it all out later."

He went back inside to dress.

Les ran up the steps. "Jessie, what happened? You guys okay? We got a report of yelling and a woman screaming. One of the Bs called it in."

Unable to speak, she burst out crying. By morning seven versions of this would be all over town.

And not one of them correct.

He took her elbow. "Come on, let's go inside. You can tell me all about it."

Pulling his t-shirt over his head, Dal hurried back into the main room in time to meet Jessie and Les coming in the door. Les had her arm and he supported her to the couch. Dal slid in beside her and hugged her. She leaned against his shoulder.

"So guys. Just what went on here tonight? Hope you didn't have a fight." The older deputy tilted his head and studied the two of them, lips curling into a grin.

"Oh, Christ. Nothing like that, Les."

Jessie agreed. "We weren't fighting. No, that wasn't it at all."

"Anyway, it got called in, so I have to make a report. Talk to me."

"Jessie, you need to tell him what you told me. Go ahead now."

She gazed at him. He nodded to encourage her and she began when the man grabbed her out of the shower all the way to shoving him off the high porch.

"He's must've been really athletic or something. Landed on his feet like a cat. I guess I didn't kill him like I thought."

"What did he look like?"

Her description was vague, but Dal didn't blame her. She must have been terrified. Sure as hell glad he'd heard her, though she'd managed to take care of things. The eye color, size, and strength was about all she came up with. Oh, and a peculiar smell on his hands. That should help if it could be identified.

Les nodded, didn't push her too hard. "Maybe tomorrow you might drop by and look at some photos."

She nodded. "Yes, I could do that. I want you to catch him. I'm afraid he'll go up to Hermitage House and try to retrieve that ledger himself. Even though he scared me, I'm glad I didn't kill him. But I sure wish I'd'a broke his leg so you could've caught him."

Les closed his notebook and tucked it into his shirt pocket. "Wouldn't've mattered if you did kill him. I mean, it would've, but it was clearly an act of self-defense. Pushing him off the porch." He rose. "I'm going out there and take a look around. Make sure he's not hanging about."

Dal made to stand but she held on to his hand.

"Best if you stay here with her. She looks pretty shook, and I would imagine he's long gone by now, but I'll be careful." On his way out the door he spoke into his walkie, clearing the call.

Dal held her close till she finally stopped shaking. Then held her some more. Sometimes she wasn't near as tough as she liked to pretend. But then who the hell was?

12
CHAPTER

In spite of the frightening appearance by Jessie's strange visitor, the weekend held promise of being peaceful. It was always difficult to get her to do anything once she'd set her mind otherwise. She was still pretty shook up over her experience. For the first time since Dal moved into the apartment at The Five Bs, she stayed the night and managed to laugh about how Bob and Barbara Blake might throw him out for indecency. No way would he allow her to go home the way she was acting. Good thing he didn't have to force the issue.

Les had returned after checking everything out to report there was no sign at all of the intruder. She slept the night locked in Dal's arms.

He made the morning coffee barefoot and wearing only his jeans while she rebuilt herself in the bathroom. He needed some time there himself. A quick shave was called for. Must be a white guy hiding in the woodpile somewhere in his heritage, cause he occasionally had to shave. But no one in the family was talking. Especially not Grandfather. Where that old coot had got to recently, he had no idea, but it did add to the peace to be free of his quoting wolf and owl legends and warning Dal the sky was in danger of falling. Still, it was good to know he could still turn on the ability to sense violence when needed.

At the kitchen sink, he gazed out the window into a glorious golden morning, fully expecting to see the old fellow perched on the hillside peering at him.

Entranced by the view, he jumped when Jessie snaked her arms around his waist. Goosebumps rode up his chest. It still bothered him how the intruder had gotten in the night before. And worse, remained hidden while they made love and slept. The man obviously had some abilities of his own, shutting down his intentions and keeping them hidden from Dal.

That would give anyone the heebie-jeebies. There was no sign of a break-in. What did he do? Walk through the wall? Things were getting plumb otherworldly.

Drawing in a long, calming breath, he turned in her arms and slipped into a full embrace, holding her close without saying anything. For once, she had nothing to say either. Just breathed against his skin in that sexy way she had when they were on the verge of something spectacular. She smelled of his deodorant, a strange sensation. Maybe she could bring some of her necessities over soon. The thought surprised him like he must be going soft or something.

The rich aroma of coffee filled the kitchen. Altogether a homey mixture that relaxed him, made him want to take her right there on the floor, inhale her sweet essence, keep her close. He cupped the back of her head with one palm, enclosed her butt with the other.

"Beautiful day. What do you want to do?" It had to be something with him so he could keep her close and safe.

"A picnic. Maybe? You working?" Her voice showed the strain she was trying to cover. She licked his ear lobe.

Holy shit. "Mmm. Just on call. If no one gets killed we can do anything you want."

She stiffened in his arms. Good going, dumbass.

"Sorry about that. First we have to get you down to the station to look at some pictures, see if you can pick out the guy from last night. Then a picnic it is. Where?"

Her teeth nibbled where she'd been licking. "In the woods."

He shivered all over, rubbed against her breasts with his bare chest. "You keep that up and we'll just stay here in bed."

At that moment he would go anywhere with her without question. Until the next time he doubted his own motives, fell victim to his stupid hang-ups. His damned guilt. He was a fucking mess. He closed his eyes and took a deep breath.

"Let's eat something and go on down to the station and get last night's business out of the way, then the weekend is ours."

She nodded, backed away from him. "Then you better turn me loose or we will indeed be back in bed. Honey Buns?"

"I think so." He patted her butt. "Oh, you didn't mean those. I have some. Coffee's ready." In one of the upper cabinets he found his stash of their favorite sweet rolls and took out four. Grinned at her. "They're small."

She folded one leg under her and sank down at the table, let him get out the mugs and fixings, saucers and buns. It was all sex talk as if neither wanted to even come close to discussing what happened last night. Best if they could just plain forget it.

His cell rang and so did hers seconds later. Brows twitching, he answered. She had about the same look when she picked up her phone.

The voice on the other end of his was Colby. *"Staties picked up Bainbridge, sitting on a rock beside the road raving something about lions and tigers and bears. They think he may be drunk. No sign of Kimble."*

It was impossible to keep from laughing. "Where they holding him?"

"Fayetteville Federal Building. He belongs to the feds."

"Of course he does."

Next to him Jessie spoke into her phone in surprise. "No kidding? Chased by Maizie? Well, now that's a story. Thanks, Parker."

Dal disconnected and faced her. "Interesting. Bainbridge?"

"Weird." She laughed. "Yep. He turned himself in. You too?"

"Uh-huh. Maizie." Thank goodness for something else to talk about.

"Yup. Sounds like Maizie found him. Said a big cat of some sort tried to eat him."

Dal chuckled. "So he's sitting on a rock out by the highway."

"Can you beat that? He steps out and thumbs a ride with a State Highway patrolman." She leaned against him laughing hysterically.

"Parker?" Dal gestured toward her phone, still unable to stop laughing.

She nodded. "He arranged with the feds for me to interview the idiot in Fayetteville. I said I would." She raised her eyebrows and shoulders. "Sorry. Raincheck?"

"Sure. I gotta go too. Did he say anything about where Kimble might be?" He hesitated a moment, then dived right in. "You realize that man who attacked you last night is connected to all this? Has to be, else why is he searching for the ledger that those two were looking for? The feds don't know about that. Maybe I'd better go with you and talk to them about what happened here while you're interviewing Bainbridge. This is developing into a strange case."

"But very interesting." She bit into her second roll and washed it down with coffee. "I need to go home and change, and feed Brad. I can meet you at the sheriff's office."

He nodded, then rose. "Wait, my unit is still missing. I have no wheels. I'll have to ride with you."

"No problem. You'll never believe what I'm driving."

"Figured you borrowed something. Hadn't really thought about it."

"Where do you suppose yours is?"

"Well, I thought Kimble and Bainbridge took it, but now I'm not so sure. Guess Kimble could still have it." He stopped dead still in the middle of the kitchen. "Marcus."

"Marcus what? That's Mister Spooky."

"Yep it is, and I'd bet he's who paid us a visit last night. Pale blue eyes, little guy, very persuasive?"

"Well, yes, you heard me describe him to Les. But that never occurred to me. Mister Spooky, the little pipsqueak, isn't exactly scary or athletic, I wouldn't think."

"I know, but size can be deceiving. I just didn't put the two things together. Not having seen him with my own eyes. I heard him, but only a perception of what he intended. He's good at hiding that."

"You mean read his mind?"

"Yep. All I picked up on was your fear."

"There was plenty of that. Nothing here is making sense."

"Not yet, but it's getting closer."

She shook her head. "Not to me, it's not. What do you suppose is in that ledger that's so important?"

"It could only be records of something illegal and my guess would be child trafficking." He took her arm, followed her out the door, and pulled it shut. "Why would anyone be so stupid as to write all that down?"

"Well, it doesn't take smarts to be a crook, just stupids."

They thumped down the stairs together. Barbara B came out the front door while they were climbing into the Jeep. Jessie hollered and waved. Barbara lifted a reluctant hand and twiddled her fingers, then picked up the Morning News and hurried back inside, sparing them a fast look just before she closed the door.

"Where did you get this?" Grinning, Dal patted the fender and slid into the Jeep beside Jessie. Eyed Barbara's slamming door. "I think we're in trouble."

"It's Parker's. I can't believe he trusted me with it. I had to go through some training before he let me go, though. Won't be long before he'll set me down for a history lesson." She stretched to peer toward the B&B. "Hope Missus B doesn't call the sex police."

Pulling into the parking at the station, she turned off the ignition but didn't move to get out. "Wonder if the daily paper has a story about Bainbridge being arrested. I'd sure love to beat them, though. It seldom happens. We won't get our issue out till Wednesday, so anything I get today could be old news by then."

"If I know you, the angle you go with will be so far out of the box they won't even have considered it."

"Why thank you." She opened the door and stepped out. "I do have Maizie, don't I? And my interview."

"And your hot vehicle." He patted the front fender, grinned, and followed her, enjoying his view of the delicate sway of her hips and the proud strut.

Colby came out the door as Jessie reached to open it. He flicked his fingers to his forehead in a mock salute. "Good morning, ma'am. Guess you've heard the news."

"Heard some, hope it's the same, unless there's more. We're just on our way to Fayetteville. Bainbridge being caught is super."

"You bet. I'm headed for Hermitage House to let them know. Wish we'd'a got Kimble too, but he's gonna be harder to catch, being so familiar with the area. They were seen together earlier. Wonder how they got separated." He hauled up short when his gaze swept over the old Jeep. "Holy shit. Like your ride. Where'd you guys find that relic?"

"I borrowed it from Parker. I sort of like it better than my newer Jeep."

"Well, it'll do stuff your newer one won't. Someone pushes it off a bluff it'll just ride the rocks and gullies and end up wheels down at the bottom."

She walked through the door he held open, waited for Dal to follow, then turned. "Wait. Did Dal tell you about the ledger?"

The two men stared at each other. Colby finally spoke. "No, why?"

She studied Dal a moment and he nodded. "Yep. Supposed to be hidden at Hermitage House. It's evidence. Supposed to be in a trunk under a window in the attic, which may be harder to find than it sounds. That place is huge, lots of windows. No telling what all junk is in the attic, or how many trunks."

"If I get the chance I'll give it a go. And I'll treat it like evidence."

"Get some pictures." Dal waved and took her arm. "Let's go in and check the photo array Les is supposed to have for you. I'm betting you tonight's supper he's your Mister Spooky."

"If he turns out to be, I can stop being so scared. To me he's a joke."

Les pulled out a chair for Jessie, and Dal settled into the corner, arms folded over his chest. The first array gained nothing, nor did the second. Then he lay down the third and the face of the man who'd accosted her in the shower the night before stared up at her. With a trembling finger she touched it.

"That's him, only he has long hair now. Yep. Mister Spooky. Marcus, the guy in the woods who thinks he's Jesus. He looks different with short hair and a t-shirt instead of that white robe, but it's him, isn't it?"

Les picked up the array and checked the IDs. "Manuel Slopes. Must've changed his name. Not Spooky not Marcus, not even Jesus."

Jessie laughed. "Just who is this Slopes?"

Les dug out his rap sheet. "Has arrests for protesting at an abortion clinic in Fayetteville, the free family clinic in Springdale where they distribute condoms, and he once chained himself to the doors of an abortion clinic in Wichita where they perform late-term abortions. Looks like he's never been violent, just passive protests. These were all eight, ten years ago. Nothing since then. He lists his occupation as Holistic Minister. Oh, come on. A bit of a stretch isn't it? Seems he has a church in El Paso, Texas. Our Mister Spooky found God."

"Slopes is his real name? Wait, arrested in Wichita? Odd coincidence."

Les rechecked the file. "Well, it looks like it. Not a common name though, is it? What about Wichita?"

She shrugged. "Just funny, that's all. I had a strange call from a woman claiming to be looking for her stolen girls. It came from Wichita. She knew me from…." Almost too late she realized Les didn't know about her previous life. He didn't seem to notice.

Dal picked up the sheets and went through them quickly. "Not only not common, I never heard of it. Born in Mexico? Huh."

Les googled the name. "Yep, as a psychic he has quite a following in El Paso. This minister thing must be something new. Probably tacked it on to get out of paying taxes. Have to tell you, though, he's not the only Slopes. There's some others but no connection. So, it looks like he's connected to our child trafficking case after all. Odd bedfellows, I'd say."

"Never can tell. He's also quite quick on his feet. He went over that railing. He must've flipped in midair, landed on his feet like a cat, and took off before Jessie could check her handiwork." Dal punched her shoulder with his fist. "Way to go."

"And we need to go unless there's anything else you need."

Les glanced at her. "Nope, we're good. I'll get this on to the feds."

She headed out the door without waiting for Dal to follow. He caught up to her at the Jeep, stood by the door after she climbed in. The wind twisted her hair in whirly-gigs. Curious at his hesitation, she swept the wild strands back. "Aren't you going up with me? Save us on gas."

The old excuse she'd once used to stay abreast of him during an investigation brought a smile to his lips. "Think I'd better get a car out of the motor pool. I've got some other things to do first and that'd just hang you up. Why don't you go on and get your story and I'll hook up with you this evening? We can go somewhere and have supper."

Odd. He hated those older vehicles on standby in the motor pool for when a newer one was incapacitated. Why would he choose to do so now unless he was going somewhere to see someone he didn't want her to know about? No use in arguing with him though. It wasn't something she could win.

"Okay, whatever you say. Want me to pick you up at your place or do you want to take one of those old clunkers to a fancy eating joint?"

He nodded. "Yeah, okay. Pick me up. We'll turn heads arriving in this." He patted the Jeep's hood. Men and their love of cars.

"Okay. By the way, her name is Gertie Jo. See you on the highway to Fayetteville then. Maybe we can drive side-by-side." Her attempt to learn where he was headed fell flat.

"Better yet, maybe they'll find my ride." He backed up, stuck his fingertips in the pockets of his jeans, and stood there as long as she could see him in the rearview mirror.

That man was up to something, but she had an assignment and shouldn't worry about it, though that was what she did. She drove out to the cabin, greeted Brad with some ear rubs and belly tickles, filled his food and water dishes, threw on some professional reporter clothes, tied her long hair back with a scarf and, dragging her backpack, jumped in the Jeep.

It was lunch time when she exited I-49 onto Business 71 and headed toward the Federal Building just off the square. There was a small sandwich shop up the street about half a block with outdoor tables. She walked there from the parking lot to grab something to eat before going to interview Taylor Bainbridge.

Lions, tigers, and bears. Oh, my.

The last time she'd seen Bainbridge he'd lied to her and Dal, presenting himself as the father of a girl who had run away from home. A girl who had later been found not to exist. He used the lie to cover up that he and his wife were a part of the human trafficking bunch stealing foster kids and selling them in Mexico. Hard to imagine those kids being sent all over the world as nothing better than slaves.

The man she'd really like to interview was Slopes. A psychic and a holistic minister. The perfect cover under which to traffic human beings. How anyone could justify doing that was beyond her understanding. On second thought, she'd hate to crawl into his mind. Him spending the night hiding in Dal's house and spying on them was creepy indeed.

It would not be easy to sit in the same room with Bainbridge either. Too bad Maizie didn't eat him rather than just scare the pants off him. But then the beautiful tiger would've paid the price that Bainbridge should pay. Hopefully he would be punished now that he was in custody. Only thing was, how come they were going to let her interview him? It didn't make sense, but someone must've pulled some strings. His wife had been in custody since the arrests out at the cave and she'd never been interviewed by anyone. It was as if she'd dropped into a deep, dark hole.

She finished off her sandwich and drink, wiped her mouth, and climbed the incline to the Federal Building that sat on the edge of one of the seven hills that cradled Fayetteville. From there one could see out across the valley and over the peaks that unfolded south to the horizon. The Boston Mountains are not truly mountains but rather a high and deeply dissected plateau. Something she'd learned researching for a story a few years ago.

At the door to the Federal Building she set her backpack on the moving belt to be x-rayed, then flashed her reporter's ID to get past two guards. It being Saturday, the courthouse was only open to those with special business. But even then, certain rules were in force and she had to obey them.

When they'd first built this courthouse, before there were incidents like 9/11, everyone just strolled in and out of the imposing building, talking, laughing, and not worrying about guards or bombs or anything else like that. The FBI and US Marshals as well as other federal organizations had offices there. No one got in with even as much as a fingernail file. It was a different world nowadays.

A man wearing a Stetson was summoned and he led her to the elevators. "Mister Bainbridge is with US Marshal Trey Ledger."

"Thank you."

The man pushed the button, stepped inside and pushed the floor number, then backed out to allow her to enter first. He never smiled even though she did because to her a smile went way further than a thank you or even the tip of a hat. He went up with her, led her to the first office on the right and tapped on the glass with one knuckle, then opened the door and gestured for her to go in. She did and was relieved to see Trey behind a desk in the sparsely furnished room. Her knees shook a little at the prospect of coming eye to eye with Bainbridge.

The used car smelled of too many hamburgers eaten on the fly, of men sweating through long working hours, of the sourness of a drunks' vomit scrubbed at with Lysol. Dal turned up the air, for all the good it did, and rolled down all the windows, coaxing the old car up toward Hermitage House. Damn that Kimble, or Bainbridge, or whoever's idea it was to steal his car. They'd better not bring it back stinking like this one.

For obvious reasons, Kimble—along with that pale-eyed son of a bitch Slopes—remained free in Grace County, unwilling to leave till they laid their hands on that ledger. It must be blasted important. With deputies keeping watch over Hermitage House, neither of them could get in there to retrieve it. At least not yet. So he'd get it for them then set a trap. Put an end to this once and for all. What he needed to do was a bit on the wrong side of the law but nothing he couldn't handle.

He parked under the spreading oak between the outbuildings and the huge plantation manor house, left the windows down to allow a breeze to continue cleansing the car, and limped up the stone pathway to the wide steps leading onto the verandah. Under his fingers the lion's-head door knocker thumped in the morning stillness. He waited with patience. It was a big house.

Deputy Burt Sample peered out the window glass, then opened the door. "Morning Dal. Hope you came to spell me. I need to get home fore Tinker runs off with the mailman."

Dal laughed and stepped into the dim foyer. Overhead, a glass chandelier hung from the ceiling. Dozens of crystals caught sunlight and threw it onto the walls in a glittering rainbow of dancing colors.

"That gal wouldn't do something like that, but yeah, I'm here to stay a while. You get on home and spend the weekend with your pretty little wife. I'll hold down the fort. I don't think it'll be for much longer."

Burt raised a brow. "Oh, is that right? That's good to hear. Say, Dal. What's going on with this family? Those little girls are just the cutest things. Who'd want to hurt them?"

"I don't know, but we're gonna find out and get everything straightened out so they can go home and have a normal life. Have you talked to Randy at all?"

"A bit, over coffee this morning."

"What'd you think of him?"

"Seems an all right guy. Real upset to be staying here, though. I get the sense he's afraid of something."

"Yeah, well, I hope we can fix that soon. You go on now. I'll stay here till Les comes on duty. He'll spend the night."

Burt trotted down the steps to his car, parked near Dal's, got in, and drove away.

Before Dal could go inside his walkie sputtered to life. A fugitive spotted. He stood there a moment, finger on the switch. It was either

Kimble or Slopes and he was tempted to take the call but he needed to retrieve the ledger.

He keyed the walkie. "Car Three, you there? You can have that. I'm up at Hermitage House."

Colby thanked him. The former marine liked the calls that might mean some excitement and was quick to follow up on them. Good for him. Dal let out a breath, and turned to see Alicia in the doorway.

"Dal, we expected Colby, but it's good to see you. The girls have asked about you several times. I think you were a big hit with them."

"That's a surprise. Kids are usually afraid of me."

"Oh, that must be your imagination."

"Hmm, or my severe looks. Everything been quiet here? No problems?"

"Not quiet exactly, the girls love to play hide'n'seek in this big ole house and they chase and giggle a lot. But Jeff likes that. Hearing them, I mean. He says he can almost see them running from room to room by listening to their chatter and laughter. Randy keeps them on the second floor out from underfoot. So, what brings you up here on the weekend?"

"I think I know what those men were searching for when they grabbed you and Jeff. If you don't mind, I'd like to go through the attic and see if my hunch is right."

"The attic? My goodness. I'm afraid it may be cobwebby and dusty up there. I haven't had the chance to clean there yet. Of course, I don't mind. I'll tell Jeff you're here, in case he hears you prowling around up there he won't panic." She followed him to the stairs. "The ladder is on the third floor at the end of the hall to your right. You can see the opening in the ceiling."

"Okay, I'm sure I can find it." He paused, caught her glance. "Don't let anyone in and if you see someone poking around you holler loud and I'll be right down. Okay?"

She nodded. "I'm not so worried with Randy here. He's so nervous he looks out the windows every little bit."

From above came the pounding of feet, the squeal of girlish giggles. He rounded the newel post on the second floor into the path of Ellie and Suzie, their dad right behind them. The two girls ran full-tilt into Dal and wrapped around his legs. Their dad hauled up short and tried to appear more sedate, but he was flushed and didn't succeed.

"Sorry about that, the girls are so full of energy and I don't want them outside till—well, you understand. Girls, turn the deputy loose. Run on and see who makes it to home base first."

With ear-piercing screams, the girls took off down the hall.

Dal watched them go. "No problem. I'm glad to see them having so much fun."

"They're so loud, I worry about them making too much noise. But Jeff and Alicia assure me it's fine as long as they quiet down by eight o'clock, which is no trouble. Still, I keep them out of the way. I didn't expect to see you here today. Is there news?"

For a moment, Dal was confused. "You mean about the fugitives?"

"I thought you might know something about my wife."

"Oh, sorry, no. I should think no news is good news in that department. Say, where does she live?"

"She was in Mountain Home. Why?" A bang followed by crying erupted down the hall. "Excuse me, I'm going to settle those urchins down a bit before they tear the place down around our ears."

Not Wichita. Interesting. That might not mean anything except who was it who called Jessie for help looking for her lost kids? And why?

The man trotted down the hall and Dal let out a huge sigh. Raising kids must take a ton of patience and energy. He climbed to the third floor and soon located the opening to the attic, pulled the rope that lowered the steps, and climbed up. A wall of heat hit him. This was going to be a hot, sticky job.

Windows all around let in patches of light, but the far corners were shadowy. Discarded furniture hovered like apparitions tied to the walls with cobwebs. He'd been right about the amount of windows, but only two sets had trunks directly under them.

He'd start there. Eliminate the obvious, according to what had been said. By the time he emptied the first huge steamer trunk he'd been through piles of clothing that appeared to come from the twenties. Men's and women's hats, shoes, and gloves shared space with stacks of yearbooks, a Bible or two, and a bundle of *Saturday Evening Post* magazines tied with string. His nose tickled and twitched from the dust and ancient smells. Nothing like the described ledger turned up. He did his best to fit everything back in, but was left with a few items that he gave up on. Who would care anyhow? He left them in a neat pile on the floor.

A smaller trunk under the colorful stained-glass window in the peak end yielded nothing either. By the time he made his way through its contents he was grimy with dust and sweat. Along the front a long chest sat between two bay windows that looked down over the entry drive. Since that didn't really fit the description he passed it by and went on to the other peak where a hump-backed trunk loomed. It was similar to those he'd seen in movies being hauled on the backs of horse drawn carriages.

Nearly an hour later and still no ledger. Maybe the man had been deliberately misleading him. Sending him on a wild goose chase. His throat was dry, his eyes burning, and his clothes wet and clinging. He was about to give up, but decided to try the chest. If that yielded nothing, he'd call it a day.

About halfway through wads of musty clothing, the leather-bound corner of a book appeared. His hands shook when he reached for it. Still, it might not be the one. He worked it out from between a stack of overlapping scrap books. Amazing how much some people kept, and then just left it all to rot. Moving into the light, he opened the book at random.

A page of neat handwriting listed locations, names, ages, gender, dollar amounts, and what must've been places delivered. He flipped several pages. At the tops of the numbered pages was a date and at the bottom a column held totaled dollar amounts.

Enough. He had to get down out of here before the heat and lack of water and the recognition of what he was looking at made him sick to his stomach. Someone had kept track of each human slave and the amount they'd sold for in neat, precise figures. He hoped by God that somewhere in here was information to prove who had been in charge of this, everyone who'd been involved. It was probably too much to hope for, but he had what he wanted and couldn't remain here. He had to get out before he choked on the hot thick air.

Just touching this vile record sent waves of disgust through him. The violent suffering of these children was embedded into each page. For the first time in weeks he was hit with a reminder of the soul-wrenching evil some people possessed. At the bottom of the steps he leaned back and gasped in great drafts of fresh air. The house was unusually quiet compared to earlier and he allowed the peaceful ambiance to settle over him before closing the entry and going downstairs.

Alicia must've heard him coming because she met him in the foyer. "Goodness, you're a mess. Let me get you a drink, you look famished."

She eyed the ledger, darted her eyes in the other direction. "Did you find what you were looking for?"

Unable to speak past his anger and disgust, he nodded. Strange how she kept looking at the wall rather than at him.

A few minutes later, he climbed into the old unit, wishing the a/c worked, and with all the windows open drove off down the mountain road. He had no desire to look in that ledger again and be exposed to such dark, insidious minds. But he had no choice.

The shabby man leaned against the chair back, wrists chained to the table top. Eyes dark so Jessie couldn't see the pupils. Demon eyes. Nothing like the smartly dressed man she'd met last year. All she needed now was for him to lick his lips in anticipation. But he didn't. He was no longer the man she'd known as Taylor Bainbridge. Something had changed him. Whether fear or a lack of hope, she didn't know.

His voice, when he spoke, frightened her.

All he said was one word. "Well?"

Her recorder lay on the table, its red eye blinking, a notepad beside it. All she had to do was open her mouth, say something. She scooted her feet on the floor, sucked in a deep breath.

"Mister Bainbridge, do you know who I am?"

He nodded, black eyes glaring. "What do you want?"

"I want to hear your side of the story. How and why you became involved with such despicable people when clearly you aren't. Despicable I mean."

His chuckle sent chills through her. "How do you know that?"

"Because, I can tell. You surely want to do what's right. How could you get involved in something like buying and selling children?"

"It's no different than farming young'uns out to foster homes where they're abused, overworked, hated. At least people who buy them see their value and care for them."

"Oh, I see. Like they didn't once beat slaves. Right? So how long have you been involved in this business?"

"Five, maybe six years now. I'm not about to tell you anything that'll get someone in trouble. I can't imagine why they allowed you to come in here and talk to me. I told them over and over, I'm just an employee. I did what I was told and got paid for it. And I'm not telling you any more than that."

"Do you have children of your own? A wife maybe?"

"Did once. She saw fit to run off and leave me. Worthless cunt."

The hated word made her eyes blink, as if he'd threatened to slap her. He was lying through his teeth, but she didn't challenge him. His wife was in the custody of the FBI and had been since the first arrests.

"So stealing kids and selling them to perverts is your payback to her? What if someone stole your children and sold them to someone who would sexually abuse them? How would you feel about that?"

He stared down at the table top, didn't answer.

"Where were you born, Mister Bainbridge?"

"What? Why do you care?"

"I'm just writing your story. All of our stories begin when we're born, don't they? Some turn in the wrong direction. I'm just curious if you had parents who loved you, brothers and sisters you would have died to protect. Did you go to school and church and play ball on Saturdays and go to movies with the girl down the street? Did you do any of those things?"

He stared over her shoulder, into something beyond the room they were in. "Oh, yeah. Once I did, but I was bored with it all. When I could, I quit school and went on the road. Looking."

She waited for him to go on, but he didn't. "Looking for what?"

"Someone, something that would stop the burning."

"Burning? I don't understand."

His fist thunked his chest hard. "Inside here. Telling me to spread the hate I felt. For myself, for everyone. No one deserves to have a good life. I didn't, so why should anyone else. And I was put here to see they don't get it. I burn, everyone burns."

For a long beat she couldn't meet his challenging stare. The bastard. God, she hoped Dal never had to go inside this one's mind. It must be maggots and rotten meat in there.

She finished the interview, getting the same kind of answers to her questions. But there was a story there. One that should serve as a warning to parents everywhere to guard their children well for here was an example of the evil and violence that awaited those who had no protection, no kindness or love. The only problem was, people continued to go through life thinking bad things only happened to other people. If they could meet and talk to this man they might change their minds. It was her job to introduce him, let them see inside him so they would take better care.

A guard came to escort him back to his holding cell and she waited till they were gone out of sight before gathering her things and leaving. Trey took one look at her, rose, and put his arms around her. She leaned against him, shaking so hard her knees wanted to buckle.

She had met evil personified and it scared the hell out of her.

13
CHAPTER

All the way back to town after leaving Hermitage House in the care of Les Howard for the night, Dal shuddered at the cruelty emanating from the ledger in the seat beside him. Now what was he going to do with it? Letting it out of his sight was not a good idea. Keeping it at his apartment wasn't either. Those people wanted it bad. Who knew how far they'd go to get it back? What the hell had he been thinking beginning this harebrained scheme in the first place? All he'd wanted was to find the damned thing. His plans never went as far as what to do with it. He hoped to use it in some way to trap Kimble and Slopes and get them arrested and under the watchful eye of the FBI.

So figure it out, dumbass.

Now he had the thing and that put him and Jessie and anyone else around him in danger. Slopes or Marcus, or whoever the hell he was, might want it bad enough to kill to get it. He didn't see Kimble as a killer, though he could be wrong. The suffering souls of all those children stolen and sold into all sorts of perversions haunted him. He hadn't counted them, didn't want to. Many were somewhere either dead or dying. Dear God, no one would ever be able to rescue all of them if they searched a hundred years. It was like shooting a BB gun at the stars with the vague hope of hitting one. All they could do was try to put a stop to it here.

Okay, calm down. Keep your mind off the monsters and figure this out. You've dealt with worse. Kids dead in back alleys with needles hanging out of their arms, babies tossed into dumpsters like so much garbage. His fragile and beautiful wife destroyed by drugs. He'd left all that to come to this peaceful place only to learn that evil had no boundaries. Grandfather told him more than once that he had been given a gift to help people and he must be grateful and use it in the best way possible. He must not run away from it. But sometimes it was so damned difficult.

Sometimes it broke his heart.

Concentrate on now and what to do. The past had no place here, would only cloud his mind. There was only now. He drove around the square twice before deciding a safe was the best place for the ledger until he could hand it over to the FBI. But not at the sheriff's office. That was too obvious and he wasn't real sure who he could trust. He parked under a canopy of trees and punched a number into his phone.

Alicia answered, her voice puzzled because he had just left there. "Is something wrong?"

"No. I need your help and I can't tell you what this is about. Does your office have a safe?"

"Of course, why?"

"Would you trust me with the combination?"

A long silence. "Dal, you understand that the files in there are private, not for anyone's eyes but mine and my clients."

"Of course, I just want to put something in there over the weekend. A place no one would know about. I'll be careful that no one sees me go in or come back out. I'll wait till after dark. Would that be okay with you? I'll pick it up Monday morning first thing, and I won't look at anything in there. You have my word on that."

"Don't tell me more. I'll access the combination from here. Call me back when you're ready to go in and I'll open it."

He had to laugh. "You'd make a good spy. Thank you, Alicia. And don't say anything about this, not even to Jeff. It'll be over and done with first thing Monday. Okay?"

"I don't like keeping things from Jeff."

"I know how you feel, but you also don't want to put him in danger. He'll want right in the middle of it just to prove he can. Tell him all about it Monday if you'd like."

He told her goodbye and stared out the windshield at the normal Saturday on the square. Farmers in town, college students strolling in the dappled shade, some kid sitting on a bench playing his guitar. So normal. He started the car and headed for the newspaper. Time to see how Jessie's interview with Bainbridge went.

The damnable ledger tucked under one arm, he went inside the newspaper office. It made him itch just to handle it, so he set it down on the desk next to hers. She glanced at him, smiled, and kept right on typing. In the middle of a thought. He'd learned how that was and leaned back in the office chair, making himself comfortable. Parker glanced out his open door and beckoned him inside his office.

"Putting in Saturday hours, huh?" Dal lowered himself in the only empty chair in the cluttered office. How the man found anything amidst the sliding piles of paper on every flat surface was amazing.

"Usually a quiet day so I like to get some work done before everyone comes in Monday. What you been up to?"

"Up at Hermitage House, checking on Alicia and Jeff and the girls."

"Found out anything more about that man's story? You realize he may be lying. He might have stolen those girls."

Dal fiddled with a button on his shirt. "He did steal them, but I think he had good cause."

"Maybe that ought to be left up to Human Services. You're treading mighty close to breaking the law."

"Don't I know it? Still, sometimes justice and mercy outweigh the law. I'm working on something else right now, but in a few days I'm going to get it all straightened out so those little girls can go home. Either with their Dad or their Mom, whichever one deserves to have them. If neither, then I'll turn them over to DHS."

Parker raised a dark brow. "I'm not one to criticize, just worried about you getting jammed up. Jessie thinks the world of you, and I think the world of her. Don't want to see her get hurt. Just be careful, is all I'm saying. I admire you for sticking up for what you think is right, no matter the danger."

The object of their conversation spoke from the doorway. "What's up?"

Dal turned to see she had the ledger in her hands. "I'll tell you about it later. You about done? How'd your interview go?" He rose and moved to take the ledger from her.

Her gaze never left the book. "Scary. Hard story to write. I've got a draft done, but I need to sleep on it, take it home and think about it. You ready to go out and eat? I'm starving." She finally dragged her attention from the blasted ledger to him.

Hell. He hadn't wanted to have to explain much to her about this, but her curiosity knew no bounds and she wouldn't let it go. So he'd have to tell her. It'd be midnight before he dared to venture to Alicia's office and hide the thing away. Meanwhile he had to keep it close. Carrying it around wasn't the best idea in the world. Suppose Slopes or Kimble were watching him? There had to be a place he could hide it till he got it safely locked away in Alicia's safe. Parker was right, he was walking a fine line and if anyone got hurt because of this it would be on him. Damned if he could let that happen, but he'd need help.

"I was wondering if—well, maybe we could just get takeout and go back to my place?"

She tilted a grin up at him. "Well, of course. If you think your reputation with the Bs will stand up under my presence for another night."

Well, damn. Now he'd done it. She was going to spend the night. He'd wanted to send her home in time to carry out his midnight tryst in secret. Any other time he'd have welcomed her presence. Now what? He couldn't just kick her out. She'd know for sure something was going on. Maybe even hang about and follow him.

"Dal? What's up? You're awfully quiet. And what is that book you're carrying around like it contains plans for launching an attack on a secret meeting of the Klan?"

This was not going to work. He could not keep anything from her and he ought to know better than to try. Best thing was to confess what he was up to and wiggle out of it when she insisted on helping.

"Okay, let's pick up something from the Red Bird and go back to my place. I'll tell you all about it." He would regret this for sure.

She wouldn't have thought too much about it if he'd left the ledger in the Jeep while they went in the Red Bird. Instead, he asked her to go in and pick up the order he'd called in earlier, he would wait for her. While they filled her order, she chatted with Wanda, then accepted the paper sack containing their food, hurried to pay her, and skedaddled outside. There was definitely something scary going on with Dal and that mysterious book and she concentrated on that. He still wouldn't talk about it till they got inside his apartment and he locked the door and closed all the shades.

"What is going on, Dal? You're acting like we're in a thriller movie or something." She emptied the sack of burgers, french fries, and onion rings out onto the table while he fetched paper plates and drinks from the fridge and they sat down. "Now give."

He told her the unbelievable story while his burger lay untouched. "So, now I have to get the damnable thing to the FBI before Kimble or Slopes learns I have it."

"So why don't we just drive over to Fayetteville and turn it in to them? What's the big deal?"

"I tried to reach someone working on the case and was told they wouldn't be back in till Monday."

"Well, can't someone else take it? Did you try Trey Ledger? He was there earlier today when I went up to interview Bainbridge."

"Nope, he's left too. They're all out looking for Kimble and Slopes. I was told to wait till Monday if it pertained to that case. So I'm stuck with the blasted evil thing till then."

"Evil? Come on, it's a ledger. It can't be evil."

He stared at her, then picked up his burger and took a huge bite. Chewed and chewed, eyes burning a hole in her direction.

Sometimes she worried about Dal, he took things so seriously. It was a lot his upbringing by that grandfather of his who haunted him even though he'd been dead for twenty years or more. She grinned at the idea. Of course he couldn't haunt him unless he was dead.

"What's so funny?"

"Nothing. Don't be mad at me. I didn't do anything." She took a long drink of her Pepsi. "So what are you going to do with the evil thing?"

"I'll handle it. Finish your food and you can go on home."

"Now you're really pissed at me. In which case I think I'll just go home now. I'm not very hungry anyway."

He glared at her. "Thought you were starved."

"I was, but I lost my appetite." If he was going to be an asshole, she'd rather be home in bed with her Kindle and to heck with him. Scooting back her chair, she gathered up her burger and fries, threw them into the empty sack, and stomped to the door. "I'll just finish this at home. Call me when you get rid of your foul mood. Or not."

"Jessie, don't be like that."

"Then tell me what you're planning on doing with that thing."

"No, I don't want you in danger."

"Okay, then. This poor helpless little woman will trot on home and crawl into her bed where she'll be safe. Sure you don't want to send a bodyguard over to protect me?"

With that she slammed out of the apartment, trotted down the staircase, and jumped in the Jeep. Out on the street, she drove half a block, turned around, and rolled back up under some trees just short of the entrance to the Five Bs. He was up to something, definitely wanted rid of her, and that wasn't about to happen. That ledger was damned important and wasn't about to get out of her sight till she learned what it was and what he was going to do. She settled in, dug out her burger, leaned back, and took a bite. Yuck. A cold hamburger wasn't one of her favorite things. Not even close.

Sometime later a car door slamming stirred her from a doze. An engine started and the cruiser rolled out of the drive into the street before the lights switched on. Luckily, he drove off in the opposite direction so she didn't have to worry about him spotting her or recognizing the Jeep. Without turning on her lights, she followed a block or so behind. He headed downtown and drove into an alley behind the Bank Building.

What in the world was he up to? Everything on the square was closed this time of night. The only places open were along College Street where the kids hung out, but downtown was dead.

He crept out of the cruiser and hugged the side of the building till he reached the square. Slipping under an awning, he continued with the same furtive behavior, slithering alongside the old bank building where several offices, including Alicia Woodsons's, were located. Jessie slipped along behind until he stopped at a side door, made a phone call, and waited a few seconds before opening the door. She ducked into the shadows, then raced to catch the closing door before it latched behind him. Hung on to it to give him time to be on his way, then slinked inside.

Alicia's offices were on the second floor. Had to be the reason he was here. She took a chance and went up the stairs. Where the hallway turned, she stopped and peeked out to see him open the door to Alicia's office.

No reason to chance him catching her by following him inside. She'd wait for him to leave. If he still had the ledger she'd be danged surprised. For some reason he was leaving it there for Alicia. Must have some evidence in it she could help him with. There was a lot he'd left out about it, that was clear. So it was a lawyer thing. Why didn't he just say so? Why so secretive and what could be dangerous?

She hurried out of the building and went down the alley to wait beside his car for him. No way would she just let this go. A warm summer breeze lifted her hair. The sky glittered with millions of stars. It would be so romantic if only he wasn't being so secretive. She leaned against the car and stared up at the streak of the Milky Way.

He must have spotted her in the dim glow from a nearby light because he hesitated, peered around, and slipped his gun from its holster. "Stay right there. What do you want?"

"What? You gonna shoot me, Dal?" She had to grin. He didn't know it was her, thought he was being ambushed.

"Jessie. Good God, what're you doing following me around? I didn't recognize you in the dark. You want to get yourself hurt or dead?"

"Well, no. I really didn't think you'd kill me."

Weapon tucked away, he rushed over and took her arm. "How'd you get here? Did anyone follow you?"

She jerked out of his grip. "Of course not. It's after midnight. Who would follow me?"

"Where's your car?"

She gestured into the darkness. "Just down there."

His grip tightened and he checked the area. "Come on."

"Turn me loose. What're you doing?"

"Taking you to your car. I want you to go home and forget all about this. Don't be writing a story about it or telling anyone about it. You understand?"

"I don't know enough to write a story."

"And it's best if you don't know any more than you do. Just go home."

When she didn't answer, he shook her. "You got that?"

"What is wrong with you? Why would I write a story about us skulking around in the middle of the night? I'm going home. You can do whatever you please. When you come to your senses maybe you'll explain this entire episode to me. Till then, I think you might need to see a shrink."

He stepped away from her, the lone light gleaming in his eyes. Without a word he turned, climbed in his car, and drove off, leaving her standing there feeling a bit foolish, and a lot sorry. She had hurt him suggesting he might be crazy. There were times when he thought he was, seeing as how he heard all those dead people suffering and saw his dead grandfather, even carried on occasional conversations with him.

When she arrived at her cabin, the outside light was out. Power must be off or else the bulb was burned out. Either way, she felt a bit uncomfortable making her way in the pitch black across the yard and up onto the porch. And where was Brad? He should be barking a greeting at her.

She stuck the key into the lock and eased the door open. It jerked out of her hand and fingers clamped around her wrist to drag her inside and slam the door.

This was getting old.

Jessie could be the most frustrating woman alive. Putting herself in danger without knowing what might happen. The important thing now was the ledger was safe and she was out of the danger zone. That safe and the combination to the door to Alicia's office couldn't be cracked without a hell of a lot of expertise. He could surely assume that neither Kimble or Slopes had that. Nor Jessie, for that matter.

All he wanted was to go home and crawl in bed. But first he'd call her. Maybe she'd answer the phone and he could talk her out of the worst of her mad. She blew hot then cold pretty fast, and thankfully not too often.

He parked under the tree outside his apartment, cut the engine, and punched her number. Voicemail came on and he frowned and hung up. Still pissed. He'd call her in the morning. Right now he needed a shower and a soft pillow.

He would've sworn he had no more than closed his eyes when the phone buzzed around on the nightstand, jerking him out of sleep. A woman's voice screaming as soon as he connected.

"Hey, settle down. Who is this? What's going on?"

His name screamed, then a babble that sounded like, "They're gone, both gone."

"Listen, I can't understand you. Who is this?"

"Alicia. It's Alicia. I can't find—the girls, they—"

"Shit. Hold on, I'm coming. Call nine-one-one." He danced into his jeans, stuck his bare feet into a beat up pair of Keds and pulled on a t-shirt while hurrying out the door and down the steps.

What happened to Les? He was always on the ball. How could anyone have gotten past him to take those little girls?

Spinning out of the yard, the tires spat grit and clods of grass and dust onto the drive. Into the street, and up the winding road to Hermitage House, slipping and sliding on every curve. Time he got there another deputy's cruiser sat out front, blue lights strobing in the darkness.

The car was still rolling when he slammed it into drive and leaped out. Someone moved around the house with a flashlight. Looked like a deputy but all that was visible was a uniform. Colby shouted from around the other side of the house.

"Nothing on this end. There's a thick hedge cutting off the back yard, need to go around the other way."

He hailed the other deputy. "Hey, Dal Starr here. What's going on?"

Another dancing flashlight and Les appeared. "Both of 'em gone. Shit, man. They had to go to the bathroom. Alicia said she'd take em. I went with them, waited outside the door. Hell, I couldn't go inside with those little girls. Next thing I know glass is breaking, she's screaming, they're screaming, and the goddamned door is locked. Imagine that? Locking the door against their guard?" He stopped, caught his breath. Opened his mouth to say more.

"Show me where they went out. Come on, Les. Calm down and show me." Colby raced past to check the back yard from the other end of the house.

Inside, Alicia sobbed and Jeff's soft voice attempted to calm her. Where the hell was their daddy? He didn't bother to ask. Hurried after Colby to the far side of the house. Stairs led to a second story outside balcony. The bathroom on the second floor had a tub set into a dormer window. Holy shit. How did they miss that obvious danger?

Colby took the steps two at a time, Dal trotting behind. Below, Les continued to flash his light over the yard, cutting a broad swath in the shadows. Glass lay shattered in the tub and on the tile floor. Bloody footprints where the girls had tried to get away. Back down and onto the stone patio. Dal flashed his light around the edges till he picked up the prints. Only the one set—he must have carried them—a bit smaller than his led across the yard to tire tracks cut into the grass… then gone. The smell of burnt gasoline drifted in the air.

"Where the hell is Randy?" Colby and Dal turned back toward the house.

Les stared out across the yard as if he could bring the girls back.

"Les, dammit, where's their daddy?" Something large and frightening tightened inside his gut.

The deputy shrugged. "He was in bed in the same room with them. Ain't seen him since. Dammit, Dal, I'm sorry. I don't know how the hell I let this happen."

"No time for that now. Check to make sure they got an Amber Alert out, and a BOLO." He shrugged. "Now. Colby, come with me. Let's check around the yard some more." Les started off. "Oh, and deputy?"

"Yeah?" He slouched as if he'd been socked in the gut.

"Include Randy in the want, describe him. He may be driving the car."

"Hell." Les took off at a run.

Some twenty or thirty minutes later, Les, Alicia, Jeff, and Dal sat in the kitchen drinking coffee and strategizing. Colby had gone back to town to round up some citizens to help contain the back roads.

Dal had called the Staties as well, but there were so many roads all through the mountains around Cedarton.

It was an impossible situation.

Alicia stopped crying and sat beside Jeff, the couple holding onto each other as if they were somehow responsible. "Do you think they're going to kill them?" She stared at Dal with bloodshot eyes.

Jeff cupped her face, stared into her tear-stained eyes, then shot a glance toward Dal.

"No, of course not. How did Randy act today, this evening? Say or do anything strange?"

"You think he did this?" Jeff rubbed Alicia's shoulder as if to calm her.

"He's not here, is he? Les said he usually accompanied the girls to the bathroom, but not this time. Why?" He didn't say anything about only one set of footprints going to the car parked out back.

"They could've taken him, too." Alicia appeared determined to defend Randy. "Did you get your little chore done?"

"What? I don't—Oh, the ledger."

"Yes, sure."

"Any connection?" She leaned toward Jeff and he whispered something. She nodded and took his hand. Said something back to him Dal couldn't hear.

What a mess. Of course it could all be connected. They wanted the ledger and could get it by threatening to hurt those little girls.

On the other hand, Randy said his wife had hired someone to find them and it could be that and nothing to do with the child trafficking case. But where the hell had Randy gotten to? And how did anyone know the girls were up here?

He excused himself and went into the kitchen. Called the sheriff's office. Mac answered.

He didn't even say hello. *"How in tarnation did this happen?"*

"Later, Mac. Listen, could you get ahold of Dave or Kathy Spacey, find out if Dave can lend us a hand with a computer search? He's pretty damned good at it and Colby is tied up with this search. We need to find Randy's wife. I've heard him call her name but can't remember it. Colby might know. She lived in Mountain Home. If she's using Randy's name, it's Drain. See if Dave can get a current phone number and address for the woman and get it to me. I know it's a lot to ask on an early Sunday morning, but it's important and I can't think of anyone else who can dig that deeply into the Internet."

"What you got in mind?"

"We need to find out if she is the one who sicced someone onto taking those girls. Eliminate that possibility. No one has even a clue where they are?"

"Nope. I've been in touch with the Staties."

"Have you been able to reach Trey or one of those FBI guys?"

"Nope."

"I think Jessie has Trey's private number. I'm gonna call her and see if she can reach out to him. We need the Marshals on this and haven't been able to get ahold of any of them. Don't know what's going on there. Who ever heard of the FBI and the US Marshals going dark?"

Mac agreed and said he'd call back soon as he found out anything.

Next he punched in Jessie's number. Again reached voicemail. Unusual for her. He tried Parker's number and roused the sleepy newspaper publisher.

"If you called to find out what time it is, you're in deep shit."

"What time is it, anyway?" Dal couldn't resist, but went on quickly before Parker could hang up on him. "What's up with Jessie? I'm trying to reach her and it goes to voicemail. She never does that. Too nosey about who might be calling."

"That is strange. Maybe she's tied up in the bathroom or taking a shower."

"At two in the morning? She ought to be in bed. She left my place last evening in a snit. We had a bit of a battle, but she was going straight home. I'm a tad worried."

"I hope this is more than an apology call you're making."

Dal hesitated several seconds. "Someone grabbed Ellie and Suzie right out of the bathroom at Hermitage House, with a deputy on the other side of the locked door."

"Good God. That's a hell of a thing. You think it might be the mother?"

"At this point that's what we're hoping."

"If it wasn't?"

"Then it could be bad. I've got something Kimble and Slopes want. Hopefully they'll call and make a deal and we can get the girls back, but so far we've heard nothing. We're a bit more than worried by now."

"If I were you I'd give it to them."

"Not that simple. It could be the means to put those pricks trafficking kids in prison for the rest of their lives."

"Have you thought that maybe you've got two separate crimes? If Jessie has disappeared, she might be the hostage being held for what you've got and Mommy could have her girls back."

Dal rubbed his forehead. "Hadn't gotten around to that."

"If I were you, I would consider it, since you can't reach her. You stay there and work on what you're doing. I'll take a run out to her place. Hell, what else do I have to do at two o'clock in the morning?"

Dal frowned. The man could walk in on trouble and be hurt. "Parker, hate to ask, but if you could come on over to the Hermitage and stay here with Alicia and Jeff to free me up to take a run out to Jessie's, I'd appreciate it. You could run into bad trouble."

"I don't mind trouble."

"Maybe so, but I can't send you out there on what should be deputy business. Do you mind?"

"Course not, be there in a jiffy. Still think I could handle it."

"I know, but it's best this way."

Parker agreed and Dal thanked him and hung up.

Alicia burst into the kitchen. "Dal? My car isn't in the garage."

"Shit." She hurried out and he followed her. "Give me your tag number and its make and model."

Pawing through her purse she came up with her registration. Waved it at him. "I know, it's supposed to be in the car, but I've never felt relaxed about that. Seems I was right. Someone steals your car, then they've got your registration as well."

He took the paper from her hand, punched in the department's number and gave them the information. "Update the BOLO. This is probably the car the girls were taken in."

Alicia disappeared into the kitchen and came back with mugs of steaming coffee on a tray since someone needed to remain at Hermitage House with the Woodsons. Dal had opted to do so, but now he'd have to run out to Jessie's, so he explained it to Alicia. The department was spread pretty thin and now all the deputies were working the girls' disappearance, those off duty being dragged out of bed to take part. Even Mac was in the field and he'd sent Tink with her husband Burt. Partners in the strictest sense of the word.

Since Duggan was out of favor, he'd been put on phone duty with strict orders to stay on the desk and relay all information immediately to Dal. Theory being that should the kidnappers call to make a deal, Dal would be able to sift the truth from lies, even on the phone. Besides, he also knew about the ledger, which no one else had knowledge of as yet. Damned if he looked forward to coming clean about it.

That could wait, and everything under control, he headed for Jessie's, fearful of what he might find.

14

CHAPTER

Getting grabbed and tossed in the trunk of a car was so cliché. Worse, Jessie always said it could never happen to her. So much for that. Cause here she was all squished up, getting a bumpy ride on a rocky road, hindquarters dented by some sort of tire iron. Didn't that one movie, she couldn't remember its title, show how the hostage had busted out the taillight and hung a rag out there to get rescued? In the pitch dark, she couldn't find any access to the taillight. Seemed to be sealed from inside. Besides, she didn't have a rag.

The air didn't smell very good. What if she got carbon monoxide poisoning? She had read about that. It was a big car, fairly new looking, so maybe she didn't need to worry about it. Her wrists and ankles were bound pretty tight and beginning to ache.

From the minute she was grabbed going into the cabin, she worked at remembering stuff. Like there was only one man. And he was stout and not too tall. If he smelled of anything in particular, it was like a cheap cologne and plenty of it. Who wears cologne when he goes on a snatch and grab? His head was shaved, but whose wasn't anymore? Anything like that she could think of for identification later.

At one point she cursed him out because she thought he might've killed Brad. He smacked her and said he didn't hurt dogs, he just turned him loose out the back door. That silly pit bull so loved to be outside, he was probably out there chasing his tail or a rabbit or a coon, not the least bit worried about his mistress being toted off in the trunk of a car. The guy's voice sounded vaguely familiar, but he made an attempt to disguise it and didn't talk much. She dealt with so many people working for the paper, that didn't help much. Her watch dial glowed so she kept track of the time. Whether that would do any good or not, she didn't know, but it gave her something to do besides panic.

Unfortunately, he wouldn't let her have her backpack and phone. So her best bet was to relax till they got where they were going, then figure a way to escape once she wasn't locked up in a car trunk anymore. That didn't work real well cause relaxing was definitely out considering the tire iron and all.

Maybe if she thought real hard about why she was in this predicament.

Okay. This was either about Randy and the girls or it was about Dal's mysterious ledger. Course, she could've made a reader so mad he'd grabbed her up, but she didn't think so. They usually only called and said things like, "That's not how it happened," or "I never said that," or "That does it, I'm cancelling my subscription to your lousy paper."

Forty-five minutes after they left her cabin the car pulled to a stop, the door slammed, and all was quiet. Surely he'd let her out soon. What if he just left her here? On the other hand, what if he didn't? She was driving herself nuts trying to second-guess this character. A while later— this time she forgot to look at her watch—voices shouted. Sounded like two men. Finally, the trunk popped open and the light revealed a man but blinded her to his features.

Against a moonlit sky, dark trees swayed in a macabre dance. A stiff breeze cooled the sweat on her face and sent her hair flying in all directions. When she struggled to move, her legs were asleep.

"Get her out of there and inside. What the hell were you thinking? I told you the kids would be enough. This one could cause us a lot of trouble." Kimble. Her captor was Sheriff Kimble.

From out of her sight the first man spoke. "I thought she could handle them kids for us. I don't want to take care of no mewling brats." Didn't recognize this one. A thick hill accent, more so than Kimble's.

A cynical laugh. "So you grabbed us a babysitter. Holy shit."

Kimble reached in, grabbed her bound wrists, and dragged her out, scraping her shins. He marched across a graveled drive and she hopped awkwardly trying to keep up.

"Hey, numbnuts. I can't walk with my ankles tied together."

He stopped, bent over and sawed at the cord with something sharp till it came loose.

Oh, crap. He had a knife.

Knife or no, it was now or never. Before he could rise, she chopped him across the back of the neck with tied wrists. He grunted, tumbled sideways, and she kicked him in the knee. An attempt to run didn't work out so well and he tackled her. Because of her bound wrists, she wasn't able to break her fall and slammed her chin on the ground hard, crunching her teeth together.

"See, what'd I tell you? All she is is trouble." The other man came into view but his back was turned so he was only a silhouette against the sky glow.

"She's gonna think trouble." Kimble kicked her, the toe of his shoe slamming into her butt, already sore.

Lucky for her that was a well-padded part of her body, but it still hurt and sent her tumbling. Little whoofty sounds came out of her mouth and nose. She rolled to a stop lying on her back peering up at him.

She would not cry but voiced a determination of his personality. "Asshole...." There was more but even she couldn't understand the words she aimed at him. He'd be sorry before this was over.

"Stop that, fool. You brought her here, now get her inside and put her with those two rug-rats. I don't want to hear anything out of any of them for the rest of the night. We need to get some sleep so we can finish this tomorrow. Come on. Get up, girl, and stop this nonsense." Kimble took her by the arm and dragged her to her feet. "Inside now, and see if you can't behave."

Head swimming, Jessie stumbled along ahead of him. The other one went up the porch steps and shoved the door open. Stepped back to usher them inside first. When he did the lamplight struck his face.

That couldn't be. Not that good ole boy who sat in the Red Bird once in a while jawing with Theron and Banjo. Theron's nephew who worked for him sometimes. He'd been a fixture around town ever since she returned to Cedarton. Everyone called him Fudge but he must have a different name. How could he be in on this? He lived back in the hills, came in to town once in a while, but didn't seem to be real bright. Besides, he had lots of hair. Now he was suddenly bald? He couldn't be a threat. What was he doing out here with Kimble? Maybe they'd hired him to help out.

Kimble pushed her past the scowling Fudge, who turned away quickly. Clouds scudded across the moon, plunging the night into darkness save for the patch of light trickling through the open door.

Too late, buddy. I have you placed now. She scurried past him, gaze glued to the floor. Best if he didn't know she recognized him. One way or another she'd get away, take those kids with her and get him hung up by his prick. She couldn't let these evil bastards put the girls in their caravan and send them off somewhere to be sold like slaves.

Shut up in the stuffy room, arms around the crying kids, something occurred to her. A great big something. Where were Randy and Jeff and Alicia and the deputy who was supposed to be protecting them? Had they killed them? No, up to this point they hadn't killed anyone and they'd had plenty of chances. Doubtful they'd start now. Sounded like they wanted that blasted ledger Dal had hidden. If she couldn't get the girls away safe, she could bargain for their freedom with information on the location of the ledger.

A window in the room let in moonlight that flickered off and on as clouds boiled into the sky. From far off thunder rumbled. She settled the girls onto a makeshift pallet on the floor, then limped to the window and tried to open it. No luck. Her fingers found no lock. The damned thing was nailed shut. She felt the heads with her fingertips.

Sliding down the wall to slump on the floor, she watched the patches of moonlight finally darken to be replaced by lightning. She fell asleep to the splashing of rain against the glass.

Brad ran to meet Dal when he drove into Jessie's yard. Distant thunder rumbled and a cool breeze sprung up to dry his sweat-soaked shirt. He took a deep breath of the rain-scented air and picked up the wiggling dog.

"What're you doing out here, buddy?" Brad licked his chin.

Parker's Jeep was parked under the oak trees near the front yard. So she was home. The yard light was out. He'd remind her to call the power company so they could come out and replace it. Lights in the house. Odd, it was pretty early for her to be up. Maybe the storm woke her. He rattled the door and it swung open.

Shit. He touched the .44 in its holster. Pulled it out. Unlike her not to lock the doors. He'd finally talked her into locking up after the scare a while back when she was shot inside her own living room. One cautious step into the dark, a pause to click the door shut at his back. It was too quiet in the house, but his mind read remnants of an act of violence and terror. No one was here now. He'd sense her presence even if she was sleeping.

Her panic and fright and an evil intent hit him square in the face when he moved into the room. Emotions hung in the air like a trailing fragrance. Dammit, something had happened to her. It was her raw fear he sensed. Whatever had happened to Ellie and Suzie had happened to Jessie too. But something was not quite the same. Another person in the mix.

Heart hammering so it almost jumped out of his chest, he pulled out his phone. Called Colby. The deputy answered.

"Colby, Jessie's gone. Someone took her. I'm having her added to the alert. I don't suppose you've heard anything?"

"Just got word. The Staties picked up Randy driving Alicia's car claiming he lit out chasing whoever took the girls to get them back, but lost them on a back road."

"Jesus. Where is he?"

"He's taking them to where he lost them. They seem to think he's telling the truth."

"So, those guys must have stolen another car or they're using mine." Dal stared out the window.

"What about Jessie? No note or anything?"

"The Jeep's here, she's not. And I can feel brutality in the air."

Colby was silent for a moment. They all knew about his weird ability to sense violence at a scene, but still had trouble believing it.

"You there?" Dal tamped down his irritation. Hell, he wouldn't believe it, either.

"Yeah. Did you call the station?"

"Not yet. Wanted you to know since you're out there looking."

"Do you have any idea where they could've taken her? Same place as the kids, do you think? Hell, that could be a dozen places."

"It makes sense. I mean, it doesn't, but you know what I mean. We don't have two crime waves, separate events going on at the same time. It's all tied together. The kidnapping of the Woodsons and Randy's girls as well as the stealing of all those kids."

"Could the girls have been taken by someone hired by their mother?"

"Hell, it could be, but I doubt it. I'm gonna call Kathy and Dave, find out what he's learned about the mother so we can touch base with her. I'll get back to you soon as I know something."

"Same here. I'm hooking up with the Staties, see if we can run down where Randy last saw those idiots."

"Keep me posted." Dal placed a call to Dave Spacey and Kathy answered right away.

"Not much he can do without a phone number or address. He's still searching in Mountain Home. Waking all the Drains there, and there are a lot. Not a very big town but big enough considering. We'll keep you posted."

"Okay, thanks. Whoever has the girls may have Jessie, so we're not real sure it's connected to the mother. But please keep digging cause I'd like to talk to her and make sure."

"My God. Jessie? What's going on anyway?"

"It's all connected to that case we worked on last fall with the FBI and the marshals. You know two of the top dogs escaped capture. We have one in custody, but there's at least another two out there who are probably involved. I can't tell you any more just yet. We're withholding some things till we know more. I'll keep you updated though. I appreciate your help on this."

"Anytime, you know that, Dal. I love Jessie like a sister. And, well, I'm sort of fond of you too, in case you didn't know it. I'd do anything for the two of you."

"Thanks, Kath, we feel the same about you. Later."

"You bet."

After going through the house and discovering Jessie's backpack and phone, he ran back out to the car, but the rising wind and approaching storm wiped out any scents he might've followed. So, if it was connected to the trafficking, then chances were Kimble and Slopes were behind the grab. And they wanted the ledger. No doubt about it. He couldn't wait to get information from Dave and Kathy before acting on that supposition.

Kimble owned a farm over in Nolton County, just across the line. He and Mac had visited the ex-sheriff there once back when it was believed he was innocent of the charges being brought against him. It was remote and a place to start. When he found Kimble and the girls he would find Jessie too. He was convinced of it.

He spun the car in a circle, kicking up gravel that spattered against the underside. His phone trilled and he pawed it off the seat. Answered with his name, voice trembling.

"What's going on, Dal?" Trey Ledger. Finally.

"Where are you?"

"Headed back to Fayetteville. Bainbridge broke and gave us a lead where we might find Kimble."

"You get him?"

"Nah. They'd both spent the night there, but he was gone."

"Where?"

"Oh, some old church in the southeast corner of the county, almost over the line. He'd been there, but was gone. Bainbridge lit out when a lion licked his face. Don't know what happened to Kimble. Your unit was there and we've brought it back to the station. We figure that moron dreamed that about a lion but we had to check it out."

"Well, that was no dream but it was a tiger. I'll explain later. Someone grabbed Jessie tonight. I'm headed for Kimble's farm hoping maybe he might be holed up there."

"No shit? Hate to be the harbinger of bad news, but we just came from there. No sign of anyone. Cattle in the pastures but the house is abandoned. Has been for a while. We checked the place out recently, but figured we'd check it again just in case."

"Abandoned? Are there still a bunch of photos on the walls?"

"I—uh—yes, I remember that. The glass has been broken on some. All over the floor like maybe kids broke in and vandalized the place, but there are a lot there."

"I'm going on out there. I seem to remember pictures of them fishing along a river and an old cabin in the background. I may be clutching at straws, but—"

"Hey, I don't blame you, buddy. Listen, I could meet you at the farm if you could use a hand."

He thanked Ledger and gave him a rundown on what he'd learned from Kathy Spacey and the latest about the Staties and Randy, then hung up.

Ahead, the road teed off toward Nolton County and Kimble's farm. Dal hit the brakes, skidded sideways so he needed both hands on the wheel. The phone fell on the floor, slid to the passenger side and came to rest against the door. No time to waste stopping, so he forgot about the call and punched the accelerator.

The storm that had threatened all night dumped sheets of water, cutting his vision down to only a few feet. Going sixty on a road built for forty-five was bad enough, but with the downpour thick as driving through a waterfall, he didn't have time to slow down and make a curve before he was already in it. The road went one way and he went another. The ground disappeared from under him and he was airborne. The older vehicle had no side airbags, but the one in the steering wheel popped out when he nosed down into a rise.

He opened his eyes hanging belly down half out the busted side window, blood blinding him. Where the hell was he and what had happened? A headlight pointed slantwise into space through a steady rain. Struggling to extricate himself from the window caused the car to tilt and groan. The door swung open, he tumbled out, one foot trapped so it felt like it was being torn from his leg when he came to an abrupt halt.

Pain blackened his vision but he hung on. Had to stay conscious. The car rocked forward then back, groaned and screeched. He had to get out. Yanked hard trying to pull his foot free. Agony shot up his leg into his back. He had to get free, or plunge off the cliff along with the car.

And this time he wouldn't survive a fall off the mountain. Both hands wrapped around his calf, he bit his lip and jerked as hard as he could. It was like ripping flesh from bone. The car tilted one last time before tearing loose with a loud squall.

Jessie awoke in the middle of the night. The storm raged. Wind tore at the old building so that it creaked and groaned. The roof leaked torrents. In the pitch dark all she could do was crawl in a crisscross until she found the two girls. Wrapped up in each other's arms, they cried softly.

"Hey, girls. Don't cry. I'm right here with you. Remember me? Jessie?" She did her best to comfort them by patting their backs and talking softly. "It's only a storm. Nothing to be afraid of."

Of course there was plenty to be afraid of, but now wasn't the time to let them know that. Just as she snuggled up closer and tried again to calm them a tree limb crashed through the window, came to rest over top of them in a sprinkling of glass.

Both girls screamed. She shushed them right away. "Are you cut? Hurt?" She lifted each one, brushing away shards of glass. No blood that she could feel. "Okay, you're fine. Listen, I think we can get out of here. Hush now and come with me. I'm going to get you out and back home."

Yeah, even if it is pouring down rain, trees falling all over the place and you have no idea where in the world you are, you're going to take them back home. Good luck with that.

"Give me your hand. Here, and here." Once she had hold of them she made her way across the room. They had to hurry. The falling tree branch would've awakened the men and they had to be gone fast.

Bright flashes of lightning showed the impossibility of that. Branches and leaf-covered limbs blocked the window almost as badly as the glass had before. She studied the predicament and listened to learn if either of the men were coming to check on them. Silence.

"Okay, girls. Stay right here while I check this out. I'm going to try to get the limb out of our way so we can crawl out."

This appeared impossible, but she had to try. She got a good hold on the main branch and wiggled it. It moved. If the limb had been broken completely away from the tree she might be able to yank it through. A sharp tug showed that it was only a smaller branch of a larger limb and most of it lay outside the wall. It had knocked out all four panes of the window though. She twisted it around till she freed all the jagged pieces of glass left in the hole. There looked to be room for them to wiggle through the opening to the outside. Rain pelted her face so hard she thought she might drown.

"Suzie, come here. If I lift you up, can you put your legs through here?" She showed her a good-sized opening in the leaves and tiny limbs.

The little girl whimpered. "No, I don't want to. I can't. It's dark out there and raining."

She hugged the child. "Okay, okay, you're right. If I go out first, would you climb through into my arms?"

Suzie shook her head. "I'm fraid of storms."

"But listen, I don't know about you, but I'm more afraid of the bad men than I am of storms." She hated to frighten the child more, but saw nothing else she could do. "Look, see I'm putting my leg through, then the other one."

She hesitated on the sill, tottering there and trying to judge how far it was to the ground. Then she grabbed hold of the branch outside the wall, swung down, and dropped. Landed in a puddle. Now all she had to do was convince the girls to follow. She figured Suzie could talk Ellie into it.

She reached up, put her hands inside the window. "Honey, get Ellie. Can you lift her up so I can pull her through?"

The frightened little face appeared above Jessie. "See, it's easy. Give me Ellie, then I can help you through and we can run away from the bad men."

Clearly Suzie wanted to escape, but at the same time she hung back from handing her little sister out into the storm. Jessie finally managed to talk Ellie into coming to the window.

She peered through the downpour, could barely see. If one of the men woke they were lost. She reached for the child. "Come on, sweetie, just lean out and I'll help you so we can get away from the scary men."

Ellie crept closer, leaned forward. "Suzie, when I have hold of her lift her feet up, would you?"

Eyes huge, the little girl nodded. "You won't go without me, will you?" Her whispered words barely carried through the storm.

Water ran over Jessie's face, soaked her clothing till it clung to her. She cupped her hands beneath Ellie's arms and lifted. "Help me, Suzie."

Together they worked Ellie out. Jessie stood her between her knees so she wouldn't panic and run away, then started the difficult job of coaxing the older girl out. The child finally leaned forward and reached into the darkness.

"Honey, I can't pull you through by your arms. Climb out feet first like I did. Sit on the sill and I'll lift you down." Holding her breath she waited while the girl did as she was told. Once sitting on the sill, legs dangling outside, she turned loose and jumped.

Jessie's heart leaped into her throat. Suzie probably weighed forty pounds or more and she hit her full in the chest, arms fastening around Jessie's neck. She staggered backward, lost hold of Ellie, and thunked down hard on her bottom, splatting water over Suzie, who sprawled on top of her.

Just as she struggled to get hold of Ellie and dislodge Suzie, a shout came from inside the room.

Oh, shit. Oh, no. All that work for nothing. She came to her knees, holding both girls by the arms. Her gaze fell below the bottom log of the cabin to total blackness. There was no foundation, just rocks piled every few feet to hold up the weight of the cabin.

On hands and knees, she dragged the girls into the darkness. "Come on, crawl under the house. Hurry. As far as we can go."

Underneath was smooth and dry and smelled of earth and animal hair. "Come on, keep going, clear back as far as we can. Maybe they'll think we ran off into the woods."

It was clearly a vague hope and would probably be the first place the men would look. What if they threw something far away from the cabin?

"Ellie, give me your shoes honey. Hurry."

By this time the child appeared so traumatized she did everything Jessie asked of her. Jessie tossed one of the little shoes just far enough it could be spotted, then threw the other one as hard as she could into the woods. It was all she could do. Together they huddled in a far corner under the cabin where rocks were stacked in both directions. At least that would help hide them.

She gathered the girls close, Ellie in her lap, Suzie under her arm, and they waited while the two men moved farther and farther away from the cabin, their shouts dying down. One of them had found the first shoe.

Three more tries swinging and grabbing at thin air and at last Dal caught hold of the back of the car seat, dragged himself painful inch by inch back inside. With the weight released from his trapped leg, he worked his foot loose from between the emergency brake and the gear shift. Another groan of metal on metal and the car began to slide.

One hand flailed toward the window on the upward side and hands grabbed his wrist, pulled him through the opening and the car fell out from under him, leaving him dangling while someone grasped his arms. He could scarcely do anything to help himself.

Far beneath him the car banged its way down the steep mountainside, clanging against rocks and smashing down saplings till the noises faded into the night. He hung tight until the echoes died away.

"I have you, Grandson. Have you." Blood filled his eyes so he couldn't see but the voice that chanted was undeniably Grandfather. He was dragged inch by inch up the steep incline onto a narrow shelf and left. Heart thundering, he collapsed on his stomach, gasping to get beyond the pain and stop his head from swimming. Then through the blood came a vision. Jessie and two children huddled in the dark while evil swirled around them and he tried to regain some semblance of reality.

"Where, Grandfather? Where are they?"

"You know, Grandson. Breaking glass will tell you."

In the silence that followed, wind twisted the canopy of tree limbs, showering great drops onto him. He lay alone on the narrow shelf, his leg on fire.

He searched for finger-holds above his head. Difficult in the dark. Dammit. Fingers clawed at slithery mud, clods broke free, rocks tumbled dangerously close. Raindrops spattered from the leaves above. The last of the storm moved on.

An owl called from a nearby tree, another answered in the distance. The shiver that skittered down his spine said only one thing. After a long absence, Grandfather's spirit had come to rescue him. That grip around his wrists was more than his imagination, less than reality. The message about broken glass important if he could decipher it. The spirit insisted on speaking in riddles. Lightning lit the ledge, showing him the way. But nothing of the old man.

Hell, why couldn't Grandfather have stayed long enough to help him crawl up this fucking bluff?

He inched forward, hands and feet finding a rock or tree root in the shelf protruding above his head. Moving slowly upward only to slide back, little by little gaining purchase to wiggle up.

Moonlight trickled around him, as if eager to point out a path. Grasping branches and small trees, he whispered a silent thank you to Grandfather and continued the long, arduous climb to the road. Once there, he straightened, took several breaths, and stretched arms and legs like a jogger finishing his run. Once more, he'd escaped death by mountain. Road firm under his feet, he headed toward Kimble's farm, dragging the injured leg.

He must've walked a mile or more before headlights approached from behind, sending his shadow up ahead like a looming giant. A siren blipped and lights blinked. Sore and weary, and damned relieved, he turned and waited for the patrol car to stop.

Colby's familiar voice hollered out the window. "Decide you needed some exercise?"

"Hell, yes. Who wants to be stuck in a stuffy car on such a beautiful night?" He opened the door and fell onto the seat. Dragged his legs in with a low groan.

"What happened?"

"You know that old cruiser we've all cussed having to drive when one of ours was disabled?"

"Yeah, what about it?"

"Well, I took care of the problem. It's at the bottom of the mountain back there a ways. Almost took me with it."

"Thought you were walking a bit slaunch-wise. Hell, man, you okay?"

"Yeah, at least I don't think anything's broke. Sure is bent some though. One thing's for sure, it's a good deal you came along when you did cause I was fixing to curl up alongside the road and catch a nap."

"I almost didn't come up here to meet you, then I talked to that Marshal and something told me it might be a good idea. Glad I did."

"Not as glad as I am." Maybe it'd be best if he didn't mention Grandfather helping him out of the car just before it tumbled off down the mountain. Most of the deputies already thought he was crazy. Hell, for all he knew, he was.

"Say, did you ever get ahold of Jessie?" Colby drove on down the road.

"Nope. I'm concerned about her, too. We'll find something at the farm, I'm sure."

"Oh, yeah, you psychic?"

"Well, at the risk of sounding loco, I might be. We'll see." He glanced sideways at the deputy, who kept his gaze straight ahead.

Colby hung a right at the access to the Kimble farm. The bright beams swept across the yard and house, all silent and dark. Weapons drawn, he and the deputy approached as if they might meet up with armed resistance.

Other than the song of crickets and night critters, nothing greeted them.

Colby stepped inside first, cleared the two front rooms while Dal crept painfully through the bedrooms and tiny bath between. The sound of broken glass underfoot drew Dal back into the living room where he pulled out his flashlight and lit the floor.

"Breaking glass will lead you." Grandfather's meaning couldn't have been more clear.

He dropped down amidst the broken glass and picture frames. The picture he remembered came into view. Scraping the fragments off, he picked it up. There stood Kimble, Mac, and old Sam Watson, with fishing poles and a line hanging full of fish held between the three. In the background and off to one side, part of a cabin, logs resting on stacked rocks in the one visible corner.

"Colby, you have a signal on your cell?"

A moment of silence. "Yeah, only three bars but that should be enough. Who do you need?"

"Mac. Might wake him up, but it's an emergency. Ask him where this picture was taken. How we get there from here. That's Sam Watson with him and Kimble. They were fishing buddies a few years back."

While Colby made the call, Dal sorted through the remainder of the pictures, all with the glass broken out. Someone must've swept them off the shelf, perhaps in anger. Nothing else there to help find the fishing cabin, but Mac would remember where it was. However, in one of the family shots of what looked like a picnic, a familiar face stared back at him. Someone he'd seen not too long ago. She was much younger in the photo, but it was definitely Bainbridge's wife, or the woman posing as her, and she had her arm around another familiar woman. One he'd seen a photo of at Kimble's farm when he and Mac had visited not long after the lawman was charged. That was Kimble's wife, who he'd claimed was dead. Considering the resemblance, they could be sisters.

Holy shit. Had the four of them, members of that evil cult, lived in the area that many years, functioning as friendly, ordinary people while they stole and sold unwanted children? It was not something he wanted to contemplate. And who was the unknown leader, who had no doubt lived amidst them too?

15
CHAPTER

Huddled in the dark dry corner under the cabin, Jessie held the two little girls, the youngest having fallen asleep with her head in Jessie's lap. Suzie stopped fussing or talking. The only sign she was okay was her steady breathing. Jessie had warned her to be quiet and she'd no doubt taken her seriously. Who could blame her with those two bastards wandering around out there looking to grab them up again?

God only knew where their dad Randy was. What his mysterious disappearance might mean was anyone's guess, one she didn't want to make. Alicia and Jeff had grown attached to the girls and were probably frantic with worry. And there was no way for her to let anyone know the children were safe. All she could do was keep them that way and get them out of this mess. Hopefully in one piece.

How long had it been since those two SOBs took off following her deliberate trail of Ellie's shoes into the woods? Should she take a chance and head in the other direction? No way would they have been dumb enough to leave the keys in their car. If Dal were here he could start the car, keys or no. But she had no idea how to do that. After they got out of this mess, she'd have him teach her that trick. It was hell not being prepared for every contingency. Left her feeling helpless. Like not having her backpack so she'd have water and nature bars. And a cell phone.

Dammit. Nothing worse than feeling this vulnerable. Sitting in the dark with two children depending solely on her and not having any idea of her next move.

A noise. A creature crawling through dry leaves. Off to her right, or from the other direction. Who could tell? Maybe a raccoon or pack rat, or worse. A snake. Fear froze her. Was it coming closer or not? Yes, yes. A snake. Oh, God, she had to get the girls out of here.

That stupid song her dad used to sing. Oh, the snakes crawl at night, that's what they do. He used it to keep her from running about the yard in the dark.

Time to do something besides sit under here in this snake-infested hole like scared babies. Well, worrying wouldn't get them out of this mess. Surely it was safe in the cabin, at least long enough to look for water and food. Safer than down here in a nest filled with snakes. There could be piles of the vipers crawling in all directions. She shuddered. Better to chance facing those two dumbasses. Besides, they would chase their own tails through the woods for hours before giving up.

She shook Ellie. "Sweetie, let's go now, okay?"

The child whimpered, clung to her.

Without a word, Suzie scrambled toward the open space outlined by light from the setting moon. The three of them crawled from under the cabin. It had stopped raining and the soppy wet grass soaked their britches. Creeping around to the back, she searched for an entry, almost tripped over the stoop in the dark. She led the girls up the steps and eased open the screen door. The wooden door stood ajar. She shushed them and led them inside.

They dared not stay here long, but at least they could get some water and a snack. The dying light helped her see around the single room. Maybe, just maybe, there'd be a telephone. One of the old-fashioned kind hung on the wall. She grabbed the receiver, hoping against hope that it was connected. No dial tone. What had she really expected?

Suzie tugged on her shirt tail. "I gotta pee."

"Me too, me too." Ellie naturally echoed her sister's need.

"I don't think there's a bathroom, just an outhouse. We'll find it in just a minute."

"No, gotta go now. Now." Both of them, one after the other. Making way too much noise.

"Girls, please be quiet. Just go out the back door and squat down in the yard. I want to find us some water."

Suzie danced around in the middle of the room. "Can't go in the yard. Dark."

"Well, then, just wet yourself. You want those men to come back and catch us?"

Ellie started bawling. Uh-oh, wrong thing to say. Kids had never been her expertise. Now what?

Ignoring the squalling, she went to what looked like a sink, but it had no faucet, just a pump off to one side. Trying to shut out the kid noise, she yanked the handle up and down. No water came out. It needed primed. To get water one had to have water. Geez.

A quick search through the single cabinet turned up some crackers but nothing else. No refrigerator. Naturally, since there was no power.

Grabbing the hand of each of the sobbing girls, she dragged them out into the yard. "You have to be quiet now or those men will come back and dig a deep hole and throw us all in it. Now come on, we have to go. You can pee in the woods. Hurry."

Her tactics hadn't done much good, but the girls did follow her and tried to be quiet, though it was evident they were terrified and couldn't control their sobbing. There must be some place they could hide till those guys got tired of looking for them and left. If they ran, chances were they'd be caught. Hiding was the best option. Back under the house? No, best to get farther away. Hopefully, they'd give up soon and come back for their car and hightail it out of here.

With eyes accustomed to the moonlit night, she searched for shadows that promised a hiding place of some sort. Down near the river was what appeared to be a shed. A line of trees off to her right offered blessed darkness. They could work their way down there. Had to get out of here. Any minute those men could circle back around.

"See those trees? That's where we're going, then you can both pee."

"I don't have to anymore." This from Ellie, the youngest. Poor baby, now she *had* wet her britches. Good thing it was warm.

"Well, I still do and I'm not squatting like a bear in the woods." Suzie stomped her foot, a gesture well-practiced by little girls.

Bet she'd heard her dad say that bear in the woods bit. Oh, great. Well, whatever, as the kids said.

"Then don't. You can just wet yourself like your sister and run around that way. I don't care."

She took off for the promising tree line, a small hand clutched in each of hers. Obviously, they weren't used to adults who didn't give in if they acted out. No doubt it was a means of control, this threatening to do something they had no intention of doing.

One thing was for sure, she was never having kids. Never. They were ornery little mutants, with no sense of decorum whatsoever.

Meanwhile, she'd take good care of these two and be very glad to turn them back over to more responsible adults as soon as possible. Hopefully without traumatizing them too badly or vice-versa.

Both girls managed to pee in the shadows of a bush once they got deep into the woods. She led them through the trees and studied the trouble that still lay ahead. About fifty feet of open ground waited between the edge of the forest and the shed. Her new hiding goal. If those men were on their way back and happened to glance toward the river, they'd see them crossing the moonlit space. They could remain where they were or head for the shelter. It was a hard decision to make but she would feel much safer in the ramshackle old building. Just in case snakes really did crawl at night, not to mention the two-legged kind.

"Suzie, I want you to go first. Stay low and out of the light as much as you can. When you get there, hide on the far side where it's really dark." She pointed and the girl nodded. "Okay, you ready?"

"You coming too?" The anxious child stood on one foot then the other, staring up at Jessie.

"Of course. You wait there and I'll bring Ellie as soon as you are safe and I don't see anyone coming. Okay?"

"What if you do?"

"Do what?"

"See someone coming. Then you gonna run the other way and leave me?" A whimper threatened to burst into loud sobs.

"No, of course not. I'll wait till they go on, then we'll come. Just wait. I won't leave you, I promise. Now don't argue with me anymore, just go. Now." She patted the little butt to get her started.

Suzie gave one long pitiful look, then darted straight across the opening, not making any effort to stay out of sight.

Nails cutting into her palms, Jessie kept watch. Someone would come swooping along and snatch the kid any minute, sure as the world, and her helpless to do anything. After the little girl disappeared unharmed into the shadow of the shed, Jessie held her position for a beat. When she felt safe to move, she picked up Ellie and darted across the open space, finding hiding places where she could.

The child hung on so tight she could barely breathe. The back of her neck rippled like there were worms under the skin, the hair on her arms stood out, her feet didn't want to take one more step, yet they did. A big hand could pounce any minute. Flight was stopped short when she banged up against the building. Hard to believe she made it without sirens going off and people yelling. For a long while the three of them huddled together until her fear abated and her legs stopped shaking.

On the far side of the shed was a window opening with no glass. She lifted Suzie and poked her through the hole.

"Just stay right there and wait for us." She picked up Ellie, pushed her through feet first. "Catch her."

When no one leaped out of the bushes to grab her she pulled up, straddled the bottom sill, and dropped inside, scraping her inner thighs on the rough lumber.

While she accomplished this the moon disappeared behind the mountains. Inside was pitch black. There were no other openings, not even a visible door. Come dawn, they should get enough light to orient themselves, but until then it was wait.

She sat down with a child on each side munching on the stale crackers. There they remained till dawn silvered the sky and morning birds started peeping. And no one came. The men must be lost or maybe they fell into a big hole or off a bluff.

Still they hunkered in place. The skin on her inner thighs burned, her muscles ached, and she wanted only a soft bed to fall asleep in. That old saying tough women loved, that they could take care of themselves, echoed through her brain. Everyone needed someone every once in a while to help with that, and she'd gladly accept any sort of aid at this very moment. Coward that she was. What she hoped for now was to hear the car start up there at the cabin and leave. If the men had returned during the night she hadn't heard them.

What now? Just how long could she remain here with these little girls? They were hungry and needed water. It was time to be brave and save them. But she didn't feel much like Wonder Woman.

A mailbox that read *Kimble* came in view in the sweep of the headlights. Odd for a fishing cabin to have a mailbox, but Dal wasn't overly concerned about that little detail. Hell, maybe the family came up here for summers. Colby cut the lights and steered up the overgrown drive. Two paths were beaten down in the weeds as if someone had recently driven in. The windows were dark but a car was nosed up against the porch. He parked on the far side.

Colby palmed his .45 and Dal nodded, pulled his weapon too. The long night was nearly over, with dawn lighting the sky above eastern peaks.

"Hope we can close this out here. I'm beat." Dal glanced at Colby's silhouette against the car window. Might be able to walk but he'd be lucky if he could run when they leaped from the car to play heroes.

He'd hung a long while by his good leg, which left him without a working one to spare.

The deputy didn't answer, just thumbed the radio. Nothing but static. Out of range. Would've been nice to get a call in, but they were on their own. All Mac knew was Colby had headed out to find Dal.

Easing the doors open then closed, they ran hunched over to the front steps. Dal took the lead into the one-room cabin and it didn't take long to clear it. Flashlights turned off they waited, one near each door.

"What do you reckon happened?" Colby kept his voice low.

"Hard to tell. The car's here, they'll be back." Dal leaned heavily against the wall.

"Why go running off if they've got the kids?"

Dal shrugged. "Maybe the girls got away and they went after them."

"Two little girls stumbling through the woods? It wouldn't take but a few minutes to catch up with them. I don't know. It's weird."

"What? You want to go haring off looking for them?" Leg on fire, Dal rose, went to the window and peered out. "It's getting light. Let's wait till we can see better, then try to track them."

"Okay, it's your call." Colby slid his butt down to the floor near the back door.

Restless, Dal feared following his example. He'd never get up if he sat down, so he parked his butt on the high counter. The room grew lighter with every minute. The cabinet gaped open and there were cracker crumbs on the top next to the dry sink. Odd. He flicked his light on, hooded it with one hand and checked the thick dust covering the floor.

"Come here." He flicked off the light till Colby joined him, then turned it back on. "Footprints. Small bare feet. Going out the back way. And there—shoes, but too small to belong to the men. What do you think?"

The deputy thought a moment. "Maybe those little girls got away and they had help."

They stared at each other, mouths whispering the same name. "Jessie."

"Holy shit. They brought Jessie here, too." Colby nodded.

A slim chance that they could save the kids with her help. What would she do? Dal had been around her enough to know she'd go to cover with those girls. Had better sense than to try to drag them through woods she wasn't familiar with. Running meant making noise and attracting attention. She was nearby somewhere.

"Out back, look around the stoop. The ground is soaked from the rain. They will have left prints."

"Well, shit." Colby did so, stared at the thick grass standing in water. "No prints here."

The sun climbed from behind the peaks, revealed their surroundings. Dal pointed. "There, down there near the river. Is that a building?"

"Looks like it. Maybe a boat dock."

"Easy does it. We don't want to walk up on them in case the men are in there too. Make them do something dangerous."

In the silence broken by a few birds happy to greet the dawn, Dal squinted to make out details of the shed. A chance the men were with them. With all that open ground, he and Colby would be spotted. He signaled to Colby to swing out to the right into the trees. Stooped to make as little a shadow as possible he followed, not sure which leg to drag until they were in the cover of the woods, then gestured again, this time to show he was going to the lower side of the shed near the river and some more trees.

Once there he could come up on one side, Colby on the other. Making no noise, he took small, cautious steps while watching the other man's shadow. The former Marine knew precisely what to do and each worked their way to the ramshackle structure. Gasping in pain, Dal held an ear against a crack between boards, listened for a long while. Nodded.

They were there.

A childish voice spoke softly, another replied. They'd best go carefully. No sense that men were in there. Still, they could be asleep.

He pointed, shook his head. The only door faced the river, the gaping window on the side. It wasn't a dock, just some kind of storage shed. Dal silently directed Colby through the door rather than chance going out into the open to the window. He still didn't get a sense of who was in there with them. Disconcerting to say the least. Was he losing his mojo?

In less than a minute muted male laughter resonated from inside. Colby emerged carrying one of the girls and Jessie came out leading the other. Sure was good to see her, but there was no time to stop to chat.

"She wanted to know if I was Batman."

Dal chuckled. "What'd you tell her?"

"I said no, you were. That I'm Robin." Colby peered into the far woods. "We'd better hightail it out of here before the Joker comes back with his gang. With me and stay low. Let's pretend they're coming out of those woods over there any minute till we get back to the cruiser."

They must've made quite an interesting lineup, the three adults and two little people hunched over, one staggering to stay on his feet, the others running like crazy through the early morning light. To keep from holding them up Dal brought up the rear, gun out and constantly checking the perimeter while Colby led the way carrying Ellie, her tiny arms locked around his neck till she must be choking him. They'd be lucky if they could pry her loose from her hero, Robin. So far no one spotted them.

Up ahead, the cruiser. With only twenty or thirty feet to go all hell broke loose. A bullet buzzed past Dal's ear so close he felt its flight. It thunked into the door of the patrol car.

"On the ground, get around to the other side and get the girls inside. Now." He fell on his face, all around him flaring red with agony, rolled to one side and fired four fast shots at their pursuers. Clawed for the car door. A bullet tore through his hand, slammed into the metal. He might as well have been hit with a ten-pound hammer over and over.

For an instant, the pain leveled out so he couldn't tell what hurt the worst. Under his touch, the car engine started and he slipped it into gear and rolled away from the moving wheels, at the same time yelling at Colby.

"Get them out of here now. Go."

Tires skidding in the wet grass, the car fishtailed and moved off. Dal wiggled on his stomach toward a mound of bushes, paused once to return fire before burrowing deep into the branches. The two men made it to their vehicle, got it turned around, and took off after the cruiser. He couldn't let them pursue and maybe shoot everyone. Battling the pain he rose, went into a firing stance, and emptied the .44 after them. Sank to the ground. He wasn't going to make it any farther. The back window shattered, the car zigged and zagged. Spreading his legs, he propped himself against a tree, slammed a full magazine into the gun using the tree trunk, and braced with both arms. Colby's car burst from the woods, blocked the other one's movement and Dal fired at the fleeing men.

They returned fire, shots flashing from the side window. Colby went down.

"Goddammit." Dal staggered to his feet, laced his last shots through the glass. Echoes faded into a deathly silence and the battered vehicle slammed to a halt against a tree. Falling to his knees he half-crawled to where Colby lay face down in the wet weeds. Blood soaked his shirt. He eased him onto his back.

From the woods Jessie and the two girls came running, their screams riddling the night.

No radio signal. He had to get the wounded deputy in the car and back to town. No way would he let him bleed out here when he'd survived the gory killing fields of Afghanistan.

"Jess, get the car. Bring it here. Now. I can't carry him."

"Are you hit?" She touched his shoulder.

"No, I'm fine. Just get the car. Okay?" He took her hand in his, gaze catching hers.

She kissed him fast. Ran. In a matter of minutes she had the car idling, the side door nearest Colby's still form. She leaped out and ran around to help drag him into the backseat. From the other car all remained quiet. Steam rose from the crushed front end.

"Jessie, help me get in. Hurry now. Forget them."

She grabbed him under the shoulders hoisted him up till he could shove himself into the driver's seat. "Girls, crawl up front with Dal. Hurry now." She boosted them over the seat and crawled in the back with Colby.

All around him turned black and he fought to stay conscious. He had to do this one last thing before passing out. Just get this man to town. He would not let him die out here like this.

To hell with the other men.

Blood soaked the t-shirt she'd placed over the wound. Colby groaned and she pressed harder. It must hurt like the very devil, but she had to make the bleeding stop. The car skidded around a curve, sped up a long hill, and careened toward Cedarton. She hung on to keep both of them from being tossed off the seat. Ahead, the firehouse where Colby would be transferred to an ambulance and taken to Harrison. In the front seat Dal spoke into the radio and a voice replied.

Thank God. It wouldn't be long to where first responders and EMTs were waiting. Colby opened his eyes, a lost, terrified look there that broke her heart. No telling what he was thinking. She grasped his bloody hand while continuing to press the shirt tight against his chest.

"Don't worry, you'll be all right. We're almost there. I can see the guys. They're going to take care of you." Her voice broke and tears flowed. She didn't even try to stop them. Sometimes you just had to cry.

He tried to speak but no sound came. If he died she'd never forgive herself. There must've been something she could've done differently. With the kids, anything. If only she hadn't insisted they take them up to Hermitage House where those assholes could lay hands on them. How had they known the girls were there? No time to ponder that now.

The car slid to a stop and everything happened so fast she couldn't keep track of it. Next thing she was standing near the ambulance not sure how she got there. Colby lay on a stretcher while Mike worked over him. Assessing him, getting him ready for the ride to the hospital. Dal sat in the open door, staring at them.

"Okay, load him up." Mike climbed inside with his patient. A couple of the other guys slammed the doors and hammered on the back. The ambulance took off, lights flashing, siren screaming. Sobbing, Jessie turned and there stood Dal propped against the patrol unit. She took him in her arms crying so hard she could scarcely breathe.

"Come on, I'm going down there. You coming? I'll need you to drive. I can't...." He sagged against her, arm across her shoulder.

She helped him into the passenger seat. He'd insisted he hadn't been shot, so what was going on? She climbed in the other side and leaned a head on his shoulder.

"So tell me what's wrong. What happened? You're hurt."

His chuckle was bitter. "Went off the road, almost went down the mountain with the car, but I got out. Had help. Tore up my leg. I'll be okay. Just need...."

He gently pried her arms loose, held both her hands in his, kissed the knuckles. "Jessie? What'd they do with the kids?"

"Don't worry. They're inside waiting for Alicia. She wants to take them home with her."

"What about those assholes?"

"They're pretty beat up. Too bad they didn't break their necks. Burt's out there now, gathering them up to take them over to the jail. After what's happened, there's no chance they'll get away or hurt anyone. I hope the bastards are all tore up and alive." She gazed at him. "And you're okay? I want you to get checked out at the hospital."

He nodded. When he didn't object she knew he was worse off than he would admit. For a moment he held very still and it was as if the entire world took a great breath before going back to normal. They were all alive. Colby would make it. He had to. She kissed Dal and he leaned back against the headrest. The sound of the receding siren echoed through the hills. She started the car and followed it down through the hills toward town.

"He'll make it, won't he?" The question barely came out.

"I don't know. A lot of blood, but it looked like a thru and thru. If it missed his lungs then—well...."

"What'll they do with those two?"

"You don't get away with shooting a law enforcement officer. Don't you worry, they'll be lucky to live till they get out of prison."

"Dal?"

"What, hon?"

She stared down the road. "No one has mentioned Randy. He disappeared. Where did he get to?"

He said nothing for a moment. "Hell, I don't know. What do you mean, he disappeared?"

"They couldn't find him after the girls were taken. No one knows where he went. You don't suppose he lied, that he really is the one in charge? I thought I'd figured out who their leader is, but you're not going to believe me."

"Try me. I really don't think Randy has the evil it takes."

"Then you'll never believe what I'm thinking. You know Fudge? Always hanging around the Red Bird, works sometimes for Theron picking tomatoes?"

"Nah. What makes you think that? He's just a good ole hill boy."

"Fraid not. Or at least I'm pretty sure I'm right. He cleans up good, loses his accent, shaves his head, and he's a different man. He was with Kimble when they threw me into the trunk. I stared him right in the eye. And if he isn't Fudge the man has a twin who likes baths and haircuts and cheap cologne more than our good ole boy."

Too late for him to reply before she turned into the emergency entrance of the hospital. The ambulance sat in peaceful silence, the doors standing open. No sign of Colby or anyone else.

She leaped out and supported him into the long hallway empty save for Mike who stood there, arms held out as if in supplication, his face white.

Her heart lurched. "He—is he okay? I mean alive?"

Mike nodded. "So far. You'd think I'd be used to it." He looked all around as if lost. "Somehow it's not the same when it's someone you care for. Yet I should care for them all."

He swayed and Dal took his elbow. "Come on, Mike. Let's go sit down for a minute. Maybe we can support each other."

"Dal, you need to see a doctor."

He waved her away. "In a little while. I'm okay."

He and Mike went into the waiting room, Dal and Jessie on either side. He dropped into a chair. Features pinched, jaw muscles bunching in an effort at control. With a groan, Dal lowered himself into another chair. They made quite a pair, each hurting in their own way.

She stared at his hand, at the purple hole through the palm. "Is that a bullet hole? Dal, you've been shot."

He held it up and stared as if just then noticing.

"I'll go find us some coffee." Jessie left and went in search of someone to take a look at Dal's injuries.

When she returned with coffee and an intern, Dal gave her a dark look, but he went with the man, leaving Jessie with Mike.

He came out of his trance a bit. "I need to get back, get the bus cleaned up." He held out his bloody hands. "And me too."

"That can wait a few minutes. Your guys are out there now." She touched his shoulder. "He's going to be all right. You'll see. He's tough."

Mike managed a weak grin. "You're right about that. Him being tough, I mean. Those guys are all tough."

She lowered herself beside Mike, neither of them saying anything. Hospital sounds went on as if nothing had happened. The smell always reminded her of suffering. Not too surprising.

"What went on out there? How did this happen?" Mike gestured around the room.

She started to answer, but a man in white who had to be a doctor approached. "Family of Colby Hanson?"

They both looked up. She couldn't speak and Mike remained quiet too.

"He's lost a lot of blood, but looks like he'll make it. No vital organs hit. We'll have him in a room in a while, but he won't be conscious for an hour or so. The nurse will give you his room number but don't go up there expecting to celebrate. He'll need to take it easy. Got that?"

"Thanks, Doc." Mike's wide grin relayed his relief.

Jessie touched him on the shoulder. "I'm going to check on Dal. He got pretty beat up when he ran his car off the road. Guess it went down the mountain and over a cliff. He said someone pulled him out just before it did, but I can't imagine who. And he got shot up there getting Colby out of danger. Didn't even mention it to me." She shook her head. There was no understanding men sometimes.

She left Mike, who joined the other EMTs. They prepared to take the ambulance back to first responder headquarters in Cedarton.

She wandered through the halls of the small hospital till she found Dal sitting on the edge of an examination table wearing a hospital gown, a white patch on his forehead, one hand wrapped, and his leg bruised, bandaged, and cut.

He gestured with an embarrassed grin. "I told them I'm okay, but they insisted on rigging me out in this. Waiting for the doc who's looking at my X-rays. He doesn't think anything's broken, just beat up pretty good. I'm okay." He held up the hand. "Went right on through."

She went to stand next to him, inching one arm around his shoulder. "Sure. Just a flesh wound or two, huh?"

He leaned into her, belying his earlier statement that he was okay.

"Who helped you out of the car, Dal?"

After a minute he spoke softly. "Grandfather."

"You're sure? I mean, you are pretty banged up. And you hit your head pretty hard."

"I guess I could be crazy, but no one else was there. I was not going to make it out, Jessie. The car was going over the edge and I couldn't get hold of anything till someone grabbed my arms and yanked me out."

She kissed his temple. No use in saying anything. She'd seen some things happen with him that were not believable. Who was she to deny this? Still, one thing had to be answered.

"Okay. Could I ask you something?"

"I guess so, but I'm not sure I can answer."

"When Steve pushed you off the mountain why didn't your grandfather help you then?"

For a long moment he was quiet. Then he took her hand in his. "He did, he sent you."

A sob caught in her throat.

The intern returned. "Nothing is broken in the leg, but you're banged up pretty good. The bullet fractured a couple of bones in your hand. You need to see your family doc for follow-up. I've written you a prescription for pain meds and you ought to take care of yourself. Sometimes torn muscles and ligaments are more painful than broken bones."

Jessie took the prescription and thanked him. Turned to Dal. "Need me to help you put on your pants?"

His attempt to grin relieved her some. "Sort of opposite of the usual, isn't it?"

16
CHAPTER

After picking up Dal's prescription, Jessie drove them in silence back to her place. Dal kept an eye on her. It had been a close call for all of them and she could fly apart. He was doing a little shaking himself. He'd been shot before and this time was only minor compared. Still, seeing Colby go down, now that was tough. They'd left the injured deputy sleeping in the hospital and when she drove straight to her place, Dal sighed with relief. Going home to an empty apartment didn't appeal to him.

After she parked, he managed to get out of the Jeep, leaning hard against the side panel. She hurried to his side, wrapped an arm around his waist, and supported him inside. He didn't object.

Lowering him to the couch, she touched him three or four times, eyes shining with tears. "I'm just going to feed and water Brad. You okay?"

The pain in his hand was like being branded. And his leg, well, one injury tended to help him ignore the other. He took the pills and drank the water she gave him, then waited while she tended to the little pit bull and moved back to his side. Again, she ran her fingers over his temple and down to his lips. He kissed her fingertips. Neither of them had spoken more than a few words since leaving the hospital. She hadn't asked him to stay. He didn't wait for permission, just stumbled along behind her, supporting himself on the walls. No way should either one of them be alone tonight. He'd make it to the bed, by god, if it killed him.

She turned right into the bathroom and when he hesitated outside the door, she pulled him in by the arm. "Hot water will be good for you." Her eyes, underlined by dark bruises, reflected their harrowing experience. Bloody clothing discarded at the hospital, she wore pink scrubs with cavorting elephants one of the nurses had given her.

Grunting, he dropped to the toilet—cold on his butt—and she cupped her palm over his cheek. He turned enough to place a kiss in her hand. There were things he thought of saying, wanted to say, but nothing fit the way he felt or explained what they had been through together. So he swallowed the words and fumbled with the buttons of his shirt. She pushed aside his fingers, bared his chest, and leaned into his shoulder, the warmth of her breath like butterfly kisses.

He touched the hem of her shirt and she pulled it up over her head, then slipped out of her bra and shoved down the baggy scrubs. She wore no panties. They had been discarded with her jeans. She toed off her shoes and kicked out of the wad of clothing. Obviously exhausted, still every move was a sensual invitation to hold each other.

Damn, he hoped she didn't have more in mind, cause it wasn't something he could manage. The admission brought a resigned sigh. Never thought he'd see the day. He might get it up, but wasn't sure what he'd do with it.

He wrapped both arms around her. Best to wait for her to make the first move. Do whatever she needed, if he could. Her cool touch across his bare belly, her lips moist on his jaw, roused a quiver of comfort that warmed him through and through. Gaze locked to his, she searched for the snap and zipper at his waistband. Eased the jeans down over his thighs. To be with her was the only thing he wanted. With a supreme effort and ignoring the jabs of pain, he pulled her close so she went to her knees. His breath hissed out.

Kneeling, she slipped off his muddy, grass-stained shoes and worked the dusty denim fabric over his feet, kissed the bruises along his leg, then turned her head so her cheek lay on his bare thigh. Locks of her hair tickled his skin and he brushed it off her face. Eyes closed, he whispered thanks to whatever gods might be listening. They were both alive, touching each other.

"Let's take a shower. It'll make you feel better." Though the whispered request came she made no move to stand, to move away from the embrace.

Odd, sitting bare-assed naked on the bathroom stool, her on her knees cheek lying on his thigh gave him such sweet comfort. Nothing she did should surprise him. She was never ordinary. By now he ought to be jumping her bones, but he couldn't move. It was as if he'd melted down. All he wanted was her and this, whatever this was.

Together.

It was so quiet in the room his breath and hers intertwined. His heart beat, hers in sync.

"Dal?"

"Hmm?"

"Let go and I'll turn on the shower."

Funny, until that moment he didn't know he held her so tight, fingers wrapped around her arms so she wouldn't pull away. Ever. Jesus, he was worn out. The damn pills made his head spin, dulled the ache in the injured leg. Made him feel somehow removed from everything, like he hovered above the two of them huddled around the stool.

"Dal? Sweetie?" She stirred enough to let him know she needed loose. On her knees on the tile floor must not be comfortable.

It was as if it would take a pry bar to turn loose of her. What the hell was wrong with him? What had that doc given him? A funny noise rolled out of his throat and he loosened his grip, let his hands slide away from her arms.

The next thing he knew she had covered his bandaged hand with a plastic bag, jockeyed him to his feet and placed him under the hot spray. Eyes closed, he wavered and she supported him. Water rained down on them. After a while she squirmed free, propped him against the wall, his head resting on folded arms. She found a bottle of body wash and filled her palm, rubbed her hands together, and massaged him from neck and shoulders all the way to his toes, touch tender over his bruised and battered legs. Dear God, her hands worked up thick lather between his legs. So damn good but all he could do was enjoy the hell out of it.

Sweet fucking mother, that felt good. Her hands rubbing soap over and under his balls, up and down his prick. Him helpless to react. Just leaning there, like maybe he'd died and gone to heaven. Once, twice, three times. He wanted… no, *had* to be inside her but he could not put forth the effort. Never had he felt this way. Drugs. Holy Hell. He had a soft hard-on. Desire shot through him to all the places a climax belonged. He was going to fall. Slid down ever so slowly, her guiding him, keeping him from hurting himself. It was as if he lay in a marshmallow bed that slowly squished down to the floor till he sat propped in the corner. Now she held the shower head and rinsed him off from stem to stern.

Her mouth moved and he watched it. Fascinating, he couldn't hear the words yet sensed that she spoke.

"You're okay, sweetheart. I'm right here. Just relax." Bouncing echoes in a tiny room.

Hot water sent rivers of soap downward over his shoulders and belly and into his crotch. God that looked weird, pooling under him, then running toward the drain in long bubbly streams.

He poked a finger into the white stuff and laughed.

"You're drunk, Dal. Must be those pills. Bet we should've told him you never even take an aspirin and one beer is your limit." She laughed. "Sure hope I can get you up from there and into bed. Hate you might have to crawl."

"Could always sleep here." The statement didn't sound like what he'd said, but he let it go. Squinting, he eyed the discarded soap bottle, fumbled with it till he got it to squirt onto her skin, then washed her in a somewhat clumsy way with one hand.

When his touch wandered between her legs she tightened her thighs around it. "Oh, my."

Well, that was nice. She squirmed till his finger slipped inside her, then closed her eyes and wiggled with enjoyment. Grinning like a big idiot, he helped her till she came with gasps of pleasure.

"Nice, huh?" His head bobbled down to rest on her shoulder.

"My baby." Her lips mumbling against his ear felt so good. Everything felt good. Her fingers trailing through his wet hair, their legs slithering around against each other, the spray raining on his head, his hand moving over her slick, soapy skin. Somehow he'd have to remember how good this felt and try it again sometime. When he was sober. He could have done this all night if he hadn't been so damnably worn out.

"You know what, sweetheart? We need to get you out from under this. The water is getting cold and I'm afraid you're falling asleep."

He heard her, he sure did. But react? Hell no. Her arms went under his. Interesting but he couldn't get his legs under him. Oh, God he felt so good. Next thing he knew she had him next to the bed and was shaking him. Must've dragged him.

"A little bit of help here, big guy. Come on, you can do it. Put your feet under you and stand up. I'll do the rest."

He did that, feeling like one of those rubber characters in a cartoon, then fell onto the bed.

He woke up to sunlight arms and legs entwined with hers. With no idea how he got there.

The heat coming in the window awoke Jessie, wrapped in Dal's arms and legs so she had trouble untangling herself. Peeking through a crevice between his legs, she read the alarm clock. Looked again. Was it seven in the morning or the evening? The bedroom was on the west side of the house, so judging by the light it must be evening. Had they slept an entire day away? Lying naked on her bed.

Memories of the past few days crowded over her. Incredulous, she stared out the window. Spring had turned to summer, the days warming, the trees unfolding full leaves so the mountains went from a feathery grey to jade green. With a great deal of care, she unwound herself from his sleeping form, his expression one of such contentment she could hardly bear to disturb him. But bodily functions could scarcely be postponed a moment longer.

She managed to get everything but her shoulders clear of his twisted legs when her elbow bumped his midsection. He came awake with a whoof, eyes searching the room for a panic-stricken moment before he saw her and went still.

"Hi, you okay?" His lopsided grin shot satisfaction through her.

"Very much so. You?"

"Uh-hum. You are quite beautiful naked in the sunshine."

"Sounds like the beginning of a poem."

He rubbed his belly. "Race you to the bathroom."

With that she shot off the bed and slammed the door before he could make it, gimpy as he was.

"Better hurry up. Can I piss off the deck?"

"Much easier than I can, so be my guest. Just don't fall off the edge. Better than a puddle in the floor."

She left the bathroom, laughing at him standing on the far end of the deck enjoying the beautiful evening, leaning on the rail and relieving himself. "One reason it's fun to live in the country. But then you don't. What would the Bs do if you peed off your porch?"

"Have me arrested for indecent exposure. I would never attempt it."

She padded onto the deck and eased her arms around his waist from behind. The purple scar that slashed down his back and thigh was surrounded by black and blue bruises from the car wreck. He looked like someone had taken a ball bat to him.

"Standing on the deck in the glow of the evening, naked as jaybirds—" He broke off when she pinched him.

"Don't quit your day job."

"What? You don't like my singing?"

"It's not that so much as it's the lyrics that are pitiful."

About that time a whippoorwill uttered its mournful cry, as if criticizing his attempts at singing, and they both broke up laughing.

"See there, the bird likes my singing, even joined me for the chorus."

"He's just welcoming the night." She went still, leaned her head back against his shoulder. "I feel so bad about Colby. If only I hadn't—"

"Nope, don't do that. The only one guilty of Colby's getting shot is the man who shot him."

"Wonder if they ever ran down Randy. I really believed him, but why did he disappear if he was telling the truth?"

"Don't know. You know what I'd like to do?"

She eyed him. "You mean naked on the deck?"

His laughter scared up several crows settling in for the evening in the top of a nearby oak. "Well, that too. Once this mess is over I'd like to go somewhere, just you and me, where we don't have to talk about or think about any of this."

From inside his cell rang. "That's mine. Guess I'd better get it." He dragged himself toward the door.

"Maybe when it's over." Unbelieving, she followed him, where they finally located the phone in the bathroom amid their clothes. Those were best discarded in the burn barrel.

Her phone was gone, along with her backpack. Must be out in the yard where Fudge had tossed it when he crammed her in the trunk.

He glanced at the caller ID. "Hey, Mac. How's it going?"

While he listened she gathered up their clothes, emptied the pockets, and took them to the laundry room. His wallet, keys, and a handful of change she piled on the folding table. His pills she took with her and walked still naked into the bedroom to dress. A pair of his jeans, left from a previous visit, hung next to hers and she took both out, laid them on the bed. Pulled hers on. When she came out he was making a pot of coffee, having a time of it with only one hand.

"That's quite a picture." She framed him between fingers and thumbs. "Naked man in kitchen. Let me finish that." She took the pot, filled it with water, and poured it into Mr. Coffee.

"Do I have any clothes here?"

"Yep, on the bed. What's up?"

"Colby is awake and seems to be on the mend. Tried to check himself out of the hospital till Mac told him if he did he'd put him on extended medical leave, so he'd just as well stay where he was for a few days. I guess they struck a deal. Anyway, Randy got in touch to see if the girls had been found. Turns out he claims he took Alicia's car to search for them when they were taken. Or at least that's his story. The girls are with Alicia and Jeff and he said he had something to do before coming back. Mac's afraid he's going after his wife. It seems Dave managed to come up with her address and phone number. No idea how. Anyway, Mac got in touch with her and she's on her way to pick up the girls. There's been an OP out against Randy for several months. Seems he met the girls after school and lit out with them. So we still don't know who's lying in this situation. Legally, she gets them, at least till it's sorted out."

"But she can swear out an order of protection without him getting to tell his side. Or am I understanding it wrong?"

"No, you're right. An ex-parte order of protection can be issued without him being present but a permanent order of protection won't be issued without a court hearing with both parties there."

"Then he could be telling the truth." She held on to her belief that Randy hadn't lied to them. "I can't believe a man with two lovely daughters could have been involved in the human trafficking scheme, so let's just hope he ran to avoid being arrested for kidnapping the girls."

"That is the lesser of the two evils." Dal went to dress and Jessie dug around in the cabinet for some Honey Buns to go with the coffee. The pills were in her jeans pocket, but maybe he ought not to take them, the way they affected him. Or she could cut one in half if he needed it for pain. She'd ask.

He returned with his pants on but not zipped or fastened and a t-shirt partway rolled over his chest. "Could use a little help here. This thing hurts like I'm holding it in a fire."

"Then you'll want one of these." She set a pill beside his mug of coffee and finished dressing him, dragging it out with pinches and nibbles.

Sitting with coffee and Honey Buns he examined the pill. "I don't remember much about last night, but what I do remember is I had no control over myself. Must be what being drunk feels like. Thank you for taking care of me."

Nodding, she studied him in silence. Hard to believe a man with his occupation had never been drunk. Interesting if true.

After they ate, she cleaned the table, went outside, and retrieved her backpack lying in the grass. Back inside she plopped down on the couch, dumped everything out on the couch. and set about refilling it and tossing wrappers, empty water bottles and the like.

"I need to go back to work Monday. Being shut up in the trunk of a car is no excuse not to report to my job. Besides, I'd say I have a whale of a story to write."

She glanced at Dal, who sat on the couch drinking more coffee and watching her with a great deal of intent. "What?"

He shook his head. "Nothing, I just—you're one amazing woman."

"Hmm. How's that?" She slipped her phone from an outside pocket and plugged it in.

"After all that's happened the last few days, after I watched you fall apart, you just pick yourself up, shake yourself off, and get back to it."

"You mean, like it was only a flesh wound? Well, that's life, isn't it? Other choices aren't too appealing. Besides, I was thinking in the middle of all that, about the people around me who keep me sane, who support me and love me. I guess I'm just fortunate that way." She stuffed some of her necessities into the backpack. Glanced up to see him still staring at her. "You okay? I mean, you did watch me fall apart and I just realized something."

His look changed to wary. "What might that be?"

"About us, I mean. You and I held each other"—she grinned—"washed each other, slept with each other, all without having sex. What we had was beyond that. It was love, don't you think? It tells me something about us."

His crooked grin amused her. "I'm afraid to ask what it might tell you. I just sensed what you needed, what we both needed was care and support. Besides, goddamn my leg hurts."

"Uh-huh. Well never fear. I'll try not to get sappy here." She chuckled. "You need to take it easy for a few days. You look sort of like an eggplant, all purple like that."

He laughed. "Nah, I'll be okay. I think it's time I got back to work too. Can you take me in? I hope my unit is back where it belongs. Begging a ride with a lowly reporter is beneath me."

Well, he sneaked right past that slick as pond scum. "Watch out, you'll end up walking to town. At least take a cane. I've got my grandpa's here somewhere. Doc said you should keep your weight off that leg for a few days. As for driving and working one-handed, well, that's going to be a bit difficult. And you'd better beware of this lowly reporter. The pen is still mightier than the sword."

"Uh-huh, if you say so." He accepted the cane and experimented with it till he could use his good hand to bear some of the weight of his injured leg.

She watched him a while, then chuckled. "I have a feeling you'll be on desk duty for a while, at least till one or the other of your battered body parts heals up a bit."

"Well, we'll see about that."

She drove him to the station house, satisfied Mac would handle him.

At the station, Sam Watson was on duty when they went in together. He grinned as if he knew a secret. Pointed at the hand-carved cane in Dal's hand. "Hear you wrecked another of our vehicles. A one-man destruction crew. Lucky you didn't break something. Nice walking stick. That snake crawling up it looks real."

"Yeah, I don't feel so lucky. Couldn't hurt much worse. Who you sitting in for?"

"Looks like I've got me a part-time job till Mac can replace Duggan. He fired the boy this morning. Anyways, I'm spelling Tink. Seems she and hubby wanted off at the same time for a change. By the way, Mac says to tell you they found your car. It's in the shop for some minor repairs and it should be out in the morning. Those idiots left it off out in the boonies in a ditch. Some kid on his way to pick up his girlfriend found it. Called in and wanted to know if there was a reward." Sam laughed. "Mac told him the reward was he didn't have to go to jail. When the kid said he wasn't going to jail, Mac told him holding a deputy's car hostage was a misdemeanor punishable by a weekend in jail or detailing all our cars."

Dal chuckled. "What'd the kid say?"

"He wanted to know what detailing was, said it didn't sound like much fun and told Mac where to find it. Anyway, it don't look like you'll be needing it right away. Mac didn't mention that old one you run off the mountain. Did say the next time this happens you get to pay the expenses." He joined Dal in a laugh.

"Before or after he fires me?" Dal turned to Jessie. "Want to go across to Grandma's and eat us a real dinner? Not in the mood for a hamburger."

"Sounds good to me. You okay to walk it?"

"Long as we don't run a marathon."

She tucked her arm under his and wiggled fingers at Sam. "Good to see you. Take care." She wanted to mention his end-run on Beth Lavender, but couldn't figure a way to do so without embarrassing someone. None of her business anyway.

The old deputy raised a hand and grinned. "Much as I can, girl. Much as I can. You do the same, you hear?"

After they were seated at Grandma's and had ordered, Jessie brought up Colby's situation. "I'm sure glad Colby is going to be okay."

"Me too. He's a good kid. You really like him, don't you?"

"I do indeed. He's interesting and tough and just plain nice. Not something you find in everyone."

He regarded her for a moment. "I like him too. My reasons may be different, though."

"Oh, and what might they be?"

"He's reliable. Says he'll do something he does it."

She propped her chin in one hand. Eyed him. "Strange, though, finding a young man with his qualifications working for a backwater sheriff's department. Makes me wonder if he has a bad record or something."

He peered over the rim of the water glass. "Backwater huh? Reckon we all have our secrets."

"I didn't mean that the way it sounded. I'm sorry, Dal. I just meant that… shoot, I'm not sure I should have to explain myself. You know how I feel about you. I have my own dirty little secrets, but you're privy to all of them, same as I know about yours."

When he remained silent, she squinted a look at him. "I do, don't I?"

He turned up the tea glass and drank deeply, then set it down and watched her for a long moment. "Hon, no one shares all their secrets. It'd be catastrophic and destructive. Now, about Colby and his dead-end job."

She sighed and drew on the tablecloth with her fork. "Okay, Mister Silent. I just think a man with Colby's qualifications and at his age could have a much better job with more opportunities to advance than this." She tapped the table with her fingers. "This is where the worn-out horses come to graze."

A grin crept across his lips. "Worn-out horses, huh? I do know what you meant though, and you do not have to explain yourself to me. You and I both have good reasons for being where we are doing what we do. I just got to thinking about what brought me here. Wondering what my life would be like if Leanne had… never mind."

She stared out the back windows across the mountains, purpling in the evening shadows. "All in all, I wouldn't trade this for what I left behind, would you?"

His hand crept across the table to cover hers. "Not for one minute."

Boy, these last few days had brought out some deep feelings between the two of them. Kind of scared him, too. Getting all touchy feely with this woman was not a good idea. They got along like wildfire in bed, but getting too serious in other ways could cause bigger problems. Living with him would be a little like residing in a cave with a bear. Not that he was mean, really, he just had a way about him made him hard to get along with on a daily basis. Plus he did not want to get married. Ever again.

Their meals arrived, and the subject turned to if the man with Kimble was really Fudge, and most of all, was he the top man or was that one yet to be encountered? Both agreed he had to be a hired hand, didn't have the get-up-and-go it took to take part in such an endeavor as human trafficking.

When they returned to the station, Dal's car was waiting complete with a wash job. "Looks like I'm back in the saddle. Want to come home with me?"

"I'm afraid the Bs have had about all they'll take of our outrageous behavior. Besides, I've got some homework to do if I'm going in to work in the morning." She stood on tiptoe, kissed his cheek. "Go home and get some sleep. You look tired. Call me after my weekly ritual at the paper is finished. Sure you can drive and get up the steps okay? I can come help you."

"Nah, I believe I can haul myself up okay. If not, I'm sure Mrs. B will be happy to assist. You helping me would prove a distraction, don't you think?"

She left in the old Jeep. After she went out of sight he took out his cell and called Mac. When the sheriff answered he went right to the point. "What's up with Randy? How'd he take you turning the girls over to his wife?"

"Not well. Hey, is this my missing deputy who can't keep ahold of his vehicle?" The old man was quiet for a beat. "Glad you weren't hurt any worse. Jessie told me the doc said you ought to stay off your feet for a few days."

"Ah, you know how docs are. Besides, it's only a flesh wound."

Mac laughed. "Is that right? Sounded like more than one to me. Go on home son, we got things covered. Let the feds handle all that other stuff. Don't you worry about Randy none, he has a mission. I think we ought to leave him alone. He needs to straighten out his wedded bliss on his own."

"Oh? You know where he's going? What he's up to?"

"He's going to take care of his business, son. Let him be. I need your help figuring this out, I'll holler. Get some rest."

"Will do. I'm going up to talk to Alicia, then you can find me at home sleeping off these pills Doc gave me. I can't think with all this cotton in my brain."

"Okay, boy. Soon as we hear something from the FBI or the Marshals, we'll help with the take-down of those yahoos. Meanwhile, it's up to them to round em up."

Hard to believe Mac was actually going to step back and let the feds do their job. Dal needed to see if he could talk Alicia into retrieving that ledger he'd left in her office. He headed out of town and up the mountain to Hermitage House.

It was awful quiet around the huge plantation. The garage door was open. A shadowy figure hustled into the darkness and out of sight. Looked like a man, but he wasn't sure. He rang the doorbell, waited a bit, rang it again, and sat down in a deck chair. Wonder where they got to? The sound of a car climbing the hill, running so quiet he only heard the crunching of tires on gravel, announced someone's arrival.

It came in sight and he waited in the chair. They obviously took the entrance to the house through the attached garage, so he gave them time to get in and rang the bell again. Alicia came to the door, looking a bit frazzled. She frowned when she saw Dal.

"Everything okay?"

"Sure. I stopped by to see if I could go to your office and pick up that ledger I left in your safe."

For a moment she stared over his shoulder as if someone she didn't want to see stood behind him. "Uh, tell you what, Dal. If you don't mind could that wait till tomorrow? Jeff isn't feeling well and I need to see to him right now. I'll go on to town in the morning and get it for you, save you a trip. I can just drop it by the station if that'd be okay."

He leaned an arm against the door jamb. "I'm sorry. Of course. I hope he feels better. I'd like to get that ledger up to Fayetteville soon as possible. The feds are going to be real interested in it."

She raised an eyebrow. "Oh? Well, I'm, uh, glad." She glanced over her shoulder. "I have to go now. See you later."

He stood there a moment after she closed the door. She sure seemed in a mood. Weary of standing, he made his slow, painful way down the steps and to his car. He would take Mac's advice and go home for a while.

The square was reasonably quiet when he drove through town, but by the time he had circumvented, things had changed.

Two black SUVs rolled past, both bearing the telltale stub of a satellite antenna. Feds cruising? Or answering a call?

How did they keep those vehicles so bright and shiny? Must run them through a special fed car wash every few hours. While he kept his eyes aimed at them, one peeled off to the left on South Street, tires squealing. The other zipped off in the other direction, leaving town on Valley Road, neither one using lights or siren. What the hell?

Nothing on the radio. Behind the wheel of his unit, he made up his mind and took off after the south bound Denali, fumbling with the steering. Good thing it was his left hand that got shot.

Goddamn feds anyway. One of these years, law enforcement departments would smarten up and start cooperating with each other. Until then it was everyone for themselves. Since the FBI and the Marshals were both out looking for the two fugitives, he figured it didn't much matter which one he kept up with.

Tailing the feds could double his chances. He asked his phone to call Trey Ledger. Might as well see what the Marshal was up to. While the phone rang in his ear, his radio burped to life. Trey went to voicemail and he disconnected to listen to the radio. Ten-thirteen at 14244 Dyer Lane. Hell, that was Ina Mae's address. He knew it well, since he'd lived at her trailer park for almost three years.

Answering the officer needs assistance radio call, he stomped the foot-feed, hung a right, and headed for Dyer Road, which bisected the lane that led to Hidden Holler Trailer Park. The black Denali disappeared in the opposite direction. Was all hell breaking loose tonight? Damn, he hoped he could stomp the brake should it become necessary.

A woman's voice shouted. *"Shots fired, shots fired."*

"Now what?" Driving and using the mic wasn't possible.

The radio went quiet. He fishtailed his vehicle onto Dyer Lane. Up ahead, off into the center of the trailer park, blue and white lights flashed into the darkening sky. Jamming on the brakes, he skidded sideways within inches of hitting the patrol car. Took both feet on the pedal. Son of a bitch, that hurt.

17
CHAPTER

The security lights in the trailer park were all off, the beams from a deputy's unit revealing a man slouched on the ground. Before Dal could leap from his car, which might or might not happen, someone carrying a long-barreled gun and wearing slouchy overalls and a big hat stepped out of the darkness.

Hand going to his weapon, Dal shouted into the night air. "Put down your gun. Now." He launched himself to his feet, more or less.

"You first." The voice that came back at him was definitely feminine and he knew who she was.

"Ina Mae, it's me. Dallas Starr. Lay your rifle down on the ground."

"Who's with you?" She swung the rifle up to point in his direction.

"I'm alone." He raised the .44. "Now please, lay that down. I don't want to have to shoot you."

"Same here, Sonny. But there's too much strange goings-on going on, if you get my drift. I'll just need to see your face fore I trust you're who you say you are."

He shuffled slowly into the light, nervous about presenting a target, but at the same time sure this woman he'd grown so close to would not shoot him once she recognized him. Hard to tell what she would do if he didn't reveal himself.

Right fast, he turned so the headlights bathed his face and spoke in a softer tone. "Ina Mae, see, it *is* me. Now lay that thing down and tell me what's going on. Is that man on the ground dead? I need to call for help."

She placed the rifle on the ground and stepped into the light with him. "Where you been boy? Haven't seen you in a coon's age. He ain't dead lessen he's got a real soft head bone."

He holstered his gun, spoke an officer-needs-assistance-code into his walkie. Didn't much blame her for being upset with him. He'd been out to visit her once or twice when he first returned to Cedarton last year, but had been too caught up in his own life lately. "Sorry about that. Been meaning to get out here and visit with you. So what happened?"

"They been hiding in one of my trailers. Thought I wouldn't notice suspicious folk coming and going from a place rented to a single party. I know who pays rent and who don't. Just cause I'm an old lady don't mean I'm stupid."

"See if he's alive, Ina Mae."

She bent down and touched fingers to the neck of the unmoving form on the ground. "Yep. Heart's beating."

"Who is this? You know him?"

"One of em visiting regularly. I come out to talk to him about coming and going in Leon's trailer and keeping a woman there. He mouthed off at me, went to draw a gun. I didn't shoot him. I hit him crosst the head with the barrel of my rifle. Must've misjudged cause he went down like he was poleaxed."

"He's a deputy. Looks like he's over from Nolton County, according to his vehicle. You sure this is one of the men visiting your trailer?"

"That there ain't one of Mac Richards's deputies. I know all of 'em. This one is not one of 'em. He comes and goes in the night. Some other feller with him here lately. I had my fill of 'em acting like they belonged here and so I challenged him. Was only going to get rent money. That's when he turned on them flashing lights and drew on me.'"

Dal bent and rolled the man over, their groans intermingling. Blood covered one side of his face. He wore a Nolton County deputy's uniform but Dal didn't recognize him. This was getting more and more confusing. What did this have to do with the two escaped fugitives and the child trafficking the FBI was investigating? Jessie said Fudge was with Kimble when they grabbed her and tossed her in the trunk of their car. This was neither. Was everyone in both counties involved in some way?

What he wanted was to get ahold of them all, drag them into the sheriff's office, and have a come-to-Jesus meeting with each and every one. Get this mess straightened out. They'd kidnapped Alicia and Jeff Woodson, then turned them loose only to grab up Ellie and Suzie Drain and Jessie. All in an effort to locate a ledger that he now had hidden in a safe at Alicia Woodson's office. And somehow it was all connected to the Cult of the Rising Moon. Most were in custody of the FBI for child trafficking. Still running loose were ex-sheriff of Nolton County Robert Kimble, an unidentified woman, a man known as Fudge, possibly the spooky Marcus, and now these folks here had got into the mix.

Maybe they'd know what it was all about.

"Ina Mae, is the woman still in one of your trailers?"

"I reckon. I ain't seen her go nowhere."

"Show me, and while I'm gone, keep an eye on this one. Only please don't kill him. Okay?"

She pointed out one of the smaller trailers down a ways where a single light burned in a window. With what was going on out here, it was doubtful the woman was still hanging around, unless she was damned stupid. Still he'd have to check her out. Looked like some of the deputies from over in Nolton County were helping their ex-sheriff. If so, they'd all be in jail soon. Human trafficking was a serious offense.

He approached the trailer. From inside soft music played. The shadow of a woman dancing moved across the window. Transfixed, he watched for a while. She looked familiar but he couldn't place her. Not young but beautiful in a delicate, ethereal way. What should he do? Knock on the door and tell her she couldn't stay? Ina Mae said she didn't belong here, so as far as the law was concerned, he could escort her out. Or could he?

It was necessary that he know more. If she was visiting the renter, then he couldn't throw her out. Not even on Ina Mae's word. It was plain he needed to know more.

Shouting from the direction of the deputy's car made up his mind for him. He scrambled back in an awkward fashion in time to see Ina Mae struggling with someone, obviously the man she'd earlier knocked out, since he was no longer lying on the ground.

"All right, you two. It's time we had a discussion. Just what the hell is going on here?"

The man stopped, still clutching Ina Mae's overall front. "I came down here to visit a friend and this old crow comes racing at me just as I get out of the car. She's screaming at me to leave before she calls the cops. When I tell her I am the cops she hits me upside the head. I don't remember anything till I just now woke up. Arrest her or I will."

"Calm down. Technically you're out of your jurisdiction, but we've always had a good relationship with our fellow officers from other counties." Dal stuck out his hand. "I'm Deputy Dallas Starr. Grace County Sheriff's Department. You are?"

"Jason Gold. Deputy Jason Gold. Nolton County Sheriff's Department. My friend Loretta is visiting here. Over there in that trailer which is lawfully rented from this... this *woman.*"

Ina Mae interrupted. "It's rented to a man by the name of Frederick Samson. I believe he's known around here as Fudge. Works at the tomato patch for Theron. Believe they're cousins or something. Has been living here in the off-season for a year or so now. Think his house burned down last winter."

I'll be damned. No such thing as a coincidence, especially not in a place as small as Cedarton. And who was this Leon? One thing at a time. "Well, I'll want to be speaking to Fudge."

"That's what I'm trying to tell you. Fudge ain't around. His friend Leon and that Loretta woman have been staying there for several weeks now. Just upped and moved in. They can't do that without my permission. They come and go in the middle of the night. Cars in and out at all hours. Disrupting everyone's sleep. Even if they was regular tenants I wouldn't allow that."

"Okay. Tell you what. We're going to go over and visit with this Loretta person and check on where Fudge might be. Then we'll see what we can do to make everyone happy. Is that okay?" Dal looked from Ina Mae to Jason Gold and when they hesitated, went on. "I asked if that's okay?"

His tone brooked no more nonsense and they both nodded. He gestured with his head. "Come on, git yourselves on over there. I can't carry you."

The two angry people stomped ahead of him to the door of the trailer where the woman named Loretta was said to be visiting. It wasn't clear who or if this was connected to the trafficking. It was time to get this nonsense ironed out and all in jail who belonged in jail. Before he fell right flat on his face.

After his second firm knock the trailer door swung open. The porch light flickered on. He peered down at a lovely petite woman. Holy shit, Robert Kimble's wife. What was her name? Anita something. Certainly not Loretta. He'd seen her in the pictures scattered on the floor at the Kimble farm. The woman was dead. Kimble had told him and Mac so when they investigated the Rising Moon cult. Now he finds her and she's almost a spitting image of Bainbridge's wife, who's already in custody with the FBI. No wonder things were confusing. Speechless for a moment, he stared over her shoulder at the shadow hovering behind her. The missing ex-sheriff himself.

Okay, so he was even more astonished.

If when he stepped inside Fudge stood there, all done up like Jessie described, then all he had to do was get backup before the three of them took him down.

"What do you want?"

Instead of replying he tried his innocent look, but he'd never been very good at lying in silence. Something about his expression always gave him away. "I'd like to talk to Robert for a moment if you don't mind."

The puzzle pieces reminded him of a blue sky and dozens of pieces with no clue how to fit them together.

The door swung open all the way. "Right here. Won't you come in?"

Every cell in his body sent out a warning. Step through that door and you're in deep shit. As if to give him room, Kimble backed against the far wall, which was only about ten feet away, holding a drink in one hand, the other in his pocket. A smirk twisted his mouth.

"Come on in, Dallas."

At that moment he made up his mind. The only way he was going through that door was if a gun was in his back. He darted sideways—fell was more like it—to put himself out of the frame. The only protection that gave him was being invisible. The trailer walls wouldn't deter the path of a bullet one iota. All this went through his mind in the blink of an eye, and the first bullet missed him by a hair. Only because he ducked and rolled off the porch, sensing that his injured leg along with the permanently bad one gave him no chance of escaping if he remained on his feet.

He hit the grass below the porch on his back with the .44 in his hand—all of which saved his life. Gunfire riddled holes from the door to the corner of the trailer. Would've cut him in half had he remained on the porch. Soon would if he didn't skedaddle. Rolling to his stomach, he belly-crawled under the trailer next to the Kimbles.

Shock waves from the enormous crack of a .30-30 rifle deafened him. By the time he regained his hearing, people were shouting and pouring out of the dozen or so trailers. Scattering every which way in the park. He peered out of his hidey hole to see Ina Mae standing spraddle-legged in the center of the drive thru, rifle at her shoulder.

The woman was crazy, making a target of herself like that. Even crazier if she killed someone with that gun.

"Get down, get down." His shout was totally ignored. He perked his ears. Dead silence followed the drum roll of echoes. Surely all hell would cut loose any moment. But it didn't. He crept back to the porch and took a quick peek above the floor.

"Come on out here, 'fore I just blow that little domicile of mine to bits. I'll do it, too." Ina Mae would do precisely what she said she would.

He had no doubt of it. He'd seen her in action against two carloads of armed men who once invaded the park looking for him. Ina Mae took no prisoners.

Her threat received no reply. She stepped into the small strip of grass between her and the trailer. Aimed the hunting rifle, shot out the window on the far side of the destroyed door and wall, racked another shell and let go again, blowing a hole halfway between the two.

Nothing. No one. Just a debris of shredded wood and insulation floating slowly to the ground.

Feeling a bit chagrined that he'd remained hidden while Ina Mae cleaned up, he pulled himself to his feet. "Stay back, Ina Mae. Don't go any closer."

He worked his way toward the porch. Before he could climb the cluttered steps sirens approached, blue and white lights lit the night sky, and patrol units lined up alongside four black SUVs, no question who that was. Men poured from every door, guns drawn.

My God. They brought an army.

"Put down the gun. Now."

Hands high, he pivoted. Hell, they were talking to Ina Mae. He holstered his weapon and hip hopped toward her. "Don't shoot. Everyone calm down and don't shoot."

"Get down. Now. On your face."

That wouldn't be too difficult considering he was practically falling on his face with every step. "Deputy Dallas Starr. The lady just took down the bad guys, so please cool it. Okay?"

"Tell her to put down her weapon, Deputy."

He shrugged. Grinned. "Well, I'll certainly try. Ina Mae, it's over. You got em. So let's just lay down our guns. Okay?"

"Son of a bitch." Her expletive sounded far and wide and was followed by laughter from the lawmen lined up, weapons aimed as if waiting to be rushed by armed outlaws. Dal took a couple of steps toward her and fell flat on his face, just like he figured he would. For an instant they must've thought he'd been shot considering the uproar. Someone in the crowd shot into the dark.

"Hold your blamed fire." At last, someone with good sense. Mac walked through the headlight beams. From his vantage point on the ground, and the lights all behind the old man decked out in his new Stetson, he sort of resembled Clint Eastwood in *The Gauntlet* coming to the rescue by wading right into the gathering of armed bad guys. He approached Ina Mae and laid a hand over the stock of her rifle.

"Git your butts around back of that trailer. If there ain't any bodies then you find those two fore they get away." He escorted Ina Mae out of danger. A guy with FBI lettered across his jacket like a bull's-eye invitation lifted Dal to his feet, then joined the deputies and feds in the search.

Reports echoed out of the destroyed shell. "No bodies in here, sir."

Les halted beside Dal. "Hey, buddy, you okay? What happened?"

Dal spread his legs to balance better. "Just a slight hitch in my get-along, deputy. Nothing serious." Be damned if he'd tell him it hurt like the fires of hell. "I could use some help though, if you don't mind. They're long gone, you know."

"Figures. Probably had a car out back and left during the melee." Les took his arm and supported him back to his unit. Tucked him into the passenger side. "Sit tight. We'll clean up the mess. No sense trying to chase after them tonight."

"Damn feds ought to be in pursuit. It's all related to the child trafficking case. Every bit of it. The kidnappings and all." Hell of a time for him to be disabled. But he was alive. And after the past few days that was a blessing.

"You think Randy was involved?"

"Nope, but him being in here with his two kidnapped kids confused the hell out of everything. Made us chase our tails when we needed to be chasing those yahoos who got away last fall. We still don't know who their leader is. And I'll be darned if I can figure out what Marcus has to do with it. But you can bet your bottom dollar he is involved."

Two feds came from behind the trailer, breathing heavily. One gasped out an explanation "They had one of them rigged-out ATVs hid out in the woods. Took off like a Harley on steroids down that mountain yonder." One pointed. "We won't ever catch em in any of these vehicles. It'll take something like one of those goddamned Bradley Tanks to do the job.

Seated sideways in the car seat, feet planted on the ground, Dal held his head in both hands and took deep breaths. Welcome to peaceful Grace County.

Jessie's phone rang before she had a chance to climb in bed after her shower. Don't answer it. Let it go to voicemail. It kept ringing.

"Crap." She lay down the book she'd picked up to read and exchanged it for the phone. "Yep?"

"Got your scanner on?"

"Parker, no I haven't. And if you're going to send me on a wild goose chase this time of the night, then fire me. Or I quit."

"Calm down. Just information only. All the deputies have been out at Hidden Holler. Shots fired. No one hurt. Bad guys got away. Now go to bed, it'll do till tomorrow."

"Parker, damn it." His grin grated in her ear.

"Just thought you'd like to know. Have a good night."

"Was Dal out there?"

"Of course."

"Crap, he's supposed to be taking it easy. I'm getting dressed and going down to the station. If I'm gonna write the story I need to be there while the guys are rehashing what happened. You knew that when you called."

"Up to you. Or I could fire you."

"Or I could quit. Hope you sleep real good." She hung up to the sound of his laughter. And someone else's. Hmm. That Lavender woman. Good for him. That'd show Sam Watson.

Dressed and climbing into the borrowed vehicle, she struggled to start the unfamiliar ignition. It finally hit, she raked around for first and popped the clutch. The rear tires spit dirt that rattled under the rear end. She could learn to love Gertie, but it wasn't a good idea. Parker would want her back. So time to hunt for a new car. Well, next week maybe.

She lounged in the intake room talking to Sam until the guys arrived. Car doors slammed, lights flashed, sirens blipped, and men talked and laughed while the testosterone flowed like water over a dam.

They punched each other, relived the happenings, and started peeling out of their vests even before they reached the locker room. Dal wasn't among them.

"Hey, fellas, what'd you do with Dal?" She flashed half a dozen photos of the deputies and volunteers.

"He opted to go on home. Think he's had enough for a while."

Mike Henley, who was a volunteer deputy as well as an EMT, approached her, popping the top on a can of Coke. "We could sure have used that old Jeep out there tonight. Perps got away down the side of South Mountain on one of those fancy ATVs and Mac is fit to be tied."

"When? Just now?"

"Oh, maybe twenty, thirty minutes why?"

"Well, why isn't someone after them?" She swung her accusatory glare from one face to another.

"Told you, we don't have a vehicle fit to pursue someone down that rough incline."

Her heart pounded in her throat. What a story. Pursuit down a mountainside after the people who had been kidnapping children and selling them. She gathered her stuff and hurried from the station, leaped into the Jeep, and headed for The Five Bs. If she drove, Dal should be fit to go along. In fact, if she didn't ask him there'd be hell to pay. Get this thing wrapped for good and all, and to heck with the feds.

The Bed and Breakfast was dark and quiet when she skid to a stop. Cutting the ignition, she raced up the steps, being as quiet as she could. Her fingers dug around in a pocket for Dal's key. Had she emptied her pockets, put everything in her clean clothes? Yep, there it was. Sticking it into the keyhole, she opened Dal's door and eased it shut behind her.

All she had to do now was keep from getting shot when she went into his bedroom. A snort from the couch drew her up. He was asleep in the living room. Dropping to her knees, she took him by the shoulder. Hissed his name, then repeated wake up several times.

He did, and if he hadn't been a bit injured, he might've knocked her across the room before he realized who she was. Instead, she grabbed his wrist and got his attention real quick.

He sat up fast. "What in God's name you doing, sneaking up on me like that?"

In a few fast sentences she told him she was going down the mountain after the escaped people and did he want to come with her.

"Are you nuts?"

"Probably, and there's no time to decide, one way or the other. You want to go or not? Gertie can do it, you know she can, the way Parker has her rigged. I'm not waiting."

He rubbed his face with the uninjured hand. "Got no choice. Can't let you go alone, and I sure can't tie you up. Just have to put my shoes on. I'm dressed." Muttering, he slipped into a pair of walking shoes and followed her, closing and locking the door behind him.

He settled into the passenger seat. There were times when he took his life in his own hands with this woman. One thing for sure, she kept his adrenaline pumping most of the time.

One way or another.

"Show me where they went into the woods."

He directed her out to Hidden Holler Trailer Park and pointed out the trailer, looking like it had been hit by an IED. Ina Mae came out on the porch when they drove through.

"Stop for a minute." He leaned out. "Seen anyone at the trailer since we all left?"

"Nope, been quiet as a graveyard. You two going down after them by yourselves?"

"I reckon. Is there a trail or path out there that you know of?"

"I'm not much of a hiker. Lots of deer around. Probably an animal trail. Don't reckon I'd want to drive it, though. You be careful, you hear?"

"We will be. Thanks, Ina Mae." He glanced at Jessie, then back to Ina Mae. "Listen, if we don't come back by morning you might call in the cavalry."

The old woman grinned. "Wish I was ten years younger, I'd just go with you. Then you wouldn't need the cavalry. Take care now, you hear?" She slapped the rear panel with fondness as if Gertie were a horse.

Jessie popped the clutch and the last words faded behind them. She followed the perimeter of the property around back of the destroyed trailer while he kept his eyes peeled for an opening where the ATV could've gone through.

"There." He pointed and she crept the Jeep between two large trees. The ATV would leave enormous tire tracks anytime they touched the ground, and there was nothing they could do about that. He could follow them.

For a while she zigzagged in and out, finding openings that led nowhere, till finally he leaned down toward the ground. "Here. The ground's soft enough from the last rain."

After about thirty feet or so the trail took a steep downturn and so did she. It was slow going, inching between boulders, trees, and sheer banks of layered shale that rattled loose behind them. Sometimes the Jeep stood on its nose, other times one side towered above their heads while they came near laying on the other side. Tree branches threatened to drag them from their seat.

Yet, foot by foot the Jeep continued to walk its way slowly down the mountainside.

"What are we going to do when we find them?"

He stared at her. "This is your party. What do you have in mind? An on-the-spot interview?"

"Not exactly. That's why I wanted you to come along. You're the law. I'm just a reporter looking for a story."

"Oh, well then. I'm sure they'd be so happy to be in your story they wouldn't mind that I'm going to arrest them."

A wheel dropped into a deep hole and they rocked to a stop. "What now?" She climbed out, bent down and checked the situation.

"What's the diagnosis?"

"Think if I can back up a bit and throw some rocks in front of the tire it'll climb out."

"Think so, huh? Well, I'll drive and you can do the rock thing." He clambered out, worked his way around the back of the vehicle, and crawled in the driver's seat. Shifted gears and rolled backward as far as he could.

She tossed rocks in front of the tire, until one by one she had a ramp of sorts built. The Jeep walked out of the hole, the rear tire dropped in and right on out. He braked to a stop, swung his legs over the side, and stood up.

"Do you have any idea where we might be headed?"

"No." She climbed onto the hood and stood, checked their surroundings. "I see some farms, houses and barns down below and off to the right. Cedarton should be back over my right shoulder. The trailer park's almost straight behind us. Up on that rise" —she pointed— "see that large roof? That would be Hermitage House. Through those trees and above is the road that comes out on Twenty-three. Yes, I have some idea where we are."

"Down below looks damned wild to me. Probably where those yahoos are hiding out. Almost inaccessible except by horses, ATV, or on foot."

She hopped off the hood and patted it. "And Gertie here."

"And what do you intend to do when and if we catch up to them? If they're cornered, they could very well turn violent. Then what do we do? I'm not exactly in shape to defend us. I suggest we get out of here and get some help."

"You're willing to let the feds get these guys?"

"Sure, why not? It's not like it's a contest or anything. Remember what happened to you the last time you went too far for a story? You almost got some people killed."

Fire in her eyes, she glared at him. "That was different and a long time ago. I'm not betraying anyone for this story. How could you bring that up?"

"Oh, I don't know. Could be I don't want to see you hurt, or myself either for that matter. Come on, Jessie. Let's get on back up the mountain before something bad happens. You can still write your story, once the feds clean up their mess. You don't think they're actually gonna be grateful to you for stealing their thunder, do you?"

"I don't care what they think. I sure don't care if they're grateful or not. Why don't you just wait here for me if you're afraid to face these people?"

"Think a minute. What are you going to do? Jump out of this ugly old Jeep, point your camera at them and yell put your hands up, then tie them to the bumper and drag them out? I don't think you've thought this out. Now that we see where they're headed, we can go fetch some help and do this the right way. The feds can call in a chopper and haul their asses out of there."

She dropped her forehead onto the cross pieces of the steering wheel. Took several deep breaths and looked around. "I know you're right. I just hate to give up."

"Yes, you do. Listen, you said that house up there on that mountain is Hermitage House. If you think about it, when those guys kidnapped Jeff and Alicia it was from over there. We followed them halfway down the mountain before catching up to them. Or at least found the two of them trussed up in that shed."

He sat there thinking for a while. What she'd said and something that had happened when he was up at Hermitage House earlier sort of locked together, like it ought to tell him something if he'd just think about it.

"This morning Alicia didn't want to take me to her office to get the ledger I locked up in her safe last week."

"Did she say why? Maybe she was just busy, or didn't want to leave Jeff for some reason."

"You're probably right. But she sure did look frazzled. And there was a man sneaking around in the garage. Say, does she remind you of anyone?"

Jessie gazed off across the holler toward the huge house on the hill. "Not that I can think of. You know, I think we can get on over there."

"Maybe in the daylight or like one of the deputies said, and maybe with a tank."

"Okay, you win. I'll turn Gertie around the first flat place we find. But come morning I'd like to take her down to that shack from the other side where Alicia and Jeff were kept prisoner. That sticks in my craw that they were kept there, then just left for us to find. Seems no rhyme or reason to it."

He agreed with that, had all along wondered about the reason for it. But sometimes criminals did stupid things for no reason.

It was close to dawn before she coaxed the tough little Jeep all the way back up the mountain to Hidden Holler. They might not have found the encampment, but it sure had been an adventure he wouldn't soon forget. And taking the trip with Jessie had proved to him just how tough she could be.

Ina Mae must've been sitting in the window watching for them because she came out on the porch. "Y'all come in and have some coffee. Made a fresh pot. You can tell me how things went. Don't look like you've got your prey tied to the hood."

Though Dal wanted only to crash for a few hours, they owed her at least a play-by-play of their trip, after all she'd done.

He touched Jessie's arm. "Let's have coffee with her."

"Sure, if you're up to it. You are supposed to be on desk duty, but I haven't seen you behind one yet."

They held hands and walked into Ina Mae's trailer that smelled of cinnamon and coffee. Seating them at her kitchen table, she produced a pan of fresh-baked cinnamon rolls. While regaling her as to their adventure on the mountain, he devoured three of them.

Jessie dropped him off at home and he dragged himself up the stairs, through the apartment, and fell face down on the bed. If he was lucky nothing would happen till he managed a nap, but then that wasn't the way this case was going.

18
CHAPTER

Much as Jessie wanted to visit Colby, who was fussing to be released from the hospital, she talked to him on her cell, then went to the newspaper office to catch up.

Plenty of stories waited for finishing touches. One she wouldn't write yet was the sad tale of Randy and his girls, who had been released to their mother despite his claim she had abused them. She denied it and since she had an order of protection it was a partially-done deal. He could present his side when they went to court. Jessie coached him on getting witnesses who would agree to testify on his behalf, and he returned to Mountain Home to do that. Left to guess who the Wichita call was from, she had to let that go for now. Their story was not something she would ever write. Such personal things didn't sit well with her or Parker. Let them handle this in private.

The fugitives continued to run free in the wilderness while the FBI, the US Marshals, the State Highway Patrol, and Grace County Deputies scoured the countryside trying to find Robert Kimble, Anita Kimble, and other unknown parties responsible for the human trafficking. That was her story and she couldn't resist writing the humorous tale of the capture of Taylor Bainbridge, who claimed to have been cornered by a large tiger. A tale that made Maizie a hero. In itself it presented a sidebar to the feature story, the escape of Robert and his wife from their hideout at Hidden Holler Trailer Park. The shootout involving Ina Mae held its own humor as well. Assuring the readers that the hero tiger responsible for the surrender of the dangerous criminal was well-enclosed in a new escape-proof cage, she wrote a story about July Jones and her animal park and urged everyone to pay all the exotic animals a visit.

She called Ina Mae and Mac for short interviews on the battle that ensued during the escape, leaving Dal till last cause he was still sleeping off the all-nighter out on the mountain. The most difficult thing for her to write, and it had always been so, was her own involvement in the pursuit when she and Dal chased the two fugitives down the treacherous mountain. She finally finished a draft she was only vaguely satisfied with and sent it to Parker's computer. He would buff up her personal stuff. To complete the day, she knocked out a couple of county news stories. By five-thirty those were finished, she had corrected Parker's edits, and called Dal to see if he was awake so she could add his comments.

He was. His quote, "The next time we corner a fugitive we'll give Ina Mae a call to handle the arrest for us," suited her story just fine. While she added it she asked him what he was doing for supper.

"First I'm going out to Hermitage House. There's something I want to check."

"That's not eating. You need to eat."

"Yes, Mother. I will when I get back."

Curiosity got the best of her. "What you going to check?"

"Well, I'm going to pick up that ledger Alicia is supposed to have brought from her office, then I want to take another look at the loft in that barn. Something isn't right up there. Supposedly, those people who used the barn for a meeting place left prior to the Woodsons moving in last fall."

"And so?"

"Well, if that's true there should've been spider webs, dust, mouse turds, pack rat nests. The place looked like someone had been living there. Not even any dust on the floor. So if someone has been using the loft regularly and more recently than that why doesn't Alicia know about it?"

"Wait, you're suggesting that Alicia must have known they were out there on a regular basis? No, you surely don't think she's involved in this?"

"I don't know. It's just something out of the ordinary. I want to check everything from a new perspective. I'll meet you at the Red Bird later."

"Oh no you don't. I'm going with you. I can't believe she'd be in on something so awful as human trafficking. She's an attorney, for goodness' sake. She wouldn't be that ignorant."

"One wouldn't think so, would they? But people who know the law are better at getting away with breaking it."

"And what about Jeff?"

He was quiet for a long beat, then a deep sigh. "I don't know, Jessie, I just don't know what to think. If you're set on coming, okay, but I don't have a search warrant and probably can't get one. I'm just trying to satisfy my curiosity about a few things."

"In other words, sneak in the back way."

"And don't get caught."

"And deny knowing anything if we do, right?"

"Precisely. And the hardest part, you can't write about it."

She hung up and chewed on the end of her pen, then popped her laptop open and googled Alicia Woodson. She was five pages into the attorney's background when a photo came up. A smiling, plump, dimpled woman with red hair. She stared at the face for a long time. Hair color could be changed, fifty pounds could be lost to present an entirely different appearance. It could be Alicia—except where did the dimples go?

Of course it wasn't. How foolish could she get? Alicia had a sister, that's all. No one with any brains would pretend to be someone they weren't in today's world of the Internet. Still, along with Dal's suspicions, it paid to think about it.

Just for the heck of it she moved on to scan through some newspaper articles about Alicia and her law office. One thing was odd. Nowhere was Jeff mentioned. You'd think a woman married to a war hero would make sure he was included in one or two articles about her.

A newspaper photo from eighteen months earlier caught her eye. Three Harper sisters posing at a fund raiser to build a shelter for homeless children in Saint Louis. She hit view and increased the size of the picture. There was Alicia, tall, thin, and a cap of dark hair, identified as Alicia Lynn Harper. The other two sisters were Kimble's wife, the plump redhead, and Bainbridge's wife. Or at least that's who they claimed to be now. Except they were identified in this photo as the Harper sisters.

Holy shit.

Hitting print, she made several copies and stuck them into her file on the trafficking case, then cut and pasted the article and photo into her computer file.

Grabbing up her backpack, she stuffed the hardcopy file inside and went out to the Jeep. Brad almost tripped her running between her feet. He leaped into the shotgun seat and sat, tongue lolling while he stared at her. She had been leaving him alone a lot. His don't-make-me-stay-home look was so cute she nodded, told him okay but he had to behave, and started the Jeep.

It was almost six thirty when she parked on the logging road deep in the woods out back of Hermitage House. Dal wasn't there yet. Should she wait or go on inside the barn? Better wait. He'd have her head if she poked around in what might soon become a crime scene. But the same thing could happen to Dal if the FBI and US Marshals found out he'd been up here.

Brad leaped from the seat and started sniffing the ground, tail going like crazy. "You stick around here, I don't want to have to chase you down."

She tossed her backpack on the hood, climbed up and re-read her files while waiting. Even now she didn't believe Alicia could possibly be involved in this dirty business. And what about her blind husband? How could she do this to him? There was clearly something screwy going on.

Dal must've parked farther off the trail, cause he came up on foot. She almost leaped off the hood when he greeted her.

Dal arrived expecting to see Jessie. She was around somewhere, that's for sure. He shut the car door with a click and hiked along the logging road. Trees thick with summer leaves made a dense barrier between him and the barn out back of Hermitage House. He could easily get in from here without being seen. Maybe that's how whoever used the place managed to come and go. It was possible. He'd go in the back, check the things he wanted to check, and get out without Alicia being the wiser. It wouldn't be dark till eight or so and by then he'd be done and gone.

When he called Alicia earlier, she'd still been in her office in town. He reminded her he wanted the ledger out of her safe and she said she hadn't forgotten. He hated like hell when someone he liked and admired had to be investigated. That was one reason he was checking out his suspicions on the QT. If he was wrong, no harm. If he was right, why then he could go to the proper authorities with his evidence and get a search warrant. What would Jeff do if she was guilty and went to prison? Poor guy had enough troubles without dealing with something like that.

By the time he found Jessie, she sat on the Jeep's hood, long legs stretched out in front of her, reading a file of some kind. He shuffled through the dry leaves so she'd hear him coming. "Hey, you."

She must've been deep in thought, because she jumped and slid to the ground. "Scared me. I thought you were a snake slithering up." In spite of her words, she smiled and gave him a hug. "You're never going to believe what I found."

He stared down into her blue eyes. "Try me."

She picked up the file copy and handed it to him. Kept still while he read the entire article and studied the picture.

"These women. That's Kimble's wife, that's Bainbridge's and this one is Alicia. I'll be damned. I knew about Kimble and Bainbridge being involved. Still can't believe it about Alicia."

"There's more. Look at their names. All have the last name of Harper. Do you suppose they all married in the past eighteen months since this photo was taken? And all three involved in a fund raiser for homeless children. Come on, Dal. How coincidental is that?"

His mind racing in all directions, Dal worked at putting the puzzle together. Finally he gazed toward the barn. "Okay, let's go in there and take a look around without disturbing anything. We should have different eyes. This has been going on for a couple of years that we know of. Probably even more. Kimble was charged last year. The cult has been around for quite a while, but these guys trafficking these kids could have been using this place as a cover even earlier. I want to know how long Hermitage House was for sale and empty. It's a perfect drop-off for the kids and hideout for everyone involved. Who knows for sure how long this has been going on? That ledger should tell us."

She gathered her things and took a few steps behind him, then stopped. "Where's Brad? Did you see him when you came up? He didn't bark."

Dal whistled. Brad came hustling from the direction of the barn, ran a few circles, then headed back the way he had come.

"I think he's trying to tell us something." Dal took off after the dog and Jessie followed along behind him to the rear access door. Brad snuffled around the bottom, then dug at the weathered boards.

Scooping the little pit up in his arms, Dal eased it open. It creaked and he paused. Listened. Jeff had especially good hearing so they had to be extra careful, even this far from the house. Besides, with Alicia in town, there was a chance he could be in the barn.

Brad wiggled. Dal was only a few steps inside when a car pulled up and parked in front of the house. Doors slammed, someone shouted. They both remained perfectly still for several minutes, then climbed the ladder into the loft to search the place more thoroughly.

At the top, Brad squirmed and he set him down. He scurried around, nose to the floor, then settled on an inner wall where he pawed at the floorboards.

"He smells someone he knows. Maybe the guy who kicked him and tossed me in his trunk. See what he's found."

Jessie chuckled. "Probably a dead possum or worse."

He smiled at her reluctance and knelt to pry at the loose boards. Shining his flashlight through the crack revealed a metal box. "Come here. Help me get this board loose."

Together they lifted the plank that wasn't nailed, but rather just placed there. The box was locked. "I don't have anything with me to open this. I do in the car. Bring it along. We can get it open, see what's in it then put it back. There's no dust or rust or cobwebs on it or in this hidey-hole." He pulled out his phone, took pictures, then handed her the box and continued his search. Other than that the place was clean. Way too clean for a barn loft.

She stared down at the box. "I—uh—thought we weren't supposed to disturb anything."

He waved his fingers, then held one over his lips, took out his phone, and dialed Alicia.

She answered on the third ring. "Say, you home yet?" He waited, nodded. "Good, I thought I'd come on out and pick up the ledger. You be home for a while? Ah, good. Give me an hour, I need some coffee to wake me up."

He grinned, told Alicia goodbye, and clicked off. Still grinning, he took Jessie's hand. "Change of plans. We're going where we can watch the house better."

"How about the hay window? It looks out across the yard. From there we can see both the front and back. You think she's going to run?"

"If she doesn't want me to have that ledger she will. She stays put, well, then we'll drive in the front way and pick it up. Change our thoughts."

Together they moved to the front of the barn and the huge opening through which bales of hay were at one time passed when this was a working farm.

"Look around you. The place looks like it's cleaned regularly. Not being a farm boy, it never occurred to me when we came up here to look around. There were a few webs in remote corners. I never thought about it till later."

"So this place has been used regularly all along, even with Alicia and Jeff staying in the house?"

"They had to know it. Know it, hell. They were a part of it."

"Even Jeff? I can't believe that."

While they talked they kept an eye on the house. As it neared dark, lights came on. Dal checked his watch.

"Well, she's hanging in there. Either going to bluff it out or she's innocent. Time we got out of here. Don't use your lights. We can still see to drive out without running into a tree or something. Keep quiet and meet me where the road goes onto the highway."

She nodded and followed him down the ladder and out the back door.

He arrived at the meeting place early. Sitting in the car, thumb tapping on the steering wheel, thoughts whirled about in his head.

The attorney was staying put. Maybe she had something up her sleeve or maybe he was way off base and she was innocent of any wrong-doing. Either way, he'd better be diligent. It took some pretty bad people to pull off human trafficking without batting an eye or worrying where those kids would end up. Right now, if he was right, they'd be cleaning up their back trail and getting ready to disappear. It was odd they'd hung around this long with the FBI and US Marshals on their heels. The good reason had to be the missing ledger. They didn't know where it was till he found it, and it was damned important to them.

He heard the Jeep coming before he saw it. Dusk had fallen under all the trees, and though the sky gleamed like polished silver, the ground was dark as the ashes from a burned-out fire.

Jessie approached and he leaned over, shoved the passenger-side door open. "Park your Jeep here and go with me. We'll just say we're on our way out to eat supper. I could've been wrong about this entire thing. I hope so. We'll just play it by ear and see."

The Woodsons were in the living room and Alicia invited the two of them to come in. "It's good to see both of you again."

Jeff rose and smiled. "I'd like to say the same."

It was quiet for a moment. Dal never knew how to take Jeff's little jokes about his blindness. They were a bit odd.

"We're on our way out to supper. I just needed to pick up that ledger. I'm taking it up to Trey in the morning. It'll pretty well close the case against Kimble and Bainbridge." He chuckled. "Now all we have to do is catch Kimble. He's really been slippery. Do you know his wife?" He aimed a deliberate gaze at Alicia.

"I don't think so." Alicia glanced at Jeff and so did Dal. He shook his head though she said nothing. A slip that filled him with disgust. Bad to steal and sell kids, also bad to pretend to be a blind veteran. He barely held his tongue.

"Well, I'll just take that ledger and we'll be on our way."

She reached under the coffee table and handed him the familiar book he'd hidden in her safe. A bit the worse for wear, it could stand a good dusting. He held it for a moment and studied the couple. They both watched him, or appeared to. With Jeff one could be fooled.

Not sure what to do at this stage, Dal fiddled with the cover, then stuck it under one arm. "Thanks, Alicia, I appreciate the help. See you guys later. Sorry to rush off, but hunger calls."

She walked with him to the door and held it open. Switched on the outside light. "Y'all come back when you can stay longer."

"We sure will. Good evening, Jeff."

Jeff raised a hand and said bye.

The door closed. Dal let out a whoosh. "I might be wrong, but I don't think he's blind."

"Why? How?"

"Never mind yet." He opened the ledger in the middle. The yellow gleam of the bulb revealed only empty pages.

"Son of a bitch." Dal stared off into the darkening evening.

"What? What is it?" He looked furious. "Dal, what's going on?"

He led her out of sight of the windows and handed her the empty ledger. Fingered his walkie. Cursed when he could get no service.

He moved back to the door, knocked. "Hey, Alicia, I forgot something. Alicia?"

The porch light went out. He tried the doorknob, but it was locked. He struggled to get down the steps, but his injuries from the accident tripped him up and he bent over, hands on his knees. "Dammit, dammit."

Jessie flipped open the ledger, which she'd been unable to see properly. In the falling darkness she couldn't make out much. White pages and it looked like there were no entries on them.

"It's not the one I gave her. Looks just like it, but that one was filled with records of their dealings. Names, dates, places, prices. All kept neatly. Enough to convict them. Jessie, see if you can spot them leaving. They're going to run. Probably out the back way."

But he was wrong because before she could head around in that direction, the garage door opened and the big sedan the couple owned screamed backward, did a fast turnaround in the yard, and disappeared down the twisting lane. Parked in the circle in front of the house, it took Dal a while to get in his car and get it started. Jessie hopped in, Brad right on her heels. The sedan's taillights were long gone by the time he maneuvered around to go after them.

He went anyway, turning on the siren and flashing lights. At the highway there was no sign of a vehicle in either direction. He headed away from Cedarton, fingered up the mic, and called in the description of the car.

Jessie kept quiet, scratching Brad's ears.

Dal muttered something she couldn't hear.

"What?"

"She switched them on me. I should have known. I've had a feeling for weeks that something was wrong, I just couldn't put my finger on what it was."

"You're right. He's not blind. Dal, my God. He's driving. It was him behind the wheel. They're both liars about who they are, what they do. This." She held up the ledger. "How did she manage one that looked just like the one you had?"

The radio crackled and Trey came on. "Officer needs assistance. One six zero zero nine Dyer Creek Road."

"That's out past Hidden Holler Park. Might as well answer it." He called in, then headed in that direction. Trey shouldn't be on their frequency. What the hell?

"I think that's awful."

"Well, yeah. What in particular?"

"Pretending to be a blind veteran. Is that against the law or something?"

Dal laughed, a bitter sound. "Not that I know of. I've heard of men going around pretending to be veterans, so no, not unless they mix in fraud or something, but it sure should be. Explains a lot though. They kidnapped themselves. It was all a ruse to make sure we kept looking the other direction. Maybe they thought we were suspicious of them or maybe they were just laying a false trail in case."

He hung a right on Dyer Creek, the rear end swinging wide one way then another. Up ahead, flashing lights lit the sky. A black Denali sat crosswise of the road, one door open. The headlights pointed over a pasture where a small herd of cattle stood mesmerized, staring toward the gathering of humans. Trey was nowhere to be seen.

A shot broke open the night. Dal shoved at his door, hunkered down, and dropped to the ground, .44 in one hand.

"Stay here, Jess. I mean that now. Get low. No nonsense. You got me?"

"I do." She opened her door, wrapped an arm around Brad, ducked down, and rolled out onto the ground and into the ditch.

Shouted voices echoed but she couldn't tell where they came from. A bullet thunked into the front fender of Dal's unit. Mac would be pissed again. Shots were exchanged while she lay in the muddy ditch, the little pit bull whining and struggling to escape. How could anyone see what they were shooting at?

Another deputy's unit skidded into the scene. Burt's. Everything was a scramble of shouts and gunfire. Who was shooting at who? No other cars on the scene. Hope the lawmen weren't aiming at each other.

Thank goodness, the firing finally stopped and a figure rose from amid the milling cattle, revealed by the headlights.

"Hold your fire. US Marshal." It was Trey and he had someone with him. Shoved him along out front. The man stumbled across the pasture, ran into the side of one of the cows, bounced off, and Trey grabbed him by one arm. She squinted to see who he was, but couldn't make much out till they got closer. He climbed through the fence, then Trey followed. Burt rose out of the shadows and grabbed the prisoner by his other arm.

They got closer and she strained to hear the conversation.

"Y'all didn't need to knock me down in the cow shit. I got it all over my clean shirt."

"Teach you to run from a Marshal. What's wrong with you, anyway?"

"I ain't done nothing. Was just out walking."

"And so when I come driving along you decided to take off through a herd of cows?"

"Why'd you chase me?"

"You match the description of someone who tossed Jessie in a car trunk a few nights ago."

"I ain't done nothing like that. She say I did?"

"And you hid behind that poor old heifer and took a shot at me." Trey pushed him up onto the road out of the ditch and Jessie rose up behind them.

"Is that Fudge you got there?"

"Miss Jessie, you tell him. I din't shove you in no car trunk. Why would I do that anyways?"

Trey poked him in the hip. "Good question. Even if you didn't do that, you shot at me. That's a Federal offense, shooting at a US Marshal."

"Aw, wait. I din't know you was that. Is that like one of them guys on the TV westerns?"

Trey shoved him up against the side of the SUV and patted him down. The poor guy was shaking like a leaf, his face and bald head smeared with fresh cow manure.

Dal and Burt came from around back of their two patrol units. "Hell, we thought you were off down yonder. You got him okay?"

Dal moved up behind Burt. Eyed Trey. "What you doing running around out here in God's country?"

Trey laughed. "I can't stay away from this peaceful little corner of Grace County."

The three men laughed some more.

"Which one of you wants this guy? He isn't going in my vehicle all smeared with cow shit like he is."

Dal looked him up and down. "I do any more damage to my car Mac's gonna send me to the house."

"You two 'spect me to haul him in? What'd he do?" Burt held his nose.

"Where do I start? Run off the road, hid in that herd of cows yonder, and took a shot at me."

Fudge slid down the side of the Denali to sit on the ground. "I wish't you guys would decide who gets me so I could rest and get outta these shitty clothes."

"Just what're you doing out here afoot in the middle of the night?" Trey's voice verged on laughter.

"If'n I tell you, will you let me go?"

Jessie wished she had her recorder. This stuff was priceless. But it was in her Jeep with her backpack. Her second wish right on top of that one was that she'd learned some type of shorthand. Did they even teach that anymore? She had no idea.

All of a sudden, Fudge hollered. "Okay, I confess. It was me throwed that paper lady in the trunk, but it was for good reason. They promised I could have a hunnert dollars if I'd haul her away for a while. Sinc't I din't have to hurt her in no way, I figgered what could it hurt? I'd already worked with them carrying those two into the woods and binding em up with duct tape. Never figgered jest why they wanted that done, but got paid for it sose what could it hurt? Now would y'all just stop arguing over who gets me and haul me somewheres where I can get shet of my shitty clothes?"

Pausing to see if the long chatter was done and amazed at what all the man had told them in such a short time, Dal muffled laughter and went to his car.

"I've got a tarp. We could wrap him in it, but I'd as soon not haul him in. He stinks. Besides, Jessie and I were on our way to eat supper when we got caught up in all this. I don't suppose they've caught the Woodsons yet."

"Wait. Jessie's here? Where is she?" Trey took out his flashlight and searched around all the cars till he found her sitting in the ditch, hysterical with laughter, Brad licking her face. He dragged her to her feet and led her up onto the road. "What's so damned funny, woman?"

Between bouts of near hysteria she tried to explain. "If this is an example of law enforcement in Grace County I hope we never have a bank robbery or anything that serious. Things have gone way downhill since we solved that murder a couple years ago." Tears ran down her cheeks. "That was quite a confession, wasn't it?"

Burt opened the door on his car. "I'm going home before I get stuck with hauling shitty Fudge here in." He waved, climbed in, and drove off.

Trey jumped in his big, shiny black SUV, hung his head out the window. "If that don't beat all. Looks like it's you Dal, whether you like it or not. I don't believe this fella has committed a Federal crime after all. Y'all take it easy." The enormous tires spit dust and bits of uprooted weeds behind the fleeing vehicle.

"Aw, Dal." Jessie bent over, shoulders shaking. When she could talk she did. "I think I'll just walk home. It's a nice night and the air smells so sweet. Come on, Brad. Let's go." She headed down the road.

"Wait a minute. That isn't fair." Hands on his hips he watched her go. Blamed woman, anyway.

She waved her hand high above her head. "You boys have a real smelly time."

19
CHAPTER

After Jessie left Dal so he could haul a cow-manure-smeared Fudge in to jail, Brad walked a good distance from her along the road, like he might catch something if he weren't careful. He must've thought she was crazy. Probably cause she couldn't stop laughing. A deep breath helped to clear the tears a bit. What a story Fudge had to tell. Too wild to be made up by a man like him. He might tell tall tales but sorry as she was to admit it, this one had to be true.

She had liked Alicia and Jeff. What a horrible thing they'd done, pretending Jeff was a hero blinded in the war. If she ever got her hands on him, she'd smack him a good one. And Alicia, pretending to be a friend of everyone in the community while leading an organization that carried out the awful things this one did. A slap was too tame for her.

What if they got away? If they did run they'd have to leave the Bainbridge couple behind. They were already in custody of the FBI. It was a cinch Trey Ledger would stay on the trail of the rest of them till he ran them down, no matter how long it took.

By the time she reached her Jeep—still parked at the lane to Hermitage House—her throat was so dry her tongue stuck to the roof of her mouth. The water in her backpack was wet if not cold and she downed half a bottle before noticing Brad panting in the seat beside her. A little pan for him sat under the seat and she poured it full.

She thought about Fudge's story and started laughing again. Brad stared at her as if he'd had quite enough.

Back in Cedarton she pulled into the Red Bird to get something to eat. Even though it was near closing time the place had a good share of folks eating one last piece of pie or drinking coffee. Worn out from the evening's ordeal, she ordered a hamburger to go. Wanda added a patty for Brad. She thanked her and rushed out before anyone she knew could strike up a conversation. There was a story to write and she wanted to get to it. Fudge's confession would have to be left out for now, but she'd go ahead and write it while it was fresh in her mind. Hopefully he'd be charged right away and she could finish it.

Too bad she couldn't quote all of his precise words, like shit, in the paper. Censoring them left out some of the humor.

While consuming the hamburger she jotted notes, finished off a piece of cheesecake from the fridge, and spent several more hours writing. Two Pepsis and two cups of coffee later, she closed her computer, took a long shower, and trooped off to bed. Lying there staring out the window, her thoughts drifted to Dal transporting the cow-shit-covered Fudge to jail. Would he ever forgive her for deserting him?

The phone woke her early the next morning. Half asleep, she fumbled around till her fingers found the thing. Must be Dal, but the voice was Parker's asking her in a teasing tone what time it was.

"Not funny. What's going on?"

"I've been getting phone calls half the night. Is it true the Woodsons are the head of our band of traffickers?"

"Uhm, partly. Well, yes. It's the Harper sisters in reality."

"Who the hell is that?"

"We don't know yet if they are actually married to the men or not. The feds have Amanda Lee supposedly married to Taylor Bainbridge. The others are still in the wind. Alicia Lynn Harper known to us as Woodson and Anna Louise Harper who in all probability is Robert Kimble's so-called wife. It's not all been straightened out yet."

"Do we have a story?"

"Yes indeed. I'm going to polish it this morning. Cross our fingers they pick up the Woodsons and the Kimbles. Oh, and by the way, Jeff is not a war hero nor is he blind. So far there's no sign of Robert and Anna since they took off from Hidden Holler Trailer Park in a hail of bullets. They headed down into the Red Mountain Wildlife Management area on this honker of an ATV. Dal and I tried to follow them in your Jeep but we couldn't get all the way down there. They got away from us slipping through some narrow crevasses."

"So the Bainbridges are the only ones in custody?"

"Yep, and I'm going to see if I can interview the two of them as soon as it's daylight."

"Sounds like I slept through the best part of this misadventure. Who's going down into the wilderness after them?"

"Last I knew Trey would lead with Dal, Burt, and Les. The FBI backed off. Said they aren't equipped for that sort of pursuit. Guess they didn't want to scratch up their shiny black SUVs. Have to wonder where their helicopter is. But you can bet they'll take plenty of credit when Trey and them bring in their prey."

"Surprised you're staying behind."

She chuckled. "I have a couple of great stories to work on, and hopefully more when they return."

"Glad you're being sensible about this."

"Why Parker, I'm always sensible. Oh, by the way, I'm afraid we put a few dents and scratches on Gertie's body. Suppose you'll have to dock my pay for a while."

He groaned, sucked in a deep breath. *"Well it was for a good cause. We'll probably win some awards from the APA for the stories."* He paused a beat or two. *"Just how bad is she?"*

"Well, we didn't break anything."

"You couldn't break anything. She's too tough for that. Go back to sleep and I'll see you when you come in. You ought to take time to go car shopping."

"As soon as the insurance check comes." And this mess is behind us. Taking time to look for a car in the midst of so much excitement wasn't on her list.

After disconnecting, she lay wide-eyed and finally gave up going back to sleep. The sky turned a salmon-hued silver along the eastern peaks and she crawled out of bed, dropped a night shirt over her head, and went to the kitchen to make some coffee. She was sitting on the deck drinking it when a pair of headlights approached down the lane. Someone else couldn't sleep either. Brad barked until the car lights shut off. Then he was quiet.

Must be Dal wanting a bit of loving before they took off in pursuit of the Kimbles and Woodsons. Clothed in the warmth of a summer breeze, she ran her fingers along the inside of her thigh and shivered with need. He had a key, so she didn't get up to go let him in. Brad wasn't barking. Dal must've scooped him up in his arms. All remained quiet. After a while she went to the railing, leaned over it to peer toward the front of the house.

"Stop kidding around, sweetie. I'm out on the deck."

Only then did a silhouette of the car catch her eye. It wasn't Dal's. Something crawled up her back bone and she rushed into the house, through to her bedroom where she kept the .38 at night. She didn't make it to the bedside table. Arms locked around her, tossed her face down onto the bed and pinned her arms behind her.

Not again. This was getting annoying. Kicking and clawing got her nowhere. Why had Brad stopped barking? He always guarded the front door. That was his job. She got a knee partially free and drove it into her attacker's stomach. He backhanded her and she saw stars but continued to fight back. Someone else came into the room and together the two subdued her. The ripping of tape and her wrists were bound. Then her ankles. Because she continued to yell they plastered a piece over her mouth. Exhausted and weary of being poked and smacked and jabbed she went limp.

Who was this? No one had a reason to grab her now. The only sounds were grunts and grumbles until they had her all taped up and ready to deliver. They picked her up by the feet and shoulders and toted her to the front door. In the weak bar of light that crossed the porch and came inside the cabin, Brad lay sprawled on the floor. She hunched her body and tried to squirm away one last time. If they'd killed her dog she'd get every last one of them.

"Stop that or I'll put you out." The voice was male and gravelly.

To hell with him. She bowed up, kicked out with both feet, and the world flashed bright for a second, then went black.

On his way to join Trey and the deputies for their appointed meeting at the station, Dal made a quick stop at the newspaper office. Surely Jessie and Parker would be there early considering all they had to write about.

Parker was in the break room brewing a pot of coffee. He glanced up when Dal bulled his way through the new door.

"Looks like we need to reinforce that door."

"Or just leave it propped open like Wendy does. Jessie's not here yet?"

"Nope. Figured she would be. I called and woke her about four this morning and she was going to come in early to get started. Haven't heard from her. Fixing to call her."

Dal dug out his phone. "I'll do it. You finish with that, it already smells good." He listened to the ring until her voice mail came on. He shrugged, disconnected, and dialed her landline this time. Usually she'd answer the second ringing in a row. But she didn't.

"Probably forgot to turn her cell on when she left the house. She hardly gets a signal out there." Parker glanced up from the brewing coffee.

"I tried her landline the second time. No dice."

"Ah, she's on her way. I'll tell her you came by. Come have a mug of this before you take off. You're gonna need it. How you getting down into the valley?"

"Nick is going with us and he has an ATV that's on steroids. Trey has one as well. We hope to arrest the entire gang. By God if we do they'll walk out in cuffs. It's gonna be a long, rough day."

"Recovered from your injuries?" Parker handed him a steaming mug.

"Ah, yeah, more or less. We have to get these people before they settle somewhere else and keep right on stealing and selling kids. It makes me sick to even think about it." He glanced at Parker. "Maybe she went right to Fayetteville to interview the Bainbridges."

Parker nodded. "Could be. I'll check up there after she's had time to get there. If she's not there, Mac can check on her. I presume he's staying here."

"Yep. He's got no business traipsing around in that rough wilderness. Besides he and Tinker have to keep watch over Cedarton."

Parker appeared calm enough, but Dal didn't like one bit not hearing from Jessie. She just didn't stay out of touch like that. Something might have happened to her. But he couldn't be in two places at one time and she often reminded him that she could handle herself. She'd light into him with both feet if he went chasing after her instead of going with Trey to help capture the Harper sisters and their bunch. When he crawled back in his unit the metal box on the floor caught his eye.

Well, shit. In all the excitement he'd forgotten all about finding that under the floorboards in the Woodson's barn. He lifted it up onto the seat. It was secured with a padlock and he didn't have time to mess around with it. There was a heavy screwdriver in the glove box. He nearly tore the lid to shreds getting inside the thing. Must be something damned important hidden in there.

The box was empty save for a single folded sheet of paper. Unfolded, it revealed three long lines of numbers. That didn't make any sense. Could be bank account numbers. Not worth much without the name of the bank. It must be important to the group, though, or they wouldn't have hidden it so well. Odd there'd been no mention of it. He folded the paper small enough to slip in his pocket, dropped the damaged box onto the floor, and headed for the sheriff's office.

He hurried inside and ran down Mac. "Have you heard from Jessie?"

Mac looked up from his desk. "Today? Nope. Why?"

"Not sure. Would you see if you can find her? Or make sure she shows up at the paper this morning? She's not answering either of her phones."

"Don't sound good, does it? You go on with those men. They're liable to need you. I'll make sure and run her down, see she's safe."

Dal nodded. "Don't tell her I sent you out looking. She doesn't take kindly to being babysat."

Mac chuckled. "That's sure the truth. I won't. I'll think of something."

He told Mac goodbye and joined Trey and the deputies in the parking lot. Nick waited there as well—with a huge ATV. Holy shit. They needed to buy some of those dudes for the sheriff's department, considering where they had to go sometimes.

He climbed in next to Nick and Les crawled onto the seat behind them. Burt and Trey mounted Trey's. Like Dal told Parker, if they captured all four, they'd handcuff them, rope them together, and drag 'em out if they had to.

The first part of the journey talk was sparse and when someone did say something they had to shout over the noise of the ATVs. Despite mufflers, they were nearly as loud as motorcycles. It took about two hours to reach the crevice that had stopped Dal and Jessie in Parker's Jeep the day before. Nick's vehicle barely skinned through, but Trey's smaller one had no problem. By that time the sun had cleared the mountain peaks and the air heated fast. Everyone sipped at their water bottles, their soaked shirts clinging to their skin.

Around noon, with the sun hanging high and hot, a wide open spot between some large sugar maples offered a good stopping place. The men were all red-faced and bathed in sweat. Dal's injured leg ached from the rough ride and he found a fallen tree to sit on. Nick sat beside him. Trey, Burt, and Les opted for a spot to stretch out in a patch of shaded grass.

Dal leaned back against a tree. "Haven't seen you in a while."

Nick had a sack-full of trail mix and passed it around. "I've been gone since January, but it's sure good to get back to a milder climate."

Dal couldn't help but wonder where Nick disappeared to off and on. He figured he was a contractor who hired out for black ops the way he handled himself. Though it seemed a bit farfetched, Jessie agreed with him.

"Yeah? Been in cold country?" Dal ate his sandwich and munched on the nuts he'd picked from the trail mix.

"Oh, hell yeah. And it's beyond me why anyone would want to live like that." He shivered. "Forty below will freeze your gizzard right out of you."

Trey chimed in. "Sounds like where they send Marshals who fuck up."

Les chuckled at Burt's remark. "Good spot for that one FBI guy. You see him fumble his gun the other night?"

Dal joined in. "Well, maybe you ought to consider a milder climate for your trips."

"Maybe so. We gonna get into a real predicament with these folks?"

Well, so much for being nosy. The man just wouldn't talk about his other life.

Mac had deputized Nick for this trip, and it wasn't the first time. Still, he refused to hire onto the Grace County Sheriff's Department. His value as a trained mountain climber and rescuer made him a good choice for a deputy and they needed to replace Duggan. With Colby laid up they were short two.

"I don't look for it to get too bad, though we did have a shoot-out at Hidden Holler Trailer Park yesterday. It was more like everyone was shooting at rocks and trees and trailers rather than people. Ina Mae all but shredded the trailer where the Kimbles were hid out, but by then they were long gone down this mountain. She conked one old boy on the noggin. Turned out to be a Nolton County Deputy."

Nick laughed. "Sounds like you ought to hire her on."

"Don't it though?" Dal finished his food and drank from his thermos. Nick had brought along a few gallons of water strapped to the back of his ATV and they all hydrated before mounting up and heading on down the mountain.

Soon as they were moving, Dal tried to call Jessie again but he had no signal. She was probably pecking away at her computer by now, happy as a reporter with the story of her life. He'd have to trust Mac to see to her.

The ride trussed up on the floor of the van proved to be hell for Jessie. After getting underway, one of the men crawled in the back, gripped her shoulders, and shook her hard.

"Where is it? What did you do with it?"

She shook her head. "What? Where is *what?*"

What was going on, anyway?

"The box. You took it from the barn. We saw you. What did you do with it?"

"I don't have it." Huh. They were watching her and Dal, but Alicia and Jeff were in Hermitage House then. So the other couple with them now had to be Robert and Anna Louise.

"We know that." The woman's strident voice took over and she slapped Jessie with the flat of her hand, then the back. Once, twice, three times.

"We'll find it." The man—no doubt Robert Kimble—hit her again and she blacked out.

When she came to, her mouth had been taped. They were on a gravel road, climbing a lot of the time before they headed down a bad excuse for a road. The van rattled and shook and coughed, while she bounced up and down, helpless to hold on. The couple carried on a conversation in a low rumble she couldn't understand.

After what seemed like forever, they pulled over and stopped. Walked away until their footsteps faded. She was dying for a drink, her throat coated with cotton. Kept telling herself not to cry. Easy to suffocate, taped like she was. Where were they taking her and why? And where had they gone? In a short time they returned, but now there were at least four of them, two women, two men. Separate voices in tone.

Well, well. The gang was all here. Everyone gathered. Now was time for Dal and the deputies to show up. Sort of like the cavalry arriving to save the day.

They climbed back in the van. She kicked the floorboards hard over and over. At last one of them paid attention.

"Shut up back there." It was a man. Jeff? She wasn't sure. "The deputy must have it, then."

"We'll get it."

They thought Dal had their precious box, or its contents. All she could think about, though, was water. She tried to say drink or water past the duct tape, but someone swatted her a good one and told her again to shut up. This time the strident female voice. She'd never met the Kimble woman. Wished she still hadn't. It was so hard not to cry from fear and anger. She sucked air through her nose, taking several deep breaths, then tried to relax. Best if she stopped fighting. It was only making matters worse. They'd have to take her out soon, then maybe she'd have a chance to get away. If she listened carefully she might hear some of what was said, get an idea what they planned.

Their ride might be one of those VW buses the hippies used to drive, all painted in crazy designs. A few words of their conversation came through between the noises made by the old van. Nothing that helped much, though. Stuff like real soon, gotta get it, don't kill. That last one gave her hope they would turn her loose.

The road grew rougher and rougher, beating her poor body black and blue. Branches scraped the sides, the noise sending chill bumps up her spine. At one point they crossed a stream, went a ways, then drove through another. The sound of water splashing drove her to distraction. What she would give to roll around in that creek. Suck up mouthfuls of the cold spring water. She had to have a drink and soon.

A long time on level ground. Must be in the valley. Voices raised, like cheering. Came to a stop. Doors opened, closed. Surely now they'd drag her out. Dump her on the ground. The words don't kill kept echoing. Please give me water. You're killing me. She could only think in bits and pieces. Or not at all.

No one came to open up and let her out. Noises died away. No. They were leaving her here. They couldn't. She bent her knees and kicked the side of the van. Once, twice, three times till her legs tingled, her knees crackled with pain.

Don't leave me here. Please don't leave me. Thoughts faded.

Silence so deep it made a noise in her ears. Her head ached. She couldn't swallow or see or move. Dear God, she couldn't move.

Hands lifted her, carried her, laid her down in grass. What were they doing? The only noise she could make was weak, a whisper. Fingers scraped the tape off her skin, mouth first. A cold wet cloth against her lips. She sucked at it like a baby at a nipple. More, more. She could say nothing, just purse her dry, cracked lips till the cloth was returned, cool and wet.

No one spoke. Fingers scraped some more, then something cut the tape away to free her wrists and ankles and last of all, remove the blindfold. Released she rolled around to sit up, opened dusty eyelashes and squinted through foggy vision. Footsteps scuttled away through rocks and gravel.

Around her the shade from an enormous oak tree. A bottle of water sat nearby. Stirred up dust lingered in the windless air. Alone. Not a sign of anyone. Though she never heard the van leave, it was gone. The sun lay behind the western mountains. She must've been out for a while. Getting to her feet wasn't possible so she sat there, leaning on one arm, holding the bottle to her mouth. The cloth lay in her lap and she used it to clean her face and wipe the dirt from her eyes.

Where was she? How would she find her way out? Nothing looked familiar. The ground around her was well trampled. They'd been here, all of them at one time. But they were gone. Vanished like fog in a windstorm.

Strange how they avoided injuring her. Why? They wanted that damned metal box she and Dal had dug from the floorboards of the barn. Then something happened that sent them fleeing before they could get anything out of her. Someone must be coming. Dal and Trey and the deputies. That had to be it. And with a caravan, even a small one, it would take a good head start to lose them. They'd been so sure they could find the box. That must mean they would hang around. At least one or two of them. So she had hope anyway, that in the end the men would catch them.

She was so godawful tired. Everything hurt. Though she stretched her legs and arms, they continued to prickle. She'd been taped up all day. The sky flared in a glorious sunset. Streaks of gold and red slashed through lavender and ash. Her eyes drifted closed. She jerked them open, but couldn't keep them there.

An ashy blanket drifted over, covering her, soothing her into a cool and silent darkness.

It was close on to dark when the two ATVs made it to the bottom of the rugged mountainside. The valley lay around them splattered in shadows and light. They dismounted from their rides. Each man carried heavy duty flashlights, side-arms, and Nick came equipped with his tool bag of special weapons.

"I hope we don't have to use any of those." Dal gestured to the closed locker. He'd seen what was in it one day last fall when they first began the pursuit of these monsters.

Nick glanced at him. "Appreciate it if you didn't—"

Dal waved away his request and they joined Trey, Burt, and Les to discuss what came next. As a US Marshal, Trey was technically in charge, so they would defer to him. Though what in the hell they could do in the dark of night was anyone's guess.

Nick removed a large zippered bag from the carry-all, opened it, and handed out head gear to each man. Trey examined his. "Night vision goggles. Hell, man."

"Don't ask. We can keep moving and catch these bastards. That is, if you have no objections, Marshal."

"I'm doing my best to think of any reason we shouldn't, but just can't come up with one. Feel like maybe you ought to swear us all to secrecy first, though."

"Yeah, well, I'll deny it, whatever comes out when this is over. I want these bastards as bad as you do, maybe more." His long delicate fingers rubbed over the headband. "My sister disappeared ten years ago and we've never found her. No matter who I talk to or where I search, she's gone like a feather in a light summer breeze." Nick turned away.

Dal cleared his throat. "Sorry man. I didn't know."

The others tried to sympathize. Strange how emotional tough men could be in certain situations. In the silence that followed, they fiddled with the night vision equipment, fitted it on their heads.

Nick helped them adjust the goggles and showed them what they'd be looking at. "If anyone flashes a bright light they turn off automatically. Ambient light or totally dark, these babies work just fine."

A few minutes later, rigged out to track and travel, the men stretched arm's-length apart across the small valley, an idling ATV on each end following the trail left by the fleeing group. An occasional footprint or marks from a tire in soft earth, easily spotted through the goggles, led them on into the darkest of night.

Be good to get some idea how many there were. About a mile along the valley floor, Trey spotted a bundle the size of a human curled knees to chin under a good-sized tree.

He signaled the line to halt. "Could be a trap. Anything comes at me shoot it." Gun in hand he trotted toward the still figure.

Dal crouched on one knee, muzzle of his .44 pointed at the sky while he scanned the surrounding countryside. All was quiet. Even the wind kept still. Trey stopped about ten feet from the bundle.

"Hey. Get up from there. Slow and easy." The person stirred, sat up.

"Help me." A woman's voice, croaking as if she had laryngitis. White bare hands clawed at the sky. "Who are you? Don't shoot me."

Clearly she couldn't see them like they could see her. She didn't appear to have a gun.

"Keep the lady covered, guys. Could be a trap. I'll get her."

Dal moved closer so he had a better view. "What's your name?" He strained to see her when she crawled to her feet and stared right at him. "Jessie, that you? This is Dal."

She stumbled toward him, reaching out, crying his name, still in a voice barely recognizable. He started for her.

Trey coming at them from the side, gun pointed at her. "Keep your eyes open, men. See anything coming at us, shoot it."

What the hell was she doing down here? Sleeping in the middle of the field, looking bedraggled and frightened. He reached her, caught her under the arms when she tripped and fell forward.

"It's Jessie, guys." He held her close, supporting most of her weight. "What're you doing out here? How'd you get here? You okay?"

Dal was barely in shape to hold up his own weight, let alone hers. Trey moved in, swept her into his arms before she hit the ground. But he didn't feel any better for Trey doing it. Pissed him off, in fact. Still, that was no way to be, under the circumstances.

"Sit in the ATV, Dal, and take her. Rest of you, eyes open." He did and Jessie wrapped her arms around his neck when they were settled in the seat.

"You okay, hon?" He nuzzled her neck, the goggles getting in the way.

Trey slipped them off Dal's head. "Find out what happened soon as she can talk. Give her some water. We need to keep moving. We're exposed, though I think if they were going to hit us they'd already have done it. Dal, you want to load her up on one of these babies and take her home?"

She squirmed and looked up. In the dark she couldn't make out faces, so Trey fitted the night vision goggles onto her head. "Now, baby, look at me and Dal. You're okay, but we need to get back on their trail or they'll get away. Now, you up to going with us or you need one of us to take you home?"

She took a drink from the bottle one of the men handed her, shook her head. "I want to go with you. Listen, there's four of them. The Kimbles and the Woodsons, far as I could tell blindfolded. They want the box we took out of the floorboards of the barn." She dragged in a long breath and drank more water. "Those bastards trussed me up and dragged me around all over the place. Didn't give me water or food, didn't even let me pee."

Everyone chuckled nervously.

She grabbed Trey's wrist. "Take me with you. I want to watch them go down."

"She can ride with me." Nick spoke for the first time since they'd run across her.

"Okay with everyone?"

Low spoken yeahs went around the group.

They loaded her up in Nick's vehicle, everyone took advantage of the stop to take a nature's break, and they were on their way in just a few minutes. All determined not to go home till they had the four fugitives in custody.

20
CHAPTER

Was she dreaming? Still lying in the dirt abandoned by those awful people instead of riding with Trey on his ATV? Maybe they'd come back and get her when they couldn't find the box they wanted. And she'd wake up and this would all be make-believe. No way to explain how Dal and Trey and the other guys found her except that it was imaginary.

But wait. When you dream you don't reason out what's happening. So this was real, weird as it seemed.

The men wore goggles that made them look like space aliens. In the night sky a fingernail moon dragged a bright planet in its wake.

What is its name? Can't remember.

On they moved, hauling her along. Bumped over rocks and through potholes. The moonset left a scattering of stars brilliant in the purple-cobalt night. Dal was one of the men hunting those bastards. She could think of nothing else to call them, for they had ruined the lives of uncountable families, of children no one else wanted and who would never be missed. And on top of that they'd killed her dog. Her faithful, so-ugly-he-was-cute dog. Poor little Brad. Tears poured for everyone and she swiped at them with anger.

They came to a halt. Why? The night simply looked dark to her, except when she squinted. A light in the woods off to the right, swinging like a lantern being carried. Even without those ugly goggles, she could see that. If they meant to hide, odd they would show themselves by carrying a light. Didn't make sense.

The machine she rode on shut down and the driver crawled off. "Stay here, Jessie. Be quiet and let us handle this. Okay? Promise me?" Trey, it was Trey.

"Yes, yes." Her words a hiss. "Go."

They left her there with the huge all-terrain vehicles. Engines ticking, cooling off in the cottony silence of the night. Even nocturnal critters feared humans and their fights. Laid low lest they become involved in the inexplicable violence.

Marcus. Marcus was real, a strange man with powers that frightened Dal. Caused him to doubt his own abilities. But whose side was he on? Was he even involved? She would ask Dal once it was all over.

Hidden in the thick trees, Dal lifted the goggles, stared at the swinging dim lantern light. What the hell? He crept to where Trey hunched behind a large tree.

Trey was good. He heard him coming. Spoke over his shoulder. "What do you think?"

"Where was the last place you saw them, other than that light?"

"There in those trees. They disappeared. But there are plenty of places to hide from our night vision. They must've figured it out. Big trees everywhere."

"Signal the others. It's a trick, a trap. We need to discuss this."

Dal nodded at the marshal, deferring to him. Only five of them, they could take these four but only if they could see them.

Trey finally spoke. "Do you see anything but that swinging light? Look all around."

A prolonged silence before all five agreed they saw nothing.

"It's hung on a low tree branch. A lure." Nick stared at the others, the green of his glasses shimmering in the dark.

Dal stood his ground, still as possible to pick out any movement. A gust of wind puffed up, rustling the leaves. Dried the sweat on his forehead. Tossed the lantern in jerks. He waited for Trey to speak again.

"Listen, they get out of here, we're not apt to find them again. This is our last chance to get these bastards. I say we force the issue. But I don't want anyone to get hurt. They've gone to ground keeping trees between us and them. No way they escaped. They're in there somewhere. What do the rest of you think?" Trey looked at each in turn, like he wanted a vote.

Dal could hold his opinion no longer. "You're all smart. What would you do in their situation?"

"Go to ground." Nick was the first to say it, but the others agreed.

"It's what Jessie did when she got away from some of this very bunch. She found a hole and crawled in it. Barely breathed. You run, they hear you, see you, catch you. We all know that."

"But what's with the lantern? Why lure us right to their hiding spot?"

Shrugs all around.

The goggled eyes stared at Dal, heads nodding. He almost laughed. All five of them, goggles pointed at each other, heads nodding.

"Only if they're prepared to stand and fight. Opinions?" Nick studied each of the bobble heads.

"Thought we are as dumb as them, would think they'd gotten away. Fooled us."

"He's right. Come on, *think*. Where was the last place any of us spotted these guys before they went out of sight?"

"We won't find em this way. They're right here. Let's settle back and outwait them."

"We quit making noise they'll come out."

"Or we lose them."

"To hell with that. I say flush them."

"Okay, a vote. We go stomping through here arm's-length apart, never mind the noise till we either flush them or step right on one of them or we wait them out."

Again the bobble heads. One by one they'd had their say. Anonymous in the night. It didn't matter who thought what, they'd voted. Dal would go along with what the other three wanted. They all knew more about this kind of manhunt than he did. Alleys and dark streets of Dallas called for a different attack altogether.

So it began. From tree to tree, covering ground fast, feet kicking up leaves and stomping, making too much noise. Like trying to scare out rabbits or quail, only this time it was human prey.

And eventually one broke and ran. Nick was the closest and he hit waist high. She screamed as she went down and the others exploded from their holes, leaves flying as they came from under their covering, scrabbled upward. Not accustomed to being hunted, they gave in to their fear, shouting as they were taken down one by one.

All four.

A bunch rolling around stirring up leaves and rocks and dirt. Grunting, cursing, hollering.

Dal soon had the two women cuffed, and Nick and Trey had grabbed the men.

Seating them on the ground, Trey knelt in front of the group. "Are there any others?"

The four stared, refused to say anything.

"Okay, let's do another check, side by side. There may be more buried in here. Then if we don't find them, I say we take these folks in. They're the ones we really want anyway."

Dal shook his head in wonderment watching another thorough search. If these folks had been armed someone would've gotten hurt. Despite the damage these people had done by kidnapping children and selling them, they refused to take a shot at anyone. An attorney, Alicia, led the pack, so she would've advised them not to shoot anyone. Hell, they probably thought that kept them from being killers. Still, they might as well be killing these kids with what they were doing to them. In some cases, the kids probably felt they'd be better off dead.

Yet Bainbridge believed they were providing better lives for those foster kids they'd grabbed by selling them to rich people. Had actually said so. What an asshole. No doubt they all believed it. But Alicia had to know better. She was in it for the money and figured they'd get away with it, cause she thought she was smarter than everyone else.

Trey did what Dal had said they would. He tied the four fugitives to the back of his ATV, one behind the other on a rope, and forced them to follow the two machines. Clamber over rocks and up inclines all the way out of the deep valley. It took the rest of the night.

Later, Trey remarked to Jessie that he wasn't really cruel to them cause they had plenty of water and he did let them stop to pee. Dal broke up over that.

Back in Cedarton, with the sun rising, Dal took Jessie home after delivering their catch to Mac to hold in the county jail for the FBI and letting everyone know they were home.

Safe in his car, she leaned back in the seat, stared out the window, tears wetting her cheeks. "If they killed Brad, they'll be sorry."

He patted her leg. "He's going to be okay, he's a tough little guy."

"I hope so." She sniffled and he could do nothing but rub her leg and get her home. She'd had a rough time. Maybe the little dog would be okay. He hoped like hell he was. Weary beyond words, he pulled up in the yard and turned off the engine. Made no move to get out. She sat there as if afraid to get out and learn the truth.

He squeezed her hand, then opened the car door. Listened for a bark, heard nothing. Dammit. He whistled, called Brad.

Heard something. Barking? Whining? Not sure, but something.

Rounding the front of the car, he pulled open her door, helped her out. "Call him, I heard something."

Instead she stumbled toward the house, sobbing.

There, he heard it again. The pit bull must be shut up in the house. He ran to the door, shoved it open, and Brad shot through his legs and leaped into Jessie's arms. Licked away her tears. She continued to cry while she hugged the ecstatic little dog.

Dal wrapped his arms around both of them, laughed with her. Together they went inside and he shut the door.

At last Jessie was able to put the dog down. While he ran excited circles throughout the house she opened the fridge, took out a Pepsi for each of them. Refilled Brad's water and food dish. Wanted to feed Dal and herself. Her stomach growled but she was too weary to drag out something to eat. Not much in there, as usual.

Instead of waiting for her to take him his drink, he moved to stand behind her, chin on her head, arms around her waist. "Which do you need the most? Shower, food, sex?"

She tapped him in the belly with her elbow, all she had the energy for. "The one thing you forgot."

"What?"

"Bed."

He chuckled, raised one hand to tickle her breast with a thumb. "Okay. This order. Shower, bed, sex, food later. Much later."

Shifting around so they were face to face. "I like it." She placed the two cans of pop back in the fridge, took his hand, and led him into the bathroom where they undressed each other, turned on the hot water, and stepped into the shower. Who held who up was anyone's guess. Once they were wet they soaped each other, sponged clean, and padded into the bedroom, each carrying a towel.

The night was hot, the windows open to a nice breeze. Wind-dried, she rolled into his arms and fell asleep with his lips touching her throat.

She awoke alone to the delicious aroma of frying bacon. Must be dreaming for sure. But the other side of the bed was empty and someone was humming a song, sort of out of tune, so it must be Dal. He talked prettier than he sang.

Stretching, she took her time sliding off the bed and slipping into shorts and a t-shirt, walked barefoot to make a stop at the bathroom, then on into the kitchen, practically drooling. Had to be someone besides Dal in the kitchen. Maybe Tinker, but he stood at the stove, bare behind toward her, apron strings tied in a bow above his butt cheeks. Turner in one hand he directed an imaginary orchestra.

"You might set the table." He must've heard her coming, turned to reveal a frilly apron covering his manly parts.

"You're cooking. And what's that?" She pointed at his get-up and broke out laughing.

"No need in being sarcastic. Didn't want hot grease spattering on my man." He gestured down his front.

"Well, in all the years I've known you, not once have you so much as turned on a cook-stove."

"I kept hoping you'd learn, but I've given up. Plates, glasses, silverware, and you might grab the orange juice."

She froze, stared at him a long moment, then tugged the fridge open. "We don't have any orange… you went *shopping?*" She covered her mouth. "Please tell me you wore clothes." Still unable to stifle a hysterical reaction.

"Yep, I did. It was either shop or sit here and starve. Get busy, woman, this is ready."

Under her breath gulps of noise that could be mistaken for choking. She took out the juice, some butter and jelly, dug around through the well-stocked appliance, then came away and set the table.

He brought a plate of bacon and over-easy eggs to her, then took a plate of toast from the oven. "Keeping it warm."

Her reaction continued when he sat down across from her. "Well, come on, help yourself and pass it to me."

Another full minute passed while she helped herself and gave him the food. "I don't believe this."

Laughing, he spread butter and jelly on two pieces of toast and handed her one. "Never thought I could rend you speechless."

"Rend me speechless? Where did you put Dal?"

"Locked him in the bedroom closet. Now eat, cause we have that one thing on the list we have to handle. Admit it'll be out of order, but hey, when it comes to sex I'll take it in any order I can get it. From you, that is. You'll note I come dressed and ready."

In that moment, holding the toast in one hand, a piece of crisp bacon in the other, she loved him more than she'd ever realized. But she couldn't say anything, just kept looking at him. Never had she seen him like this.

"What?" He grinned.

Before she could reply Brad jumped on her leg and begged for a piece of the meat. She gave it to him and grabbed another.

Why in the world had he kept his cooking ability from her for so long? Not to mention this sense of humor, this craziness she found endearing. Surely not because he thought she might learn how to cook in the interim. Whatever the reason, it was hilarious and she couldn't help but joke with him for the remainder of the delicious breakfast.

Together they washed and dried the dishes, then he took her hand and led her to the bedroom.

Her breasts were most beautiful, fascinating because she kept them disguised, not like some women who put their pair on display. The rest of her body wasn't exactly shameful either. It too was a well-kept secret, so much so that each time they made love he was spellbound at the loveliness she kept so well hidden.

Dal traced around each nipple with the tip of his finger, then trailed down between her ribs to the center of her belly. She shivered under his touch and goose bumps broke out along the path he drew. Her body was surprisingly hairless, with a small golden patch in the triangle between her thighs. He bent forward and placed his lips there, moved to taste of her. A touch delicate as moisture-laden honeysuckle.

Her noises revealed delight much like the purring of a cat. The more he explored, the more intense her reaction. She rolled her head from one side to the other, purred some more, raised her well-rounded hips, and breathed in and out through pouted lips. When she came it was with a shout of pleasure.

"Oh God, come here, come here." Hands cupped on both sides of his face, she eased his mouth to one breast where he feasted deeply before she moved him to the other. After a while she wrapped her legs around his waist and gathered him inside, took him deep into the dark sweetness of her most secret chamber. Massaged his pulsing and eager member.

"Your turn, my love. Your turn."

He plunged into the heady cavern, rotated in long, sensuous motions. An erotic dance of pleasure intensified beyond all imagination, a heat flared hot, then hotter.

Just hold on, baby. Don't let go. Keep holding on till the world ends.

Why could he only think those words, not say them? Why didn't he take her, keep her? Forever. But all he dared do was think them. He dare not bind himself to her, care so much that what she did mattered more than anything he might do. That what happened to her hurt more than what happened to him. Dear God, don't let that come to be.

Later they took a shower together again, and his memory of the lovemaking made him so hard she had to help him tame the passion.

He dropped her off at the newspaper and was backing out of the parking when the fire alarms went off and his radio blared the news.

Hermitage House was on fire.

Most of the town tried to get there. So much so that the roads were blocked for miles in all directions. First responders, volunteer firemen, residents eager to help, all raced to the site, some hanging onto the sides of both the fire and water trucks, others in pickups, the beds filled to overflowing.

Hermitage House burned with a brilliance one would expect of such a beautiful and important structure. For hours, while hoses sprayed water, the flames continued to reach into the cloudless sky, so hot it was hours before the fire died down to a billowing of smoke.

The mansion had stood high on the hill above town for more than a century and was gone in a few hours.

And these were some of the words Jessie used in her story of the fire. No one injured or killed. All told six people ended in the Federal lockup. The Harper sisters and their cohorts, Taylor Bainbridge, Robert Kimble, and Jeff Woodson. He the most shamed for his part in acting like a hero and blind veteran. For this he actually apologized while they dragged him through the square to the jail. Mrs. Yingling, widow of Cameron, a soldier killed in Iraq, threw rocks at him when he said he was sorry. No apologies from Alicia Woodson, who held her head high, as if she had nothing to be ashamed of. If there were more involved on the periphery, they fled the county and the state.

Who brought about the fall of Hermitage House? Though Parker insisted and Jessie asked the question of the many even remotely connected to the plot, no one ever learned the truth. Was the fire set or the result of fate? Arson investigators were silent and sifted the remains for weeks. Then they were gone and the yellow crime scene tape fluttered away in the wind of a midnight storm.

The ledger that would incriminate the three couples was never found, but Dave Spacey figured out the numbers hidden in the box. A bank in some obscure island country no one had ever heard of and couldn't pronounce or spell held over a million dollars and as of the last article it had not been decided where the money would go.

Jessie wrote about the basement and cavern discovered after the ashes of Hermitage house cooled. An underground route that ran from under the house to the barn. Possibly left over from slavery days and thought to be part of the Underground Railroad route through which slaves were sneaked from the South to the North over one hundred-fifty years earlier. A bitter irony, some said.

Alicia bragged of having hatched the idea of stealing unwanted children and selling them and offered to write a book about it. Once begun, she wouldn't stop talking. How she dreamed up a blind war hero and lived in the midst of her criminal enterprises.

Jessie's interviews were with Bainbridge and Kimble, who revealed how none of the couples were married, they were only together to blend into the community. Even Kimble, who had told everyone his wife had died, wasn't married to Anna Louise Harper. It was one of the few truths he'd told. His wife had died while visiting her mother out in California.

There was enough evidence to charge the couples with Federal crimes. Taking the children out of the United States into Mexico where they were sold. Even without the ledger the feds had an iron-clad case.

Jessie stretched and sighed, stared at the computer screen and typed—30—at the bottom of the last of her four-week series. The most exciting story she'd ever written, but not the most satisfying.

Still, it just went to show, sometimes it was hard to tell the good guys from the bad. She hadn't faced Alicia, whom she had considered a friend, and didn't want to.

Jessie shoved back her hair, sent the final chapter of the series to Parker's computer, and stuffed her backpack. She had a date with Dal to go dancing out at the Country Square. It had been too long since they been dancing, or even had an actual date, for that matter.

For a few minutes she paused to enjoy the sun beside her new acquisition, Gertie Jo the second, a gleaming, almost-new Jeep Cherokee. From across the way Mike hollered. "Finished for the day, huh?"

"Yep, it's been quite an exciting few weeks. I'm glad it's over with. Dal and I are going dancing."

"Well, have fun. When you gonna give in and go dancing with me? I'm better at it than that ole Dallas boy."

She laughed. "You wanna bet?"

"Did they ever find that spooky Marcus character?"

"Nope. He went as he came. Like a puff of smoke. Turned out he had nothing to do with the child trafficking."

"Maybe he was a ghost."

"You know, I wouldn't be surprised."

He laughed and waved and went back to washing the fire engine. She crawled behind the wheel. Things in Cedarton were getting back to normal slowly but surely.

A horn sounded and she slammed on the brakes, leaned out the window. All she needed was another insurance claim.

"Hey, Jessie, it's me. Randy. You on your way home?"

Turning off the ignition, she leaped out and ran back to the car blocking her way. "I'm so glad to see you, we've all been wondering what happened."

Two little girls cried out her name from the backseat.

"Hey, Ellie. Suzie. How are you?"

As always, Ellie did the talking. "We are fine, Miss Jessie. Daddy says we're going to live here soon as we find a house. He has a job."

"Well, that's mighty fine. Randy, that's such good news. How did this all happen?"

"It's a long story. I'm sorry to hold you up. I was late getting into town. I'd hoped you might know of a place I could rent till I get on my feet."

"Hang on just a minute." She ran to the paper box in front of the office and pulled out a copy of that week's issue. "I think there's a couple of houses listed in here."

Ignoring the headlines and above-the-fold final feature story on the fall of Hermitage House, she paged to the classifieds. "Yes, here they are. The Jasper house out on Maple is sort of big and old, but if you're real handy you could fix it up. The other one is more expensive but in better shape. It's here in town."

He took the paper. "Thanks. I'll give them a call."

"You might just go on out to the Jasper's. They're trying to move out and should be home. You could just take a look around. I know they wouldn't mind." She glanced at her watch. "Look, I've got a date tonight. We need to get together and hear all your news."

"That'd be great. I go to work Monday for the sheriff's department, so we'll be seeing you around."

"Randy, that's fantastic. Wait, how did you get the girls? Or, I guess you got them."

"It was a no-brainer. I had some eyewitnesses who agreed to speak up for me, then my ex-wife's new boyfriend decided to move to California and told her if she wanted to go along she could, but he didn't want any B-R-A-T-S." He spelled the last word.

"And she went and left her K-I-D-S?"

"Yeah, believe that?"

"Good for you and them. Listen, why don't you come out Sunday? I'll order up something good to eat." She laughed. "I don't cook, you know."

"Never would've guessed it. Sounds great."

"Maybe we'll just have a BBQ and ask all the guys out so you can get better acquainted with everyone. And hear all the news since last you were here. I hope you will no longer be Cedarton's hermit."

"No way. That sounds super. Can I bring something?"

"Not this time, but keep in mind, ever after you will be called upon."

He laughed, she told the girls goodbye, backed out, and drove down the street behind him.

On her way out of town, she glanced in the rearview mirror. From high on the hill, the stone chimneys of Hermitage House reflected like gravestones marking the burial site of a culture come and gone. All that remained of the regal Southern mansion.

She headed home where Dal was meeting her. Before they went dancing, he was going to teach her how to start a car without keys. He'd told her it wasn't quite as easy as when someone did it in the movies or on TV, but it could be done, with the right tools and a lot of patience.

Much between the two of them met that requirement.

Velda Brotherton writes from her home perched on the side of a mountain against the Ozark National Forest. Branded as *Sexy, Dark and Gritty*, her work embraces the lives of gutsy women and heroes who are strong enough to deserve them. After a stint writing for a New York publisher, she has settled comfortably in with small publishers to produce novels in several genres. She enjoys reading mysteries, but it never occurred to her she could write them until Dal Starr and Jessie West emerged from her background in the newspaper business, and the *Twist of Poe* mysteries were born.

Facebook: Author Velda Brotherton
Twitter: @veldabrotherton
http://www.veldabrotherton.com

www.ingramcontent.com/pod-product-compliance
Lightning Source LLC
Chambersburg PA
CBHW030557020726
47494CB00005B/1645